WILD BRIDE

Lady Berenice couldn't believe she was being forced to marry a man she'd never met. How was she to know she would encounter her unknown fiancé during an ill-advised visit to a tavern? Now he dared to treat her with scorn! But her heart betrayed her and his heated kisses aroused a shameless desire for the rogue she now called husband... The last woman, Sebastian, Comte Lajeaunesse, wanted as a wife was this hell-raising beauty. Little did he dream that her sensual touch would spark a lifelong passion...

WILD BRIDE

WILD BRIDE

Wild Bride

by

Jeanne Montague

Black Satin Romance
Long Preston, North Yorkshire,
England.

British Library Cataloguing in Publication Data.

Montague, Jeanne
  Wild bride.

A catalogue record for this book is
available from the British Library

ISBN 1-86110-039-6

Black Satin Romance is an imprint of
Library Magna Books Ltd.
Printed and bound in Great Britain by
T.J. International Ltd., Cornwall, PL28 8RW.

ONE

The great, crested coach juddered to a screeching halt with a force that jerked its occupants from their seats and flung them to the floor. An unladylike oath shot from the lips of the youngest and—as many men would attest—the prettiest of the two women inside. She scrambled to her feet, threw up the glass window and leaned out, shaking her fist at the driver perched high on his box out front.

'Do that but once more, Thomas, and I'll wring your poxy nose off!' she shouted above the tumult of the London streets.

Letting the reins of his four-horse team trail idly, Thomas broke off from his rip-roaring exchange of insults with the hulking drayman whose cart was jammed against their vehicle, to acknowledge this rebuke. They were stuck fast in a snarl of traffic, a swearing, sweating conglomeration of coal wagons, farm carts piled with hay or vegetables, impatient horsemen, chairmen struggling along under the burden of the sedan, all jostling the carriages of the élite, whose liveried attendants shouted ill-natured jibes at belligerent hackney-drivers.

'Calm down, Berenice, do, before you have the vapors,' drawled her companion, regaining her languid pose on the deeply cushioned velvet seat and patting her elegant bonnet into place

7

on her high-piled golden curls.

Berenice took her advice, a smile lifting her lips, determined that nothing should mar this shopping spree with Lucinda Clayton. It was such a relief to escape the fussy attentions of chaperons, ladies' maids, and spying servants. Of course, Papa would be furious if he knew. She sighed deeply, wishing as so often before, that she had been born plain Berenice Rossiter, instead of being the only daughter of the Marquis of Church Stretton. He was a stern, uncompromising man, who worried about her unduly and considered her to be frivolous and light-minded. This was not true, but sometimes his restrictions made her rebellious, bringing out all that was headstrong and willful in her nature.

In many ways, he had no one to blame but himself for lavishing so much care on her. From birth, Berenice had been indulged in every possible way. Perhaps it was the Marquis's muddled notion that by so doing he could recompense her for the fact that her mother had died while giving her life. He was ambitious for her, and she was treated like a princess and waited on hand and foot. He had even given her a doll's house that looked like King George III's palace in miniature, hung with tiny tapestries, furnished in walnut, and peopled by wax dolls dressed to resemble the royal family. She also had a white pony to ride in Hyde Park or round the great estate of Stretton Court in the county of Wiltshire.

It was as well for her that she had an older

brother, Damian, Viscount Norwood, or else all the Marquis's hopes would have been centered entirely on her. As it was, he had two children to fret over, for Damian was almost as hot-headed as herself. The strait-laced old nobleman was wont to stamp about, muttering darkly that he did not know what the younger generation were coming to; that their heads were stuffed full of revolutionary ideas and that they lacked dignity and decorum and respect for their parents.

Even so, being Lady Berenice was a heavy responsibility. Her destiny had been decided when she was a baby, but this did not make it any easier to accept. She brooded on this as the coach lurched into motion, only half listening to Lucinda's chatter. In all honesty, she could not say that her papa had been cruel. He was a proud, rather cold man, but the worst accusation she could bring against him was his lack of understanding where she and Damian were concerned, evidenced in the damning fact that he had given her away in marriage many years before to a man whom she had never met.

Her education, her training, had been geared to the day when she would be old enough to take her place at the side of her husband, a colonial aristocrat, Comte Sebastian Lajeaunesse. Thus, when she was in the cradle, she had been married by proxy to a youth of thirteen—property, money and religion being of prime importance. Neither of the principal participants had been consulted as to their wishes. The Marquis and the Comte's father had been friends and business associates, and this was considered enough to make a satisfactory alliance between the two houses. Even the ravaging upheaval of the French Revolution eleven years earlier, had not obstructed these plans. The Lajeaunesse family, forced to flee the vengeance of the mob, had sailed for America. It would be this strange New World that Berenice would travel to when her husband came to fetch her.

As her nursery attendants had predicted early, Berenice had grown into a woman of peerless beauty, with very dark brown curling tresses shot with fiery tints, and the most brilliant, wide-spaced eyes of deep sapphire blue. There was something vital and alive about her piquant face, with its high cheekbones, broad forehead, arched brows and those compelling eyes under the sweep of long, black lashes. Of medium height, she carried herself regally, head held high, little chin lifted at a determined angle. Yet she was more than a society belle. Those privileged to know her recognized that she was sensitive, intelligent and well-educated, as well as bedeviled by a fierce temper, self-willed, rash and capable of great caprices, even wild injustices where her emotions were involved. But she possessed a melting charm, a heart generous and warm, a nature deep, and instincts untamed and passionate.

Now this explosive mixture of conflicting elements was churning within her, so that her expression changed, eyes stormy, brows winging together in a frown, lower lip rolled out in a pout.

Lucinda noticed it, remarking, 'La, what ails you this morning, child? You're in an almighty pet, I declare.'

Berenice bounced up energetically, gloved hands locked together within her sable muff. 'Wouldn't you be distressed if you were about to be confronted by a bridegroom who's a complete stranger? He's expected any day, you know, and I must depart to the wilds of Carolina with him! I'll warrant he's a bent, spindle-shanked sort of fellow—and terribly old! Why, he must be all of thirty!'

Lucinda nodded sagely, the ostrich feathers in her beribboned hat dipping and bobbing. Both ladies were of the opinion that a man of such an advanced age must be in his dotage. 'I understand that he's very rich,' she murmured, by way of compensation.

'Fie! So am I! Don't think to soften the blow by talk of his wealth, Lucinda!' Berenice flashed angrily. 'I hate the idea of marrying him! Should I run away? Can't you help me?'

Lucinda was twenty, three years her senior, and worldly-wise. If anyone could aid Berenice, then she was the person to do it. Although the Marquis was finding it increasingly difficult to control his daughter, in spite of having the assistance of a whole troop of servants, Berenice dared not openly defy him. She was a thorn in his side—such a lively girl with a reckless lust for life who could not be kept under lock and key.

There were a host of entertainments to which she and Damian were constantly invited—balls

11

and masques and pleasure parties on barges down the Thames were the order of the day. The Marquis himself refused to attend these frivolities, but often the kindly wife of some acquaintance would offer to keep an eye on Berenice, promising to take good care of her. Given her many and varied social engagements, it was inevitable that she should meet people who were not excessively concerned in preserving her innocence. Lucinda was amongst these. She had been an actress, and was now the mistress of a duke, residing in a house in the fashionable West End of London.

She had taken Berenice under her wing, teaching her all the mannerisms of a lady of quality, introducing her to her own dressmaker and, more valuable still, advising on how to treat the dandies who had begun to court her. Lucinda was well versed on that particular subject. In straightforward, uninhibited language, she had told her the basic facts of life. Berenice, naïve and inexperienced, listened avidly. She was not only virgin in body—she still had a virgin mind, quite innocent or, more exactly, ignorant. No one else had seen fit to enlighten her.

Although she had known there was a physical act between men and women, because of her immured youth, she had had no accurate expectations until she met Lucinda. When that sophisticated courtesan spoke frankly, it had seemed so simple to Berenice. Of course that was what happened. And she had been filled with sudden stabbing desire. She wanted it to happen to her! But Lucinda kept the fops firmly at bay. It was not her intention that they should debauch her friend, merely that she should have some fun. But then, Berenice thought wickedly, Lucinda did not know about Peregrine.

He was a mutual friend, but no one suspected that he was wooing Berenice ardently. Sir Peregrine Baxter was one of the most eligible bachelors in town. She leaned her head back against the maroon lining of the coach and closed her eyes, dreaming of him and of those brief meetings which had made the past weeks so exciting.

She had been attracted to him at first sight. He was tall and slender, with fair hair dressed in that casual, ruffled style so popular among the beaux. His eyes were brown, humorous and adoring, and he cut a dash, always attired in the very latest mode, with tightly tailored breeches and velvet jackets, fine Flemish lace frothing at his wrists and throat. Because she was so closely chaperoned, she had never really been alone with him, but he fancied himself as a poet, writing verses in praise of her, which he had delivered to the house with great bouquets of flowers. Berenice was flattered, and touched by such devotion, though occasionally she thought that his tongue was just a little too glib. Then he would murmur a compliment into her ear or she would feel the smoothness of his cheek against hers in a greeting kiss, and she would forget her misgivings. Yet a tiny, lingering doubt remained, preventing her from confiding in Lucinda, lest some word from that lady's sharp tongue should shatter her happiness.

Lucinda was tapping her on the knee with her fan, interrupting her reverie. 'Dearest, we're nearing the Old Man coffeehouse. Shall we stop and see if any of the gentlemen are inside?'

Berenice's lids flicked open and she regarded her with sparkling azure eyes, her lips quirked into an impish smile. The Old Man's was popular as a meeting place for the young bucks, who idled away their mornings talking of fashions and amours, cockfighting, horse racing and the latest gossip concerning the Prince of Wales and his mistresses. The town beaux were amusing but rakish. The coffeehouse would have been forbidden if her chaperon, Miss Harriet Osborne, had been present, but they had already dropped her off to take tea with a friend, the prospect of a good gossip tempting her away from her duty. Miss Osborne was the latest in a string of companions, Berenice being too trying for these unfortunate women to remain in her service long.

It was a rainy May morning, the wind whipping across the crowded streets, stirring the rubbish in the gutters and tearing at the rags which clothed the beggars. But the weather caused no inconvenience to Berenice and Lucinda who were warmly clad in high-waisted, simple dresses of patterned wool. The long, straight skirts were concealed beneath full-length, fur-edged pelisses, with gloves and cozy muffs to keep their fingers protected.

As the shiny black coach, picked out with yellow lines and bearing the Stretton arms, drew up outside the coffeehouse, half a dozen brilliantly attired gentlemen hurried to meet them. They were a permissive, high-spirited company, and Berenice was still ingenuous and easily impressed. Lucinda, however, saw them in a more realistic light, as garrulous freeloaders who eked out their incomes by gaming, living on their wits, their style and bravura.

— 'Dear ladies!' exclaimed one. Berenice's heart skipped a beat at the sight of him—it was Peregrine. He dragged open the door and clambered in, seating himself beside her, while his companions hung at the opening, smelling high of brandy and lavender water. 'So delightful to see you, most beautiful votaries of Venus!'

He leaned over to plant a kiss on her cheek, and Berenice could feel the hot blush rising up her throat to her forehead. She was aware of Lucinda's eagle eye upon her, and struggled to feign indifference. He was certainly good-looking in a slightly effeminate way, wearing pantaloons, very tight-fitting and reaching to his calves, a red and white striped jacket loosely open over an exquisitely decorated waistcoat, and a stiff, intricately folded white stock fastened beneath his chin. Silk stockings and black pumps completed this stunning ensemble, and he had removed his high-crowned beaver hat on entry, tucking it under his arm.

In spite of his foppery, there was something frank and charming about the smiling eyes that regarded Berenice with unconcealed pleasure as he chatted on. 'You, my dear, are the talk of the town this morning, strike me dumb if you ain't!'

15

he admonished playfully, wagging a beringed finger at her.

'Me?' Berenice gave a puzzled little frown. Good Heavens! What had she done now? A sudden uneasy qualm stirred her stomach.

The beaux laughed, winking and elbowing one another. One fell from the carriage step and had to be hauled up again. 'D'you mean to sit there so demurely and tell me that you don't know, madam? That, I can't believe!' continued Peregrine, raising the quizzing glass that hung on a black velvet ribbon round his neck and staring at her in a most disconcerting way.

'Stop teasing, Peregrine, and proceed with the story, since you're plainly dying to tell it,' Lucinda commented, bored by his hints, knowing how these young bloods loved to be the bearers of tidings, particularly if it was to someone else's detriment.

Peregrine smirked at her. 'Don't rush me—a good tale should not be hurried, Duchess—' He broke off to clap himself on the brow in mock alarm. 'Ah, forgive me—a slip of the tongue—you can't use that title, can you, dearest?' He cocked a peaked eyebrow at her, grinning puckishly, then flipped open his silver snuffbox, took a pinch between thumb and forefinger, applied it to each nostril, sniffed delicately and then used his lawn handkerchief.

Lucinda's eyes were frosty. 'Don't play games with me, sir. You know perfectly well that I'm the Duke's whore,' she said grittily, while the gentlemen tittered. 'And that his wife is still alive, damn her!'

'So you've not heard about the duel?' Peregrine asked blandly, smiling into Berenice's eyes in a way that made her melt inside, and lazily tucking his handkerchief into his cuff.

'A duel!' she paled and sat up sharply, hoping against all hope that her worst fears were not about to be realized.

'Ah—' Having captured his audience, Peregrine launched into the details with relish. 'It was on Hampstead Heath at dawn today, between Captain Simon Curtis and Chevalier Duval. I believe you know that Curtis challenged him, don't you, Lady Berenice?'

Berenice went hot and cold, her heart pounding so hard that it made her breasts shake beneath her concealing coat. Oh, yes, she knew that these two silly young men had quarreled over her, both wanting to escort her to a concert. But she had not thought they were in deadly earnest.

'What happened?' she breathed, eyes wide with alarm.

Peregrine took advantage of her fright to reach over and clasp one of her hands in his. 'Curtis pinked the Frenchie in the arm—he's a renowned swordsman. I know he's the son of an escaped aristocrat and all that but we're at war with France. Then the constables arrived—someone must have tipped them off—most unsportsmanlike, don't-cher-know—and they had to make a run for it. Curtis has ridden pell-mell for his estate in Norfolk, and the Chevalier galloped to Holyhead to take the first packet

17

boat to Ireland. It's all over town, my dear.'

There was an edict against dueling, but the hot-blooded gentlemen took little notice and were quick to fall out over a point of honor some real or imagined insult. Pistols were in vogue, but some still preferred to meet with rapiers. This latest scandal would be a nine-day wonder, of course, but it would damage her reputation and her father would be furious if he came to hear of it.

Berenice bit her lip in vexation; she had hardly encouraged Curtis and Duval at all. Perhaps she had flirted with them a little, but had never dreamed it would come to this. Supposing her bridegroom arrived just now when this hot piece of gossip was on everyone's tongue? Too late she regretted her thoughtlessness which, once again, had led her into dangerous waters.

'Don't look so distraught, my love.' Lucinda was beaming her approval. 'It's the ambition of every belle to have at least one duel fought on her account.'

But Berenice shook her head, beset by doubts, swaying towards Peregrine momentarily, longing to bury her face against the lace ruffles on his chest and cry. She felt swamped and uncertain, knowing deep inside that she only plunged into the reckless gaiety of the social scene in order to stave off the fear of a loveless marriage that loomed ever nearer. She was trapped. Terror of the future made her heart flutter like that of a bird in a snare.

Peregrine yearned to comfort her, surprised

18

by this uprush of concern, and alarmed to discover how fond he was of the lovely Berenice, disappointed yet relieved to know that it was hopeless. She was already promised to another. He had tried, but failed to resist the temptation of seeing her, recognizing her innocence and aware of his own profligate life. Son of a country squire, he had come to London to seek his destiny, fancying his chances as a playwright, trading on the goodwill of wealthy relatives. He led a precarious, ne'er-do-well existence, always in debt, but always on the threshold of some ingeniously conceived fortune which never materialized.

Unseen by Berenice, a rueful smile played over his mouth as he chided himself for his uncharacteristic gallantry towards her. He found something infinitely bewitching and irresistible about her. It was not only her perfection of face and figure, it was her personality which was so dazzling that she eclipsed every other woman when she swept into a room. She shone like a flame, with that burnished hair, those eloquent eyes, that provocative body with its flowing grace of movement. Peregrine was in his twenties, and had already lost much of his idealism, yet in her he saw all the goddesses of his dreams. Distressed to see her downcast by his news, for he had thought she would be pleased to be the center of so much attention, he racked his brain to find a diversion to cheer her.

'Sweetest lady, don't look so glum,' he ventured gently. 'You're as pale as a ghost. There's a tavern near here which serves a very passable sherry-sack. That will put color in your cheeks.'

It was not considered proper for a young lady to enter an inn, unless it was a posting house during a journey, and then only under the supervision of some responsible person. This applied particularly to a hostelry such as the Rose and Crown, which was situated near the theater in Drury Lane. It was frequented by actors and women of notorious reputation, but Berenice was feeling too despondent to argue—the Marquis would be furious when he heard about the duel—she was already doomed, so might as well be hung for a sheep as a lamb.

Soon the coach was swinging beneath an arch and clattering into a paved courtyard at the rear of the tavern, which enclosed the cobbled yard on each side. Open galleries ran round the four stories, with stairs reaching down to ground level. Several maidservants leaned over the balustrade, idling instead of getting on with their work, calling out to those below. As soon as the carriage stopped, a postilion leapt into action, opening the doors and unfolding the iron step to allow the occupants to alight. Peregrine held out a crooked arm to Berenice, who tested the tips of her fingers on his sleeve, the other hand holding up her skirt. Wide-eyed and apprehensive, she permitted him to conduct her into the taproom. Lucinda swept along beside them, talking in a loud, affected voice and drawing attention to herself.

The room was well lit and comfortable, a

welcoming refuge from the dull weather. A log fire blazed in the wide hearth, and the newcomers occupied settles close by. The place was crowded, every seat and table taken. Berenice peered around curiously at the men, who were drinking, dicing or playing cards. There were several women, too, strident, overpainted and garishly attired ladies who no doubt trod the boards at the adjacent theater. She fidgeted nervously, knowing that she had no business being there, but this feeling of guilt made her even more defiant. Tossing up her head, chin lifted militantly, she let her pelisse fall open over her full breasts which were revealed by the fashionably scooped neckline, as she was adopting a brazen manner as she discoursed with her friends.

After several glasses of wine, she became even more reckless, spurred on by the risqué talk buzzing around their table. The members of the *ton* who had joined them were gossiping waspishly with a worldly air of elegant abandon. Flirtation, or so it seemed to Berenice as she listened, had become something of an art, seductions strategically planned, the more involved and devious the better. Truth and honor were words to be mocked, and there was nothing on earth more important to that dissolute group than showy clothes, wit delivered with a bite, and dubious assignations. Steadily, they grew noisier and louder, the dandies leaning back in their chairs, shouting orders over their shoulders to the obsequious landlord. Amidst the din, Berenice looked up sharply as a commotion

21

in the doorway heralded the entrance of another guest.

A sudden silence descended over the room as he strode across to the fire, rapping out a command to a waiter in passing. He was the tallest man Berenice had ever seen, standing at least six foot four and powerfully built, the breadth of his shoulders emphasized by the caped cloak which swirled around him, reaching halfway down his black top-boots. He leaned against the oaken overmantel as he removed his curly brimmed hat, knocking the drizzle from it before handing it to a manservant who had followed quietly behind him. He loosened his cloak to display a blue cloth jacket and buckskin breeches that fitted his sleek hips snugly, a braided waistcoat, and a smart, military-styled black silk stock tied around a stand-up collar beneath his firm, square jaw.

There was something formidable, even alarming in his mien. His features were strikingly handsome, but harsh and ruthless, too, with pronounced cheekbones, a hawklike nose, and piercing green eyes staring out from under curving brows. His hair was black, and swept back in deep waves to curl at the nape of his neck.

Across that crowded room, his eyes locked on Berenice for a second. She met that first glance with a jolt that shook her to the marrow. The flagrant virility of the man hit her with the force of a physical blow. He was a truly magnificent creature, long-limbed and whipcord lean, his every movement graceful as a panther's, full of barely restrained violence and passion. His sheer size made him overpowering. He dominated the taproom. There was a freshness about him which contrasted sharply with the fops who flitted in their fashionable half world. His tanned skin and serviceable clothing suggested that he preferred to be outdoors, unlike the dandies who draped themselves in elegant poses, admiring their own pretty images in the mirrors hanging against the paneled walls.

The stranger drank his ale silently, eyeing the group around Berenice, his finely chiseled lips curling sardonically as scraps of their conversation drifted across to him. Every male there, had been aware of him from the moment he entered, though pretending otherwise. Now, resentful of being put in the shade, they became wary, waiting for someone to make the first move.

Peregrine would do so. He was tipsy and took offense at the stranger's hard, ironic smile. He stood up, swaying unsteadily as he shouted rashly, 'You there, sir! D'you find something amusing, eh? Or are you ogling our ladies?'

The tall man did not budge, but his lips tightened and his eyes grew cold as steel. Then he flickered a glance over Lucinda and Berenice. 'Ladies, sir? I see no ladies. Only a pair of gaudy jill-flirts!' he replied.

His voice was accented—a foreign intonation that Berenice could not place, but it was deep, commanding and, despite the obvious insult, held a quality which sent a shiver down her spine. Peregrine's expression darkened. Egged on by his troublemaking comrades, he stood before the traveler, one hand on his hip, the other lifting his lorgnette to one eye, looking him up and down in a slow, insolent way, before remarking,

'Sink me, friends, it has a tongue in its head after all. I took it to be some deuced savage who couldn't converse with a cultured gentleman, strike me dumb!'

His cronies whooped, doubling up with mirth at this barbed sally. There was a split-second pause, then the stranger's right arm shot out, his massive hand closing in a vicelike grip on Peregrine's upper arm, lifting him high off his feet and shaking him as a terrier shakes a rat. For an eternity he seemed to hold him there, shoulder high, his left fist clenched in front of the fop's nose, as he said in clipped tones, 'Would you care to repeat that, sir? More clearly, so that I can hear it and decide exactly what I'm going to do with you!'

'I was jesting, nothing more!' Peregrine panted. 'You're a foreigner, perhaps, and not accustomed to our humor? Dammit, there's no need to manhandle a fellow so!'

The big man set him down on the floor, with a force that made his teeth rattle. 'If you want satisfaction,' he ground out. 'I'll be happy to oblige. Elect your seconds, and I'll put them in touch with my own!'

Peregrine shook his head, shrinking back against the table, massaging his bruised arm. Lucinda rose to her feet, alert to the storm warnings, gathering up the fops and shepherding them towards the door before further mayhem broke out. As she passed, followed closely by Berenice, she flashed the stranger an inviting look. He returned her glance with one of undisguised scorn, but as Berenice made to pass, he suddenly swooped, seized her and drew her up close to him.

Startled and wildly indignant, she met the stare of his heavy-lidded eyes, her own slanting blue ones bright and challenging. A taunting smile curved that sensual mouth hovering above hers, and he said, in measured tones, 'Humm, as pretty a ladybird as ever I've seen. You should choose your companions more carefully. That bunch of mincing coxcombs can offer you scant protection. I think I deserve some recompense for their rudeness.'

Abruptly he abandoned his lazy pose and she knew a thrill, half terror, half anticipation, as his mouth fastened on hers in a demanding kiss that banished for all time her girlish fancies about romantic love. He pressed his lips contemptuously on hers, that kiss suggestive of his conviction that she was a harlot. Crushed to his muscular body, she could feel the hardness of the thighs pressed against her own. A strange, pleasurable warmth flooded through her, coupled with shame that he should treat her in such a manner before a crowd of amused onlookers.

She struggled, desperate to break his hold, wrenching her mouth away, then pounding at his chest with futile fists. When he raised his dark head, she was petrified by the raw, untamed desire she saw flaring in his emerald eyes. With a strength that surprised them both, she wrested free from his arms and stood back, breasts heaving under the flimsy covering, glaring up at the huge man towering over her.

His face was tight with passion and, eyes narrowed to glittering slits, he asked, 'What price d'you put on your favors, madame? What will it cost me to bed you?'

Infuriated beyond fear or reason, she gave an outraged gasp. 'How dare you!' she blazed, exploding into a boiling rage that eclipsed caution. Without thought of the consequences, she swung up her hand and slapped him across his mocking face.

His head jerked back with the force of her blow and, with great self-control, he resisted the impulse to wring her slender white neck. Instead, he smiled icily, folding his arms across his chest. 'Little firebrand! What's this game you're playing?'

Speechless with indignation, she satisfied herself by giving him a caustic glare and making for the door, where Lucinda was waiting. Berenice was trembling now. Her only thought was to put as much distance as possible between herself and that dreadful man, and to forget his kiss, of which she was far more terrified than any physical harm he might do her.

Even when she was in the safety of the coach, with Lucinda attempting to smooth her ruffled feathers, she could not shake off the memory of that burning embrace. It was as if he had put a brand on her, and she resented it furiously. She was also seething because he had mistaken her for a prostitute.

'How dare he?' she shouted, almost in tears. 'How *could* he? I don't look in the least like a whore, do I?'

'Of course, you don't, sweeting,' Lucinda assured her. 'Try to forget about him. He's nothing but an ill-mannered oaf.'

Peregrine was nettled because he'd been made to look like a fool in public, and he flopped down beside Berenice, exclaiming indignantly, 'What a bully! 'Pon my honor, it comes to something when a gentleman can't take a drink without being set upon. Did he hurt you, dear lady? Gad, but I'd like to run him through for his impudence!'

'No, he didn't hurt me, and it's a trifle late for heroics, isn't it?' Berenice was even cross with Peregrine. It had been the most disturbing experience of her life.

Suddenly they were interrupted by a violent racket from the street. The far door of the coach was wrenched open, and a girl leapt in, hair disheveled, eyes wild and desperate.

'Please, ma'am!' she entreated Berenice. 'Tell 'em I'm your maid!' Her pretty face was intense, her voice pleading. 'Oh, God! Here they come! Please, ma'am—help me!'

She gave Berenice one last look filled with misery and alarm, then shrank back into a corner, pulling the hood of her cloak over her springy red curls. Berenice stared at her in astonishment, forgetting her own problems for the moment. Then the door was thrown wide and a blue-uniformed constable pushed his head in. There were a couple at his back, armed, and plainly intent on making an arrest.

At the sight of these keepers of law and order with whom, for reasons of his own, he did not wish to become embroiled, Peregrine said to Berenice, 'I'll meet you in the grotto tonight,' before he scrambled out of the other door, missing his footing and cursing as he slipped in the rain-washed muck at the side of the road.

The leading officer made a salute. 'Begging your pardon, your ladyship, but that wench just stole a bolt of cloth. I arrest you, in the name of King George!' he shouted, lunging across Berenice towards the girl, who cowered away, her skirts drawn tightly around her.

Suddenly furious, remembering that it was just such an official who had almost caught the duelists and thus implicated her in a scandal, Berenice brought down her fan with a hearty smack on his wrist. 'Hands off, sir! She's my maid!'

Berenice knew crime flourished in the city and that, due to the shortage of members of the Watch, it went largely unpunished. She had also heard that when offenders were caught, they were treated savagely. This poor creature would doubtless be flung into Newgate Gaol to await trial, and then publicly hanged for theft. From where she sat, Berenice could feel her trembling.

The constable, plainly surprised, drew back. 'Well, madam, far be it from me to call a lady a liar, but I saw her take the silk myself and make a run for it. So I'll thank you to let me perform my duty.'

Berenice already disliked his red, pompous face and became even more indignant when he leaned further in, grabbing the girl by the ankle and trying to drag her towards him. She had had quite enough of high-handed bullies for one day! A crowd had begun to gather in the street outside the tavern, relishing a brush with the unpopular constables. Berenice moved fast, giving him a sharp kick in the belly with the toe of her shoe, followed by a hard shove that toppled him back and out through the door into the arms of his disgruntled minions. The throng of spectators gave a roar of delighted laughter.

Berenice rapped briskly on the paneling behind her, shouting: 'Drive on, Thomas!' and the carriage rolled away.

Lucinda turned to her, amazed. 'Child, was that wise? I've never thought you the champion of the poor and needy.'

'There you're wrong, Lucinda. I've often taken food and clothing to the cottagers on my father's estate. It seems terribly unfair for them to have so little when we have so much.'

'Good heavens! Have you been reading Rousseau?' Lucinda exclaimed, surprised by this aspect of her friend's character that she had no idea existed.

'I couldn't let them take her,' Berenice protested, though unable to explain the sudden impulse.

The girl was staring at her, hazel eyes glowing with gratitude. 'Oh, ma'am, how ever can I repay you? But for you, I'd have been in that stinking prison by now. I was in this draper's shop, you see, and saw a length of cloth. I've still got it here, under my cloak. You can have it, if you want—as thanks.'

She held out a bundle of shimmering pink silk, but Berenice shook her head. Lucinda was eyeing the fabric and the girl with suspicion. 'What did you want with it?' she questioned sharply.

'It wasn't for me, madam. What would I be doing with such fine stuff? But I'm starving—haven't had a bite to eat for two days—not since I was kicked out of my last job. I know a fellow down in St. Giles—the Rookery, ma'am, where the criminals live,' the girl replied hurriedly, seeing Berenice's puzzled expression.

Lucinda made an impatient gesture, eyes flinty. 'You don't have to tell me anything about that squalid fleapit—crawling with pickpockets, whores and the greedy pimps who bleed them dry. I've lived there.'

Berenice was dumbstruck; she had not known this part of Lucinda's past. It was nigh impossible to picture that dainty being with the milk white skin and gorgeous clothes in the sordid alleys of St. Giles.

'You've never spoken of this before. I didn't know,' she managed to blurt out.

Lucinda shrugged. 'It's not the kind of thing one boasts about. I've succeeded in forgetting it—till now.'

The young thief recovered herself, and

30

continued her story. 'As I was saying, milady, this fence would've bought it from me, at his own price, of course, and far less than its true worth—but I'd have been able to buy food and lodgings for a few days, till I found a new position.'

Now that she had a chance to study her, Berenice saw that the girl was neat, though rather grubby, with a cheerful oval face, pert snub nose, merry eyes and a lively manner. She guessed their ages to be about the same, and took an instant liking to her. 'Have you really nowhere to go?' she asked.

'No, ma'am, nor no kin neither,' came the prompt reply. Berenice reached for her reticule, intending to give her some money and send her on her way. Then a thought struck her. 'What was your former employment?'

'I was maid to a lady, may it please you, ma'am.'

'Why did you lose your place?' Lucinda, less trusting than Berenice, fixed her with a stern eye.

The girl grinned cheekily, then tried to suppress it, but her bubbling humor broke through. 'I was turned out, madam.'

'For stealing?' Berenice asked quickly, for she was about to yield to another impulse and wanted an assurance that the girl was basically honest.

'Lord love you, no, ma'am!' The eyes which regarded her were wide and innocent. 'I'm a good girl, I am—'cept when I'm starving to death, like now. No, my mistress accused me

31

of leading her husband astray—but it weren't like that—'twas t'other way about. He wanted to roger me, and gave me no peace—forever pestering me, he was, and I didn't fancy him a jot, the silly old fool! That's the truth, ma'am, I swear it.'

'What do they call you?' Berenice's lips twitched in response to the mischievous glint in the girl's eyes. It was easy to believe that her master had found such gamin charm a great temptation.

'Dulcie Riley, ma'am.' She showed no hesitation in giving her name, which convinced Berenice of her sincerity.

'Don't believe her, my dear. I'll wager that's not what she was baptized,' put in the cynical Lucinda. 'She's probably had so many names that she can't remember her real one.'

Berenice chose to ignore this, saying, 'Well, Dulcie, you'd best come home with me. I'm seeking a personal servant as my present one is leaving to be married soon. How would you like to take her place?' She brought this out firmly, closing her ears to Lucinda's disapproving snort.

Doubt, hope and joy chased themselves over Dulcie's face in rapid succession. She clasped her hands together, leaning towards Berenice. 'Oh, my lady! I'd be so proud to work for you. Thank you a thousand times. I'll never forget your kindness. I'll do anything for you—just name it!'

It had been a most eventful morning, Berenice decided, as she bade farewell to Lucinda who alighted outside her smart residence in a pleasant, tree-shaded square. She had lost two suitors, though Peregrine remained, and now, it seemed, she had gained a most devoted ally, too. Resolutely, she put from her mind the memory of the ruthless face with glittering green eyes and firm mouth that had roused such uncomfortable and tumultuous feelings within her. It would be as well if she never set eyes on that despicable blackguard again, she told herself sternly. He was an arrogant, conceited, domineering villain. Her cheeks flushed as she remembered that humiliating scene in the tavern.

She had no time to brood on it further, for as the carriage drew up at the imposing wrought-iron gates of the town house, all thought was banished from her mind with an unpleasant shock. There, parked on the cobbles, was her father's best coach, a well-sprung, immaculately maintained conveyance. He had returned from the country earlier than expected. Her father, the Marquis, the only man in the world to whom she bowed her proud head.

TWO

After instructing one of the postilions to take Dulcie to the servants' quarters, and promising to see her later, Berenice entered the magnificent house between the fluted columns which flanked the front door. It was opened for her by the porter, bearing his tipstaff.

33

She walked swiftly over the tiled floor of the hall, past walls hung with mirrors in ornate frames, past statues—some in niches, and others holding aloft brass girandoles with nests of candles, to be lit after dark. The curving staircase lay ahead, and Berenice mounted its wide shallow steps on trembling legs, praying fervently that the Marquis had not yet heard about the duel. Yet she knew this to be a faint hope, for the servants were a tale-bearing tribe, ever ready to exaggerate the escapades of Lady Berenice and Viscount Norwood, and if they did not do so, then there was always Miss Osborne with her tattling tongue. It was a relief to remember that the companion would be staying at her friend's house for the night. One less enemy in the camp.

When she reached her bedchamber, she was greeted with enthusiastic yaps by her miniature spaniel, Sheba. She swept the fluffy bundle of liver-and-white fur into her arms and smiled affectionately as she was lashed by a feathery tail and licked on the nose by a curling pink tongue. Her maid, Millicent, was there, busy laying out an evening gown in her usual quiet, obedient and boring fashion, preoccupied as she was with her impending marriage to one of the butlers. Berenice found herself missing the lilting chatter of Dulcie, and made a mental note to replace Millicent as soon as possible.

Pulling the pins from her round-brimmed hat with its circlet of ribbons and feathers, she tossed it on to the bed, a fine four-poster with barley-sugar twist supports and muslin drapes.

Like everything else in that airy, spacious room, the bed conformed to the vogue for Chinoiserie. The walls were covered in hand-painted paper, a riot of pagodas, stylized chrysanthemums, and brilliantly plumaged birds, motifs that were echoed in the curtains at the tall, narrow windows. The chairs and dressing table, made of mahogany inlaid with boxwood, owed their perfection to that master craftsman, Hepplewhite.

Berenice gained solace from this atmosphere of warm, friendly security as she peeled off her gloves and stretched out her slender fingers before the coal fire glowing in the pink-veined marble fireplace. She strolled to the window overlooking the lovingly tended gardens at the back of the mansion, but now she was jumpy again, heaving an anxious sigh and twisting her rings nervously in anticipation of a summons by her father. Millicent came across to help her out of her pelisse.

Beneath it Berenice wore a dark green, floral-patterned gown, its long sleeves fastened with tiny buttons at the wrists. High-waisted, with a softly gathered skirt, its décolletage was trimmed with ivory lace, the color a perfect foil for her shining dark hair. Placing a cashmere shawl over her mistress's shoulders, the maid knelt to take off the buttoned boots and replace them with black kid, flat-heeled pumps.

Berenice viewed herself critically in the swing mirror of her dressing table, adding a dusting of pale pink powder to her cheeks. She dared not carmine her lips, so bit them instead to deepen their natural rosy hue, half expecting them to look crushed and bruised after the stranger's kiss. She shivered, angry with herself for being so affected, yet nothing—not even harsh thoughts—could banish him from her memory. It was as if his face and form were branded into her brain. With a small moan of defeat, she dwelt upon their brief meeting. A thrill of fright and something else, as yet unrecognizable, raced through her veins as she recalled his tall, wide-shouldered body, the casual elegance of his dress, the aura of male passion of which she had been so aware when he held her in his arms.

Lingering at the window again, she fought to control her confused emotions, postponing the evil hour when she would have to face the Marquis. She fixed her eyes on the terrace, forcing herself to concentrate on the green lawns between clipped box-yews, the ornamental pond with its fountain spraying up into the grey afternoon. Here, as at Stretton Court, her father had indulged his love of baroque architecture. There were mazes and sundials, even a mock temple, beneath which lay the grotto where she had agreed to meet Peregrine that night. She stirred restlessly, remembering his soft, persuasive wooing, while Millicent gave her a final spray of perfume and put her fan and purse into her hands. Then the maid opened the door, stood back, and Berenice glided out.

As she made her way to the drawing room, she was hardly conscious of the succession of flunkies in their smart black and gold livery.

They were an ever-present background to her life, and she took them for granted. Silent, unobtrusive, they smoothed the paths of their noble employers, attending to lowly chores and household duties.

When she reached the hall, one of the footmen bowed solemnly before her, saying, 'His lordship wishes to see you in the library, my lady.'

Her stomach gave a lurch, but she merely nodded and changed direction, bravely attempting to convince herself that this was nothing more than a parent's natural desire to see his daughter after an absence. She paused at the door, then knocked with a confidence which she was far from feeling. The clipped accents of the Marquis bade her enter.

Lord Herbert Rossiter, Tenth Marquis of Church Stretton, was an imposing figure. He stood before the richly swagged marble hearth, facing the door and giving Berenice a searching glance as she stepped over the threshold. As usual, he was wearing black velvet with a simple silver trim, contrasting vividly with his pristine linen. There was nothing ostentatious about his clothing, but each item was faultlessly tailored and of impeccable taste. Black silk hose and gleaming shoes with shiny steel buckles completed his outfit, the whole topped by a silver grey powdered wig in the old-fashioned style, with a ribboned queue at the back.

Stern, austere and aloof, the Marquis always rose early and, when not working on his accounts or riding, was to be found studying in his beloved library. He did not approve of the gambling fever that had seized the nobility, and was never seen at the gaming tables or the races, considering such occupations to be both vulgar and a wicked waste of time and money. He demanded the same seemly behavior from members of staff—and his children.

Berenice quailed, but held her head high as she dipped him a curtsy. 'Good afternoon, Papa. I trust your journey hasn't fatigued you overmuch.' In reality, she was wishing that he was so exhausted that he might be confined to his room for several days, thus avoiding stories of her doings.

Her eyes traversed the library, cursing her own sensitivity which made her only too aware of something in the air which boded ill. It was a room of modest size, its walls almost completely lined with shelves containing leather-bound volumes. Above the mantelpiece, in a gilt frame, hung a portrait of an earlier Marquis, a starchy old gentleman sporting a stiff ruff in the Elizabethan style, his features resembling those of her father—the same aristocratic nose, and cold eyes which seemed to be staring at her with a jaundiced look.

The Marquis gave a cool nod, rocking slightly on his heels before the blaze, hands clasped under the full tails of his coat. His narrow face was set in those disapproving lines which she recognized only too clearly.

'The journey did not distress me, miss—but the news with which I was greeted on my return has worried me greatly,' he said levelly.

Berenice could not bear the reproach in his

eyes, for she loved him and wished to win his approbation, but the only way she seemed able to please him was by becoming as scholarly and learned, as serious and God-fearing as himself, a hard task for a young girl tormented by headstrong impulses. A hot wave of rebellious anger surged within her. What right had he to address her as if she were an erring kitchen drab? She was Berenice—a living, breathing being, with a need for consideration and love. Peregrine understood this, and she yearned to see him, impatient for the night and their secret tryst. She only wished that he were there to support her now, but that was a wild fantasy; the Marquis would merely sneer and call him a popinjay.

It was difficult for her to remain controlled with such unrest churning inside her, but she managed to saunter towards her father, her eyes turned warily to his face. Her generous mouth was unusually tight, but she said, sweetly enough, 'What alarming news is this, Papa? Some trouble concerning your shipping ventures? Or perhaps your architect has failed to find the correct Palladian columns for Stretton Court?'

The Marquis thought he detected insolence in this enquiry. 'Don't be pert!' His voice cut like a lash. 'You're well aware of the incident to which I refer. There's been a duel between two gentlemen of the town, and you were the cause of it. What have you to say for yourself?'

Berenice immediately fended off his question with another. 'Who told you this, Papa?' she demanded, facing him defiantly. She had inherited his strong temper along with his haughty nose.

'It was the housekeeper,' he barked, scowling at her. Berenice longed to flee the room. His temper was notoriously short, and all quaked before his outbursts, which were usually directed at incompetence or dishonesty, two failings which he would not tolerate.

I suspected as much, thought Berenice angrily. That prattling old busybody would not miss the chance to blacken my name and ingratiate herself with Papa. Aloud she said, 'I'm surprised that you stooped to heed the gossip of underlings. What more can I add, since you choose to take her word against mine?'

'I'll not countenance it, Berenice!' he thundered, jabbing a finger at her. 'You go out and about with Lucinda Clayton, that woman who calls herself an actress, but is known by all as a painted fly-by-night!'

'She's my friend!' Berenice rounded on him. 'And our escorts are noblemen.'

'That's as may be,' he answered darkly. 'But you're already committed, miss, and don't forget it!'

'Aye, committed to a marriage that I don't want and which has been forced on me!' she cried, eyes sparkling with tears that she was too proud to shed. 'Oh, Papa, couldn't I have been given a choice?'

They had been over this many times and always he had clung steadfastly to his determination that the alliance should take place,

40

refusing to be swayed by the protests of a girl whom he considered to be too young to know her own mind. This was how marriages had been arranged down the centuries, and he saw no good reason for changing the established rule. The Marquis squared his shoulders and gazed sternly at his youngest child, seeing her beauty, her slender, full-bosomed body, her aristocratic birth showing in her bearing, the faintly regal tilt of her head and the set of her chin. It was only in the azure eyes that a certain vulnerability betrayed itself—that, and the trembling softness of her mouth.

The sight of her caught at his heart, for she resembled her mother whom he had loved. Memories flooded up within him, threatening to weaken his resolve. 'It's too late now. Your bridegroom has already arrived,' he snapped.

Berenice took a step back, hands clasped against her breasts, eyes widening in the fading light. Shocks of fear rippled through her, the blind panic of a trapped animal. 'He's here? In London?' she gasped, the color draining from her face, leaving it alabaster white.

The Marquis experienced a pang at having broken the news so harshly. But dammit, he thought, most girls would be overjoyed at the prospect of such a wealthy match! What the devil ailed her?

'He'll be dining with us tonight,' he continued. 'I expect your attendance—and no tantrums. Is that understood?'

She nodded dumbly, a terrible sense of inevitability paralyzing her mind. Whatever she

41

said or did, the same fate awaited her—that marriage which had hung over her like a storm cloud for years, shadowing her youth. Now it had come—the day that she had been dreading. She was to meet the man destined to be her husband and, all too soon, the ceremony would be performed that would bind them together forever. Whether they felt liking or loathing for one another was quite immaterial. It had been ordained. And she would have to leave her homeland—England, with its gentle, misty landscapes, its damp, soft climate, its pale, fresh springs, the flaming, hay-sweet days of high summer, golden autumns and snow-powdered winters. All that was so dear and familiar to her would now be exchanged for a vast, unknown and terrifying country far away across the ocean. America! Where huge tracts were still unexplored and inhabited by Indians. Uncivilized. Uncultured. And she would be wedded to a stranger!

She fought to choke back the sob that was gathering in her chest, digging her pointed nails into the palms of her hands. She refused to give way to tears in front of this unbending man who called himself a father and yet, without a qualm, could send his only daughter miles away to a foreign shore. She gave him one final, agonized glance, then stormed to the door.

His voice arrested her. 'I shall expect your presence at seven o'clock precisely,' he reminded.

Berenice almost screamed with frustration. Never mind that her heart was breaking! Oh, no—let the skies fall, the earth stop spinning, they must dine at seven! 'Very well, Papa,' she hissed through clenched teeth, then closed the door behind her.

A manservant, who had been eavesdropping, jumped back guiltily. Berenice gave him a withering look and brushed past, skirts held high as she ran up the stairs to the privacy of her chamber, impelled by rage and despair. For minutes, she stared at her reflection in the mirror, hands pressed flat on the surface of the dressing table, as if seeking an answer to her problems. Very soon, she would be a stranger even to herself—Madame la Comtesse—yet she could form no mental picture of her future life. She had learned French during the course of her education, but had never visited France. England had been at war with that country since 1793, and how she wished that the Lajeaunesse brood had never escaped to the New World. An arrangement made so long before the outbreak of hostilities would then have been easily broken, but now her future husband was no longer a Frenchman—he was an American.

She found no help in the sight of her own familiar face staring back at her. Oh, that she might avoid her fate! Fearful, disjointed thoughts buzzed in her head like a swarm of angry bees. What would he look like? She imagined him to be elderly, short and dark, like some of the *emigrés* who had settled in England after the Revolution. How could she bear it? If she were to be unhappy, there would be no escape. And Peregrine, dear, romantic Peregrine! Pain lanced her at the thought of leaving him. It was impossible. She must talk to him tonight. Perhaps they could elope before it was too late.

How long she stayed thus, lost in a wilderness of misery, she did not know. She was disturbed at last by the quiet entry of Millicent, who had come to prepare her for dinner. Like an animated doll, Berenice suffered herself to be bathed in the brass tub filled with warm, delicately scented water. The tub stood on a rug before the hearth and the flickering flames dancing over her, joining the glow of the many candles set in holders round the room. Under Millicent's gentle ministrations, Berenice relaxed a little. But still the thought burned in her mind that soon such privacy would be denied her. At any time it could be invaded by her husband. Her soul cringed, a blush staining her cheeks at the idea of a stranger viewing her body—and to be sure, he would expect much more than mere looking.

The idea revolted her, yet she was impatient with her own inexperience, angry with those who had given her such a sheltered upbringing. Surely they were to blame for the fact that she was now filled with this irrational terror? Oh, Lucinda had talked of the sexual act—cynical, worldly, she had held up three mirrors in which Berenice might see the male creature. The husband—usually a drunken, tight-fisted wretch with no awareness of his wife's feelings; the lover—willing to be a humble doormat on

44

which his adored one could wipe her dainty shoes, buying her presents, writing poems in her honor. Did Peregrine come into this category? Then there was the other man—the vile seducer, pouncing on virgins. Lucinda had been careful to warn her against all three, but her advice made Berenice's head whirl.

Once the bathing was over, she sat on a stool before the dressing table, wrapped in a thick white towel, while Millicent brushed her luxuriant hair before piling it on top of her head in a cascade of ringlets. Then she was dusted lavishly with perfumed powder and helped into a gossamer-thin chemise. The gown followed next, a simple white muslin sheath with—just under the bosom—a pink satin ribbon which allowed the skirt to fall straight to the ground. The Grecian effect was completed by the low, square neckline and short, puffed sleeves. Millicent then rolled white stockings up Berenice's legs, fastened them with buckled garters, and slipped a pair of pink satin pumps on her feet.

The gilt clock on the mantel struck a quarter to seven. Berenice started, so nervous that the palms of her hands began to sweat beneath the lacy mittens. Hurriedly, she added a touch of rouge to her lips and cheeks, whilst her maid placed a bandeau ornamented with a single, curling white ostrich plume on her curls. She was ready to go down. Ready? Dear God, she thought, I'll never be ready for this evening's work!

The great crystal chandeliers in the hall were ablaze with a multitude of candles as Berenice walked silently across the mosaic tiles and stood, trembling, at the door of the anteroom. Her heart was thudding hard and she felt cold, though the night was not exceptionally chilly and the house was well heated, with fires burning in almost every chamber. An ice pall seemed to enfold her, an inner, apprehensive shivering that would not be stilled. A starchy footman, wearing formal livery and a white-powdered wig, flung wide the door with a flourish and announced her. Just for an instant, Berenice hesitated, dazzled by the glare of light which illuminated the room, the whole scene reflected to infinity in the long mirrors. Her father was standing near the mahogany sideboard with her brother, Damian, surrounded by his guests. He broke free, stepping forward to meet her, accompanied by one of them.

'Ah, my dear daughter,' he said, his voice rising above the murmur of voices. He sounded pleased, though rather guarded, as if unsure of her reaction. 'It gives me great joy to introduce you to your bridegroom, who has come all the way from America to fetch you. Comte Sebastian Lajeaunesse, allow me to present your bride-to-be—Lady Berenice.'

For a second of pure horror, she thought that she was dreaming. Or that the entire world had gone mad. She stood speechless, rooted to the spot with astonishment. Then fear blanched her cheeks, and she breathed unsteadily. Standing before her, with the same mocking smile twisting his mouth, was the arrogant devil who had accosted her in the tavern. She shook her head

46

in a tiny gesture of denial, as recognition flashed between them.

Sebastian recovered first, bowing gracefully over her hand and raising it to his lips. The touch of his fingers on hers, the press of his mouth against the lace, was like a burning fire shooting up her arm into her pounding heart. Almost rudely, she dragged her hand away, while the Marquis watched, his smile thinning, puzzled by her violent gesture. The guests clustered round, offering their congratulations, lifting their glasses of champagne in a toast. Merciful heaven, thought Berenice despairingly, everyone seems delighted, except me. Then, glancing shyly up at Sebastian, she was surprised and not a little piqued to catch him viewing her with the blackest scowl that she had ever seen. Obviously, he was as appalled at the prospect of the marriage as herself. It was most unflattering. Mentally she chalked up another mark against him.

Sebastian caught the meaning of her expression and, aware of the Marquis's stare, offered her his arm, drawing her apart from the crowd. 'Well madame, here's a fine jest!' he began, a mirthless smile on his mouth. 'The circumstances are somewhat different from when we last met, eh?' His dark brows were raised in a haughty manner, his green eyes watching her suspiciously.

Berenice took her hand from his arm, uncomfortably conscious that every eye was on them and that the guests were smiling indulgently, nodding and winking to assure the

47

Marquis that matters were progressing smoothly. Sebastian was so large and overpowering that she found it difficult to breathe. He towered at least twelve inches over her modest five feet four, and she felt dwarfed. Yet she had to admit grudgingly that he was quite devastatingly handsome. He was dressed in a superbly fitting jacket of claret velvet, over a black satin waistcoat from which hung a collection of gold fobs, and white breeches which reached the tops of his highly polished Hessian boots. His ruffled shirt front and stock were of the finest lawn his dark, intensely masculine face perfectly shaven, his hair glossy and stylish. He was the acme of refined, confident aristocracy, and she should have rejoiced that she was promised to such a man—but she did not.

'Why did it have to be *you?*' she whispered fiercely.

He laughed softly, unpleasantly. 'Why indeed? Do you suppose it gives me pleasure to find that my future wife is a flighty ladybird who frequents low taverns with a collection of prancing fops?'

Their hostility was so intense that it seemed the air crackled about them. Berenice tossed her dark curls, mulishly resolving not to bother explaining to him her reason for going there. If he thought her promiscuous—well, let him! The thick-witted colonial!

Sebastian was as bewildered and angry as she by the turn of events. He had disembarked in the port of London early that morning and immediately sent a message to Elsewood House. The trip had been planned for some time, and he had sent the Marquis a letter weeks before, giving the approximate date of arrival. But it seemed the old man had kept the news to himself. Now, instead of the genteel English lady whom Sebastian had expected to meet, he found himself face to face with the harpy who had infuriated him in the taproom of the Rose and Crown.

Oh, she was lovely enough, there was no doubt of that. The creature who glared at him so defiantly was positively queenly, but wayward and probably spoilt, too—a society butterfly, accustomed to the fawning attentions of the gallants. He harbored serious doubts as to her virtue. Even as far away as Carolina, word had reached him of the licentious behavior in Court circles, of the orgies and entertainments given at Carlton House, Prince George's palace in London, and the high jinks that took place at Brighton, the seaside resort which his raffish Royal Highness had made so popular. How could Berenice have remained pure with so many temptations abounding?

The thought gave him an uneasy feeling in the gut and, had he not been convinced otherwise, he might have imagined it to be jealousy. No, it couldn't be that, he told himself severely; it was more likely a question of pride and family honor. He didn't intend to make a wanton the mistress of his vast, wealthy, hard-won acres. And yet there was no way out; the documents had been signed and all that remained was the wedding ceremony—and the consummation. His mind lingered on that thought, savoring it, quick

49

desire leaping in him as he remembered the honeyed sweetness of her mouth when he had forced his kiss upon her. Now he regarded her slowly, speculatively, in a way that brought the color to her cheeks.

Dieu, he would make her his bride and then bend the little minx to his will, he vowed silently. Already he could feel the strong pull of an allure of which she herself was only half conscious. His eyes roved over her face, her throat, and then moved lower to her bodice, which was cut so low across the bosom as to leave her shoulders bare and hardly cover the young, upthrusting breasts.

'Stop looking at me like that,' she muttered, terror, a sense of outrage, and an odd, tingling excitement warring in her.

He chuckled coolly, so sure of himself that she stabbed about in her mind for something witty and hurtful to say, but was at a loss for words, coherent thought deserting her. There was wicked amusement on his swarthy, handsome face as he whispered,

'I have every right to look at you—and more. In a short while every inch of you will belong to me.'

'Oh, you're insufferable!' she hissed, longing to tell him exactly what she thought of him, but the Marquis was glancing across at them anxiously, and dinner was about to be served.

Berenice dreaded the grueling hours ahead, during which she would have not only to endure Sebastian's odious company, but pretend to everyone that she was delighted to do so. Her

50

loyalty to her father demanded that she did not make a scene, or give those present a tasty tidbit of scandal to spread abroad. As it was, she was sure they were looking at her askance. Maybe they had heard about the duel. Did Sebastian know of it, too?

To add to her chagrin, Peregrine arrived just as they were about to be seated, in the company of Lady Chard, an old friend of the family. Berenice had quite forgotten that he was her ladyship's nephew, and had certainly not expected him to be invited. In the midst of the buzz of greetings and introductions, she was acutely conscious of the angry glance of recognition exchanged between him and Sebastian. She fought for composure, finding it impossible to meet her fiancé's eye.

She had been placed beside him at the long oval table, opposite the Marquis, a sea of snowy damask cloth, sparkling cut glass and glittering silver dishes and condiments stretching out between them. The many courses were served by a fleet of footmen, and there was an enormous variety of food. Dining was a leisurely affair, lasting two or three hours. The Marquis selected his guests with care, particularly on such an important occasion as this. It was a time for intellectual exchange, and the ramifications of European politics came under discussion, along with many other matters. On each topic Sebastian seemed remarkably well informed, his comments shrewd and intelligent. The Marquis dwelt briefly on lighter subjects, too—the works of writers and artists—but always in a serious vein. He did not encourage gossip or waste time on trivia. Tonight there was also another fascinating theme—America. There in their midst was a man who could give firsthand information: Monsieur le Comte.

'Pray, sir, do tell us about it,' gushed Lady Chard, leaning forward eagerly, the mottled skin of her breasts rising against the frills of her elaborate bodice.

Like many of the older generation, she scorned the modern trend for skimpy, immodest dresses and clung to the outmoded panniers which stuck out on either side of her portly waist, supporting yards of material. She rolled her eyes at Sebastian with heavy encouragement, the topmost curls of her absurd hairpiece quivering. She was flanked by her plain, dumpy daughters, Jane and Sarah, who were simpering at him in a way which disgusted Berenice. How could they be so deceived by his good looks and facile charm? She knew him for what he really was—a blackguard who had insulted her.

'Will Monsieur le Comte's adventures be fit for the ears of young ladies?' Berenice broke in, her serene expression hiding her desire to denigrate him in any way possible. 'I've been led to understand that America is peopled by slaves, Indians, and criminals running from justice.' Her voice rang with sweet reasonableness, but her eyes met Sebastian's with a warning glare.

A ripple of consternation at such boldness passed round the table; some laughed, thinking that she jested. Sebastian looked at her steadily, relaxed and easy in his chair, long legs stretched out, a wineglass in one lean, tanned hand.

'It's far more civilized than you imagine, Lady Berenice,' he said quietly. 'I'll admit there are still huge regions as yet uncharted, but the towns flourish. Why, we even have musical concerts and plays. Of course, there've been troubles—strife between the settlers—the War of Independence—but that was long ago. It's a place of golden opportunity, a prodigal land where game and fish abound. Animals are in abundant supply, and one of my main sources of income is the fur trade.'

'A trapper!' commented Berenice scornfully. The wine had gone to her head, making her reckless. On her lips the words were transformed into an insult.

'Among other things,' he answered drily, raising his glass to his lips and studying her over the rim. 'I also own acres of timber, rice and tobacco fields, a fine plantation house called Oakwood Hall, and a mansion in Charleston. A piece of the coast also belongs to me—a quiet spot known as Mobby Cove. I've a manor there too, a rambling old building known as Buckhorn House, to visit on my hunting trips. In all, we colonials live much as the gentry do here. Southerners in particular delight in the title of "the Quality." '

Lady Chard listened rapturously, then exclaimed, 'Oh, I know something of this, sir. I have a sister living in Georgetown. She married into a very fine family—such good blood!'

They sound as if they're discussing thoroughbreds, thought Berenice gloomily. Soon the talk became more general, but she found it impossible to do more than pick at her food, nerves jangling each time Sebastian spoke or moved, and she was constantly sneaking a glance down the table to where Peregrine was paying court to his aunt. He looked suave in a blue tail coat, the cuffs flashing with rhinestone buttons, a smile hovering about his lips as he toasted Berenice silently. He dropped an eyelid in a brief, conspiratorial wink and she shifted her gaze demurely to her plate. In so doing she missed the expression on Sebastian's face, for little escaped his hunter's eye. Seeing the intimacy between her and Peregrine, his features set so that they appeared to be carved out of granite.

The Marquis, meanwhile, was in an expansive mood. He had quite taken to his proposed son-in-law, liking his down-to-earth approach to trade, his general air of confidence without vulgar brashness. Satisfied with the match, he chose to ignore Berenice's sulky mouth and to concentrate instead on enjoying the company of his friends. There was his architect, a voluble Italian, quick of speech and gesture, full of ideas for turning Stretton Court into a monument for posterity. Next to him sat Lady Chard, and then Damian, that fine young sprig of the House of Rossiter—tall and straight, boyish still, but showing manly promise in his carriage and voice. Damian was pleasantly good-looking, though he lacked his sister's singular beauty. He resembled her nonetheless, the same nose, eyes of a paler blue, hair a shade darker. The

54

Marquis knew of the devotion between them; they were forever supporting one another in madcap schemes.

'And when is the wedding to take place?' enquired Lady Chard, smiling patronizingly at Berenice. 'So exciting, my dear. I'll be only too happy to advise and assist. I'm much experienced in such matters, I assure you, having already seen three of my girls walk down the aisle as lovely brides. I dare say that these two will follow before long.' She beamed proudly on her blushing daughters, while Berenice seethed.

'I have to leave for America without too much delay,' announced Sebastian, subjecting them his most dazzling smile, which put the giggling girls in a flutter. 'Though I would like to see something of England.'

'So you shall, my dear sir,' the Marquis declared. 'I think a trip to Bath will be in order, and I'd like to take you to Stretton Court, my family seat in Wiltshire. I'm sure this can be arranged.'

'Thank you, my lord.' Sebastian inclined his head, lips curling in a pleasant smile.

'I suggest that we go next week, stay for a few days, and then return to London for the wedding. Let me see, the preparations should be completed within the month.' The Marquis brought this out firmly, daring Berenice to argue.

There was a second's silence, then everyone began to talk at once, expressing their approval of the plan—everyone, that is, except Berenice.

She was aware only of the bleak look on Peregrine's face, the flash of anger which he quickly controlled.

'So soon?' questioned Damian, alarmed by the pinched appearance of his sister's mouth, his sympathy reaching out to her.

'I have decided.' The Marquis thumped his fist on the table, making the glasses clink. He turned to Sebastian. 'Does this suit you, monsieur?'

Sebastian nodded, glancing under his brows at Berenice. 'Admirably, sir. It will give me ample time to stock my ship with merchandise. What does my betrothed think?'

Berenice felt crushed, wanting to cry, unable to swim against the remorseless tide of events. Of what value was her opinion? No one would listen. 'I'm sensible of my duty,' she replied. 'Even were I to wish it otherwise, it is a daughter's part to obey her father's commands.' She directed her words to Peregrine, though not daring to look his way, praying that he might understand.

Damian, however, was only too aware of her state of mind. They had discussed the situation over and over. She gave him a tremulous smile which touched his heart with sadness. Plainly, meeting Sebastian had done nothing to alter her views. The idea of her going reluctantly to a foreign land was repugnant to him, but go she must and he resolved to support her. He swung round to his father, his fresh young face alight with enthusiasm.

'Can I go too, sir? I'd like to accompany my

sister. What an adventure! Please give me your blessing!'

The elderly nobleman's face softened as he regarded his son, then he patted him benignly on the shoulder. 'You have it, my boy. Had it not been for this deuced war, you'd have done your grand tour of Europe long before now. It will be good for you to travel the world before settling down to manage the estates when I pass on.'

'Ah, don't speak of dying, sir!' Damian's face was a mixture of delight at having got his way and regret that the Marquis should mention death. Berenice felt a pang, too, noting that their father had aged of late and was stooping a little, yet his dignity remained and with it an air of authority impossible to gainsay.

'You'll enjoy your stay with us, I'm sure,' promised Sebastian, conscious of the emotions that seemed to ripple over the features of brother and sister. 'There's a lively social life in town, and good hunting in the forests. You'll be able to come trapping with me, and see some Indians. Some of my best friends are Indians.'

Indians! thought Berenice sourly. Fit companions for the likes of him! Oh, he appears civilized now—sickeningly sophisticated! But I know the real villain beneath that show.

Though fond of Peregrine, Lady Chard had grown weary of supporting her spendthrift nephew and had decided, some time ago, that what he needed was a purpose in life. With a sudden flash of inspiration; 'Why don't you go too, Peregrine?' she suggested. 'Aunt Agatha will be overjoyed to see you. You could stay with her in Georgetown.'

Berenice waited breathlessly for his reply, hope springing up in her breast. But his thin face expressed almost as much surprise and alarm as if Lady Chard had just proposed that he should fly to the moon. 'I've never thought of it!' he stuttered. 'America! Gad's life—!'

'Oh, come on, old fellow!' Damian urged, fired by the idea. 'It'll be a tremendous lark! And company for Berenice.'

'It takes a certain verve and courage to journey so far—particularly if we visit the backwoods.' Sebastian's deep, foreign-sounding voice cut across the conversation. 'Do you have such qualities, sir?'

His eyes glittered, and Berenice was again uneasily conscious of the force which emanated from him, instinctively recognizing that he would be a merciless adversary. Peregrine threw him an angry glance, still smarting from his ignominious defeat in the tavern. He hated the implication that he was not man enough for the colonies.

'You'll not find me lacking in resolution, sir,' he snapped.

Lady Chard clapped her hands gleefully. 'Then it's settled! We shall have a memorable wedding, after which you dear young people will all go adventuring. I'll expect you to write regularly, Peregrine, and mind that you bring me back a handsome present!'

Everyone laughed and the atmosphere lightened. The meal over, the ladies retired to the drawing room, while the men lingered over port and further talk. There Lady Chard took the opportunity to air her views about Sebastian.

'My word, how fortunate you are!' she gushed, settling her hooped skirts over a serpentine-shaped couch.

'You think so?' Berenice flicked open her lace fan and stirred the air between them, knowing that she could not escape a half-hour of questions and innuendos.

'What a fine man! Isn't he, girls?' the stout, motherly lady drew her daughters into the discussion.

'Oh, yes, Mama! Mighty fine!' they chorused, last year's debutantes who, as yet, had no suitors.

'How can you be so sure? None of us know him. He could be the biggest rogue under the sun.' Berenice sat rigidly on the edge of a gilt-framed chair, a tight smile pasted across her face.

'You jest, of course? He's no such thing.' Lady Chard leaned over and rested a plump hand on Berenice's knee, the skin whitened in an attempt to emulate the freshness of youth. 'I can tell, my dear. I'm experienced in such matters. Why, it shows in every inch of him—such breeding, such spectacular good looks—such a gentleman—and such wealth! If only my girls could find someone like him!'

'Oh, Mama, if only we could!' they sighed in unison, staring at Berenice enviously with their silly, grape-shaped eyes.

Later, they were joined by the gentlemen,

and some of them played whist, while the Marquis strolled on the terrace with Sebastian, engrossed in conversation. Feigning reluctance, all giggles and bashful protests, Jane and Sarah were persuaded to sing a duet, accompanied on the harpsichord by Berenice, the applause sounding false to her for she considered the girls' performances excruciating.

At last the evening dragged to a close and it was time to retire. As she stood beside her father, bidding the visitors good night, she managed to whisper a reminder in Peregrine's ear, 'The temple, at midnight.' His hand touched hers and he nodded, a flame glowing in the depths of his eyes.

'I have invited the Comte to stay here as our guest,' the Marquis announced, delighted with this man, whom he had found astute and knowledgeable.

'You are too kind,' Sebastian bowed. 'I shall, of course, find suitable lodgings when we return from Bath.'

'Why did Papa do that?' she murmured crossly to Damian as he gave her a kiss good night.

'He likes him, and so do I,' her brother countered, annoying her so much that she pushed him away.

'He's bewitched you, too, has he? Well, he's not pulled the wool over my eyes,' she countered. 'I hope his chamber is as far away from mine as possible.'

'It won't be for much longer,' Damian reminded with a grin.

'Don't!' she shuddered, and ran up the staircase.

She paused when she reached the top, one hand on the newel post, glancing back and seeing how the candlelight glimmered on Sebastian's black hair, turning it to silver, as he bent his head respectfully, listening to something the Marquis was saying. The sound of his voice as he replied to her father sent a chill through her. She whirled round and fled for the sanctity of her bedroom.

THREE

When Berenice entered her room, she found Millicent shaking the pillows from their decorative daytime coverings and smoothing them out before arranging them neatly at the folded edge of the lace-trimmed sheet. Then she helped Berenice unpin her hair so that it flowed in a curling mass almost to her waist, and assisted her to undress and don her nightgown and robe.

All the time, inside her, Berenice was conscious of an expectant hush and a sense of waiting. Soon she dismissed Millicent, who left her propped up in bed. Picking up a book from the side table, she leaned closer to the china candlestick. It was impossible to settle down and read, and her eyes roamed the room, taking in the details; the Persian rugs,

61

the massive armoire containing her clothes, the looped-back bed curtains, the firelight dancing across the ceiling.

Downstairs, the long-case clock in the hall chimed a quarter to twelve. Berenice got up and crept to the window, her filmy gown and negligee billowing behind her. She stared through the panes into the night beyond. It had stopped raining, and a shard of moonlight notched between the clouds and lit the garden. The mundane objects outside seemed mysterious, the lawns, the paved walks, the statues with their blind eyes. Berenice shivered in anticipation and fear, wondering if Peregrine was out there under the dripping trees. She could just glimpse the mock temple, its cupola silhouetted between a break in the trees. The house was silent, yet filled with Sebastian's presence, even though the guest wing was on the other side of the building and she hoped that he might be asleep.

Berating herself for her cowardice, she went to a recess and took down a lantern from a top shelf, lighting the candle within before throwing an enveloping cloak over her night attire and leaving the room. Gliding along the corridor and down the stairs, she entered the deserted drawing room, the beam of her lantern flickering weakly over the waxed floor that seemed to stretch out endlessly before her. To her intense relief, she found that the key had been left in the double glass doors.

It was the work of seconds to let herself out, cross the terrace and run down the shallow steps. The dew of the smooth grass struck damp through her thin slippers. She circled the pond and headed for the grove. It was gloomy there, and the artificial ruined pillars of the temple reared over her. Fear made her mouth dry, and she gave an involuntary scream, nearly dropping the lantern when someone moved towards her, dark as the night itself, wrapped in a cloak.

Arms came about her, and Peregrine was murmuring in her ear. 'Darling, I thought you were never coming.'

Relief washed through her, and she pressed her cheek against the velvety texture of his coat, smelling the laundered freshness of his linen, the scent of his skin, the pomade he used on his hair. It was a poignant reminder of all she had to lose.

'Oh, what are we to do?' She clung to him frantically, catching her breath on a sob.

His lips found her forehead, her cheeks. 'My sweet—my angel,' he whispered, one finger softly brushing back the little curls from her brow, a soothing touch of comfort and concern. 'Don't distress yourself. Fate has decreed that we're not to be parted. Lady Chard has promised me money for the trip. Indeed, it proves a blessing in disguise. There are gambling debts outstanding, and several gentlemen who are getting rather ugly and demanding their dues. It'll be wise for me to skip the country for a while.'

Doubts began to assail her and she drew away, pouting up at him. 'Is this the only reason? I thought it was for my sake.'

'Of course I'm doing it for you, my love,' he

added hurriedly. 'We'll have time to plan our future.'

The future! A chill swept over her, though her body burned. She gave a moan of anguish. 'But what of my husband?'

His arm tightened round her. Out of reach of Sebastian's hard stare and sarcastic tongue, he could be bold. 'Damn the boorish fellow! At least I'll be there to see that he doesn't ill-treat you.'

Was that all he intended to do? It was a cruel disappointment. She longed to tell him of her half-formed plan for an elopement, yet she was shy, for he had never mentioned marriage, had not even said that he loved her, except through the fulsome phrases of his poems. Conscious of his body close to hers in the darkness, she sighed as his lips found her mouth, lips which were warm and gentle, so unlike those plundering ones of Sebastian. She recalled the intense sensations that his kiss had roused in her. Peregrine's embrace caused no such havoc.

She was suddenly concerned at her own lack of ardor. She did not burn—she merely felt restful with him, as one would feel in the arms of a parent or a brother, safe and at peace. She looked at him when he lifted his head, listening to her own heartbeats, waiting to feel that goose-flesh prickle of her skin which had tormented her at Sebastian's touch. She remained placid, unmoved. She liked to hold his hand, enjoyed his kisses and his company, but was it love, that mysterious thing for which she had been waiting so long?

Keeping an arm about her, Peregrine guided her down a flight of rough-hewn steps to the grotto. Once, this had been a natural cavern through which a stream flowed, but the Marquis had enlarged it, turning it into a fairy-tale cave, its walls sparkling with East Indian shells and semi-precious stones. The stream, redirected, now formed miniature waterfalls, cascading into a series of stone basins and culminating in one large pool where a mossy, green-bronze Neptune sported with buxom mermaids.

Peregrine released her just long enough to hang the lantern on a hook hammered into an overhanging rock, then he spread his cloak across a bed of dried ferns on a level plateau above the water and drew her down on to it. She sank into his arms, though still struggling to voice the idea forming in her mind.

'Peregrine,' she began, embarrassed and a trifle irritated. Surely, he should have been the one to suggest that they elope? 'Why can't we run away together?'

He grew still for a moment, his breath tickling her ear. A sudden panic seized him. So she was serious! For his part, he loved the idea of being in love and was ever ready to write of its glories and thrill to its drama, but the reality scared him half to death. He much preferred to set his adored one on a pedestal, far removed from the bawdy-house trollops whom he visited for physical relief. Then he said, 'Elope? But I'm not a rich man, beloved.'

Berenice scrambled up on her knees beside him as he sprawled on the cloak, her face alive with eagerness. 'There are always my jewels!'

His expression was wary in the dim light, as he continued to stroke her fingers, but said doubtfully, 'Sell them, do you mean?'

He was practical enough to know that they would need far more than the proceeds from a few gems. The legal position was uncertain, too. Berenice had already been married to Sebastian by proxy and all that remained was the church ceremony. His brain ached with the complexity of it. Adore Berenice though he might, did he really want to embark on such a course?

Berenice sensed his tepidity and felt hurt and angry. The bold hero of the romance books she devoured would not have been so tardy. He would have jumped at the chance to save his lady! Nothing would have stopped him making passionate love to her, claiming her as his own, and snatching her from under Sebastian's nose. In her heart, she admitted that she had come there tonight with the intention of giving herself to Peregrine, thus settling the matter. Faced with a dishonored bride, Sebastian would be forced to release her.

Or would he? With a shiver, she recalled that angular, harsh-looking face and piercing green eyes that glinted so wickedly, sapping her strength and filling her with painful giddiness. She could well imagine that, denied the satisfaction of taking her virginity, he would insist on keeping her prisoner and making her life a living hell, solely in order to be revenged.

'Oh, Peregrine, don't leave me! I'm frightened!' she implored, suddenly seized with unreasoning panic.

He reached for her again, stroking the bare shoulder beneath her wrap, his hands sliding lower, moving over the pliant body in his arms. Previously he had been unable to make love to ladies of quality—perhaps tonight would be different. Used to the offices of whores, who knew how to arouse him and expected nothing but payment in return, Peregrine was impotent with any other type of woman, no matter how much he wanted her. Tonight, however, he was aware of desire, and to this was added the pleasure of imagining himself performing gallant deeds in America, maybe saving Berenice from savage Indians! It made him feel virile and manly. He kissed her face, tasting her tears, excited by them.

Berenice began to experience misgivings. They had rarely been alone during their courtship, and had done little more than exchange fervent glances, touch fingertips and snatch a few chaste kisses. The idea of yielding to him had been all very fine in the cloistered seclusion of her chamber, but now that they were together, she was having second thoughts. Beneath her nightwear, she was naked, every curve and hollow exposed to his exploring fingers. She tried to push him away, but he groaned as if in pain.

'Please, Berenice—don't stop me, I beg you. I need you—I want you—'

She longed to give in, but at the same time

she was frightened. His face was so handsome and sensitive, his fair hair tousled, making him look boyish. How could she refuse him? Then she became aware that he had stopped caressing her, his head flung up and a listening look on his face.

'Hush!' he whispered warningly. 'There's someone outside.' He jerked away from her, stumbling to his feet. She heard him cursing beneath his breath; then she, too, was aware of a voice, recognizing it as belonging to Barnaby, the watchman. He had arrived at the grotto's entrance, his challenge bouncing off the shimmering walls.

'Is anyone down there?'

Berenice moved quickly, wrapping her cloak about her as she went to meet him before he descended the steps and discovered them. She almost collided with him. His startled face peered out from under his tricorn hat. He held a lantern in one sturdy fist, a blunderbuss in the other.

'Barnaby!' she said crisply, assuming her most commanding manner. 'It's Lady Berenice. I'm searching for Sheba. Have you seen her? I fear that the moonlight has lured her out to chase rabbits, the naughty little dog.'

'No, ma'am, I ain't seen nothing of her. Indeed, you shouldn't be roaming here alone, milady—too many footpads and rough persons abroad in the darkness. They might do you mischief. Shall I escort you to the house?'

'Wait for me in the garden,' she ordered haughtily. 'I must fetch my lantern.'

Puffing and grumbling to himself, Barnaby saluted, turned and shuffled off into the gloom. She raced back to the grotto, where Peregrine stood in the shadows. 'I have to go, my love,' she said quietly, oddly relieved by the interruption.

'So soon?' he protested. 'You're always snatched away from me.'

'It won't be like that in future, I promise.' She gazed at him seriously, stirred by his sorrowful looks, his words, his passion. 'You will come to America, won't you?'

He nodded, and she leaned against him for a moment. His lips brushed hers briefly and then she left him, her lantern casting sweeping light and shadows over the grotto as she ran.

For Barnaby's benefit, she called Sheba's name frequently on the way back to the house, pretending that she saw her in nearby bushes and ordering him to poke about in fruitless search. He escorted her to the steps of the terrace and then stumped towards the kitchen with a final warning to be sure to lock the door securely. Berenice breathed a deep sigh of relief as she sought the darkness of the drawing room, believing herself safe at last. She had barely taken a step inside when a figure appeared in the gloom, and she gave a smothered shriek as Sebastian materialized in front of her. His hand shot out to grip her arm, while with the other he wrested the lantern from her and placed it on a table.

His voice cut through the night air, cool, sardonic, menacing. 'Where have you been, madame? Enjoying a midnight stroll?'

She was shaking, her pulse jumping madly, but she tugged at her arm indignantly. 'How dare you spy on me? I thought you were asleep!'

He gave a low chuckle, tightening his hold and making her wince. 'The devil you did! Creeping out to meet your lover, were you? That damned weakling, Peregrine!'

'We're not married yet, sir!' she retorted, though she could feel the guilty color rush to her cheeks.

'Ah, but we soon will be, *ma chérie,* and I'm going to make damned sure that no seducer's hands roam over my property before or after the ceremony, even if I have to chain you to the bedpost to prevent it!' Though his exterior seemed to be relaxed and controlled, Berenice caught the chill gleam in his eyes and was horribly aware that her future husband was in an extremely dangerous mood.

He was so big, so awe-inspiring! And he looked even larger in semiundress, for he had discarded the velvet jacket and satin waistcoat he had worn earlier. His white shirt was now open to the waist, showing an expanse of chest covered with a curling mat of black hair. He still wore his tight breeches and boots of soft leather, but there was something untamed about him, as if the trappings of the gentleman had been set aside. Berenice felt a bolt of pure, primitive fear, both for herself and for Peregrine.

'He's a good friend—nothing more. We speak of poetry, of music and the theater.

70

He offers me companionship and intellectual exchange—things which I doubt someone like you could understand,' she said bitingly, chin at a haughty tilt.

A disbelieving snort greeted her prim words. 'Do you really expect me to accept such nonsense?' he stated flatly. 'That idiot fancies himself in love with you. It's obvious by the way he looks at you, in the stupid manner in which he runs to obey your smallest, most foolish whim. I know! I've watched him all evening.'

'Then why did you agree to him accompanying us to America?' she asked, while inwardly she was wondering why she was bothering to argue with this barbarian.

She barely knew the man, and yet here they were, quarreling as if their relationship was one of long standing. Fight it though she might, she had the queerest sensation that they had met before, far away in the mists of time. All that was wild and reckless in her soul responded to the same qualities in his. He disturbed and perplexed her, and she had the awful suspicion that there would never be calm, serene waters in her existence again.

An ugly expression twisted his mouth. 'It'll amuse me to have him come along. There should be rare sport in watching him adjust to life on board ship—so dandified, so supercilious! And a real treat to introduce him to the backwoodsmen and trappers. They'll make mincemeat of him!'

'You're cruel and horrible!' She shuddered away, but he would not let her go, making her aware of the closeness of his body as he slid

71

his arms under her cloak.

'Oh, I am, there's no doubt of it,' he murmured suavely. 'I'm a—how do you English put it? A cad? A bounder? As you'll presently find out.'

Annoying she might be, but Sebastian could not deny that she was lovely. His hand brushed against her naked shoulder, so cool, so soft, and he felt an overwhelming urge to stroke it, yet at the same time he was furiously angry with her. How dare that little hellcat play fast and loose when she was about to become his wife! Certainly she was not in the least the compliant, meek creature he had expected.

He had arrived ready to do his best as a husband, to look after his wife, provide for her, asking only that she give him children, run his household efficiently, and take her place beside him in Charleston society. He had not expected love—had closed his mind to that painful emotion long ago—besides which, it was a factor considered irrelevant in arranged marriages. Husbands were expected to indulge their lusts elsewhere, in the timeworn tradition. It had been far from encouraging to find such a dazzling, wayward hussy as his intended bride, and it had thrown him, quite upsetting his carefully laid plans.

During dinner, he had become convinced that she was up to something, and had retired to his room in a surly mood, drinking brandy and brooding darkly on the puzzling enigma of women. Sebastian had had his fair share of amorous encounters, and it seemed to him that from babyhood girls were taught that their strength lie in secrecy and duplicity. Even when they lay in his arms and whispered of love, he had the sneaking suspicion that they were deceiving him. He had not always felt like this. Just once he had allowed himself the unspeakable folly of falling in love, and that had ended in betrayal and disaster.

He stared down at Berenice with frowning black brows and harshly compressed lips, in his mind's eye seeing once more the alluring features of Giselle, the woman who had broken his heart during the French Revolution. Crazy for power, she had been willing to send anyone to the guillotine if it would help her get her greedy hands on wealth, power and authority. *Women!* And this one was no different, sneaking out in the dead of night for a sordid rendezvous with an effete dandy.

'You're hurting me!' Berenice's voice brought him back to the present.

He relaxed his hold slightly, irked that she had the power to arouse in him memories of the past which he had thought securely buried, forever. And yet, looking at the pale blur of her face, he was moved despite himself by the vulnerability which shone in those eyes. A feeling which he had thought dead stirred achingly in the region of his chest, and his fingers reached out to wind themselves in the glossy mane of hair that streamed across her shoulders. Before he realized what he was doing, he raised a fragrant tress to his lips.

'*M'amie,* you are exceedingly beautiful,' he

said in a low, husky voice, its timbre sending shivers down her spine. Then, frightened of such a show of weakness, he deliberately ruined the moment by adding, 'As desirable a little cocotte as any I've visited in the brothels of New Orleans.'

Berenice flinched and, stammering with rage, she cried, 'Oh, how I hate you! I don't want to be your wife!'

His eyes narrowed and hardened. 'Your wishes don't come into it, you silly child! It's purely dynastic. It's a matter of business and the amalgamation of two powerful families. What you or I feel about it personally is of no account!'

'You're insufferable!' Her temper, difficult to control at the best of times, now flared up.

She longed to hit him, to kick and scratch him, shock him into realizing that she was a person, not a chattel to be passed around! With a snarl, she drove hard at his chest and broke away, ready to spring across the floor and escape. But Sebastian was too quick for her. She heard a rip as he caught a handful of her gown and dragged her back to him, twisting and kicking like a fiend. Her struggles were useless. His arms closed about her like iron bands, binding her hands at her sides, forcing her to be still, mastering her squirming body effortlessly in a firm embrace.

'Mon enfant,' he breathed into her hair. 'Do you think to run back to your pretty-boy lover, eh? Don't try, for if you do, I'll wring your lovely neck. I'll never wear cuckold's horns.'

Before she had a chance to speak, he bent his head and captured her lips with his. Berenice was astonished by this tender caress. She had expected violence, but instead, his mouth was surprisingly sweet, closing softly over hers with a tenderness which moved her strangely. She fought to control the trembling, melting feeling that flowed through her, as her body of its own volition molded itself to his muscular form. Never before had she been kissed like that, feeling the surprise of his exploring tongue. It sent fiery shocks along her nerves, and she had the alarming desire to let her arms creep about his neck and hold him fast. With a great effort of will, she prevented herself from doing so, trying to escape his lips, but his hands came up, holding her head firmly, unwilling to relinquish the witchery of her mouth. Frantic with fury at her own response, she succeeded in tearing herself from his grip.

'No! No!' she panted, bewildered by the uprush of feeling which was turning her into a wanton, despite her loathing for him.

What sort of a woman was she, to be reduced to an animal by his kisses—an animal seeking nothing but the satisfaction of her lowest instincts? Unable even to think clearly, she was aware of his lips trailing over her face, her throat, his hands pushing aside the low neckline of her nightgown to bare her breasts to his touch.

'But yes! Yes! How very dramatic!' he mocked.

That mockery was the most cruel thing of all,

75

for it told her plainly that though he lusted for her, he despised her. Driven by devils of fear and pride, Sebastian placed a firm hand on her buttocks and pressed her thigh into his groin, letting her feel the hardness of his desire, almost taunting her with it.

She gave a smothered cry. Dramatic or no, this mustn't continue. 'You're no gentleman, sir. Let me go!' she demanded.

As if from a distance she heard him chuckle deeply and growl out; *'Non, mon trésor.* This is what life is about. I'll conquer you, vixen. You'll learn to enjoy it, when I'm your lord and master.'

His assured confidence in her final submission fanned the flames of her rage and gave her added strength. She stood facing him in the moonlight that poured through the windows, her skin shining like ivory between the front of her cloak.

Her voice was low and ominous as she said, 'You think you've won, don't you? But I haven't even started fighting yet!'

Giving him no chance to delay her, she raced across the floor, tearing open the door and making a dash for her room, convinced that Sebastian was in pursuit. With a great sigh of relief she finally slammed her door shut behind her and rammed the bolt home. Shedding tears of temper, she could not think of words bad enough to describe him. He was the exact kind of vile bully she loathed. Insensitive! Thick-skinned! No one was going to order her about and tell her what to do. Why, oh why, was her father so mercenary, so eager to lay hands on a share of the profits from Sebastian's cargo of smuggled furs? He had money enough.

Trade! The odious word which had been bandied about over the dinner table. Trade was the answer! Trade, with which no true gentleman would deign to associate himself. But times were changing, and Sebastian was considered a desirable adjunct to the family because he had run a boatload of those soft, pliable and infinitely salable skins out of his country, beneath the noses of the American excise officers. She was to be sacrificed on the altar of Mammon.

Sheba was sound asleep in her basket and did not stir as Berenice tossed off her robe and jumped into the high, canopied bed, the cold sheets making her shudder. Her mind was racing in confusion. She was unsure of Peregrine, though trying to convince herself otherwise, and unable to shake off the memory of Sebastian's strong arms and demanding mouth. Men! She hated them, and her fiancé above all. In the silence of the still room, she rolled on her back, one knee pressed into the other as if to preserve her virginity for as long as possible—tense, her heart fluttering, thinking ahead to the awful reality of the bridal couch.

Sebastian would possess her body. The idea appalled her. It would be a violation of her flesh—the very flesh she had viewed as a sacred vessel for a poet, like Peregrine. A mass of complex emotions rushed across her consciousness as her sleepless eyes stared up at the tester. Her mind skimmed over every detail of her conversations with Sebastian. No matter what she did or how uncharitable her thoughts, she could not banish him from her mind. It was as if he had indeed put a seal upon her when he subjected her to his kisses. She groaned aloud, burying her face in the pillows as if to escape the dreaded moment which was drawing ever closer.

The two carriages raced down the course at breakneck speed, hooves thudding on turf and iron-shod wheels rumbling. Light, high vehicles, fast and dangerous, each was drawn by a pair of sweating horses, matched black and dappled greys straining between the shafts.

The spectators yelled with excitement, for many had put money on the outcome. They were ranged along the edge of the grass that spread out like a great green carpet in front of the half-moon terrace of stately, white stone houses that made up Bath's magnificent Royal Crescent. Above were clear blue skies, the sun shining on the exhilarating and rather scandalous spectacle of Lady Berenice Rossiter pitting her phaeton against that of the champion, Sir Hugh Caldwell.

Berenice was aware of the crowd, though every bit of her mind and body was concentrated on giving Hugh the trouncing he richly deserved. How dare he so much as hint that she was incapable of handling a high-flyer? She had accepted his challenge, eager to prove herself his match, but chiefly motivated by the knowledge that Sebastian, who was away visiting Church Stretton with her father, would be infuriated when he heard about it.

Bath had buzzed when the news of the race had leaked out, the *ton* relishing this latest bit of gossip about Berenice. It had been enough that two men had fought a duel over her and that she was visiting the city in the company of her American fiancé. Then, as soon as his back was turned, she had thrown down the gauntlet to one of the finest sportsmen in the field of racing. Wagers had been laid and a large throng had gathered to witness the event.

I'll not let him beat me! Berenice vowed as, gloved hands clenched on the reins, she encouraged her team to give of their best, leaving Hugh behind. It was of paramount importance that she be the victor in this contest. If she did not succeed, then it would mean that, once again, she had been beaten by a man. In a muddled way, it was as if she were challenging Sebastian himself, showing him that she had a will of her own that he would never, never subdue.

Hugh cursed, used his whip, sent his greys plunging in pursuit. Berenice gave a quick glance back. He was gaining, his expression one of astonishment mingled with admiration. His horses were full out, ears flat, tails and manes streaming, nostrils dilated and eyes rolling. Berenice, however, had kept a little in reserve, and now she gave her blacks their heads. The phaetons thundered down the homestretch and, with a sudden burst of speed, she reached the finish line, winning by a hair's breadth. Amidst tumultuous cheers, she tossed the reins to her groom and climbed down, cheeks glowing, hair disarrayed beneath her low-crowned topper.

Damian swung her up and kissed her, shouting, 'Well done, Sister!'

Hugh sprang from his carriage, elbowing his way through the people who clustered around her. 'Congratulations, Lady Berenice!' he exclaimed with genuine pleasure. A sportsman to the bone, he took his defeat like the Corinthian he was.

'She bested you, without a shadow of doubt!' Damian said proudly. 'My sister has a way with horses.'

'Who'd have thought it? Old Hugh yielding his laurels to a lady,' remarked another dandy, wearing beige breeches and a wasp-waisted jacket. 'And a deuced pretty one, by Jove. Are you going to suggest a return race?'

'That is for the victor to decide,' Hugh replied, bowing to her, the expression in his eyes putting Damian on the alert.

He had been given strict instructions to look after her, and had only agreed to the race in order to put a smile on her face instead of a frown. No doubt he would be in hot water when his father came home.

Berenice laughed up at Hugh, honor satisfied. 'Perhaps, sir, or there again, perhaps not.' Then a shadow passed over her features, as she added, 'My fiancé returns shortly.'

She turned, patted her horses and gave the groom special instructions as to their care. They must be walked back to their stables, rubbed down, given water and a good feed of oats. These proud animals had done well; she would miss them and wondered if she'd find their like in Carolina or, indeed, if she would be allowed to ride. She tossed up her head in defiance. Sebastian would have a hard time stopping her! More than the achievement of winning this race was the knowledge that he would now be forced to acknowledge that she was someone to be reckoned with. He must already be aware of this, for during the few days he had stayed with her in Bath, her popularity had been obvious. No ball, soirée or card party was complete without her presence. He had kept his distance since the night she had met Peregrine, and she had made certain that they were never alone. It was with immense relief that she had seen him ride off with the Marquis, but now her freedom was nearly at an end. Soon he'd return, and it would start over, that tension between them that turned everything into a battlefield.

'A penny for your thoughts,' Hugh's light-hearted voice drew her back to the present.

'They aren't worth even that much, sir,' she answered, a droop to her coral lips.

'Indeed? How sad,' he rejoined. 'Aren't you looking forward to being married?'

'No, sir, I am not.' She walked beside him beneath the trees, enjoying the shade after the heat and passion of the race, and desperately trying to hold it to memory for always—the verdure, the flowers, the sunshine, stately Bath, the Queen City of the West, and further out, the little villages and peaceful shires, so soon to be snatched from her grasp for all time, for she could not visualize surviving in America, or ever returning to her homeland.

They reached a spot where Damian had organized a picnic. His friends were reclining on rugs and cushions while servants bustled, erecting folding tables and spreading them with damask cloths, then serving this open-air feast. Champagne corks popped like miniature artillery, after the dark green bottles had been lifted from ice buckets. Glasses were raised to Berenice—their Diana of the Chase, and none was more fervent in his praise than Hugh.

'Who taught you to drive with such skill, my lady?' he asked, angling to sit beside her, though Damian occupied the space on the other side, self-appointed guardian of her morals.

'My father,' she answered, resting against the bole of a spreading oak, neatly booted feet crossed at the ankles beneath the hem of her black velvet riding habit.

'Ah, not that tall, savage-looking fellow who never left your side when you first arrived in Bath?' Hugh took a dish of strawberries and cream from the tray of a passing footman and handed it to her. 'Seemed to me he was unwarrantably possessive. Didn't like you dancing with any of us fellows.'

That's putting it mildly, Berenice thought. Sebastian would hide me in a nunnery, if he had his way. It was only because he knew that Peregrine wasn't expected here that he allowed my father to persuade him to visit the manor.

And even then, I was left in the care of two jailors—Damian and Miss Osborne.

'He has the right to restrict her, sir,' Damian declared forcefully. 'He is the man Berenice is about to marry. Didn't you know?' He was giving Hugh fair warning that she was out of bounds.

'Perhaps I did,' Hugh answered languidly, passing his enameled snuffbox, then saying to Berenice. 'My dear, we'll be distraught to lose you, but you'll be here for a few more days, won't you?'

'I am, and so will he,' she replied, cross with Damian for acting like a duenna.

'He's an interesting person,' Damian said slowly, tearing up a blade of grass, sticking it between his teeth and chewing reflectively. 'I'm looking forward to going to America with him.'

'It's all right for you!' Berenice rapped out. 'You don't have to marry the odious fellow!'

She glanced around her nervously, almost expecting to see Sebastian pop up from behind the bushes. She had no idea when the Marquis planned to return, but it could not be long, as they were going back to London at the weekend. The wedding! It was coming ever closer and no more acceptable to Berenice than before. This idyll would soon be over, the lull before the storm. No more gallivanting with the beaux—no more fun of any kind.

Seated on the grass, the strawberries untouched in her lap, she was roused from her musings by a commotion from the direction of the Royal Crescent. Looking across, she saw a stout lady advancing towards her purposefully. She wore a cerise silk gown and, while the vogue for skimpy tubelike dresses with raised waists suited those of willowy build, they gave her the appearance of a pouter-pigeon. Dulcie Riley trotted behind her.

'Oh, dear, it's Miss Osborne. Such a tiresome person,' Berenice groaned. 'No doubt she's come to chastise me for my immodest behavior. Can't you stave her off, Damian?'

'I'll do what I can,' he promised, ready to defend her against all comers. 'But you know what she's like.'

'Lady Berenice!' Miss Osborne boomed. 'Lady Berenice! What *has* been going on?'

Berenice heaved a sigh and rose, a slender figure in black with a white cravat around her throat, a complete contrast to Miss Osborne, who stopped in front of her, hot and bothered, her cheeks quivering with indignation beneath the brim of her feather-laden bonnet. She felt the responsibility for this young hoyden keenly, terrified of the Marquis, and even more so of the Comte. If anything should happen to Berenice while they were away, Harriet Osborne's life wouldn't be worth a pin, and she could certainly forget any hope of receiving good references.

'Didn't I tell you that I intended to ride this morning?' Berenice replied coolly, and her lips twitched as she caught Dulcie's eye. Millicent had been dismissed and Dulcie promoted to her position, an arrangement which suited both her and Berenice very well. Now she had been

84

detailed to accompany Miss Osborne and hold the lacy parasol aloft to protect that lady's complexion.

'Ride, yes! Race, no! I've never heard of anything so unseemly,' Miss Osborne panted. Any movement other than a leisurely stroll rendered her breathless, and it was a warm day. She thanked her stars that she'd be free of this troublesome chit soon, seeking a new post as companion to a much more refined young girl.

'You don't approve?' Berenice prevaricated, knowing that the race would have been impossible, had not Miss Osborne been confined to her bed over the past twenty-four hours.

'Approve?' Miss Osborne raised her eyes and hands to heaven as if beseeching aid. 'It was wrong of you, milady, very wrong indeed, and quite unkind. You were aware that I was ill. Goodness knows that I suffer dreadfully, but keep this to myself and never complain. I'm in frail health, not at all robust, and you took unfair advantage. What is your father going to say about this? As for the Comte! I dare not think!'

Berenice suspected that the chaperon's indisposition was due to an overindulgence in bonbons and too-frequent visits to Sally Lunn's cake shop in Old Lilliput Alley. Miss Osborne did not have a delicate constitution, merely a greedy one.

'I hope you're feeling better now,' she murmured dutifully, catching Dulcie's eye again.

'Yes, I am, and just as well by the look of things,' Miss Osborne grumbled opening her fan and waving it across her perspiring face. 'I dread to think what will happen when your fiancé comes back. You really make my life most difficult. It's a blessing that you're getting married so that I can leave. I really can't be looking after so headstrong a person as yourself, my lady. I pity the Comte, I really do, and him such a fine man, too.'

'Strong words, Miss Osborne! I'm certain that Lady Berenice will be devastated to be deprived of your devotion. Pray calm yourself, madam.' Damian winked at Berenice and tried to calm the outraged lady.

'You knew about this, my lord?' she asked accusingly, never at ease with either of these lively young springs of the house of Rossiter. 'You encouraged her ladyship in this reckless venture?'

'No harm intended, Miss Osborne, I assure you.' Damian could charm the birds from the trees if he put his mind to it. 'I'll take the blame, never fear. Now, why don't you sit down and partake of a glass of this excellent wine?'

'We can't stay. You have guests, my lord.'

'Guests? I wasn't expecting callers this morning.' Damian was puzzled, wondering who, among his many acquaintances, they might be.

He was in command of the Royal Crescent establishment during his father's absence, under the guidance of the housekeeper, the butler and Miss Osborne and, had Berenice not been in such a bad mood, would have carried out the Marquis's instructions to the letter.

'Baron and Baroness Edington have driven over from Carters Grange to congratulate Lady Berenice on her forthcoming wedding,' the chaperon informed him smugly, as if to say—you should have been about your duties, young sir, not arranging phaeton races.

Berenice brightened when she heard the name of the couple who had always taken a keen interest in the welfare of the Marquis's motherless children. It would be good to see them again. Maybe she could tell them how unhappy she was, and beg them to speak with her father. Surely, it might be possible to call the whole thing off, even at this eleventh hour?

'Come on, Damian!' Berenice was already heading across the green.

She ran the last part of the way, leaving grass and trees behind and crossing the cobbled street. Coaches rattled past, and people were strolling along the wide pavements. She reached the massive front door of their residence first, but it was her brother who hammered on it with the brass, lion-headed knocker.

'Don't you think you should change before you receive them?' he suggested, casting an eye at her dishevelment.

'No!' she snapped.

The door was opened by a footman wearing the Rossiter livery and, without pausing to see if Damian was following, she hurried through the hall and burst into the grey-hung drawing room, full of gilt chairs and mirrors and porcelain vases from which rose leaves spilled on to lacquered cabinets. The first person she saw was Lady Olivia Edington, seated on a couch by the bay windows that faced the garden.

She was a pretty woman in her midthirties who had always treated Berenice and Damian with the utmost kindness. Many were the happy holidays they had spent at Carters Grange, the Baron's family seat in Somerset. Lady Olivia was sweet-natured and practical, completely lacking that air of boredom and helplessness which many ladies of her class affected. In her childhood, Berenice had often worked beside her in stillroom and kitchen, learning how to distill perfumes from flower heads, to use herb extracts for medicines and salves, to preserve fruits and prepare delicious dishes.

'Ah, there you are, my dears,' said the middle-aged gentleman who stood up as Berenice made her entrance, with Damian close behind her. 'They tell me that the Marquis is at Stretton Court. No matter, we're mighty pleased to see you. Ain't that so, madam?' and he turned to his wife, who beamed at him.

'I'm very glad you came,' Berenice answered, dipping a curtsy as Damian swept off his hat and made a leg. But tears pricked her eyelids and she wanted to break down and cry.

The Baron was of small build, yet possessed a natural dignity. But if his wife favored high fashion, he stuck to old-fashioned styles, wearing a formal full-skirted coat, white breeches, white stockings and black shoes. His waistcoat was long, its somber hue brightened by gold threadwork, and instead of the high stock favored by the *ton*, he wore a lace-frilled cravat. His hair, grey at the temples and tied in a queue behind, was lightly powdered in a manner that was outdated. Berenice loved him, and looked on him as if he were a favorite uncle, though they were unrelated.

Now he cocked a bushy eyebrow in her direction, saying, 'What ails your companion? She seems in an almighty fluster.'

'I've no idea.' Berenice looked him straight in his twinkling eyes. 'I've only been out racing a high-perch phaeton, my lord.'

'What does your fiancé say about this?' Lady Olivia came over and slipped an arm round her.

'He doesn't know,' Berenice confessed, glad that they were there, needing them desperately to protect her from Sebastian's wrath and, most of all, to try talking her father out of the marriage arrangements.

'I'm sure he won't mind,' Damian said, though having a pretty good idea that he would. 'Berenice needed something to distract her. She's worried about the wedding.'

Lady Olivia's wise grey eyes rested on Berenice, then she turned to her husband, saying, 'Haven't you business to attend to in town, sir?'

He looked puzzled. 'Have I, m'dear?'

'Yes, I think so, but even if you haven't, couldn't you visit your club or go to the pump room or something. I want to talk to Berenice and Damian,' his wife answered firmly.

He grimaced, recognized her signals, but had a final grumble. 'Dash it, madam, you know I can't abide those addle-pated foplings and foolish women parading in their fallalls, but all right. No doubt you have much chitchatting to do over the wedding plans and all that.'

When the door closed behind him, Lady Olivia sat down again and addressed Berenice. 'What's the matter?'

'Everything!' she cried, striking her fist into her palm and pacing the room. 'That man my father wants me to marry! He's impossible! I don't want to do it—or go to America!'

'You'd better tell me all about it,' Lady Olivia advised, exchanging a worried glance with Damian, knowing Berenice's hot temper of old. It had often landed her in trouble. Privately, she thought Herbert Rossiter a fool if he imagined for one moment that he could bully his daughter into an alliance that was against her wishes.

Berenice's fury abated, and with it her spirit. She drooped against the side table, and tears spilled over, running down her cheeks. 'He's hateful! I won't marry him!'

'It's bound to be hard for you. Any venture into matrimony is. Why, I cried for days when I was first a bride, but it passed and I began to enjoy it.' Lady Olivia smiled at the memory of her own foolishness.

'Lucinda says all men are vile,' Berenice sniffed, dabbing her cheeks with a scrap of lace handkerchief.

Lady Olivia's eyes sharpened, and her face

took on a serious expression. 'I suppose you refer to Lucinda Clayton. She has, perforce, a biased view in my opinion. Your father is right when he says that she isn't the sort of woman you should mix with.'

'I agree,' Damian nodded, seated on a corner of the table, one slim leg braced on the floor, the other swinging idly. 'I think you should give Sebastian a chance, Berenice. You may find he won't seem so bad when he returns from Church Stretton.'

'Do you really think so?' Berenice asked dubiously.

Damian grinned encouragingly. 'I'm certain of it. You've hardly had time to get to know him, have you? Take it slowly, don't expect too much. Rome wasn't built in a day. I wouldn't be surprised to find that he's as nervous as you are.'

Berenice stared at him in astonishment. 'Him? Nervous? He's the most arrogant man alive.'

Lady Olivia laughed. 'Oh, my dear, you are so young and have much to learn about men—or people in general, for that matter. Things are not always what they seem.'

A parlormaid arrived with the tea tray, and by the time Berenice had drunk a cup and eaten a couple of iced cakes, she was feeling more optimistic. The Edingtons had come in the nick of time, it seemed, giving her the support she needed so badly. They decided to go down to the town to meet the Baron after Berenice had changed her attire.

Soon they were in a curricle clopping sedately

towards Gay Street, along the Paragon and down steep Milsom Street towards the Abbey Churchyard. There it stopped and, bidding the driver wait for them, Berenice stepped out. Arm in arm with Damian, she strolled across the broad piazza and passed beneath the columns of the pump room.

As usual for this time of the year, it was crowded. There was a quite bewildering variety of silk gowns, cotton dresses, feathered hats, and flowered bonnets. Gentlemen in tight pantaloons walked to and fro, flourishing Malacca canes, quizzing glasses and snuffboxes. Gouty old men in wheelchairs were being pushed along by harassed servants, while bedizened dowagers chanced their luck at the card tables.

'La, such a crush!' Lady Olivia exclaimed, then waved across the room. 'Oh, look—I spy the Baron.'

Berenice glanced to where she pointed, and froze. There, his black head inclined towards the Baron and her father, was Sebastian. Damian saw him at the same moment, a smile breaking over his face.

'He's here! He's come back!' he shouted, and elbowed his way through the throng so that Lady Olivia and his sister might pass.

Traitor! Berenice thought bleakly. It's as if he likes, perhaps admires, Sebastian!

The pump room was even more crowded by now, and the noise swelled above the music of the string quartet seated on a stage under a shell-shaped arch—chatter and laughter, the swish of silks, the air heavy with the smell of sweat, of lavender, jasmine water or frangipani.

Sebastian found it overpowering and unpleasant, coming so soon after the fresh air and space of the Stretton Court estate, a place that had brought a breath of home to him—reminiscent of the rolling pasturelands, the plains and forests, lakes and hills of South Carolina. He found society, and the *ton* in particular, immensely shallow. Even the fact that England was engaged in a dragging war seemed to have made little difference to them. They might lose fathers, brothers, sons and husbands in battle, yet as far as he could tell on short acquaintance, the élite still drifted from London to Brighton and thence to Bath, in their relentless pursuit of pleasure.

He had returned from the country refreshed, vowing to be nicer to Berenice and, if possible, make a clean start, only to find her in that empty, gossipy, fashion-mad world epitomized by the company gathered beneath the glass dome of the pump room. And, from what he had just heard, she had been involved in another scandal.

'You must try a glass of those miraculous waters that gush, hot and steaming, from the springs deep beneath the building. Very beneficial for the health, my boy,' Baron Edington was in the middle of expounding, when Sebastian spotted Berenice coming across the room.

He was aware that Damian was with her, and an unknown lady, but his attention was riveted on Berenice, and Berenice alone. The crowd thinned and he could see her clearly—that dark-haired beauty with the lovely, lissom figure. She was clad in a white lawn gown belted beneath her breasts, the bodice a low oval, making his palms itch to touch that ivory skin. The whole effect was one of extreme simplicity, following the trend that required ladies to look like milkmaids, appealing to his recent rural experiences. No jewels, no ornamentation, although a yellow stole of oriental pattern lay over her arm. On her head she wore a bonnet, of natural straw, with a shovel brim banded by a wide pink ribbon ending in a large bow.

How innocent she looked! How deceptively prim! Sebastian almost ground his teeth in rage as he recalled the news that had greeted him on his arrival. It was on everyone's lips, and they were falling all over themselves in their eagerness to let him know of it. She had, only that morning, taken part in a phaeton race.

FOUR

'Your servant, madame.' Sebastian gave an ironic bow, hand on his heart, mocking the conventions that insisted on this greeting.

'Monsieur le Comte.' Berenice sank into a low curtsy, more from the weakness of her knees than formality. He raised her, the grip of his fingers a shade too tight.

While the Marquis was introducing him to

94

the Baron and Baroness, Berenice stood there nervously, distrusting, his suave manner and amiability. Did he know about the race? Was he playing with her, as a cat will play with a mouse? It distressed her to think that he had recently come from Stretton Court, that beloved old manor where she was wont to roam barefoot through the grounds if the fancy took her, to gallop across the downs to her heart's content. How dared he walk in its gardens, enjoy its long gallery, breathe that sacred air? It was as if his presence would have polluted it, leaving a poisonous miasma in its wake.

She sneaked a glance at his craggy profile as he conversed with Lady Olivia. Once again, she was forced to admit that he was a handsome man, his curling hair holding the sheen of a raven's wing, his body displayed in a bottle-green coat that fitted his shoulders without a flaw, short at the waist in front, flaring into tails behind. His breeches clung closely, emphasizing the strength of his muscular legs, and ending in gleaming top-boots. The ruffles on his shirt front were spotless, as was the stiff collar that reached his sideburns, and a gold fob dangled from a chain across his brocade waistcoat. As the fops might have said he was 'rigged out in the latest stare,' the current slang for being dressed in the height of fashion.

He was talking to Lady Olivia with practiced ease, his manners perfect, and she was obviously taken with him. Berenice viewed this as the deepest betrayal, her resentment gathering by the second. Was he a magician who cast a spell on everyone he met? It was desperately unfair! Only she, it seemed, had been subjected to his brutality, and no one paid the slightest attention or took her seriously when she tried to tell them that he was wicked.

The Marquis beckoned Damian to one side and began to address him in a low tone. Berenice could tell by her brother's expression that their father was questioning him sternly. She could feel the sweat breaking out at her armpits and down her back. He knew about the race! They both knew! Then why was Sebastian being so calm?

A moment later, she had her answer. 'I hear that you've been riding, madame?' he said suddenly, his tone light because Lady Olivia was listening.

Now for it, Berenice thought. She gave him a ravishing smile as if she hadn't a care in the world. 'Why, yes, sir, you're well informed. I declare, you've not been back in Bath an hour and the gossips have already stolen my thunder. I was so looking forward to telling you myself.'

'Were you indeed?' One of his dark brows swooped up. 'A high-flyer, I understand. Zounds! I'd have laid a monkey on you had I known. Did you win?'

'I did,' Berenice managed to splutter, though thunderstruck. He'd have wagered five hundred pounds against her skill? What had happened to the man while he was down in Wiltshire? Was he moonstruck?

Sebastian found it gratifying to see her silenced

by this unexpected praise, much more so than had he given vent to a show of rage. He smiled to himself darkly, vowing to keep her guessing as to what he might do under any given circumstance. Perhaps the way to deal with this shrew was to spike her guns. He had even succeeded in calming the Marquis, pretending that he did not object to Berenice's escapade, and was proud of her success, though he could not prevent the old man from taking his son to task.

Berenice recovered slightly, though remaining suspicious, even when he said, 'Can I get you something, ladies? Syllabub, tea, or a glass of lemonade?' and escorted the party across a tiled passageway and into a reception room where refreshments were being served.

Later, as they drove to the Royal Crescent in the curricle, he rested an arm along the back of the seat behind her and asked, 'May I see the horses that bore you to victory?'

'If you really want to.' She was still uncertain, expecting this to be a trick, the change in him too sudden and uncharacteristic.

They dropped the others off at the front door and rode with the coachman to the stables. There Berenice led Sebastian to where her blacks rested in their stalls. They whinnied as she spoke softly to them and rubbed their long, shining noses. Knowing that there was usually a treat in her pocket, they nudged her with their great heads and she laughed, producing sugar lumps which they licked from the flat of her hand with wet, rasping tongues.

'They love you,' Sebastian observed, one booted foot resting on the lower paling as he watched her.

'I've had them since they were foals. They were born at Stretton Court.' She rubbed her cheek against the muzzle of the biggest horse, who was also the leader.

'You'll be sad to leave them.' For the first time, Sebastian found himself considering her side of the bargain. He had learned a lot about her and her background while in Wiltshire.

'Naturally, I shall be sad.' She could not trust herself to look at him, this stranger who held her destiny in his hands.

'I can see that you have an empathy with animals.' The sunlight shafting from a window high above lit his face.

'Yes,' she answered simply, trembling as he stepped closer. 'I've been brought up with them—horses, dogs...'

'And children? You love children, too?' His hand closed over hers where it lay on the edge of the stall.

'Doesn't everyone?' she prevaricated, aware of his meaning and unable to stop the color rushing up into her face. 'I've often played with Lady Olivia's little ones.'

'That's good, *chérie*,' he murmured. 'I'm glad.' Then, mercurially, his softened mood changed and he released her. 'Sir Peregrine hasn't been here during my absence, has he?'

'No,' she answered, feeling guilty as she remembered that though Peregrine had not been dancing attendance, Hugh had.

'You've had no young man escorting you?'
So stern his expression, making him un-
approachable.

'Sometimes,' she admitted, then added hastily,
'But always with Damian or Miss Osborne
chaperoning me. Why are you so suspicious?'

'You've given me cause.' Sebastian moved
restlessly, going back to the horses, running
expert hands over their sleek black sides
and, surprisingly, for they were choosy as
to whose caresses they permitted, the highly
strung animals accepted his homage.

'That is your opinion, sir,' she declared
with that hubris which threatened to ruin any
tentative overtures he might be tempted to
make. 'You forget that Peregrine was my friend
long before you came barging into my life.
Until I'm given proof that he's unworthy,
then I'll continue to regard him as a harmless
acquaintance.'

He gave a harsh bark of laughter. 'Hoity-toity!
Will you, madame? Just keep him out of your
bed, that's all!'

Before she could stop him, he swung her up
in his arms as effortlessly as if she was made of
thistledown, and deposited her high on top of
a bale of straw. He was still laughing, his face
level with her own, so close that she could see
the curl of his thick lashes, the fineness of his
tanned skin.

'Get me down, sir!' she cried in fury.

'If you promise to behave yourself,' he
chuckled. 'Do you promise?'

'I promise you nothing!' she declared, her

eyes, even her hair seeming to spark with temper.

'Then you'll have to stay there,' he said and sat astride a bentwood chair, folding his arms over the back and resting his chin on them, staring up at her.

'Oh, you—*you!*' she stammered, then, refusing to let him have the last word, hitched up her skirts and began to scramble down.

Sebastian did not move a muscle or offer aid, merely sitting there enjoying the unexpected view of long bare legs, and fine-boned feet and ankles in flat strappy sandals, with lacing that crisscrossed halfway to her perfect knees. *Ma foi!* He thought, aware of an ache in his groin. Roll on the wedding night! She's a haughty, troublesome minx, but I'll marry her, come what may.

Landing in an inelegant heap, Berenice leapt up, rearranged her skirts, flung her stole over one shoulder and darted out of the stable, across the yard and into the house. Sebastian followed more slowly, planning his next move and half inclined to invite her out to dinner that night. But just as he entered the hall, he saw the porter handing her a parcel. She seemed surprised, saw him watching her and lifted it with a mystified shrug. He followed her as she carried it into the drawing room, tearing off the wrapping as she went. Inside was a long box which she placed on the buhl table before raising the lid.

There, cocooned in tissue paper, was a beautiful riding whip with an intricately carved bone handle. A card lay alongside, and on it

100

was written, 'To the most lovely of charioteers! Use this when next you ride out and think of me, the one who desires you above all else.' It was unsigned.

'What the devil—?' Sebastian's brows swooped down in a fearsome scowl.

'I'm as astonished as you,' she faltered, completely nonplussed. 'I've no idea who sent it.'

'Haven't you? Are there so many men flinging themselves at your feet, and sending you expensive gifts?' He looked angry enough to strike her.

Damnation! she was thinking. Why did this have to happen now? Had someone done it on purpose? She knew that the fops had a spiteful streak. No doubt everyone in Bath was aware that Sebastian had arrived. Those among the young gentlemen who had met him had taken offense at his brusque manner. Any of them could have sent the whip to stir up trouble.

'I swear to you that I don't know the identity of the sender,' she whispered, even as she wondered why she was bothering to convince him. 'As soon as I find the culprit, I'll return it, and I'll certainly never use it.'

'That you won't!' he agreed with a taut smile, taking it from her hands, replacing it in the box and closing the lid with a snap. 'For if you do, then you'll bear its stripes yourself, I promise you.'

With that, he turned on his heel and stalked off, leaving her standing in the center of the room, unsure whether to laugh or cry.

During the next three weeks, Berenice was kept virtually a prisoner in Elsewood House while the preparations for the wedding went ahead. Lady Chard had put herself at the helm, persuading the Marquis that his daughter needed a capable, experienced woman to call upon at such a time. For his part he was more than willing to hand Berenice over to that forthright, positive lady, finding her storms, tantrums and petulant looks altogether too much for him. Berenice was behaving atrociously, and knew it! They were forcing her into an alliance repugnant to her, therefore she was being as obstructive as she knew how. Lady Chard ignored every scene, assuring the worried Marquis that it was merely bridal nerves, a young girl's natural bashfulness which would melt away as soon as she belonged to her husband. The Marquis, knowing his daughter better than she did, was not convinced.

Lady Olivia had spoken with him at length when they met in Bath, but even her eloquence had been of no avail. Dogmatic and immovable, it had ended with him losing his temper and telling her to mind her own business. Upset, and unable to assist the girl whom she loved dearly, Lady Olivia had not even been able to help her prepare for the ordeal. One of her children was consumptive and she and the Baron were about to take him to Switzerland in search of a cure.

Berenice had hardly seen the author of her misfortunes since the day of the race.

As soon as they had arrived in London, Damian arranged for Sebastian to rent an apartment, hoping for a more favorable result if the couple were kept apart. He took him everywhere, to the exclusive gentlemen's clubs, the coffeehouses, the gambling dens, cockfights, wrestling matches, prizefights, and the theaters. He was eager to show this knowledgeable colonial the sights of London, and equally eager to hear tales from one who could vividly remember the social whirl of Paris before the taking of the Bastille and the downfall of the aristocrats.

When her brother called to see her a week into their arrival, Berenice listened sourly to his accounts of their escapes. 'The apartment is very fine and well appointed. It's near Whitehall and has a cheerful view over St. James's Park. We were at Brooks's Club from three in the afternoon yesterday till four o'clock this morning, playing *rouge et noir,*' he said, yawning widely and stretching till his joints cracked.

'How nice for you,' she replied acidly, as she lay on the scroll-backed couch, exhausted from too much shopping.

Really, the clothes that one needed for one's trousseau. It was ridiculous! Anyone would think she was taking a journey to Timbuktu instead of America, where, she was assured, the townspeople were moderately civilized.

'It was. Nice, I mean,' Damian continued, grinning across at her and helping himself to hot coffee and buttered crumpets, served in her boudoir. 'He's a topping chap, a real out-and-outer. I wish you'd give him a chance, Berenice.'

'Don't start!' she warned, blue eyes sparking.

'Well, if you don't appreciate him, there are plenty who do,' he said, shooting her a glance to see her reaction.

He was not disappointed. 'What do you mean?' she demanded, sitting up, and glaring at him.

'You should just see the women when we go to the Ranelagh Rotunda. They practically line up to dance with him.'

'You've taken him to the Pleasure Gardens? Why? You know very well that it's a place where whores ply their trade.' Somehow, the idea of Sebastian setting foot there made her seethe.

'Why should you bother about that? You've made it plain that you detest him. Why shouldn't he find consolation elsewhere?' said the practical Damian, but he was watching her closely, wondering how she really felt at the thought of her fiancé in the arms of another woman. He turned the screw a notch tighter, adding, 'The Cyprians are agog! I swear if he entered any School of Venus, they'd entertain him without payment.'

She knew that he was referring to the prostitutes who operated in houses of ill fame, and this made her angrier still. 'I don't care! Tell him that, if you like, but make it clear that I don't want to catch a dose of the pox, so he'd better be selective in his fornication,' she shouted

104

and, picking up her bonnet, flounced out of the room.

Rousing Miss Osborne from a nap, she rushed off to the dressmaker to keep an appointment for a fitting. There she bumped into Lucinda who could talk of nothing except Sebastian.

'My dear,' she gushed, half in and half out of a new creation, in a curtained niche at the back of the shop. 'He's taken the town by storm. All the ladies are languishing over his good looks, his fascinating accent, and that thrilling air of the hardened traveler and adventurer that positively oozes out of him.'

'Really?' Berenice managed to sound bored, standing before the mirror as the couturier pinned and tucked, altered and fastened, apparently deaf to these exchanges between his customers.

'Oh, yes—really! I met him when I was having supper at Vauxhall Gardens the other evening. Damian introduced us, bless him. Your Sebastian is a ravishing creature!' Lucinda rolled up her eyes to express vast admiration, standing there in her chemise. 'A quite magnificent savage. La, I'd change my duke for him any day—or night!'

'You're welcome to him!'

'Lady Berenice, stay still, I beg you!' The couturier exclaimed pettishly, gesturing with his manicured hands.

'Haven't you nearly finished! Merciful heavens! How much more must I endure?' Berenice cried impatiently.

'But madame, this bonnet is just right for

the ensemble. Too, too divine!' he exclaimed, taking it from the hat stand and placing it on her head.

Though it had seemed so attractive only yesterday, the spray of white and purple feathers attached to a velvet base had suddenly lost its charm. Berenice snatched it off and threw it to the floor, shouting, 'It's hateful! Take it away!'

Lucinda's flow was not to be stemmed, particularly as Berenice displayed such an interesting reaction. 'I saw him in Mrs. Jermaine's box at Drury Lane Theatre the night before last. My dear, she couldn't keep her hands off him, and you know what she's like!'

Berenice did indeed know about her. Mrs. Jermaine was a notorious demirep who ran her own exclusive bordello in Mayfair, which was frequented by the highest gentlemen in the land. She was rumored to be insatiable, with the appetites of an alley cat, and the gossips reported that the Prince himself patronized her temple of love.

Berenice went home in a despondent state. It seemed that she hadn't a friend in the world. Only Dulcie lent a sympathetic ear to her new mistress's complaints. Though not totally conversant with every aspect of the situation, being new to her post, Dulcie gave Berenice her unquestioning support, never forgetting that she had saved her from the constables. And, intrigue being the stuff of life to her, she played Cupid, bearing secret messages for Berenice and Peregrine. Although they were never able to be alone, his letters were balm to Berenice's bruised feelings, speaking of love and promising his undying devotion.

Meanwhile, she was caught up in the fever of preparations, incarcerated for hours with the dressmaker, Lady Chard and a host of attendants. Her chamber came to resemble a gown and milliner's shop, glorious materials, silks, muslins and velvets draped over every available piece of furniture, fashion plates littering the floor. The day before the wedding, Dulcie set about the monumental task of packing all but a few of Berenice's belongings into trunks and boxes.

There were a dozen gorgeous dresses, both for day and evening wear; nightgowns of the sheerest tiffany, with matching robes trimmed with lace; several pairs of dainty slippers in satin or kid, flat pumps on which the wearer glided like a ballet dancer. She was careful not to forget the smart blue riding habit, the skirt long and full, its hem edged with gold braid, to be worn with dashing boots. There were hats like turbans and bonnets with poke brims, muslin caps and headbands, wide-brimmed creations swirling with feathers, chemises and silk shifts, long gloves, stockings and garters, not to mention a case overflowing with jewelry. Sebastian's bride was not going to the Americas ill equipped. No one, surely, could have had more extensive and costly accoutrements.

But the bride-to-be sat miserably amidst this finery on the eve of her wedding, almost in tears. After Dulcie had bathed her and washed her hair, brushing it dry so that it resembled a silken mantle falling over her shoulders, Berenice huddled by the fire in a state of blackest gloom. Although she had been feeling soothed by Dulcie's devoted attentions, she now wore a woeful expression. The sight of the wedding gown suspended on a hanger near the armoire added to her depression. She fetched a deep sigh.

Dulcie looked up from folding garments and laying them in a leather valise. 'What's the matter, my lady? You should be excited about tomorrow. Such sighs, such moping, it's bound to bring bad luck,' she said with slight reproval in her voice.

'Oh, Dulcie, you know what's troubling me.' Berenice began to pace the room restlessly. 'How can I marry a man I dislike so much?'

Dulcie gave her a sharp look, her normally cheerful face worried beneath the frill of her white cap. 'I realize that he's upset you, but perhaps that's just his way. Men are clumsy boobies, I've found, sometimes rough in their wooing. They can't see ahead like we women, and are only concerned with the here and now.'

'But I love Peregrine,' Berenice wailed. 'I don't want to belong to anyone else.' Her face hardened with resolve as she voiced the idea that had been brewing in her head for some days. 'I'm quite determined to refuse the Comte consummation. Then he'll have to release me eventually, and seek an annulment.'

Dulcie blew out her cheeks and shook her head doubtfully. 'I don't think he's the sort of man to take a rebuff kindly. He may force you.'

Berenice stopped dead in her tracks. 'Resort to rape, do you mean? Surely he couldn't be so base?' Her voice rose as fear raced through her. Her skin crept, tightening her scalp. If he should try to touch her like that she'd kill him!

'Don't count on it, madam,' cautioned her maid, alarmed by the sight of her mistress's flushed cheeks and feverishly bright eyes.

'I'm going to deny him, so don't waste your breath in attempting to dissuade me,' Berenice replied, and sprang into action, rushing to the escritoire and scribbling a note to Peregrine, sanding it, and slipping it into an envelope. Then she melted a lump of sealing wax at the candle, dropped a blood-red blob on to the fold and pressed her crested ring against it.

'You want me to take it to the hiding place now, tonight?' Dulcie asked, shaking her head. 'How d'you know Sir Peregrine will go there?'

'I'm sure he'll be expecting a final note from me, and I want him to know of my intentions.'

Though considering this to be rash, Dulcie kept her peace as she drew back the covers so that Berenice could climb into the four-poster. Then amusement curved her lips as she could not help remarking, 'You won't need me tomorrow night. There'll be someone else to help you into bed.'

'Be silent!'

Temper blazed in Berenice's eyes and the maid scooted to the door, carrying the letter. 'All right, milady. I'll deliver it. Don't fret!' she cried, ducking to avoid the pillow that came hurtling towards her.

Berenice slumped back, her rage dying abruptly. She knew that Dulcie had her welfare at heart, but she could not reconcile herself to the fact that this was to be her last night of blessed privacy. Hereafter, Sebastian would expect to stride into the bedroom whenever he chose, to take her whether or not she was willing, to put children into her womb which she had not the slightest desire to bear him. Damn him! Oh, Peregrine, where are you? she mourned, no longer able to fight that feeling of desperation. Couldn't you have rescued me from this plight?

She clung to the notion of refusing Sebastian marital rights. It seemed the only way. There were so many hurdles to cross if she and Peregrine were to find happiness and peace in each other's arms—almost insurmountable hurdles, which it would take courage and ingenuity to overcome.

Tears welled up, trickling across her temples into her hair, as a great wave of lonely helplessness washed over her. Even Sheba was gone, her basket empty and forlorn. Berenice had given her to Lucinda, guessing that the pampered little dog would be as unhappy in America as she anticipated being. She wept in earnest now, the future enveloping her like a black cloud.

110

A bride's tears, she thought, hiding her face in the pillow. Surely an unfortunate omen?

Dulcie, ever resourceful, had become adept at slipping out to the grotto after dark. Streetwise, surviving on her wits since her childhood, she had no difficulty in avoiding the watchmen, opening locks with a hairpin if need be, tiptoeing across the terrace, keeping well to the shadows, and traversing the lawn. It was easier than usual that night, as everyone was fully occupied with the wedding arrangements—servants burnishing the silver, the butler about his important work in the wine cellar, the housekeeper in a flurry over the linen, the flowers, the reception.

Dulcie ran along the path leading to the mock temple, intent on completing her task as quickly as possible and then going to bed. Tomorrow would be an exacting day, and she had been up since six that morning. She reached the steps, found the cunningly concealed aperture near its entrance—a crack covered by a stone, and tucked the note inside. All done, and she was halfway through the return journey when she was aware of a dark shape against the blackness of the trees, standing almost in her path.

Dulcie had never lacked courage, and now she doubled up her fists, and faced whatever lurked there. 'Who is it?' she demanded tersely. 'Don't try to hide. I can see you. Show yourself.'

As the figure stepped out into the moonlight, she could see that it was a tall man, someone vaguely familiar, but who? Then he spoke and she straightened, displeased to see him but relieved that it was not a robber.

'Miss Dulcie. It's me, Quico, the Comte's manservant,' he said, his voice deep, and with a heavy accent.

'What are you doing here?' Oh, Lord, has he been following me? she thought. But, no, surely not? They were in the garden close to the house, nowhere near the grotto.

'I like to walk at night. At home, my master and me often hunt in the hours before sunup.'

He had come closer on silent feet, moving with unnerving swiftness, part of the shadows, made up of darkness. Dulcie tingled with fear. She had noticed him often, hanging around the house, appearing without warning, upsetting the other servants who did not trust him. The Comte's man—an Indian, so they said—one who'd slice your head off with a tomahawk as soon as look at you!

Now, by the light of the moon, Dulcie stared up into his narrow, unsmiling face with the wide, flat cheekbones and aquiline nose, and it was as if his black eyes missed nothing. He was clad in a broadcloth suit, his thick, straight, blue-black hair tied back, yet in the lonely rustling night, she could almost imagine him wearing feathers and doeskin.

Dulcie stiffened her spine and decided to brazen it out. 'Well, Quico, if you enjoy a walk, then so do I. That's why I'm here, taking the air, so I'll be on my way.'

She started off in the direction of the back door, annoyed to find him padding along behind her. She stopped so abruptly that they almost collided, and stood there with arms akimbo and shouted, 'Can't you leave me be?'

He was like a solid wall, his face gleaming in the dimness, as he answered steadily, 'You are a lone female. I go with you and see that you come to no harm.'

Dulcie stamped her foot in rage. 'I can look after myself. Can't you get that into your thick skull?' And she started off again, only to find him trailing her.

Giving a yell of exasperation, she blasted him with a final glare, then ran inside and slammed the door after her.

Since early morning, Berenice had been surrounded by women engaged in the solemn, almost ritualistic process of attiring the bride. When they had finished, she stood for some time before the pier glass, hardly able to believe that the image thrown back was herself, and finding a modicum of consolation in this fact. It was like wearing a fancy-dress costume or a mask behind which one could say or do things otherwise impossible. Comtesse Lajeaunesse did not yet exist, yet she was no longer Lady Berenice Rossiter. In the meantime she could hide inside the person of this faultlessly dressed, unfeeling stranger.

Her attendants, however, were overcome by the beautiful spectacle, for Berenice fulfilled every woman's dream of how a bride should look. Her gown was of ivory slipper-satin, encrusted with silver embroidery and seed pearls round the hem and train. It had a deep neckline, tiny sleeves and a high waist set just under the bust. White kid gloves reached beyond her elbows, and her sepia ringlets clustered beneath a full-length veil, held in place by a diamond tiara. In the coach, she wore a wrap of Arctic fox, a present from Sebastian, but discarded it at the church porch, giving it to Dulcie to hold. Carrying a posy of orange blossom from the hothouses of Stretton Court, she stepped inside, followed by Lady Chard's daughters, enthusiastic if somewhat gauche bridesmaids, and a collection of younger relatives acting as pages and flower girls.

The Marquis's guests were so elaborately dressed that they might have been in masquerade costumes. Berenice took comfort in that thought; it was as if this ceremony which she was attending so reluctantly was nothing more than a grotesque charade. The congregation coughed and shuffled, then as the organ music swelled, all eyes were turned towards her as she began to walk down the aisle on her father's arm. Her face was waxen, her eyes like blue jewels, glimpsed through the transparent veil. She resembled a breathtakingly beautiful statue, cold and unresponsive. In fact, she had deliberately cut off thought and feeling, knowing that it was the only way she could get through the ordeal. Soon, she would be given away by her father to that foreigner whose tall, straight back she could see as he waited for her before the altar.

The music soared, the sweet, innocent treble voices of the choirboys reaching soulful

114

perfection, and Berenice stood, as if turned to ice, at Sebastian's side. She did not look at him but kept her eyes fixed on the shining gold vessels, the candlesticks, the censers, the trappings of a religion which was about to bind her to the man she hated. The service commenced, but Berenice's thoughts were a world away, straying off into a wasteland of desolation. She made the responses dully, unthinkingly, only coming back to life when she felt the thick golden ring placed on her finger.

As the priest gave the final benediction, Berenice turned her head slowly, as if drawn by a magnet, and met Sebastian's eyes. He was nearly as pale as she, the color quite drained from his tanned cheeks, and there was something in his deep, enigmatic glance which sent a strange sensation shivering through her, a feeling of regret that this could not have happened at some other time, in different circumstances. Who knows? She might have loved him then.

He lifted her veil, bent his head and kissed her full on the mouth, taking her frozen fingers in his hard, warm ones. Berenice had the dizzy feeling of falling through space. Everything around her began to spin, seen through a mist of tears, and his hand became a lifeline to which she clung. It lasted for a fraction of a second, no more, then she was once again in command of herself, allowing him to lead her to the door of the magnificent church, her fingers resting on the velvet sleeve of his jacket, while he kept his profile firmly towards her. She glanced neither to the right or left, fighting the urge to break down.

Outside, the capricious English weather held sway. An hour of sunshine had given way to black clouds, heavy and threatening. Dulcie flung the fur wrap about her mistress as a crowd of well-wishers gathered round the couple, showering them with rice—the first of those prolonged and ludicrous activities without which it was popularly assumed the knot would fail to be properly tied. For a moment Berenice panicked, staring wildly at the smiling faces, meeting the knowing eyes. She knew what they were thinking—picturing in their minds Sebastian and herself alone in the bridal chamber. Then the wedding party piled into carriages waiting to convey them to Elsewood House for the reception.

Berenice and Sebastian did not exchange a single word on the journey. She gave him a glance from the corner of her eye, but he seemed abstracted, making no move to speak to her or touch her. He was with her in body, but his spirit was miles away. A fine start to married life, she thought, with my husband so moody and distant. But of what, or more to the point, of *whom* did he dream? Was he wishing Mrs. Jermaine sat there in her place, or some other woman? She knew more about the activities of her servants than she did of him. And now she was shackled to the man!

She flushed as she remembered how he had behaved to her on the first evening of their meeting, the things he had said—almost calling her a whore. And how he had held her, letting her feel his desire, making her know that he wanted her. Her skin itched as if it had been infected by his touch. He had treated her, not as a woman, but as an instrument of pleasure, something to be callously used and then discarded.

The great town residence was aglow. Musicians played for dancing while flunkies moved among the guests, bearing salvers of refreshments from the buffet tables set up in the salon. Peregrine was there, and Berenice was smitten with jealousy when she saw how he was admired by the gaggles of bewitching ladies who descended upon him with little shrieks of welcome, each one arrayed in gorgeous gowns of every hue, with feathers in their hair and jewels sparkling. The men, too, were like peacocks displaying their plumes, strutting about the huge room under the lofty, plaster-encrusted ceilings where cut-glass chandeliers hung, their crystal drops throwing off a myriad, rainbow-hued scintillations.

Observing Peregrine, whilst not appearing to do so, Berenice saw him strolling around, talking easily to people and laughing. That laughter cut her to the quick. How could he act so casually if the contents of his letters were to be believed and he really was devastated by her marriage? She wondered if he had received her last *billet-doux*. There was no way of finding out, for she could not snatch a moment's conversation with him, so besieged was she by guests offering congratulations, wanting to kiss her, to press her hand. She moved like a clockwork doll, curtsying gracefully, and turning on a bright, false smile whenever she was addressed by her hateful new title, Madame la Comtesse.

The Marquis, after quietly assuring himself that all was going well, had now retired to a corner with several cronies, and as Berenice passed, she caught scraps of conversation concerning politics or building. Lady Chard was in her element, introducing Jane and Sarah to every bachelor in sight, with further weddings in mind. Sebastian circulated casually among the throng, charming, smooth and gracious.

Berenice could see that she was much envied, and even she had to concede that he was looking remarkably distinguished in a black velvet jacket and matching breeches. Silk hose, and leather shoes with cut-steel buckles completed this formal attire, with a court sword hanging at his left hip. The snowy linen at his throat contrasted with his gypsy-tinted skin, and not a single gentleman present could rival him.

'The two-faced scoundrel!' Berenice muttered to Dulcie who walked behind her, carrying her fan and the fur wrap. 'Do you notice the way he smiles and bows? So courteous! It'll be a different story when we're alone.'

Dulcie made soothing noises, and brought her another glass of wine. Berenice found that she was more than a little tipsy, grateful for anything that would dull the painful edges of sensation. Damian and Peregrine came up to her and they were unsteady, too, leaning on each other's shoulders.

Her brother raised his glass to her. 'Here's to your happiness, my dear sister,' then seeing her bleak look and the drawn expression round her mouth, he slipped an arm about her comfortingly, adding, 'Cheer up! He's not such a bad fellow, you know. One of the best, in fact. Jolly good company, what?'

Berenice impatiently pushed him away, glaring at both of them. 'You're not the one who's wedded to the damned varlet!'

Peregrine was smiling at her, his eyes glazed, speech a trifle slurred. 'Let's drink to America! The land of plenty, where we'll find our fortunes!'

Berenice longed to see him to take some action—to make a scene, challenge Sebastian to a duel—anything! She had begun to find his calm acceptance of her marriage deeply insulting. Did he, or did he not, love her? His letters declared an abiding passion, but his actions proved the opposite. She did not know what to believe anymore, and wished that he would leave, turning her shoulder to avoid seeing him, thankful when he and Damian finally staggered away.

The guests had taken their fill of the lavish buffet, the speeches had been made, the toasts drunk, and now another merry group bore down on Berenice, carrying her to Sebastian and insisting that the two of them lead the dancing. A space was cleared, the guests formed a circle, and with a mocking glint in his eyes, he bowed over his bride's hand. The musicians struck up a minuet, and he led her through the intricate steps. Sounds of appreciation rippled round the spectators as they watched that handsome man and his unusually lovely wife. The maidens sighed wistfully, and the older women shed sentimental tears. Everyone seemed to be saying what a splendid couple they made.

Holding her head high, Berenice stared up into Sebastian's amused eyes, and he murmured from the side of his mouth, '*Venez m'amie*—come along, sweetheart—smile! This must surely be the wedding of the year! A perfect love match!'

If only, she mourned, surely two of the saddest words in the world. How much she wished that she loved the man she had married. When she was younger, she had dreamed of being a happy bride, and perhaps, fleetingly, there had been moments when Sebastian offered the hope that this dream might yet be fulfilled. That in itself had proved another illusion to be dashed to pieces by a chance remark, an unkind gesture, a betrayal of trust.

It was getting late now, and people began to move away, with the exception of the hard core of determined party-goers. In the large hall, servants were helping guests into their cloaks, and with a reluctant, backward glance at the rapidly thinning crowd, Berenice suffered herself to be conducted upstairs by Lady Chard and the bridesmaids. An apartment had been placed at the disposal of the newlyweds, it being deemed unnecessary for them to sleep at a hotel, since they were sailing next day. Elsewood House was large enough to accommodate a dozen couples, and Berenice was totally indifferent as to where the wedding night should be spent. All she wanted was to sink into merciful oblivion and wake when it was over, or perhaps, never wake again.

Dulcie undressed her, while Lady Chard and the other women flitted about, emitting excited squeaks and giggles, fixing ridiculous true-lovers' knots of ribbon to the bed drapes, and scattering corn and other pagan symbols of fertility. Berenice found it barbaric, indecent! She wished they would leave, yet longed to detain them, if only to put off for as long as possible the moment when she would be alone with Sebastian.

The nightgown was of a soft, cornflower blue, the material diaphanous, clinging to Berenice's breasts, then swirling into foaming yards at her feet. It was fastened on the shoulders with two slender ribbon bows, a seductive garment, designed for one purpose only—as an adjunct to a night of passion. She took one look in the mirror and almost ordered Dulcie to seek out something plain and conservative, shocked by the sight of her body gleaming through the fabric. Hurriedly, she thrust her arms into the matching negligee, which had ballooning sleeves drawn into a cuff, and a long train which floated behind her. But even these two layers did not conceal her limbs properly, and she still felt naked and extremely unprotected.

Her hair was unpinned now, coiling about her cheeks, across her shoulders and breasts, making her look childlike. Lady Chard, on her

121

way out, paused at her side, her stiff-hooped skirts rustling, saying quietly,

'My dear, you are so pale! Are you nervous? But of course, you would be. It's natural, maidenly modesty. Most commendable. There are far too many brazen flirts about these days.' She leaned closer so that Berenice could see the fard which plastered her face, and the two bright spots of rouge on either flabby cheek. 'Is there anything you wish to know? A motherless girl like yourself—has anyone taken the trouble to prepare you? Do you know what to expect?'

There was sympathy in her voice, but also another quality which Berenice found most distasteful. A note of triumph. It was as if that good lady took delight in welcoming yet another victim to the altar of the marriage bed. Berenice recoiled. The last person with whom she wished to discuss so intimate a subject was Lady Chard.

'I'm not ignorant, thank you, madam. Please don't worry about me,' she said, casting an agitated look at Dulcie, whose lips were quivering with amusement.

Lady Chard drew herself up, rather offended. 'Oh, well, if that's the case, I'll leave you. But be brave. Face up to the assault with courage. Men are brutes and we poor females have to do our duty. Good night, Comtesse.'

With that she rounded up her companions and they made their farewells with kisses and good wishes, chattering like a flock of starlings as they rustled out of the door. Dulcie added another log to the fire, then tidied away her mistress's clothes, removing the china basin of water in which she had freshened herself. Berenice made every excuse she could think of to detain her, all too aware of Sebastian in the adjoining room, which connected with the bridal chamber by a pair of high, cedarwood doors. She guessed that he would also be preparing, no doubt helped by that Indian valet of his, a sinister, poker-faced man whom she found most intimidating.

Dulcie wanted to have her installed in the bed, looking radiantly seductive, but Berenice took the big padded chair by the fire. She and Sebastian must have a serious talk—on this she was quite adamant.

When she was alone at last, the sudden silence pressed on her ears painfully. The sound of the coaches on the cobbles below could scarcely be heard, and the light from their link torches penetrated only a narrow gap in the brocade curtains. The embers of the fire cast an orange glow over the painted ceiling, rendering ruddy the fluffy clouds, coy cherubs and plump goddesses of that mythical, Olympian landscape. Dully, Berenice stared at the heavy gold ring which hung like a lump of lead on her finger. So it was true. They were legally, irrevocably married, but the worst was still to come. The suspense seemed to hurt her physically, under the heart, and she found it difficult to breathe. Her pulse almost stopped in terror when the dividing door opened on oiled hinges and Sebastian crossed the threshold. For a second, their eyes met, his hard and wary, hers almost black with anguish.

He had changed into a deep purple East India robe, decorated with intricate motifs, the sleeves wide, the collar made of sable, a gold sash fastening it together at his lean waist. The effect was outlandish, adding to his distinctly foreign appearance. Oh no, there was nothing English about Comte Lajeaunesse.

Moving with fluid grace, he came over to where she sat rooted to the chair, staring back at him like a snared wild thing. Sebastian did not like that look. As a trapper he had seen it too often. His mouth thinned, eyes lingering on those parted lips, then sliding down to the swell of her breasts tantalizingly glimpsed through the thin material.

Dieu, she's bewitching! he thought, experiencing a sudden ache in the region of his heart, a sense of loss and deep regret that this couldn't have been otherwise. If only she would have come willingly, even rapturously, to his bed!

Sebastian might deny it on the surface, making a very thorough job of convincing the world that he was a hardened cynic, but within the depths of his soul, he knew that he would never be truly healed or whole again until he loved, selflessly and completely, as he had done when a young man. Recently there had been flashes, insight, almost inspiration when he had thought—Berenice? But no, hot on this had arrived indisputable evidence of her treachery. At that very moment, he held such proof in his hand, a proof so damning that even the impulsiveness of youth could not excuse her.

His eyes were cold as a northern sea, his face rock hard, as he reminded himself, deliberately and bitterly, that life wasn't a fairy-tale romance, and love merely a sweet-sounding lie put about by poets and dreamers.

Berenice, who had been watching him with her hands clenched on the arms of the chair, shrank back with a start as he suddenly bent over her and thrust a scrap of paper under her nose, snarling,

'Well, my virgin bride, do you recognize this?'

For a second her brain recorded nothing, then she saw what it was. In that lean brown fist lay her last letter to Peregrine. She made a grab for it, but he feinted neatly, his free hand shooting out to grip her wrist.

'That's mine! Give it to me!' she protested.

'So, you confess it! I'll give you a point for courage, *mon amour*,' he purred, though his eyes were green slits of rage.

After the first rush of guilty astonishment, Berenice was consumed with fury. Twisting her wrist in his hand, she spat out, 'Let go of me!' But he merely tightened his hold. She felt so small, so helpless. The top of her head barely reached his shoulder, yet for all his size, she met his gaze boldly. 'How dare you tamper with my letters? Is this how wedded life will be? Am I to be permitted no privacy? No friends? Do you look on me as a piece of property?'

'That is precisely how I see you,' he answered crisply. 'You're as much my property as the slaves on my plantation. This deal has cost me much time and money. Your father's a clever man and he drove a hard bargain. I fully intend to get my money's worth out of you, madame. As for the letter, it's the work of a lying, conniving little cheat, who dares take marriage vows while fully intending to shirk her duty. You've written as much. Listen to this!'

With her hand still clamped tightly in his, he held the incriminating evidence towards the candlestick and began to read aloud, his sarcasm making Berenice's cheeks flame with indignation, as he mouthed the words jeeringly, ' "My beloved Peregrine. You say that you cannot endure the thought of another man enjoying my embrace. Believe me when I promise that no one but you shall do so. I will never share a couch with that odious Frenchman, and I wait for you, my love, to rescue me." '

With a snort of disgust, Sebastian flung the letter down and seized her angrily by the shoulders, while Berenice's eyes flashed fire. It horrified her to think that her note had been discovered, for she and Dulcie had been so sure that the hiding place was safe. There could be only one explanation.

'You've been spying on me again!' Her lips drew back over her even white teeth. 'Using that damned valet, I suppose! The fellow is forever prowling silently about, like a demonic shadow!'

'Do you think I'd trust such as you? Don't play the simpleton, *chérie*. You made it easy, leaving a trail a blind man could follow. The

126

grotto indeed! How very trite!' As he spoke, his accent became more marked. He now seemed more alien than ever, his hair falling across his brow untidily.

'Very well, sir. Accept that I hate you and love Peregrine. What are you going to do about it?' she challenged.

Seeing her exquisite beauty, he felt desire claw at him anew. He yearned to stop her spirited words with kisses, to crush the very breath from her. As he felt the press of her breasts against his chest, the intoxicating perfume of her hair wafted up, rousing him beyond bearing. He could have been so happy with her, had her nature been different. Here she was, on the threshold of glorious womanhood, with those heavy coils of glossy hair above and about a face of winning loveliness, yet she was a harpy. A damned slut who had probably been rogered by every debauched rake in town!

He had heard about the duel, had met those sly glances in the places of entertainment, and been told of Hugh Caldwell's part in the phaeton race. There was no doubt in Sebastian's mind that it was he who had sent Berenice the riding whip. Clearly it was thought that here was some slow-witted colonial come over to take Rossiter's wanton daughter off his hands. A dark ember of rage had burned in his breast as he had outfaced the scoffers, his arrogant features so intimidating that they had been embarrassed into silence, but the slur remained, festering within him. When Quico brought him that clandestine letter last night, he had longed first to upbraid her, then smash his fist into Peregrine's face. He had given way to neither impulse, biding his time throughout the wedding, watchful as a lynx, but if his friends back home in America had seen him, they would have recognized the signs and taken warning. For when Sebastian was cool and quiet, he was at his most deadly.

Now, with Berenice helpless under his hands, his hard-won reserve snapped. She was his lawful, wedded wife. He could do with her as he willed and no one would condemn him. She needed a sharp lesson, one which she would not forget in a hurry.

'Do you suppose I'll take your schoolgirl infatuation seriously?' he rasped. 'Or that ridiculous vow of chastity? A little late for that, I should have thought. Oh, and by the by, should we by chance be blessed with a happy event before the allotted nine-month period, I shall, of course, disown the child. I'm not a complete imbecile, you know, and can count very well.'

This insulting remark added oil to the fire of Berenice's wrath. How dare he besmirch her innocent relationship with Peregrine? 'In that case, sir,' she said slowly, 'I should tell everyone that you were the father, and the baby premature. I might even add that you anticipated the ceremony, and seduced me on the day you arrived in England.'

'You're brazen enough for such lies!' The look on his face took her off guard. It was a flash of pain, quickly suppressed.

Her heart was thumping madly and she could see that the situation was getting out of control. She wished she had not drunk quite so much wine, senses stirred by the intimacy of this warm, candle-shaded room, furious with her body's betrayal as her nerves tingled in response to the heat of him burning through her nightgown. His fingers began to play up and down her spine, familiarizing themselves with her curves.

'Don't do that!' she rasped out, fighting to keep the memory of Peregrine firmly in mind. 'You wouldn't be so dishonorable as to force yourself on me against my will.'

A grim smile touched his lips as he replied, 'Would I not?'

Suddenly she was filled with the most horrible conviction that he was perfectly capable of carrying out such a threat. Fear swept her. In a few moments the mystery would be revealed. Would he be as malicious as she feared? 'This is ludicrous,' she began, finding it difficult to speak with those warm fingers stroking her neck.

'I agree, *ma doucette.*' Again she heard the maddening mockery in his voice. 'I can't fathom this nunlike reticence, not from a woman who's had so much experience.'

His deprecating tone was the goad she needed. She tore herself from his arms and danced out of his reach, snatching up a little silver paper knife from the dressing table. 'You devil! I could stab you to death and feel no remorse!' she shouted. 'I warn you, if you touch me again, I'll kill you and then myself!'

'You should be on the stage,' Sebastian said, leaning back against the bedpost, arms folded over his chest, bare feet crossed negligently at the ankles. 'But, as we're not at the theater, I suggest that you put the knife down before you cut yourself. Keep it for its intended purpose—opening letters from your lovers.'

With a forceful oath, she hurled herself at him, catching him off balance. Her arm swung back and the blade flashed in a downward arc, slicing through the sleeve of his robe and nicking the skin beneath.

'She-devil!' he grated, and closed on her, grabbing the wrist that held the weapon and twisting her arm behind her. 'Drop it!' he commanded, but Berenice thrashed frantically, trying to jab him in the groin with her knee.

In their struggles, they knocked against the sofa table and sent it flying. The candle guttered out, glasses and decanter crashed to the floor. Yet Berenice could make little impression on those iron muscles, and Sebastian scarcely felt her blows. As his grip tightened about her wrist her fingers slowly opened. The knife dropped to the carpet.

She was conscious that her robe had come apart, leaving only one layer between her and complete nudity. His had also fallen open, exposing the broad chest with its flowing muscles, the powerful shoulders, the pelt of curling black hair spreading downwards, crossing his belly, circling his navel, going lower. It was the first time she had seen a man naked, and she was fascinated by the sight of his arousal, so animal in its need.

It must be the wine! she thought dizzily. It was as if her and thighs had developed a will of their own—her mouth and tongue, too. Physically she yearned for his embrace, though her puritan mind and romantic heart rebelled.

Sebastian took her in his arms, stared down into her exquisite face, and gave a low, seductive growl. 'I'm going to have you, *m'amie.'*

He swept her up and laid her down upon their marriage-bed. He quickly flung himself beside her. His hands caressed her body and inflamed her senses. Instinctively, she folded her arms around her. 'Oh, please—' she moaned; half-shamed and half-overcome by the sensations her husband aroused.

Sebastian, kneeling above her, took hold of her wrists, slowly eased them apart, and feasted his eyes on her.

'You're so beautiful, there's no need to hide yourself from me. I am your husband now,' he whispered huskily into her ear.

She turned her head to the side in an attempt to avoid his mouth, knowing that a kiss would be her undoing, that a kiss would make her lose control and give in to the carnal pleasures he promised. He pinned her down with one thigh thrown over her legs, holding her face between his hands and kissing the soft full moisture of her lips. He knew how and when to apply the pressure of his tongue, and when to withdraw it, leaving her staring up at him with wide, bewildered eyes. He began to caress

131

her, hands moving over her skin—the slim waist, the flat stomach, going higher till he cupped her breast. She was unprepared for the spasm of desire this caused. Involuntarily, she thrust her breast upwards into his hand. With a smile, he moved his thumb gently on the hardened nipple, expecting her to admit her desire.

Uncharacteristically, Sebastian had not taken her mind and soul into consideration, those parts of her which craved more than fleshly pleasures. With a moan, she pulled away, but he was not to be thwarted. His hand traveled across her belly, feeling for the dark triangle between her legs, and Berenice, though shocked, experienced a sensation like no other. His mouth was on her breasts, tongue licking over the nipples till she thought she might faint from pleasure. For a moment she was mindless, instinct overcoming her scruples, a rushing feeling beginning at the base of her spine, coursing its way into her thighs and gathering in intensity between them. She shuddered and he looked down at her lax limbs, her half-closed eyes, her wet, parted mouth. He sank upon her lips like a man dying of thirst.

His hand kept up its persuasive, fondling rhythm, and she longed for him to continue, though not knowing what to expect next—only aware of a burning need driving her, making her writhe beneath him. His breath was like fire on her skin, and now he was moving against her, one of her legs caught fast between his strong thighs as she rose, whirling, straining towards the brink of fulfillment. He then kneeled between her legs, took her chin in his hand, looked in her eyes and whispered, 'Surrender, *ma chérie.*' At that she relaxed momentarily, long enough for him to enter into the most sensitive part of her. Her eyes grew wide, staring up at him, amazed at the rush of sensations.

Berenice caught a glimpse of his face above her beaded with sweat. His head was back, his expression that of a tortured saint. His big body bucked and shuddered and a groan escaped him as he spent himself within her. For an instant he lay heavily on her, then moved away slightly, his hand caressing her cheek.

He had stopped too soon, she needed him to continue, now tormented by the tingling between her legs that seemed unsated. Her nipples were still hard and she pressed them against the soft hairs of his chest. Sensation welled in her loins. She realized he was the cure for her ache but she couldn't bear it. To surrender to him! Never.

As if receptive to the furor churning inside her, Sebastian moved away. Freed from those imprisoning arms, Berenice gave a muffled sob and shifted to the far corner of the bed, dragging the covers about her and turning her back to him. Silence, like a third presence in the room, settled about them. The fire flickered, its light like golden demons dancing within the mirrors. Plunged into a dark well of misery and confusion, Berenice could no longer contain her tears, crying into the pillow, but very softly.

The pain throbbing between her thighs was as nothing compared to the graver wounds to her self-esteem. Her body, that old friend whom she had pampered and cared for so lovingly all these years, had behaved with an abandon of which she was deeply ashamed. Guiltily, she realized that she had quite forgotten Peregrine. How could she have done such a thing? Did all those happy hours spent in the music room, while she played the harpsichord and he stood turning the pages of the music book, mean nothing? And what of those days in the garden, when he had recited his stanzas, whilst she indulged in the most ladylike occupation of sketching flowers? How could she have forgotten such tender, elevated moments, in the rutting heat of the bed?

Sebastian stirred, the mattress sagging on one side as he flung back the bedclothes and stood up. Berenice was acutely aware of him, feeling a leap of apprehension. What was he going to do now? She turned her head and peeked through her fingers, unable to do other than admire his splendid physique as he padded towards the connecting doors, the firelight bathing him in crimson—those wide shoulders, that smooth-skinned back tapering to a slim waist—the long, well-shaped legs. Was he leaving her? She felt like a discarded trollop, left alone midst the tangled sheets. All the dreadful stories she had heard about husbands came back to her; how they used their wives solely to slake their lusts, careless of their finer feelings and offering no sweet love words. Surely, it would have been different with Peregrine?

She closed her eyes and tried to recapture

the uplifting emotion she had felt for him. Had he been there in Sebastian's place, it would have been a marriage of true minds. He would have made her his chaste goddess again, raised above the gross reality of the body, with its base demands. Tears began afresh, seeping between her long lashes, streaking her cheeks.

Lost in self-pity, she did not hear Sebastian return, moving silently on hunter's feet, and she gave a start when he slid into bed. She waited stiffly, steeling herself for another touch, but he simply pulled the pillows behind his head, as he leaned back and lighted a cheroot. The fragrant smoke curled up towards the tester. She recognized it as that strange smell which always hung about him like a wicked aura, whispering of danger, its exotic odor tickling her nostrils whenever they were together. It was nothing more sinister than tobacco.

Under its relaxing fumes, Sebastian lay quietly musing on what had just transpired. He was annoyed with himself, having reduced his bride to tears. The carnal experience had been most rewarding, but it had given way to sadness, a sense of isolation that he found difficult to fathom. So, she had been a virgin after all. He did not like the uncomfortable knowledge that he had misjudged her. *Dieu!* but she had given the impression that she was a jilt! Why hadn't she told him? The nagging voice of conscience reminded him that even if she had, he would never have believed her. A tight smile played about his mouth, and his eyes narrowed as he lazily watched the smoke rings, yet Berenice's sorrow was disturbing him more than he liked to admit. In the stillness, he could hear her tears falling on the pillow and feel her convulsive sobs.

The shoulder turned so resolutely towards him had a silken sheen—he had noted earlier that her skin was particularly fine—clear and soft as a child's. Sometimes she seemed like a little girl who needed care. Memory stabbed him and he grimaced. Dammit, his thoughts were getting out of control again, wandering down paths best left untrod.

Once, there had been just such a child—his daughter, Lisette. He remembered her fluffy curls, those eyes which had been as green as his own. She was two years old when he last saw her. For a long while now he had known that she was dead, neglected by that witch Giselle, who had been too preoccupied with fostering her own ambitions to love his baby born out of wedlock.

Despite his auspicious beginning as heir to a great French family with a chateau near Chambord, a magnificent house in Paris and business interests in America, life for Sebastian had had its setbacks. In the course of the Revolution, the chateau had been attacked and vandalized by the enraged peasants, and he and his parents had barely escaped with their lives. After gathering together as much money and as many valuables as possible, they had taken horse for Dieppe, there embarking on one of the Lajeaunesse merchant ships bound for the colonies. South Carolina had welcomed them, and the stately plantation of Oakwood Hall had given them a home and a new life, but it had been too much for the elderly Comte and his delicate wife. Within a year they both were dead, and Sebastian had inherited everything.

Because the plantation had been left in the hands of stewards and distant, ineffectual relatives for so long, it had fallen sadly in production, and it had taken Sebastian years of hard work and shrewd management to put it back on its feet. Money had been of the essence, and he had been forced to join many an illicit enterprise to obtain it. With this capital, he had planted acres of tobacco and rice, and steadily built up his task force of slaves and freemen.

Many and varied had been his associates—pirates, smugglers and trappers. And he had made friends among the Cherokee Indians, who helped supply the ever-growing demand for beaver, fox, deer and bearskins, those furs so coveted by the wealthy and fashionable. Inevitably he had made enemies, too, but he had never been short of loyal fellows to follow him.

Berenice's continued sobbing impinged on his thoughts. He stubbed out his cheroot and slipped a hand on to her shoulder, trying to ease her around. *'Mon coeur,'* he said softly. 'Don't cry so bitterly. Am I such a villain that you'll break your little heart because I made love to you?'

137

Berenice recoiled instantly from his touch, shrinking to the outer limits of the bed.

'You did not make love to me, sir, you attacked me,' she said through her tears. With a downward slant to his mouth, Sebastian looked at her curled woefully there, her abundant hair a tangled halo about her head. Anger, remorse and regret merged in his mind. He had a guilty feeling that he could have behaved in a more gentlemanly way, using the charm of which he was fully capable, had he not been so blinded by pride. Her active dislike was most unflattering to a lover of his renown. He was not used to such a reaction. Women were usually more than willing to accept his advances. How dare she prefer Peregrine!

'Very well, madame, I see that you're determined to continue in this manner,' he said with a cutting edge to his voice. He rose from the bed; slipped his arms into his robe, knotted the girdle round his waist and stood for a moment with one large hand resting on the bedpost, scowling in perplexed annoyance at her small, huddled form. 'I don't judge you to be a cold woman—only a reluctant one—to me, at any rate. But you'll have to accept that I am master now.'

At that she started up, dragging the sheet over her breasts, her face a mask of desperation. 'Never in a thousand years! I hate you! I despise you! Go away!'

He wanted to stroke her hair, to wipe away her angry tears, to assure her that he did not intend to be a brute, but he knew that if he touched her again it would end in him taking her. He would make love to her not only because he desired her, but also to break through that barrier of ice which she was deliberately creating. Women! They were devils put on the earth to torment men. With a snort of disdain, he swung on his heel and left the room.

Berenice jumped as she heard the dividing door slam between them. She choked on her furious sobs. He was so sure of himself. So confident in his power over her. So he thought he could bend her, did he? She would show him! Her chance would come, sooner or later, and she would be ready to take it. She would escape, and Peregrine with her.

The thought soothed her, and she stopped crying. She told herself firmly that she was delighted Sebastian had taken himself off. She did not want him there, mocking and tormenting her, making her body behave in a brazen fashion. But as she lay with the silk sheets brushing sensually over her nakedness, she remembered with half shame, half pleasure, the way in which she had responded to him. For in spite of everything, he had made her conscious of the enjoyment a man might give a woman, and she had an inkling of the power of her own attractions.

The complexity of it was too much. With an exhausted sigh, she curled into a ball, and much sooner than she had expected, slumber overcame her.

FIVE

It seemed that she had only been asleep for a few moments before she was awakened by Dulcie, standing by the bed holding a breakfast tray. Berenice flung an arm over her eyes to shut out the early sunshine which crept between the curtains.

Recollection rushed back and she groaned, sitting up sluggishly, wanting nothing more than to sleep forever, to forget yesterday and its implications. Dulcie, crisply efficient in her brown cotton dress, neat pinafore and cap, eyed her with amusement, obviously bursting with curiosity about the wedding night. Berenice sourly disregarded her, sipping her coffee with a sulky expression and wondering where Sebastian could be.

Dulcie supplied the answer. 'He was up at crack of dawn, madam—gone down to the docks to make sure the cargo is aboard. I've finished packing and everything is ready.' Her bubbling vitality burst out, a wide smile lifting her pretty features. 'Ooh, aren't you excited? I never dreamed I'd be going on a sea voyage—not as a passenger, that is. I might have been transported in the old days, if you know what I mean—sold as a bond servant because I'd been a thief. But I never thought to go as an honest traveler.'

Berenice wished she could feel an iota of her maid's enthusiasm, instead, filled with gloomy musings, she got out of bed and commenced dressing. Days before, they had decided what she should wear, so that everything else could be stored in the trunks. There was no time to have a bath and remove the musky odor of Sebastian's sweat, which still clung to her skin, so she washed carefully and then slipped into her chemise, allowing Dulcie to drop the gown over her head. It was of fine moss-green bargé, the neckline modestly covered by a lace fichu. Because the day was chilly, she added a matching spencer to her outfit, short-bodiced and buttoning down the front, with long tight sleeves.

Seated before her mirror for the last time, she became completely absorbed as she worked on her face, rubbing rich, scented cream into her skin, then wiping the surplus away with a napkin before using a hare's foot to add a touch of rouge to her cheeks. She dipped a tiny brush in a pot of carmine and painted her mouth, then darkened her wing-shaped brows and brushed her lashes upwards.

This ritual never failed to calm her, even this morning when she needed reassurance so desperately. Dulcie was hovering with unwonted nervousness as she worked on her mistress's hair. She was unnaturally clumsy, dropping pins and combs, swooping to pick them up, apologetic and flustered. Eventually she managed to finish, leaving Berenice's dark locks arranged in ringlets, topped by a stylish hat.

'He got hold of my last letter to Sir Peregrine,' Berenice announced, staring at her maid's reflection in the glass. 'Showed it to me last night, taunted me with it, used it as an excuse to treat me diabolically.'

'Did he, milady?' Dulcie was not convinced that her mistress was as outraged as she liked to appear. She packed the cosmetics in a small leather case, then said, 'It was that servant of his, that Quico. He stole it. Hanging around in the garden, he was.'

'Then I was right!' Somehow this justified her actions. 'Sebastian had set the damned fellow to spy on me! You'll have to watch him, Dulcie, for I've every intention of continuing my liaison with Sir Peregrine.'

'Anything you say, madam,' Dulcie agreed, to pacify her.

'Good. We'll foil them yet—Sebastian and his rascally servant!'

Sorrowfully aware that there was no way she could delay her departure further, Berenice gave a final, unnecessary tweak to her hat. Dulcie held out the green velvet coat and, unable to postpone the dreaded moment of departure any longer, Berenice picked up her gloves, taking a look round the room which had witnessed her initiation into the mysteries of sex. Here she had lost her maidenhead but instead of glorying in her husband's conquest, she felt nothing but resentment. Tears gathered in her eyes, and she blinked hard to stop them, checking her hand luggage and making sure she had packed her diary. There would be plenty of time for her to make entries in it, and she had a lot to write about.

A servant came to announce that the coach was outside. He was followed by a stream of footmen to heave down the luggage. Damian was waiting in the hall, booted and cloaked, issuing instructions, very masterful of a sudden. The servants lined up to bid them godspeed, and the Marquis, feeling his years, stepped forward to embrace his children for what might be the last time.

It was a sad and solemn moment. Berenice pressed her cheek to his, her heart aching. What was there to say? The only words filling her mind were, Father, don't send me away! But her lips remained sealed. The proprieties had to be observed.

She was glad when the ordeal was over. Unable to cope with further inroads on her emotions, she was relieved when they were settled in the carriage and clattering away towards the wharf where Sebastian's ship, *La Foudre*, lay at anchor. While Berenice and Dulcie stood uncertainly on the cobbled quayside, Damian organized the loading of the trunks. Sebastian was nowhere to be seen—much to Berenice's joy. Nervously she faced the curious stares of the conglomeration of people thronging the waterfront, for with her fine clothes and exceptional beauty she stood out like a jewel in a muddy gutter. It was a seedy area and, in the normal course of things, a well-bred woman would not have set foot there.

As she became more accustomed to her

surroundings, Berenice could not suppress a quiver of anticipation as she took in the strange sights and sounds. Her nostrils detected a salty tang in the air, for there was a sea breeze even this far up the Thames. A dozen aromatic odors wafted from the holds of the vessels moored in the harbor—spices and hides, the pungent scent of resin from felled pines—a fascinating mixture that whispered of adventures far away in exotic places. Dulcie was fairly hopping with glee, hardly able to wait to walk the decks of *La Foudre,* and soon Damian reappeared, escorting them up the gangplank of this merchantman, owned by Sebastian.

They were conducted down a companionway and into the main cabin, a long, low apartment situated in the stern, where the officers and passengers ate and spent their leisure. On the other side of the gangway were several staterooms, and Berenice was shown into the largest of these, which she was to share with her husband. Dulcie started to unpack one of the trunks, the rest of the luggage having been stowed below decks, and the strictly masculine cabin soon became strewn with female garments as the maid set about making it as comfortable as possible for her mistress.

Berenice ordered her to desist, unbearably tense, finding the atmosphere claustrophobic— the small space filled with Sebastian's things, his hand apparent everywhere in the choice of furnishings, and his clothing already stowed in the cupboards. She insisted that they go on deck again, and Dulcie was nothing loath, intoxicated by the sight of so many bronzed and muscular seamen. Even the thought of the cramped conditions of the weeks ahead did not dampen her enthusiasm.

The two women were standing at the quarterdeck rail, watching the activity below, with Dulcie keeping up a lively commentary, when Berenice hushed her, seeing Sebastian in close conversation with a short, stocky man whose air of authority singled him out as the captain. Even when her husband moved beyond range, she could still hear his voice every now and again, issuing orders and arguing with the mate about the precise placing of the cargo. Damian was following him about, completely absorbed in all that was taking place, having quite lost his heart to *La Foudre*.

Peregrine arrived late, accompanied by a noisy coachload of young people who spilled out on to the quay, shouting and hallooing, giving him a rousing send-off. Berenice was not too pleased to see him being warmly embraced by a sumptuous redhead, and keenly resented her air of intimacy. Even when he came and sought her out, her manner remained cool, though this derived partly from her own shame at having betrayed her vow and yielded to Sebastian. Did Peregrine realize what had happened? she wondered. Was there something different about her now? An aura which suggested that she was no longer a virgin?

Lecturing herself on her foolish fancies, she retired to the cabin, there to toy with the packed lunch Dulcie had thoughtfully brought with her.

145

After this she tried to rest, a difficult task, as there was so much noise above, below and on every side as the ship was prepared to sail on the tide. Berenice would have given almost anything to see Lady Olivia walk through the door, or even Miss Osborne, that most tedious of companions, but she had left Elsewood House directly after the wedding reception. As a Comtesse and respectable married lady, Berenice no longer required a chaperon. Paradoxically, she would now have welcomed the presence of a duenna in the room when a man was there, provided that man was Sebastian, whereas at one time she had kicked violently against this convention, considering it a stupid, old-fashioned curb on her freedom.

She settled herself in a chair, a foreign-looking item covered with stamped Spanish leather and trimmed with shaggy fringe held in place with brass-headed pins, and she drew her diary from the depths of her reticule. Lately, there had been few entries in this journal, which she had vowed to keep regularly when Lucinda gave it to her on her last birthday. In the beginning, the novelty of it had made her write every day, and, flipping back to the early pages, she found accounts of galas, fêtes, and boat trips on the river at Richmond. Then it had petered out.

Reading these made her cry. How happy her life had been, how carefree! She could almost hear Lucinda saying when they met for the last time,

'Don't forget the journal, my child. Write about everything that happens to you, and show it to me one day. Oh, and I shall expect letters, and will be mortally offended if I don't receive them.'

'Will you write back?' Berenice had asked, petting Sheba before placing her in her friend's arms.

'Of course I shall!' There had been tears streaking Lucinda's rouged cheeks. 'And I'll be at the church to throw confetti, even if I've not been invited to the reception.'

Now Berenice wiped away the wetness that bedewed her own face, found a pencil, opened the book and started to scrawl.

'I'm on board the ship. No, that's not how I wanted to start. I'm his wife! Last night I learned what it is like to be rogered by a man. Oh, Lucinda, if you ever read this, I know you'll expect salacious details, such as you love to devour from those racy books that you keep in your bedroom, but I can't describe it. There's nothing new I can tell you anyway. You're an experienced mistress. All I know is that I feel as battered as a vessel that's been in a storm. Not bodily, maybe, but spiritually.'

She cried a lot more after this, resting her head in her hands—the diary had fallen to the floor. Dulcie came in shortly after, clucking over Berenice like a hen with a single chick, soothing, solicitous, genuinely in distress.

'Oh, come, my lady, cheer up do. You must put on a brave face, as supper is about to be served and you've strangers to meet. It's necessary for you to change and appear calm and collected. Wash your face and let's choose a dress for the occasion, shall we?'

Berenice permitted herself to be treated like a child, doing as her maid suggested. Sebastian had not approached her all day, but he appeared in the stateroom as she was just about to depart, and her heart sank. He seemed immense in that confined space, suffocatingly so. As he bowed to her solemnly, she could not prevent a flush from coloring her face.

'Madame, I'm sorry I did not welcome you aboard, but I've been very busy. I trust you are rested and ready for the voyage,' he said, as formal as a bishop.

Berenice, acutely conscious of what had taken place at their last meeting, made a special effort to remain icy cool. 'Thank you, sir. I'm as ready as I ever shall be,' she replied, and went to pass him, but he stood in the way.

'A word of warning, my dear wife.' His voice was clipped, his eyes piercing hers. 'You'll remain in the officers' area of the ship, and only appear on deck once a day for exercise. The forecastle is the seamen's quarters, and you will *never* go there. We're in for a long journey, and you're far too beautiful. I don't want a mutiny on my hands before we're halfway across the Atlantic.' He frowned in Dulcie's direction. 'And the same applies to you, girl. Keep away from the crew.'

Berenice opened her mouth to argue, but there was something about the set of his lips that silenced her. Now that he was on board his ship, he bore an even stronger air of authority. She shivered, guessing that he would be a stern

148

disciplinarian who would deal mercilessly with malcontents. But there was one rebel whom he would find impossible to browbeat—and that was her.

'You underestimate my intelligence,' she answered. 'I know how to conduct myself. So does Dulcie.'

'Let us hope so, *chérie*,' he replied. 'We've an arduous haul ahead of us and it'll be as well if tempers remain unfrayed. Sir Peregrine had best watch that acid tongue of his. There are those here who'll not be as tolerant as myself of his airs and graces.'

Whenever he mentioned Peregrine, his voice took on an unpleasant, sneering tone which riled Berenice, but before she could retort, she was interrupted by the soft-footed Quico descending the steps, bearing a message for his master. Berenice glared at the manservant, hating him for his part in betraying her, but Quico merely watched her with expressionless eyes, his face impassive.

'Come, Dulcie,' Berenice said, but as she went to leave, a ray of dying sunlight struck through one of the thick glass portholes and flashed on the gold wedding ring on her finger. It was as if the band grew tighter.

Needing air, Berenice drew her sequined shawl about her shoulders and stepped out on the quarterdeck, which lifted and fell beneath her feet. She could feel the slow vibration, hear the rush of waves against the rudder, and the creaking of the ropes. The great spread of canvas puffed out overhead, bearing *La Foudre* downriver towards the sea. The sun was sinking, a fiery ball balanced on the horizon, and night was falling in grey mists upon the water. On either side, there was a spangle of lights along the distant bank. Berenice felt a lonely ache in her chest. Soon she would see the last of England, perhaps forever.

'Oh, Dulcie—' she gasped, her hand reaching out and meeting that of her maid.

'I'm here, my lady. I'll never leave you,' Dulcie whispered, then a bell sounded, summoning them to supper.

Below deck, the main cabin was lit by lanterns swaying gently on gimbals. It was a large room with windows curving along its width. In the center an oak table was clamped to the floor, with chairs around it, also bolted firmly to prevent them moving during a storm. The furnishings were of fine quality, woodwork and metal fittings gleaming. Berenice was later to discover that this sense of order permeated the entire ship. The food was well prepared and imaginative, cooked in the galley on the other side of the gangway and served by two uniformed stewards. There was nothing slipshod about the running of that vessel. Berenice could not help being impressed, though she was unable to decide whether the credit should go to the owner or to the gritty little man who was introduced to her as Captain Ogilvie.

Seated at table, she studied the officers, the captain, thickset, sparing of speech, gazing at her disconcertingly from under beetling brows, and two younger men, Mr. Croft and Mr. Manson, the former middle-sized with a neatly clipped beard, and the latter a sturdy individual with chubby pink cheeks and sparse fair hair. All three wore dark blue jackets ornamented with rows of brass buttons, white cloth breeches, white hose and black leather shoes. Their cravats and shirt cuffs were snow white, their appearance spruce, their manner gravely courteous. Croft and Manson were American, but Ogilvie had Scottish connections, and each of them was dedicated, heart and soul, to the sea.

The meal progressed sedately, though Berenice ate little, too aware of Sebastian lounging at the head of the board, conversing easily with the other men. As she half listened to what was being said, she watched the play of light over his strongly-cut features, fascinated by his lean hand holding the stem of his brandy glass, remembering how it had been to have those same fingers fondling her body. An expression of half-derisive amusement curved his lips as he caught her gaze, and she flushed scarlet, convinced that he read her thoughts.

Damian, meanwhile, was chattering ani-matedly with the mariners, wanting to know everything about life on board ship. 'Where will be our first port of call?' he asked.

'The Canary Islands,' Sebastian rejoined promptly, tapping on the stem of his glass with his fingernail. A steward leapt forward to refill his glass. 'We're to pick up a consignment of wine there. America is the most fruitful place in the world, but still it can't produce good vintage.'

'So you import it,' put in Damian brightly,

thinking he had a grasp of the situation.

With a deepening of his sardonic smile, Sebastian exchanged a glance with Ogilvie. 'You could put it that way,' he replied.

He neglected to add that he had a greedy customsman in his pocket who was ready to turn a blind eye to smuggling, for a substantial consideration. Sebastian had it down to a fine art, loading up with Spanish wine in the Canaries, then putting in at Madeira to take aboard a few additional casks of local brew for the inspectors at Charleston to sample, thus diverting them from the illicit hogsheads stowed deeper in the hold.

'Your ship is lighter and speedier than most merchantmen, isn't she?' Damian went on, his boyish face eager. As he spoke, he gave Berenice a reassuring smile, unable to understand her sullen looks. In his opinion Sebastian was an excellent sort of chap.

'*Oui*, I've had her fitted out that way,' Sebastian nodded, a glint in his eyes. 'And she's well armed, too.'

'But why?' Damian was puzzled. There was so much he wanted to learn. He had completely fallen under the spell of the older man, whom he saw as a fearless leader, his high-powered personality inspiring confidence and unswerving loyalty.

Sebastian abandoned his lazy pose, sitting up and resting an elbow on the table, one hand cupping his chin. 'Pirates!' he said crisply.

'Pirates?' Both Damian and Peregrine said together.

'They're still the scourge of the seas.' Sebastian smiled darkly at their surprise, enjoying the private joke between himself and Ogilvie. Both of them had followed that trade in their time, never averse to capturing an easy, profitable prey, but not for a long while now, confining lawless activities to smuggling.

'They prowl the coast of Africa,' he continued. 'And if we fell into their hands, the men would probably end up at the oars as galley slaves. Whilst you, madame,' and here he nodded towards Berenice, 'might find yourself in a sultan's harem. How would you like that, eh?'

Dulcie, standing behind her mistress's chair, gave a frightened squeak, but Berenice was certainly not about to give him the satisfaction of knowing that he had alarmed her. She shrugged her white shoulders that were bared by the midnight blue gown she wore, her eyes taking on its dark hue as she gave him back stare for stare.

'I don't know what that would entail, but it seems to me that we women endure all manner of slavery, even in a so-called Christian society. Aren't we expected to subject ourself to our husbands?' she remarked pointedly, glad to see the hardening of his mouth. Her barb had struck home.

'*Touché!*' murmured Peregrine behind his hand.

He was seated at her side, elegant as ever, and had been keeping up a barbed commentary throughout the evening, sharpening his wit at the expense of the less sophisticated seamen, whilst they, with raised brows and tight jaws, formed their own unflattering opinion of him. He used the occasion as a stage, monopolizing Berenice with singular lack of prudence, pantomiming with his shapely hands.

Sebastian was nobody's fool and, alert to his game, eyed him as if he were a peculiarly unwholesome species of insect. Angrily, he marveled at his wife's interest in him. Surely she could not be such a simpleton as to be deceived by his pinchbeck glitter? It was offensive to realize that she actually preferred the company of that shallow poser. To his horror, he found himself simmering with resentment, and something perilously close to jealousy. His possessiveness made him long to lock her away so that no other man could embrace her even in his dreams. And there she sat, as demure as a nun, turning the full glory of her smile in Peregrine's direction, whereas every time Sebastian caught her eye, it was to meet a look of withering contempt.

Peregrine was not slow in sensing the discord between them, and emboldened by Berenice's obvious approval, he said conversationally, but with a sneering edge, 'Jove! I'm mighty eager to set eyes on America. Lady Chard's given me letters of introduction to the very best families in Georgetown. How do you think I'll fare, Comte? Shall I make my fortune in your fabled country?'

An ominous silence followed, then Sebastian raised one black, curving eyebrow and stared down his patrician nose at the fop. 'There are opportunities for any amount of rogues in the New World,' he drawled slowly. 'It's so big that the useless ones get lost among men of guts and determination.'

Peregrine's face paled and his supercilious expression became more marked. His fingers played nervously with a pellet of bread on his plate. 'Is that how you came to be there, sir? A runagate from France?' he ventured boldly, eyes sliding to Berenice, watching her reaction.

Sebastian took a cheroot from a silver box, and the steward lit it for him. He did not deign to answer for a moment, drawing the smoke back into his lungs, then exhaling it through flared nostrils before saying,

'My family have had connections with Carolina for over two hundred years. A branch of my House settled there. I took it as my home when it was no longer possible for me to remain in *la belle France*. My situation is somewhat different from your own, *mon ami*. I was not leaving my country to avoid my creditors—merely my enemies, who would have killed me.'

There was a cold malevolence in his eyes that crushed Peregrine. Of a sudden, the air seemed so charged with violence that it almost sizzled. Captain Ogilvie hurriedly changed the subject and they talked of less personal matters, but Berenice was uncomfortably conscious of the two men scowling at each other down the length of the table. Dear God, they'd only just begun the journey and already there was trouble brewing! Her head began to ache dully, and she refused another glass of wine, begging that they might excuse her, and retiring to her cabin.

In that alien sleeping place, Dulcie helped her get ready for the night. She took a white gown from the valise, chaste in style, with long full sleeves and a yoke which fastened high at the throat, but the novicelike aspect of this garment was purely superficial, since the material was virtually transparent. Chiding Dulcie wearily, having asked her to make sure and pack a nightdress made of sensible and nonrevealing flannel, Berenice pulled a dressing gown over it. She found it difficult to stand, staggering against the slant of the deck, for they had reached open water and the sea was choppy. She wondered if she would ever get used to the motion, depressed by the prospect of being imprisoned in this stateroom which bore Sebastian's stamp so clearly.

It was uncompromisingly male, but splendidly appointed, the padded lockers covered in chocolate brown plush edged with gold fringe. There were cupboards cunningly contrived between the bulkheads, and a secretaire which, when Berenice opened it to take a peek, revealed quills and sunken inkwells, every article decorated with silver chasing. The decor showed style and taste and a flair for color and texture, the embroidered panels glowing against the dark wood, the carved, gilded mirror set to catch the light, the expertly executed paintings—all were an astonishing revelation of Sebastian's diverse character.

In contrast to this sophistication, the sanitary arrangements were primitive: a simple chamber pot in a commode, a china bowl set on a washstand, the contents of both being borne aloft and flung overboard. Berenice, however, was not unduly dismayed by this. Even in the great houses of England, the privy usually consisted of nothing more complicated than a tiny closet on the ground floor with a hole dug deep in the earth, topped by a boxlike seat. As for bathing, only a very few rich eccentrics went in for the newfangled tubs, with water on tap, and drainage.

'Oh, madam, I'm queasy,' Dulcie complained, hand to her brow. 'May I go and lie down?'

Berenice was having trouble controlling her own stomach, and she nodded dismally. This was all she needed—a bout of *mal de mer!* The feeling was growing stronger. Her stomach rose. Sour saliva ran into her mouth and swimming flecks of faintness almost blinded her. She barely managed to reach the porthole, flinging it wide and leaning out, dizzied by the spume racing far below. She vomited violently, pouring her supper into the void, then crouching, shivering, clutching the edge of the window with icy fingers.

Somehow she found herself on the bed with its damask drapes and tasseled velvet quilt. Groaning, sweating, her head pounding as if it was being beaten by hammers, she crawled beneath the covers. Every item in the cabin seemed to be swaying, and even when she closed her eyes, she could still see them; the lanterns, her gown on a hanger, the polished wooden floor shifting, tilting, then dropping down sharply. Berenice huddled on her side, knees drawn up, too ill to weep, pressing the heel of her hand against her temple to assuage the pain.

Sebastian came in late after gambling with Damian and Peregrine. He was angry, more than half convinced that the dandy was a cardsharp, but unable as yet to prove it. He crossed the cabin swiftly, tossing his cravat over one of the high-backed chairs, shrugging his shoulders out of his jacket and stabbing a glance at the still figure on the bed, partly covered by the quilt. Her slender shoulders were turned towards him, the dip of her waist softly curving upwards to the sharper swell of her hip, the outline of her buttocks clearly defined.

Desire rose thick in him, urging him to lean over and feast his eyes on her sleeping face and those fragrant curls—wonderful scented curls—hiding each ear, and that delectable mouth parted over the small, even teeth. His hand hovered above her, ready to lift aside the bedclothes, but just at that moment she stirred, moaning feverishly. Peering closer, he was struck by the deathly pallor of her skin. When he touched her forehead, he found that she was feverish. Conscious that he was there, her lids flew open, eyes shining with unnatural brilliance but, even in her extremity, she shrank away from him.

'What ails you?' he said, hurt by this demonstration of loathing.

She shook her head, unable to speak, and he guessed the reason for her indisposition. The sea was rough and he had gathered that she'd never sailed before. His feelings changed abruptly to compassion, tenderness taking him unawares as he laid her back gently, after turning the hot pillow so that she might rest on the cool underside of it. He went to the medicine chest and mixed her a herbal draught, then propped her up against his shoulder, coaxing her to drink. After this, he filled the basin with water and carefully sponged her face and throat.

Berenice was hardly aware of what was happening, the blinding headache rendering her semiconscious. As he let his eyes take their fill of her body, provocatively bare beneath the nightgown, Sebastian realized that she was as much a girl as a woman, an innocent seductress. Was it a fortune to have such a combination as a wife!

He frowned, distrustful of these feelings of pity and tenderness which overcame him. He was growing mawkish! As he smoothed back her dark hair that streamed across the pillow, he was astonished when she snuggled gratefully into the curve of his arm. This simple, trusting gesture moved him deeply.

He checked himself and shifted away from her, angry and disturbed. This was ridiculous! He was Lajeaunesse, pirate and smuggler, one of the toughest, most experienced scouts and craftiest trappers, schooled by the Cherokee Indians. How his ruffianly associates would jeer if they could see him now. Lajeaunesse, on a bed with a lovely woman playing her nursemaid.

Berenice felt him withdraw, perceiving him through the soothing mists of laudanum that he had added to his potion. Dimly, she was aware of the presence of someone comforting and warm and immensely reassuring, yet she refused to believe it could be Sebastian. Finally her tired brain gave up the struggle, allowing her to sink into sleep.

She was ill for days, so miserable that death would have been a blessing. She never thought to survive the ordeal. Dulcie, too, was completely incapacitated, and judging from the groans and complaints issuing from Peregrine's cabin, he had also fallen victim to seasickness. By the time they sighted the Canary Islands, off the coast of Africa, Berenice was able to stagger to the rail of *La Foudre*. She gazed down shakily at the sea, swelling, falling so monotonously, remembering how she had begged God to still those dreadful waters, promising anything if only He would!

She leaned against a bulwark, while *La Foudre* danced through the waves, seeming to flirt with them, rearing and plunging like a skittish filly. Ahead lay the misted shape of an island, lying like a pink cloud on the horizon. Land! Was it really land at last? Suddenly she wanted to find Sebastian, to beg that he might let her go ashore, if only for a brief time, to feel the blessing of solid earth beneath her feet. The wind was whipping the cobwebs from her mind, and now she began to remember, seeing vague pictures of him bending over her, tenderness softening his eyes, his hands as gentle as a woman's. She shook her head to clear it. No, she must have been dreaming. How could her mocking, black-hearted husband have turned into a ministering angel? The idea was absurd, and she dismissed it as a hallucination wrought by her delirium.

She did not have to seek him, for he appeared at her side, throwing his boat cloak round her as he said, 'Be careful, *chérie*. You are weak, and might take a chill.'

'I want to go ashore. I need to feel land under my feet, not this terrible, heaving water! Can I disembark?' She was pleading, pride lost, begging him for this one favor.

He looked down into her wan face, the eyes huge and set in blue-smudged circles. 'Not yet, *doucette*. We don't stay long in Tenerife. The wine is brought out to us, but when we reach Madeira we'll stop off for a spell. I'll take you there myself, and we'll visit an old friend of mine, Don Santos,' he promised, then ruffled her hair gently. 'Poor darling—seasickness is a dreadful affliction, is it not?'

'And Dulcie can come as well? She's been ill, too.'

Sebastian shrugged and smiled, happy to indulge her. It pleased him to have her dependent on him, no longer snapping and snarling, for once. 'Of course. I'm not so dreadful a monster, you see.'

Then Berenice pushed her luck, adding, 'Can

we take Peregrine with us? Dulcie tells me that he's been awfully sick.'

Sebastian withdrew the arm that had been steadying her against the swell. 'If it is your wish, madame,' he answered frostily.

'It is, sir.' Her hands gripped the rail before her, the cloak still wrapped close, but there was something missing now—the warmth of Sebastian's body.

At six o'clock in the morning the lookout in the crow's nest sighted land. The silent ship came to life. Men started swabbing the decks, swilling down the stairs, polishing rails and cleaning everything. They worked with a will, singing as they did so; everyone was happy at the prospect of shore leave.

Within two hours, Berenice was standing on deck, waiting to land in Madeira. Beside her stood a white-faced, still nauseous Dulcie, watching the native rafts streaming out from the harbor, loaded with barrels which Sebastian's men then heaved aboard. They were taking on fresh water as well as wine, and this provided an opportunity to make other purchases. In the forechains the steward and the cook were receiving a bombardment of pidgin English from a cluster of vessels laden with fruit and vegetables, bumping and scraping alongside, manned by whites and half-castes, all of them nearly tumbling into the pellucid, jade green sea in their eagerness to sell. Little blue and red rowing boats were bobbing about, with boys diving from them for silver coins thrown by those on the ship. They never missed, but it looked extremely dangerous and Berenice feared for them, even as she encouraged their daring by tossing money in.

The weather was delightfully warm, and Berenice's hair was gently stirred by the breeze which sweetly tempered the sun's heat. The waters of the bay were so different from the crashing waves further out, deceptively calm-looking. In the distance she could see mountains topped with clouds and houses dotting the green hillside like patches of snow. Peregrine ventured forth, crawling up the companionway, with a bilious tinge to his skin, looking very much the worse for wear. He and Berenice commiserated with one another. They were used to traveling by barge on the Thames—indeed it was often the quickest mode of transport in London, but this had been their first experience of vast oceanic omnipotence.

Damian, on the other hand, had proved to be a born sailor, unaffected by the sickness that had laid them low, spending most of his time with the helmsman, glorying in the mountainous waves and stiff, exhilarating wind. Now he came across the deck towards them, adopting the rolling gait of the seasoned mariner.

'Are you recovered, Sister,' he cried, shirt thrown open at the neck, a knitted jelly-bag cap placed jauntily on one side of his head.

'A little,' she answered, bored by his enthusiasm for everything nautical. 'I'm looking forward to walking on dry land.'

'You'll get used to the motion in no time,' he predicted, with the annoying conviction of someone who has found his sea legs with no difficulty. He sat astride a bollard, sniffing the wind and acting as if he had always been a seafarer.

'It's fine for those with a cast-iron constitution,' Peregrine grumbled, eyeing him resentfully. 'Personally, I can't even enjoy a pinch of snuff at the moment. Everything makes me want to spew.'

'Captain Ogilvie'll soon turn you into a jolly jack-tar!' Damian seemed to have lost his usual sensitivity concerning other people's feelings.

Peregrine shuddered. 'No, thank you very much. I don't want to spend the rest of my days condemned to sleep in a hammock and live on weevil-infested biscuits, salt pork and brackish water, expected to play the sea-wife into the bargain, and flogged with the cat-o'-nine-tails for the smallest misdemeanor.'

Damian laughed. 'You exaggerate, Peregrine. I should think it's a most exciting career. Sebastian's been teaching me navigation, and we're traveling on the quickest route to America. It's called the Verrazano Course.'

'Oh, dear. Is it far?' Dulcie looked distinctly worried, and Peregrine moaned at the prospect.

'Miles, or rather knots, I should say!' Damian rejoined gleefully. 'And the crossing can be stormy!'

Berenice folded her arms about her uneasy stomach and moved closer to Peregrine. 'We'll

164

be feeling better soon, I'm sure,' she said consolingly.

She was unaware that Sebastian was watching them from high among the shrouds where he was inspecting the rigging, and unaware also of the furious expression on his face, as he saw her reach out and place her hand on that of the beau. He bawled for a boat to be lowered and came down the rope at a rapid rate, hand over hand, agile as a monkey, barefooted and wearing white linen trousers and shirt.

'Time to go, madame,' he said crisply. 'Are you ready for this?'

'I'm ready, sir,' she answered, with much more confidence than she felt.

She had never been called upon to do anything more frightening than climb down the ladder that swayed and bumped against the ship's precipitous side. The longboat seemed to be a hundred miles below. In the end, Sebastian lost patience with her timidity. She was lifted bodily and thrown across his shoulder. Then, with one arm like a steel band under her buttocks and his other hand coming up to clamp across her spine, he paused, judged the right moment between the waves and then jumped nimbly into the restless pinnace moving up and down at alarming speed beneath them.

'Wait for me, my lady!' Dulcie screamed, but before she had finished speaking, Quico had lifted her high in his wiry arms.

'Put me down!' the maid gasped, outraged.

'You want to fall?' Quico answered laconically.

' 'Course I don't, you great cork-brained loon!'

'Then you do as I say!' And before she knew what was happening, Dulcie found herself upended and hanging somewhere between the ship and the sea, until at last her feet encountered the longboat's decking.

There was a strong swell running and the pinnace, manned by eight oarsmen, rolled about in the waves, nearly toppling over and swamping its occupants, but eventually they reached the shore and Sebastian helped Berenice up some slippery stone steps to the quay. She stood there shaking, and it felt as if she were still on *La Foudre,* her balance not yet adjusted. She was glad when he held her arm, never letting go as he guided her along the cobbled wharfside where traders waited, offering wicker tables, chairs, baskets and local lace.

The women wore traditional costume, the rich-textured skirts and waistcoats thick with embroidery, their linen decorated with broderie anglaise. But there were a large number of beggars, too, even more than those Berenice had seen in the London streets. The diseased and deformed children being shamelessly exploited upset her, and she emptied her purse as she moved among them. Somehow it seemed worse in that tropical paradise where the sea and sky were so blue, and the flowers so abundant.

'Don't take it to heart, Berenice,' Sebastian advised, as he conducted her to where a carriage awaited them. 'Some are genuine, but there are a lot of fakes. You'll have to toughen up. I'll wager that Dulcie can tell the real from the false.'

He stopped when a girl approached carrying a basket, astonished the smiling, dark-skinned beauty by buying every orchid and exotic strelitzia she possessed, and then handed them to an equally surprised Berenice.

'For me!' she asked on a note of wonder.

'For you,' he answered with a slow smile.

The landau, too, was another surprise, sparkling with crimson varnish picked out with gold paint, its housings a glittering tribute to the lorimer's art. Every time the four scrupulously groomed gray horses shifted between the shafts they set silver bells jingling. This open vehicle was driven by a black, uniformed coachman with a massive tricorn hat perched on top of his hair, and there were two postilions in red livery standing on the step at the rear.

One of them leapt down to open the door and unfolded the step so that Sebastian's party could climb in. Dulcie sat opposite her mistress, but Quico jumped up beside the coachman on his lofty box. The whip cracked, the horses started forward and the conveyance rolled away from the quay, passing plodding oxcarts with straw-hatted drivers, and sledges that came careering down the steep cobbled side streets.

They left the main thoroughfare and drove towards the outskirts of the port, entering a wide, tree-shaded avenue. On either side were walled gardens with iron grilled gates through which Berenice glimpsed cool patios, green lawns and fountains. Everywhere there were flowers, drooping over fences, rioting on rookeries, tumbling out of ornamental earthenware crocks and climbing the fronts of the white-walled houses.

They arrived at a pair of imposing gates which opened inwards, apparently moved by some invisible agency. A graveled drive snaked ahead, ending in a semicircle in front of a set of wide, stone steps leading up to the verandah of a large house, with elaborate iron balconies and patterns of blue tiles ornamenting its facade.

A man came down to greet them, very tall, lean and old, but erect as a lance. He was hatless, his silver-white hair falling to the shoulders of his dove gray jacket. He wore matching trousers and a purple patterned waistcoat over which flowed the ends of a loosely tied cravat. He held out his arms as Sebastian alighted, crying, 'Monsieur le Comte! Welcome, welcome! My house is your house, as we say in Spain.'

'Don Santos. How good it is to see you again.' Sebastian took his hand, shaking it warmly.

He stepped back to the carriage and Berenice descended, her fingertips resting on his extended fingers. The heat beat down from a molten sky and she unfurled her parasol, holding it over her head. The venerable nobleman smiled at her charmingly.

'Your wife, monsieur?' he asked, dark eyes twinkling in a face scribbled all over with a fine network of wrinkles.

'My wife, señor.'

'I am honored, Comtesse. I see before me

168

a woman fair as the morning, with the grace of the forest deer, and the classical beauty of Aspasia of Athens or Lucrezia of Rome. Please to enter,' and Don Santos bowed her up the steps, across the verandah and into a cool, arched and spacious hall.

Somewhat overwhelmed by this effusive greeting, Berenice moved slowly over the terra-cotta tiled floor, appreciating the feeling of light and air that the Don's magnificent house provided. And this increased as he conducted them through room after room, each one finer than the last and filled with treasures.

They had luncheon on a balcony overlooking the garden and the bay, and Berenice had never seen such a beautiful view. It was nothing like England. It occurred to her that the Garden of Eden might have resembled this place before the Fall of Man. The Don was a gentleman, cultured and well educated, a noble of the old school before the world turned topsy-turvy with the French Revolution, when, for the first time since England in 1649, a people had risen up against their monarch and assassinated him.

'And this was in your country, madame,' the Don reminded as he and Sebastian discussed the situation in France and the leadership of Napoleon Bonaparte. 'The Parliament of King Charles I rebelled and there was civil war.'

'I know a little history, sir. My ancestors supported the king, and suffered consequentially during the interregnum that followed his execution,' she replied, resting her arm on the table which was made of Carrara marble.

Everything in the house was of the finest quality. A superb lunch had been served on Minton china, and they had drunk the wine for which the island was famous, from crystal goblets banded with gold. The wall behind the balcony was faced with colored *azulejo* tiles from Portugal—primrose, azure, apple green, rust red—sparkling like precious stones in the strong sunlight. Sebastian fitted these surroundings perfectly, able to adapt himself to any situation, still casually dressed in white linen, but this seemed to be the attire favored by most gentlemen in this tropical climate.

The Don smiled at her kindly, obviously enjoying the company of an educated Englishwoman. 'I am a great admirer of your homeland,' he said, snapping his fingers at a footman who came forward bearing a silver coffeepot, delicate porcelain cups, and a carafe of brandy. 'And particularly of your writers—Dr. Johnson, and of course, the peerless William Shakespeare. One can do nothing but marvel at the depth of his understanding of human nature. Don't you agree?'

Berenice nodded, while ferreting though her mind for something wise and witty to say. In actual fact, she had read little of the Bard of Avon's works, though she had seen them performed on the stage. It came flooding back to her now—the candle-lit theater, the fops in the pit, the great ladies in their boxes. Could it have been but a few weeks ago? It seemed like another world, an era before Sebastian burst into her life like some fiery, destructive comet.

170

'I have seen the actor Edmund Kean perform at Drury Lane Theater,' she said, stirring the air with a peacock feather fan.

'You have?' The Don's dark eyes shone and his face lit up, making him look much younger. 'Pray what was the role he played?'

Berenice had to think about this for a moment, then daylight dawned and, 'Richard III,' she replied triumphantly. She'd show that arrogant Frenchman that he wasn't the Don's only learned guest.

He was sitting there with an inscrutable expression on his handsome features, and she noticed that his skin was already browner—like a gypsy, she thought with a sneer—some tinker who should be living on the roadside with his cart, his pots and pans.

'Ah, how wonderful, madame!' The Don exclaimed, throwing up his tapering hands, most impressed. 'I've always wanted to see that performed. Perhaps Shakespeare's finest masterpiece—such characterization!'

This spurred Berenice to even greater heights. 'Have you read *Vathek* by William Beckford?' she asked, leaning back in her chair, her white gown shimmering with color reflected from the blossoms trailing round the columns that supported the roof.

'I have indeed. A strange and mystic tale,' the old man replied, delighted to have found a fellow enthusiast. He smiled across the table at Sebastian. 'Have you read it?'

'I always have a copy among my baggage, no matter where I go,' Sebastian answered, and

171

Berenice thought crossly—he *would*.

'I adore such Gothic romances,' she put in quickly, aware that her husband was stealing her thunder.

'Would you call it that?' Sebastian demurred, accepting the cup of strong black coffee the footman offered. 'I'd say it was difficult to classify, for comedy alternates with scenes of Oriental magnificence and cruelty during the Caliph Vathek's adventures. Don't you agree, madame?'

'I suppose you have a point,' she agreed, wishing that she had read the wretched book in its entirety, but she had become bored halfway through and thrown it aside for something more entertaining.

Sebastian's green eyes twinkled. One eyebrow lifted in a question mark and she knew that he knew that she'd not finished the beastly thing. Don Santos was a shrewd man who had seen much of life, been married three times and raised a large family. It did not take a genius to realize that all was not well between the honeymoon couple. As an old friend of the Lajeaunesse family and Sebastian's godfather, he had watched him grow up, recognized his admirable qualities but was not blind to his faults, the chief of which was overweening pride.

He knew all about the marriage, and had lectured Sebastian against impetuosity when he had called in at Madeira on his way to fetch his bride, but feared that his advice had fallen on deaf ears. Something had happened in France during the Revolution, Don Santos was not sure what, but he had noticed an alarming change in Sebastian over the years. He was hard, tough, ruthless on many counts. He had a good business head on him, and the Don never hesitated to supply him with wine from his extensive vineyards, though under no illusion as to the other sources, well aware that Sebastian enjoyed the thrill and profit of smuggling.

But the girl? Ah, how lovely she was, and Don Santos permitted himself the pleasure of looking at her. So charming in her extravagantly long and flowing white muslin gown, with its high belt and tiny sleeves picked out with silk flowers, a transparent lawn stole, and exaggerated, very wide-brimmed straw hat worn over loosely dressed hair. He was afforded a glimpse of small naked feet in strappy sandals, and applauded these graceful, quasi-Greek styles which European women wore now, so much more attractive than the tight stays, panniers and powdered wigs favored when he was a young man. One could almost imagine that girls walked abroad in their nightgowns these days, and though in his seventies he was neither incapable nor impotent, as his twenty-year-old mulatto mistress would have attested, had it been proper to have her present at table.

The afternoon passed pleasantly and, in the cool of early evening, Don Santos took his guests to view his vineyards, and Berenice enjoyed the stroll through those carefully cultivated acres where, in the dimness of his cellar, they sampled some of his finest vintage. Soothed by the wine and the company of such a courtly gentleman, Berenice walked through the garden later, on Sebastian's arm. Damian and Peregrine had delayed in the cellar for yet another glass, listening to the Don discoursing on grapes, and the methods used to transform them into nectar fit for the gods.

'This is a beautiful place,' Berenice remarked, as they paused by the balustrade on a terrace that gave an uninterrupted view of the harbor.

Never in her life had she seen such a spectacular sunset, and she watched, awed. Now towering clouds edged with dazzling colors began to gather on the horizon. They cast a carmine reflection on the sea, seeming to flood it with torrents of flame, the air luminous and clear. Details stood out sharply, while a dozen different songbirds gave their final calls as they went to roost.

'Yes, it is lovely,' Sebastian agreed. 'I wish we could see the dawn come up together, for then the sea is pearly with pink mist.'

'Is Carolina anything like it?' she asked softly, still held in a kind of spell brought about by this awareness of the glory of nature.

'No, but it has its own attractions,' he answered, lighting up a cheroot. He braced one foot on the lower stone rail, leaned his elbow on it and studied the sunset for a while as he smoked, then asked, 'You're feeling better, madame?'

'Oh, yes. It's because I'm ashore.' She sneaked a glance at him, wondering—wishing, she didn't quite know what. He had been different all afternoon. Don Santos seemed to be a calming influence. 'Can we stay here tonight?' she added, trying not to sound too eager.

'No.' He finished the cheroot and ground the butt under his heel. 'I can't delay, and we'll sail when the tide turns.'

'Must we? If you cared about me, you'd know that I need longer to get over my illness—' she began, then stopped short as an impatient expression settled on his strongly carved features.

'Berenice, you are accustomed to having your own way,' he declared. 'It is time you learned that there are more important issues than yourself. Sailing a vessel, for example. One is ruled by the tides, by the winds and weather. Nature does not wait for the whims and fancies of a spoilt girl.'

'Time and tide wait for no man,' she quipped sarcastically, her spirits sinking, all the good feeling engendered by their visit to the Don evaporating as she perceived that he had changed again, once more the single-minded master of a vessel.

'Precisely.' That hard edge was back in his voice, the one she disliked so heartily.

Swallowing her disappointment, she concentrated on the purple night clouds which were consuming the dying sun. A flock of parrots made a flamboyant show against the red sky. There was an absolute stillness everywhere.

Sebastian was very aware of her standing so tantalizingly close to him. He wanted to remain there, imagined taking her to that white draped room which he always used when staying with Don Santos, so cool, the fragrance of flowers drifting in at the arched windows. The bed was so wide, and they could hide away within it, the mosquito netting pulled around them like a tent. Berenice and himself, loving one another, finding each other—was it possible? Yet he had his duty to *La Foudre* and to Captain Ogilvie. The ship must be made ready to sail.

'Berenice,' he whispered, and touched her arm.

She looked up at him. His skin was so tanned in that strange, unearthly light, contrasting strongly with the white of his linen. A great, dark man, and she did not know what to expect from him.

'Yes, Sebastian?' she said, his Christian name still strange to her lips.

'Look here,' he blurted out. 'I'm sorry we can't delay. It's impossible, *chérie.*'

An apology! From him! This was extraordinary and she could not believe the evidence of her own ears. Was this some sort of trick? Was he lulling her into a false sense of security? It was sad to be so suspicious of the man to whom she was married. They stood there, staring into each other's eyes, for a heartbeat, no more, then suddenly loud, laughing voices sounded across the terrace. Damian and Peregrine came charging towards them.

'I say! Can't we go down to the town and find a taverna, or whatever they call inns here,' Damian exclaimed, then pulled up as he saw

176

his sister and her husband standing as close as lovers.

'Yes, let's. Do tell us where to find one, Comte,' Peregrine chimed in, too tipsy to notice anything untoward.

Don Santos had followed more slowly, leaning on his cane. He had tried to stop the young men, delaying them as long as he was able, trusting in the magic of the evening to cast its enchantment over the couple. Now he saw that it was too late. The spell had been broken. Sebastian spun round angrily, snarling,

'No one is going anywhere. We must return to the ship.'

'You're such a spoilsport,' Peregrine complained, daring to do so, protected by the Don's presence. 'It will be our last chance to have any fun for weeks.'

'We'll make our own amusement,' Berenice declared, glad of the interruption, no longer having to struggle with those tumultuous emotions that had been urging her to reach out towards Sebastian and draw him into her arms.

Peregrine brightened. 'So we will, dear lady. What say we have a game of backgammon when we get to the ship? And later I'll play my flute and you shall sing to entertain us.'

'That will be lovely,' Berenice answered, and after bidding farewell to the Don, she left the house, her arms linked with her brother and Peregrine.

'Don't let it worry you, my friend,' the Don advised as he walked slowly with Sebastian towards the waiting landau. 'She is young and lively. You must be patient.'

'Patient! One needs the patience of a saint with someone like her,' he ground out. 'She's impossible. Her father, the Marquis has overindulged her, señor.'

Don Santos smiled faintly, when they stood at the top of the steps, Berenice's laughter ringing out as she climbed into the coach. 'She's headstrong, yes,' he agreed, clapping Sebastian on the shoulder affectionately. 'But I can't see you married to someone without spirit. You're used to breaking horses, *amigo*. Does not the most difficult one prove to be the finest in the end?'

Sebastian did not answer, his mood dark as he said good-night to his old friend and joined the others in the coach. Quico slipped out of the shadows and sprang up behind, clinging on as the vehicle swung off down the drive.

SIX

The mid-Atlantic weather was diabolical. Berenice found it a miracle that the frail craft managed to stay afloat on those mountainous seas, bobbing like a cork on the giant swell. But the seamen knew their business, going about their duties quite unperturbed, and when she voiced her fears to Captain Ogilvie, he smiled broadly, and said,

'Don't worry, madame, this crossing is mild compared to some I've known. Why, bless you, there have been times when the seas have risen above the masts. You should try rounding the Horn. Now there're seas for you, if you like.'

'I wouldn't like to, thank you, Captain. These are quite high enough for me,' she replied briskly, and scurried back to her stateroom.

Now that she had recovered from sickness and could see that they were not about to sink, the days passed monotonously. She hardly saw Sebastian, and for this, at least, she was grateful. He spent most of his time with the navigator or with Ogilvie. At night he could be found in the forecastle with those sailors who were off duty, dicing, yarning and smoking. He hardly ever came near her cabin, sending Quico for anything he might require.

Sometimes she conversed with the officers, Mr. Croft and Mr. Manson, but they were usually preoccupied. She had not realized just how much work was involved in running a ship and how strict the routine was. Even Damian had become engrossed in it, so she idled in the main cabin with Peregrine, yawning over faro or hazard, reminiscing about London and sighing for the gay life they had once enjoyed. Sometimes she would listlessly occupy herself with her embroidery, whilst he declaimed passages of poetry from his notebook.

'It's wonderful to be with you, dearest lady,' he would say, that perfectly groomed, personable young man, a link with home. 'There's nothing I desire so greatly as to spend my days by your side. We share so many interests.'

'How true,' she would reply earnestly, looking up from her sewing to smile across at him. 'Richness of mind, tenderness of spirit—the rapport of true minds. Indeed, and these are to be prized above all else. Read me that poem of yours again, I pray you.'

Dulcie also helped her pass the time, and Berenice, on discovering that the maid had never received any form of learning, decided to teach her the rudiments of reading, writing and arithmetic. This proved to be rewarding, for the girl was bright, absorbing knowledge like a sponge, and enormously proud of these new achievements.

Yet Berenice was aware that something was missing, and struggled unsuccessfully to recapture that sense of completeness she had once known. She might toy with her stitchery, write in her diary, enter into deep discussions with Peregrine, and hear Dulcie at her lessons, but her ears were ever alert for sounds that indicated Sebastian's approach. She told herself firmly that it was fear that had instilled in her this extraordinary sensitivity to his whereabouts. It couldn't possibly be interest, could it?

One evening, when the ship was speeding forward, thrust by the strong force of the trade winds, Berenice sat with Peregrine after supper, trying to concentrate on her sewing, but feeling restless. Sebastian had gone out to the crew's quarters, directly the meal was over. He was so difficult to understand, stern in matters of discipline aboard, yet sometimes he would cast off his mantle of rank completely and fraternize with the men. When taking the air on deck, she had often seen him laughing with them, capping their crude sallies with his own, seated on a coil of rope with a crowd around him, hirsute, tattooed sailors listening in rapt silence as he gave a lively account of some naval action in which he had been involved.

Tonight Quico had fetched a guitar from among his master's effects in the cabin and, strolling on the poop deck with Dulcie after supper, Berenice had looked over the rail, seeing him perched on the hatch coaming below, with a polyglot collection of mariners gathered round. She was astonished to hear him singing tuneful French songs to entertain them. He had a rich, baritone voice, its timbre ringing out under the stars. It had disturbed her, or maybe it was the magic of the night, with a full moon hanging in the indigo sky.

Restless and uneasy, Berenice returned to the main cabin. She tried to settle, but could not, and finally flung her silks into her work basket, cut off Peregrine in mid-flow—he had been reading his latest poem aloud, and bade him an abrupt good-night.

She had grown to detest the stateroom after spending so many lonely nights there, staring into the dimness, seeing Sebastian's belongings and knowing that, in his eyes, she was just another chattel. The awful part was that she could never be certain if he might come stalking in, catching her half dressed, and she chafed because she was not allowed to lock the door or forbid him entry. Yet it seemed that he preferred the company of his low-born crew.

The cabin was deserted, Dulcie having gone to meet the amiable Mr. Manson, with whom she was fostering a romance. Berenice was pleased to manage without her, finding even her presence irksome, with her eternal talk of love, her sighs over the pleasant-looking young officer, her hints that Berenice would do well to curb her baneful glares and be pleasant when Sebastian was near.

She undressed swiftly, letting her gown slide to her feet, leaving it there in a careless heap for Dulcie to retrieve later. Pulling her chemise over her head, she sat on the low stool to untie the satin ribbons which fastened her black pumps. Her body always startled her whenever she saw it on dressing or preparing for bed. It always seemed so much bigger when naked, as if clothing restricted it and, freed, it expanded, stretching like a sensuous animal.

She passed a hand down the long sweep of her thigh, past her dimpled knees, the soft swell of her calves, gently stroking her fine-boned feet. It was a dangerous thing, this body of hers. Already it had betrayed her high aspirations, and even now it tingled pleasantly at her touch and, for one perilous moment, she allowed herself to imagine the caresses of a man she could love.

Not Sebastian, of course. That was unthinkable. Yet she trembled at the memory of how her desires had conquered her most virginal resolutions, recalling the tautness she had felt as he entered her, and then the relief which had seemed to gush from her heart, flooding every part of her. She checked these wanton images sternly. Surely the soul should be at one with the flesh at such a time? These thoughts continued to plague her, however, even when she jumped resolutely into bed and tried to sleep. Impossible. With a sigh, she picked up a book from the bedside and leaned closer to the candle. It was an outdated periodical, *The Ladies Magazine, or Entertaining Companion for the Fair Sex,* and contained fashion drawings, but Berenice had looked at them a hundred times before. She started to read the copy again—muffs were *à la mode* (not in a hot climate, she decided)—and there was a wealth of hats to choose from.

She yawned and snuggled down, the magazine propped on her chest. Soon, her lids began to droop, the book to sink. Half dreams smothered her mind. She saw faces of people she did not know and heard snippets of conversation that vanished when she surfaced. Sinking back again, her limbs felt weighted—so warm—so comfortable—sleep—

Suddenly she was shocked into wakefulness. There was the clump of boots outside the door. It opened wide and Sebastian entered. Berenice kept her eyes tightly shut, feigning slumber.

Sebastian paused on the threshold, wondering why he was there. Thus far he had not troubled her at night, telling himself that it was because of her indisposition, that he had been too occupied with the ship, taking his turn at the wheel, spending watches under the stars. Now he faced the truth. He had been deliberately avoiding her. What an idiot you are, he thought. You have every right to sleep with her. The situation is farcical.

That evening he had been drinking strong, dark rum, becoming increasingly annoyed at her rejection. She was his wife, and he had only once possessed her. It offended his masculinity, and even the knowledge that she had depended on him during her sickness could not fully compensate for the hatred that stared at him from her eyes whenever they met. How dare she hate him? What had he ever done to hurt her? He'd stopped her making a fool of herself with Peregrine. Was that ground for such childish behavior? Writing love notes to the fop! That, Sebastian, could not forgive.

His senses had been enflamed by the hours he had just passed with the crew. He had played to them, and drunk more than he should have, and not failed to notice how their conversation always veered round to the subject of women. They were weary of the voyage, longing for the touch, taste and smell of woman flesh. Such were the tortures of a long journey. He had been wise to warn Berenice to keep out of their sight. He felt it himself—that insistent urge for physical relief.

The sailors had swapped tales of their amatory exploits, anticipating the brothels of Carolina. It was of gorgeous black women that they talked, and the milk white flesh of harlots shipped over from Europe—half-breeds, too, were gaudy, accommodating wenches who crowded the jetties whenever a ship put into port. They had begged Sebastian to sing about women, and he had obliged, skillfully turning their lustful thoughts into sentimental channels, reminding them of wives and children at home. But it had done him no good, serving only to bring to mind Berenice and her close proximity. Why in hell's name should he suffer frustration when he had his own doxy aboard?

With sudden resolution, he pulled off his jacket and strode over to the bed, the need to embrace her so strong that it was like a bodily pain. 'Are you awake?' he demanded.

Berenice knew it was useless to playact. She bounced up in bed angrily, eyes sparking, hair tumbling about her bare shoulders, her nightgown disordered. 'Yes, I am! Thanks to you stamping in here like a regiment of soldiers!'

He bowed mockingly. 'My deepest regrets for such a boorish intrusion, madame. My manners must upset your delicate sensibilities. How fortunate that I arranged for your lap dog, Sir Peregrine, to come along, too, so that while I attend to such prosaic matters as ensuring that we reach America in one piece, you can enjoy cloud-cuckoo-land with him!' he said nastily, and took a long pull at the bottle in his hand. 'And may I bring to your notice that this is also *my* cabin?'

'Would you like me to move into another?' she inquired frostily. 'I'll be only too happy to oblige you.'

A crooked grin curved his mouth. 'There's no question of that, *ma doucette*. I've discipline

185

to maintain, and I'd be the laughingstock of the ship if it was thought that I couldn't control my own wife.'

He set the bottle down on the locker and started to undress, pulling the white shirt out from his belt, unbuttoning it and throwing it off. Berenice stared apprehensively at his naked torso, but averted her eyes quickly when she saw him unbuckle his belt and then sit on the bed to wrench at his boots.

With a mouth gone suddenly dry, she retreated to the far side till she was pressed up against the paneling, but when he stood up to divest himself of his breeches, her control snapped. 'What d'you think you're doing?'

He chuckled, standing naked before her, legs slightly spread to balance his weight against the ship's slow roll, one hand on his hip, the other lifting the bottle to his lips again. 'I should have thought it obvious, *m'amie*. I'm about to get into bed with you.'

'You've been drinking,' she accused, thoroughly alarmed by the glitter in his eyes and the purposeful way in which he was folding back the covers.

'Not a lot,' he replied calmly, settling in beside her and pulling the sheet over his sun-bronzed chest. 'But just enough to make me see clearly that you're acting like an idiot, and that I'm an even greater fool for putting up with it.'

His desire was mounting by the second. He could not think, all his senses concentrated on Berenice. He was drunk not so much

186

with rum, as with passion. It was as if her body was a magnet, drawing him to her. He was transported by the perfume that breathed from her skin—roses coupled with a sweetness that was all her own. What other men had responded to such seduction? he wondered dazedly. Peregrine? Or that damned coxcomb who had sent her the riding whip? Others, of whom he knew nothing?

The thought was like a hot iron twisting his gut. He'd been too soft with her—letting her simper and flutter her eyelashes at that rat, Peregrine! *Fripouille!* Whilst in London he had learned many things about the popular beau, things which he was perfectly certain Berenice could not possibly know and still admire him.

Having recovered a little from the shock of finding him there beside her, Berenice stabbed around for a way of escape, but she was penned between the wall and him. How could she get off the bed and out of the cabin with any show of dignity? Did pride matter anymore? No, all that mattered was putting as much space between them as possible.

Then, they could talk, she supposed. She'd already rehearsed what she would say to him. Sebastian, I don't love you. I don't even respect or like you. Annul the marriage.

She made a dash for the bottom of the bed, but Sebastian reached out a long arm, and her feet became enmeshed in the bedcovers. It gave him pleasure to see her anger, to hear her quick breathing and watch the rise and fall of her breasts.

'Go away,' she panted, trying to free herself. 'No,' he said, wondering what to do with her now he had caught her. He'd never had to resort to force to make a woman want him, and he didn't intend to start now. Talk to her? He could try. Plain talking, perhaps. So, 'I'm sick of seeing you wearing that tragic air of martyrdom,' he began, then fury clouded his resolve as she lay there, glaring up at him. *'Mon Dieu!* I'll give you something to be martyred about! I've treated you far too softly. You're just a woman—only worth the taking.'

He caught her by the chin, meaning to kiss her mouth. She squirmed aside, but despite her struggles he pressed his lips on hers, so baffled by her that he gave up the idea of sensible discussion, doing that which he managed to convince himself any proper man would do in his place.

She wrenched her mouth away, saying coldly, 'How can you, when you know that I don't love you?'

For answer, Sebastian placed his palm over one of her breasts. 'Love!' he muttered thickly. 'What do you know of love? Do you really believe Peregrine's lies? That mincing fop's more in love with himself than with any woman, yet he seeks to sneak between another man's sheets and enjoy another man's wife! You know nothing of life or love. But I do, and I will teach you.'

Protestations were a waste of breath—Berenice knew that, and already her heart was beating madly at the touch of his hand. Feeling her

188

shiver, Sebastian's excitement mounted, the heat and hardness of his desire pressing insistently against her. He ran his lips over her throat and shoulders, and her struggles became feeble, then died out altogether. Ripples of pleasure coursed through her as his mouth sought hers again, wooing her into enjoyment, as if in apology for his recent harshness. All the time his hand was playing with her, as if on a finely tuned instrument, making her glow inside, blinding her to everything but the tension gathering with fierce intensity. Sebastian whipped away the gossamer garment that covered her, eyes glowing as they looked at her nakedness.

'Oh, *m'amie*—you have the most perfect breasts!' He kissed them softly. 'Why have you been so cold to me? I've never harmed you. Come, let me show you the deep delight a man can give a woman.'

His words roused her as much as his touch, and, moved by some irresistible inner force, her arms went round his neck, fingers buried in his black curls, forgetful of all except this tumult in her blood. Sebastian recognized that her resistance was dying. He went slowly, savoring each caress, controlling his own need, determined that this time she should enjoy the encounter. There was still a tantalizingly virginal quality about her which spoke of her inexperience, and it was a challenge to his prowess that he accepted with joy.

With a finger he gently touched her eyelashes and the blue-veined lids, ran it slowly back and forth along her parted lips, then continued its tender journey, down her chin and throat. Her body was flushed with silver in the soft candlelight, that slender, hairless body with the coral-tipped breasts that slipped so neatly into his hand. His lips traveled to her nipples, and Berenice was overwhelmed by a piercingly sweet sensation as his tongue encircled one, then the other.

Her own hand, hesitant to begin with, then more bold, skimmed over his chest, smoothing the tanned skin, moving slowly down, driven by the strong desire to grasp that shaft of male power. It was as if she were seeing him for the first time. With her pulse pounding, she felt him with her fingertips, delight washing through her as she heard him sigh with pleasure as her hand went to where he most craved her touch.

'Little witch!' he breathed into her ear, the words sending shivers down her spine. 'That's right—but not too much, or this will be over before we've begun. Explore me, as I explore you. We must learn to know one another, *ma chérie?*'

He ran his hand over her, measuring the narrow waist and back, the flat stomach, finding the warm darkness between her legs. She gave a start, then relaxed letting him have his way, allowing his fingers to do what they willed. A strange heat bloomed and expanded within her and she abandoned herself eagerly to this compelling need, feeling it mounting, gathering in great waves, receding, then crashing back to bear her to higher and higher peaks. She was drowning, being consumed by burning waves of sensation; behind her closed eyes crimson waters billowed, filling her with a most desperate want.

She was biting his shoulders and neck, the lobes of his ears, drawing the flesh into her mouth greedily, and her hands arched on his back, nails scratching up and down, while his spell-binding touch continued its maddening rhythm. She could not escape it—did not want to—feeling that she would die if he stopped. But Sebastian did not stop: he used all his skills as a lover to give Berenice her first taste of sexual completion. She cared for nothing at that moment but that this surging feeling to go on, until it rose to an explosive crest of ecstasy that left her shuddering and dewed with sweat.

Hearing the cry which escaped her lips, Sebastian raised himself, spreading her legs and thrusting deep within her, and Berenice, still floating on a heady cloud, clasped him to her, needing that powerful force stretching her, filling her, her hips pushing up to meet him, her body moist and welcoming. The furor of his passion echoed her own as he moved faster, giving full rein to his own desire which he had held back until she was ready. She was swept along with him, home on the raging tide of his fulfillment until finally he grew still, lying with his head in the hollow of her shoulder.

Slowly, she came back to reality, aware of the thump of his heart that gradually returned to normal as his passion ebbed. She opened her eyes, and the cabin swung back into focus.

Once more, she was conscious of the movement of the ship, hearing the lapping of the waves against the hull. From somewhere aloft came the subdued exchange of voices as an officer took the dogwatch. Then silence—a deep pool of silence in which there was only Sebastian and herself.

Regretfully, he slid from her, gathering her close to his body, resting one hand on her breast. Berenice was bewildered, exhausted after the storm of passion. Was this what making love meant? Nibbling at the outer edge of her consciousness was the nagging feeling that once again her body had betrayed her, her idealism still insisting that there should be more than mere animal lust. She tried to move away, but Sebastian only rumbled with laughter, holding her closer, half asleep himself. Berenice sighed, too tired to worry further. She would think about it tomorrow, she decided, and allowed the gentle rocking of *La Foudre* to lull her to sleep.

The wide, muddy river lapped lazily at the piles of the quay, and the humid air pressed down on the crowd jostling at the harborside. The gangway formed a swaying bridge from the deck of *La Foudre* linking it with Charleston, and Berenice stood by the bulwarks, her parasol opened and held high, its gold-tasseled fringe stirring in the breeze, her face shaded to cool violet, only her teeth showing white.

Slowly, she surveyed the green arc of land which was to be her home from now on.

The wharf shimmered in the hazy heat and it seemed as if the earth was melting. The bay was immense, the Carolina shore most intricately cut by estuaries, sounds and creeks, and far off rose dark hills, misty under the flossy blue sky.

Berenice was nervous, stomach fluttering, and she held Sebastian's arm tightly till they were safely across the gangplank. Her knees were weak, that shaky feeling persisting at the unusual sensation of land under her feet, the cobbles burning like hot coals through the soles of her shoes, yet she stubbornly released her grip on her husband's sleeve, hating to admit her dependence on him. Sebastian frowned as she withdrew and she saw his jaw tighten while his eyes flashed, but if he thought she was going to behave like a rapturous bride inspired with interest in her new home, then he was very much mistaken. Determined to annoy him even further, she made a small moue of displeasure, glancing with haughty distaste around the landing stage.

The usual seaport riff-raff lingered there, accosting the passengers as they stepped ashore with offers of food, lodgings, and entertainment. On all sides was the brisk bustle of crews preparing either to disembark or set sail; gangs of laborers moving supplies on to the boats or into the warehouses; wagons pulled by teams of shire horses, hauling loads of casks and bales along the garbage-strewn wharf.

To Berenice's astonishment, she found a large, elegant carriage awaiting them, complete with four Cleveland grays, and a crest on its varnished doors. The coachman, smartly turned out in matching gray livery, hailed Sebastian, and a couple of footmen jumped down from the back, immediately setting to work loading up the baggage. Somehow, she had not expected this, having a vague notion that the colonies were still rough places, and half expecting a farm cart. It surprised her to see that, apart from the heat and the preponderance of dark-skinned workers, she could have been standing in an English port. She was even more astounded when suddenly, from a side street, another vehicle came into view, traveling at breakneck speed and scattering the crowd with supreme disregard for life and limb.

She recognized it at once. It was a crane-necked phaeton, similar to the one she had driven in Bath, a dashing, sporting conveyance, its body perched precariously high on upright springs. Spirited white horses ran tossing their heads in front as their hooves rang over the cobbles. The driver reined in skillfully just in time to avoid a collision with the coach, and leapt down, seizing Sebastian in an affectionate hug, while Berenice stared, open-mouthed. When they had finished thumping each other on the shoulders, the newcomer swung round to her, his bright, penetrating blue eyes going over her with unconcealed delight.

With a grin, Sebastian presented her. 'Madame, this is Dr. Greg Lattimer, one of my oldest friends. Greg—meet my wife, Berenice.'

Greg bowed and swept off his beaver hat.

'Welcome to Carolina, ma'am. And may I say that our colony will be enriched by such a beautiful addition?'

Berenice saw before her a tall, loose-limbed young man, whose Southern drawl was intriguing. Even someone as fastidious as Peregrine could not have faulted his costume, which was cut in the latest style; a mulberry hued tail-coat with cream satin lapels, a gold fob and chain dangling below a fancy waistcoat, and a lace-trimmed jabot and high stock collar. Fawn linen breeches met the tops of his black boots. His hair was of that white blond which looks permanently bleached by the sun, and he wore it in a deliberately negligent cut, curling about his ears, its fairness contrasting with the darkly bronzed skin of his lean handsome face.

Berenice was fascinated by his dandified clothing and his studious occupation. 'Are you really a doctor?' she asked.

He smiled, and she caught a glimpse of the steely quality beneath his lazy pose. 'Sure am. Did my training at medical school in New England,' he replied.

He appeared to be so cultured and friendly, that her drooping spirits revived and she gave him a dazzling glance, 'I'd like to hear more about that, Dr. Lattimer,' she said.

He grinned more widely than ever, and hung his arm round Sebastian's shoulders. 'You're a deuced lucky chap, my friend.'

'I admire your vehicle,' she went on, walking closer to it and running her fingers over its high sides. 'I owned one just like it.'

'You did?' Greg expressed surprise, then shrugged. 'You had a jockey to race it?'

'No, sir—I raced it myself.'

Greg whistled softly, and raised his brows at Sebastian. Beneath that deceptively languid manner, the young doctor was astute and, knowing Sebastian as he did, he wondered what he thought about his bride taking the reins of such a conveyance. If she tried a thing like that in Carolina, she would come up against the female members of the Quality, who did not approve of young women behaving like hoydens.

'I'd like to introduce you to my brother-in-law, Lord Damian, Viscount Norwood,' Sebastian said, then could not avoid presenting Peregrine, too. 'And Sir Peregrine Baxter. They've both come to try their fortunes in America.'

'Pleased to meet you,' Greg answered, shaking hands with both men. 'Now fill me in on the news. What's happening in the old country?'

Sebastian recounted information that he had read in the English newspapers or discussed in the clubs, then he said, 'How are things at Oakwood Hall? Has the plantation prospered during my absence?'

'Nothing to worry about there, my friend,' Greg answered slowly, leaning on his tapering, silver-knobbed cane. 'But Darby Modiford's hanging around Mobby Cove.'

A startling change came over Sebastian. He tensed, frowning darkly. 'Modiford! What the devil is he up to?'

'Villainy, I'll wager,' Greg replied.

196

'We can't talk here,' Sebastian said crisply. 'Come to Meeting Street. I've already sent instructions for the house to be made ready.' And he snapped into action, barking an order to the coachman.

Berenice found herself bundled unceremoniously into the carriage, Dulcie beside her and Damian and Peregrine on the opposite seat, with Quico on guard at the back. Sebastian leaped into the phaeton with Greg, and it careered ahead, leading the way through the winding dockside streets. Berenice was disgruntled. She had wanted to ride in it and cause a stir, making her entrance into Charleston with a flourish, but this had been denied her. Peering through the window of the carriage, she received a jumbled impression of shops and narrow houses, reminiscent of England in architecture, some adorned with wrought-iron balconies, others having dormer windows and long wooden verandahs. Gardens could be seen between white wooden gates, and trees lined the pleasant avenues, the air heavy with the fragrance of magnolia.

The town house belonging to Sebastian was one of a row of tall, stylish residences which owed a lot to the influence of Robert Adam, the English colonials having brought much of the old way of life with them during their settling over the past two hundred years. The Quality were proud of their lineage, and though they had lost much of their power since the War of Independence, they still maintained their sense of superiority.

Berenice could not fail to be impressed by the mansion, despite her prejudice against anything in which Sebastian had had a hand. There were so many features which reminded her of Elsewood House; the same design of the rooms; the furnishings and fabrics imported from Europe; the carving of wooden-pedimented doorways and all in the graceful classical style. As she gazed about the tiled hall, she tried to hide her pleasure from Sebastian who, however, merely paused long enough to order wine and refreshments to be served in the library.

Berenice and Dulcie were met at the bottom step of the beautiful staircase by a young slave attired in a gaily patterned skirt and white blouse, her head covered by a red-and-white striped bandanna. Each of his servants had greeted Sebastian with genuine pleasure, and Berenice had been forced to look on sourly as one face after another lit up with smiles at the master's approach. She wondered about his charismatic appeal—that charm which he could turn on and off at will. Certainly he showed precious little of it to her, certainly not in the daytime.

As he glanced down at her, he cocked one eyebrow mockingly, reading her annoyed expression and correctly guessing its cause. 'This warm welcome surprises you, *mon trésor?* You see, there are those who don't find me such an ogre.'

'Your relationship with your servants is of no possible interest to me, sir,' she replied with maddening condescension. 'All I care about at present is a bath, and privacy in which to change for dinner.'

Instead of rising to the bait, Sebastian bowed and strode off in the direction of the library, while Damian and Peregrine were conducted to their respective chambers by an extremely tall, thin servant dressed in the same immaculate gray uniform as the coachman. The maidservant detailed to assist Berenice was friendly, her lisping voice reminding her obscurely of Greg's. Perhaps Greg had been brought up by black nursemaids, his soft drawl acquired from them.

'What's your name?' Berenice asked impressed by the girl's smile.

'Chloë, ma'am,' she answered, bobbing a curtsy.

'Well, then, Chloë, we'll need your help in getting to know the customs here. This is my personal maid, Dulcie Riley.'

'How d'you do?' said Dulcie ungraciously, jealous of her intimate relationship with her mistress.

'Have you ever visited England, Chloë?' Berenice ignored Dulcie's huffiness, fascinated by the girl.

Berenice had attended prize fights where the contestants were often Africans, and had also seen them employed as footmen. Several of her lady friends in London had had black page boys, keeping them rather as one might a pet. This had made Berenice uncomfortable. She felt it wrong to treat a human being as a fashion accessory, and she had stopped Lucinda from purchasing a slave from the slave auctions.

Having now met Chloë, she intended to get to know her.

Chloë seemed equally intrigued by this Englishwoman, proud to be of service to the Comte's wife. 'No, ma'am, but I'd sure like to,' she answered shyly.

'I'll see what can be arranged, and maybe take you with me when I go to home sometime in the future,' Berenice promised, though wondering sadly if Sebastian had any intention of returning there.

Dulcie walked stiffly at the servant's side as they progressed up the stairs, not sure that she approved of having colored people as fellow servants. Her sunny world had been a little dimmed by her dear mistress's unhappiness of late. Too often she had heard her weeping, seen her red eyes and wan face, and far too often her ears had been scorched by the newly married couple's blistering arguments, which it had been impossible to avoid in the close confines of the ship. Dulcie had noted that the times Sebastian shared Berenice's bed were few. Most nights he had spent with his men, or slept in a hammock slung between two bulkheads. Sadly, she had shaken her head as she smoothed the sheets after Berenice got up—she would have been far happier if they had been rumpled—the sure sign of a rollicking night of love.

The bedchamber was magnificent, as luxurious a suite as money and good taste could devise. Dulcie soon forgot her gloom, dancing round it, exclaiming in delight, even talking animatedly with Chloë, but Berenice obstinately refused to share her excitement. What was she to expect from Sebastian henceforth? Would he be sharing this room with her? Her feelings on the matter were confused, part of her wanting to sleep alone, but another part, one which she did not like to acknowledge, wanting to repeat the nights they had spent in each other's arms. Stonily, she stared at the Turkish rugs strewn over the highly polished parquet, trying not to look at the grandiose mahogany bedstead, but feeling her gaze drawn towards it, nonetheless.

How wide it was! With three shallow steps leading up to it, and a gilded headboard carved with plump cupids and sheaves of corn, blatant symbols of fecundity. The tester was domed like the tent of an Eastern potentate, its yellow silk draped from the four turned posts and gathered into the center, round a circular mirror. Berenice blushed as she imagined the scene which might later be reflected there. The matching silk curtains were looped back, the heavily fringed brocade coverlet folded over the sheet to show two lace-frilled pillows waiting expectantly.

With an effort of will, she turned her attention to the other furnishings. There were neat side tables and beautiful Chippendale chairs; a fantastically carved armoire for her clothing; a dressing table with triple mirrors and silver toilet articles. At the far end of the chamber stood a fireplace of white marble, carved with an Egyptian motif, its overmantel bearing a large Venetian looking glass which reflected the whole impressive apartment.

Berenice paced uneasily to the windows, hung

with curtains in the same shade as those of the bed, staring moodily out at the wide lawns, watching the sun sinking behind the towering oaks. There was despair in her heart. She was a captive in this exotic, splendid golden cage—as much a prisoner as a poor wretch awaiting execution in Newgate. There was nowhere she could run from that complex devil who had married her.

Dulcie, meanwhile, was accepting Chloë's tentative overtures though she was still inclined to look down on her from her lofty position as lady's maid to the Comtesse. Certainly, her manner was dictatorial as she ordered a bath to be prepared. Berenice languidly sipped a tumbler of iced lemonade which had been brought to her on a mahogany tray. Without enthusiasm, she watched her maid begin to unpack. Dulcie clicked her tongue over the creases in her mistress's gowns caused by being too long in the trunk, whilst Chloë assisted her, her helpfulness gradually winning her over. A large copper tub was placed in the center of the room, and servants entered in solemn procession, bearing buckets of steaming water to fill it. Dulcie fussed, tested the temperature, then dismissed everyone and coaxed Berenice to undress.

She was tempted to refuse to attend the dinner party, but did not quite dare; she had learned to fear Sebastian's evil moods and black temper. As she stripped and sank into the soothing tub of scented water, she thought about him. As the voyage progressed it had been impossible to avoid spending time with him, and as the days had passed and his company had become more tolerable, her manner had grown less frosty. In a ferment of uncertainty, she had waited every night, lying tensely in bed, listening for his step.

Usually he had come in late, fixed the hammock in place and thrown himself into it without a word. Often when she had awakened in the morning, he had been gone. What would he expect of her now? That she behave impeccably? A perfect lady to impress Charleston society? Did he think that he had been successful in banishing her feelings for Peregrine? If he did, he was mistaken, for she had been cultivating that gentleman's regard most assiduously, spending many a moonlit evening with him on the quarterdeck, studying the stars. A hazy plan buzzed in her brain of going with him when he went to visit his aunt in Georgetown. A crazy scheme, of course, for the scandal would be appalling, yet the alternative of remaining here with Sebastian was even more unsettling.

She soaped herself thoughtfully, while Dulcie went round taking a taper to the candles. It was nearly dark outside, night enfolding the house, the sky scattered with stars like specks of silver set against velvet. Through the open windows of the balcony, she could hear the cool splash of a fountain and the whirr of insects, a monotonous hum to which her ear soon became accustomed. It was an almost tropical night, so different from the cool, calm evenings of England, so soft, so muted. Here, her soul responded to a primitive element beneath the facade of civilization imposed by homesick Europeans. First they had settled around the coasts, then they had pushed inland; yet beyond, there still lay hundreds of miles of untamed forests, sweeping savannahs, plains and mountains, where the Indians held sway. Berenice could feel it—savage, barbarous. It terrified her, and Sebastian was a part of it.

Suddenly, the doors between his dressing room and the bedchamber swung open, and he was framed there. With a startled gasp, she held the sponge against her breasts, returning his stare. 'Sir, I'm at my toilet—' she spluttered indignantly, but he only gave a bark of laughter, and went over to the bed, sprawling on the golden quilt, propping himself on one elbow to watch her.

Seeing his white linen shirt gaping open to the waist, Berenice was prey to an unnerving desire to run her hands over his muscular chest, her fingers remembering the feel of him, her inward ear recalling his groans of pleasure when she had touched him intimately. Now he was eyeing her insolently, much as a sultan might amuse himself by gloating over the favorite of his seraglio. In one hand he held a glass of rum, and in the other a thin brown cheroot, the pungent scent drifted lightly in the air.

It was not easy to be dignified under the circumstances but Berenice did her best, saying primly, 'I would prefer that you don't smoke when you're in my room. I thought that gentlemen confined such activity to occasions

204

when they're with friends who also like tobacco.'

'I'll do as I damned please,' he growled ungraciously, still perusing her with eyes like liquid fire.

He had just come from the library downstairs where Greg had been enthusiastic about her, instead of getting to grips with the problem of Darby Modiford. It seemed that she bewitched every man she met. He had the gravest doubts about letting her loose among the rakish sons of the Quality. He was further angered because he hungered for her so much, even though every word she addressed to him was in the nature of a thinly veiled insult. It was odious! He had always had a reputation for remaining heart-whole, never getting deeply involved with any woman, and yet here he was, put on the rack by this flighty minx.

He jerked his head towards Dulcie, barking, 'Get out!'

Dulcie was indignant. 'But, sir—madam needs me to complete her attiring,' she argued, looking to Berenice for support.

He waved a hand at her imperiously, repeating, 'Out—out, you saucy wench—or I'll put you on the market as a bondservant.'

With one final look at her mistress, Dulcie fled. Berenice sat in the rapidly cooling water, struck speechless by such high-handedness. Then her temper surged up and she shouted, 'This is an outrage! How dare you order my servant about? By God, is this how Americans treat their wives? Have I no rights?'

'Very few.'

He lounged to his feet, tall and dominating in his shirt sleeves, beige breeches and top-boots. He strolled over to stand very close to the tub, staring down at the seething, naked girl within it. Her loveliness struck at some deep, sensitive core in his being which responded to all things rare and beautiful, but it also roused his carnality—a combustible element that got the better of his good resolutions.

His eyes traveled down the heart-shaped face, meeting her questioning gaze, skimming to the fine column of her throat, the bare shoulders shiny with water, to the curves of her breasts, plainly visible amongst the frothy soapsuds. Her curls had been piled on top of her head, little tendrils wisping round the back of her neck. He reached out a hand, letting his fingers play on that sensitive area. He ached to go further, to caress the womanly softness of her, to hold her close and ease the emotional need that made his heart ache. But he knew that he might have to argue with her first. Was this the only way? Would there ever be a time when she would come to him willingly, asking his forgiveness for her behavior, confessing that she loved him? Only then might he exorcise the demon that dwelt inside him, and know peace. But she denied him. It was like talking to a statue—she was so cold, so withdrawn.

'You're a monster, sir! An untutored savage. Do you think I'll let you treat me this way?' she hissed.

A spasm of pain shook him, and though he

knew it was entirely the wrong thing to say, 'I am master here!' he snarled. 'You'll do as I command!'

Too infuriated to remain seated, Berenice grabbed the big white towel from a nearby chair and, holding it like a shield before her, stood up. Quickly folding it about her, she stepped from the bath, the water dribbling down her calves and making puddles on the rug.

'I've never had the misfortune to meet anyone as vicious as you,' she said, walking regally away from him, though her knees had turned to jelly.

Sebastian watched her go, seeing the proud, erect back, the beckoning fullness of her hips. 'You have really no notion of how truly vicious I could be, if I put my mind to it,' he retorted, and in two strides he caught up with her, swinging her round to face him.

Berenice was hampered by having to keep a tight grip on the towel, and weakened by his nearness. His intoxicating male scent was filling her head and warming her blood, evoking a strong desire which made her long to melt into his arms, but she had no intention of doing so. Through the folds of the towel and his tight breeches, she could feel the now-familiar hardening, which spoke more eloquently of his desire than any words.

He was holding her with one strong hand behind her neck, the other sliding down her back to her hips, pressing her against him. Horrified by her own urges, Berenice longed to grind her body into his, to open, enfold, gather every part of him close to her, to possess and be possessed in turn, forgetting everything in mad, delirious union. The heat of hunger bounded eagerly through her, and Sebastian felt that sudden yielding which made her heavy in his arms.

'It's as well that I married you, Berenice,' he whispered, his lips close to her ear. 'For if not, then I would've had to make you my concubine. You were designed for love. Don't deny it—let the warmth of your nature flood up. Believe me, I can give you more pleasure than you've ever dreamed existed.'

His words suddenly brought her out of her hazy trance and stung her once more into fury. *'Married!* Can you call this, marriage? A few phrases mumbled by a priest to a woman who had no choice in the matter! A fine marriage!'

Sebastian knew only one way to silence her spiteful tongue. His mouth fastened on hers and, without breaking that deepening kiss, he swung her up and tumbled her on to the bed, stretching himself beside her. But Berenice rolled away from him, lying half on her stomach, half on her side, her right arm outstretched, the left doubled under her. Her long dark hair, glinting with reddish streaks of light, swept over her shoulders, partly hiding her face. Seeing her so vulnerable, so pathetic, sprawling like a broken doll, Sebastian nearly lost his desire and was filled with a most uncharacteristic urge to touch her cheek with a chaste kiss and tiptoe away. He checked the impulse.

How d'you know that she's not pretending? he

asked himself angrily. You've already discovered that beneath this virginal shrinking, there's a hot caldron of boiling passion.

Urged on, he placed a hand on her shoulder. Berenice moaned and shook her head, curling into a ball. It was only by doing this that she could stop herself from flinging her arms about his neck and pulling him down on her. She felt his hand slide down her spine, exploring the curve of her rounded buttocks. She pressed her face harder into the pillow, hands clenched. She would not give in to him—would not accept the bondage which her own feelings would impose on her if she allowed herself to commit the unspeakable folly of enjoying him—wanting him! He would destroy her if she gave him that much power, and she would never have a moment's peace, wanting nothing but to live forever in his presence, tormented, jealous, out of her mind with love. She could not bear such a fate.

Sebastian's touch became infinitely gentle, disarming her, seducing her from her purpose. He gathered her resisting body close to his, and for several minutes they were molded together. Berenice was conscious of the hard length of his form, his chest against her back, her hips pressing into his stomach, his legs following the curved position of hers. One of his hands came across her, finding her breasts, teasing the nipples, while she giddily tried to break the web of desire that he was weaving so insistently around her.

His lips were moving over that delicate spot

where her shoulders joined her neck, and she was sinking, falling into the well of passion. It was the beginning again—her body taking over, refusing to be denied. She nearly cried out in protest when he left her for a second to take off his clothes, then he was back, fondling her again and her thighs relaxed, falling open as his hand wandered down over her belly. An uncontrollable fire now raged deep inside her, and she heard a voice pleading with him not to stop. He gave her what she wanted, his fingers settling into that rhythm which roused her to fever pitch, taking her over the edge of ecstasy. Then, while she was still whirling with pleasure, she felt him entering her welcoming body, his hands firm on her hips, holding her steady. Every fiber of her being seemed to tingle with joy as she felt him achieve the heights.

Sebastian knew that this time it had been different. It was almost as if they had reached out and touched souls. He lay totally relaxed at her side, stunned by the way in which she had offered herself to his desire. Dear God, it was incredible! Could it be true? With a trembling finger, he stroked her cheek, wanting to explore each part of her, knowing that he could live for a thousand years and never exhaust the subtlety of her form and face. There seemed to be magic under her skin—every touch, each caress revealing new treasures. But why should it mean so much to him? He had made love to countless women. Why should his hand shake now, as if with fear?

He raised himself on one arm and looked

down at her as she lay prone on her back. She breathed slowly, deeply, her mouth slightly parted in a blissful smile, seeming to purr under his caressing fingertips. Yet always at the back of his mind, persistent, inescapable, was the thought—Is she acting? Was her surrender real or feigned? His heart became heavy. Dare he allow himself to fall into the snare of love again?

As the ecstasy faded, Berenice returned to reality with something of a start. She opened her eyes and saw the canopy stretching above her, the color rushing to her face as she caught sight of their reflections in the ceiling mirror. A satiated couple stared down at her, their limbs entwined, magnolia white skin molded to that of bronze—her hair was tangled wildly about her, and he was looking at her with a sensual smile curving his lips.

Sebastian's grin deepened as he watched the expression of alarm cross her features. 'The mirror shocks you, *mon amour?* In time, you'll learn to enjoy watching us make love.'

'Stop saying such dreadful things!' She sat up smartly, glad that the room was dimly lit, hiding her embarrassment.

Sebastian threw back his head and roared with laughter. 'What a hypocrite you are! Pretending to be so demure.'

She scrambled into her negligee, and thrust her feet into a pair of backless mules, wishing he would go away. Perched on the stool before the toilet table, she began to brush her hair with firm strokes, as if by restoring order to her appearance she could control her seesaw emotions and pretend that nothing had happened just now.

'May I send for Dulcie?' She tossed this over her shoulder, stumbling with the words. What does one say to a man after such an encounter?

'Not yet.' Sebastian threw back the covers and stood up, reached for his breeches and stepped into them. 'I've something for you.'

Opening a drawer in the bedside table, he took out a flat, oblong velvet case, and came towards her. She saw his image in the looking glass and, just for an instant, an unidentifiable emotion flickered in his eyes, then, just as swiftly, it was gone.

Smiling down at her, he put the box in her hands. Surprised and puzzled, Berenice pressed the catch and lifted the lid. She caught her breath with wonder as the candlelight winked on sapphires and diamonds, sparkling against a dark satin lining. Sebastian was moved by her genuine delight, watching as she reverently picked up the heavy pendant earrings set in gold filigree, hooking the wires into her pierced lobes, head to one side, studying her reflection. Even though she was in *déshabille*, with the negligee shrugged on carelessly, the effect was stunning. He took up the matching necklace, laying it about her throat and fastening the clasp, then pulled her back against him, sliding his hands into her robe.

'I knew that these jewels were made for you, *mon coeur*,' he murmured. 'They're fit for a queen—and the exact color of your eyes.'

212

She could not speak for the tightening of her throat, deeply stirred by this unexpected gift, and the fact that he could be charming—even fascinating—the kind of man it would be fatally easy to love, not hate. His tenderness undermined her resolve, and she almost wished he had remained a harsh, cold-faced stranger. That was easier to deal with. The will to fight was draining out of her as his warm breath touched her ear and he nibbled gently at the base of her neck, sending shivers through her.

She found her tongue at last. 'Thank you, sir. You do me much honor and I'm grateful.' The stilted speech was not what she wanted to say. She had no choice but to hide behind formality, unable to give voice to the giant emotion that was squeezing her heart.

Sebastian mistook her frigid air, suspecting that she was playing games again. He released her, a puzzled expression in his green eyes. 'You'll wear them at dinner. I would also like you to play for my guests later. There's a pianoforte in the music room. Having heard you perform on the harpsichord, I know that you're most accomplished.'

When Berenice went into the dining room later, the breathless cessation of conversation instantly told her that she had made a successful entrance. The half-a-dozen gentlemen gathered there suddenly paused, their glasses poised, cigars half lifted to their lips. Every eye was upon her, and Berenice advanced proudly; she looked ravishing and she knew it, taking a certain cold pleasure in the passions she could

213

arouse. Sebastian wanted her to be a pretty toy, an enviable possession. So be it, and he would have to suffer the prick of seeing that other men desired her, too.

She had taken special care with her appearance, and wore a gown of blue tiffany over a thin, tubular silk slip. Following the current, daring vogue, she was naked beneath. The dress, she knew, was provocative, revealing bare shoulders and much of her bosom. The waistline was high, again drawing attention to her breasts, the sleeves known as *bretelles,* or shoulder-straps. The skirt was long, and whispered into a train at the back, and the ensemble had a classical simplicity, the Grecian influence emphasized by her hair, dressed high in a profusion of loose curls with a riband entwined in them.

She seemed to glide in, moving silently in kid sandals, with straps crossing her bare feet. The effect was light and graceful, and Berenice floated across the room as if she had just stepped down from Mount Olympus, a delectable goddess of love.

Sebastian could feel his body betraying him even as he came to give her his arm and introduce her. Her perfume was evocative of the hour they had spent together earlier. It aroused him so much that he could barely prevent the passion from showing in his eyes as he gazed down into her lovely, wayward face. Her wide brow was hidden beneath the gush of curls, soft tendrils coiling over each ear, and the gems he had given her scintillated in the candlelight. The flowerlike texture of her skin made her slanting azure eyes seem huge, the lashes darkened with kohl.

His gaze lingered on her full, freshly painted mouth—a mouth made for kissing—the lower lip pouting slightly with a certain childish petulance, an air of scorn. Her slender throat and perfect shoulders seemed so white as to be almost transparent, and so soft that he ached to caress them, not with lust, but with sheer wonderment at their perfection.

Disconcerted by the emotions tormenting him, he escorted her to the table and presented her to his friends, then made sure that everyone was comfortably seated. Damian was there, seeming completely at home, talking eagerly with Colonel George Perkins, a retired soldier who lived on memories of his struggles with the Indians.

'Those were the days, eh, Lajeaunesse?' he included Sebastian in the conversation, a great hulk of a man with the rubicund nose and veined cheeks of the heavy drinker, who still sported a fine military moustache, and wore a red broadcloth jacket cut in the style of a uniform.

'We did share some interesting campaigns, I'll admit,' Sebastian replied slowly. 'But now I tend to think we should have left the Indians alone. It's their country, after all, and they show a fine respect for it, understanding nature in a way which we have lost through becoming civilized, so-called.'

'Maybe you're right,' the colonel conceded,

215

though rather unwillingly. 'Life's a riddle, ain't it?'

'A riddle, indeed. You've never said a truer word, Colonel. Don't you agree, Sir Peregrine?' Greg chimed in.

An amusing if unpredictable dinner companion, he had decided to exercise his wit on Peregrine, testing him out, indulging in verbal fencing. He did not like the way the dandy looked at Berenice, nor she at him, for that matter. He had guessed on talking with Sebastian, although that gentleman always played close to his chest, that all was not well on the marital scene.

Peregrine was not at ease, eyes wide, ears open, as he listened to the colonel, and then vouchsafed, 'Life, my dear sir, is composed of conundrums, stap me, if it isn't?' He passed Greg his snuffbox, wary of the young doctor.

'What do you do, sir, by way of occupation?' Greg asked, sniffing at the little dune of snuff at the base of his thumb.

'Do, sir? Do? Why, a gentleman is not called upon to *do* anything, is he?' Peregrine asked with a superior smile.

'I beg to differ.' Greg handed back the gilt box. 'I'm a gentleman, sir, and I do a great deal. As a doctor I'm called out at all times of the night or day. I deal with sickness, accidents, gunshot wounds, arrow wounds, and the birthing of babies.'

'Dear me,' Peregrine permitted himself a fleeting shudder. 'It sounds quite horrendous.'

Greg's humorous mouth turned up at the

216

corners as he enjoyed the dandy's discomfiture. 'Yep! It sometimes is,' he rejoined. 'Why, only the other day I was called to attend a lady who was having difficulty delivering her child. I took one look, got the opium out of my medical bag, made sure that the poor soul was woozy and then performed a Caesarean section, right there on her kitchen table.'

'Please—' Peregrine lifted his handkerchief to his mouth. 'You'll put me off my food.'

'My patient recovered splendidly. But you don't want to hear about my work, do you?' He grinned at Berenice, including her in the conversation. 'Tell me the latest fashion fads in England. Is it true that the more daring of the *demimonde* dampen their underskirts so that their dresses cling more closely to their figures?'

'Quite true. The idea came from France,' she answered, slanting a glance at Sebastian to see how he was taking this, 'where I understand one person to have said that the garment that best suits a woman is nudity.'

'Have you done this, Comtesse?' Greg questioned, amused by his friend's scowl.

'Yes, of course.' She never had, but was not about to let Sebastian know this.

His head went up and he stared at her hard. 'Then, madame, it's a wonder that you didn't have pneumonia!'

Servingmen brought forth a vast array of dishes, starting with oysters stewed in cream and followed by fish sauces, and game served with a bewildering choice of vegetables. 'The cuisine has that undeniable excellence which is the mark of a master chef,' Damian commented, accepting a second helping.

'I brought the chef with me out of Paris at the Revolution,' Sebastian confessed. 'And he has remained loyal ever since, though many a hostess among the Quality has attempted to lure him away.'

The talk was general, light and informative, and Greg assured the new arrivals that they would soon find themselves at ease in Charleston. 'Society is waiting to meet you,' he said, smiling at Berenice and making no secret of his admiration. 'You'll be all the rage—fêted everywhere at first, but pretty soon you'll fall into our way of life—the big houses, the plantations, the elegantly dressed ladies and educated, sporting men. I've never been to England, but I guess you won't find it so very different.'

'I should say not,' put in Colonel Perkins, his eyes twinkling across the table at her. 'Our young folk have a great time—there'll be picnics and balls—barbecues beside the creeks. You'll get along just fine, m'dear. And you, young sirs,' he turned to Damian and Peregrine. 'Why, there's a mint of fun awaiting you—and such hunting as you've never had back home.'

They lit up cigars, the meal over at last and that mellow stage reached when the port was circulating. Had there been any other women present, Berenice would have taken them to the drawing room, but this appeared to be a strictly masculine meeting.

'Hunting will come later, Colonel,' Sebastian

said. 'First, I have to arrange an expedition to deal with Darby Modiford.'

'Modiford?' The protuberant eyes widened, and the colonel reached for his glass. 'Is that cuttlefish on the rampage again?'

'He sure is,' drawled Greg, accepting Peregrine's snuffbox again and touching a dab to each nostril. 'He's taken advantage of Sebastian's being out of the country for a spell.'

Colonel Perkins frowned, rolling out his lower lip. 'What's he been up to?'

'Apparently, he's anchored in Mobby Cove, and is terrorizing the neighborhood,' Sebastian replied, his face hardening ominously. 'He's after my blood. Thinks I cheated him on our last venture, which is a damned lie! We split the profits. Everything was done according to the articles which we'd both drawn up and signed. He can't seek me out in Charleston, for the obvious reason that he'd be arrested on sight, but he knows damn well that I'll go to Mobby Cove. I have to look after my people there.'

The colonel shook his gray head dubiously. 'I warned you at the time, my boy—told you not to have any truck with that pirate. But would you listen? Would you hell! You can be mighty stubborn, Sebastian—I'll say it to your face. Smuggling's one thing—and we've all indulged in that—but piracy's a different kettle of fish entirely.'

'Aw, come on, Colonel! You know that it's been going on as long as there've been settlers here,' broke in Greg. 'Bless me—the eminent citizens of New York did very well out of that

219

old ruffian, Captain William Kidd, who holed up on Long Island. He's become a legend. You can't blame Sebastian for being a pirate. Anyhow—it was a while back.'

Berenice sat as if turned to marble, appalled that they should be talking of such a crime with apparent calm. She cast a look of appeal at Damian, but was horrified to see him sitting there with a smug, rather knowing smile on his face, as if he had heard about Sebastian's illegal exploits before, and only admired him the more for them. Peregrine said nothing, steepling his fingertips together, a watchful expression in his eyes. He caught her glance and raised an eyebrow significantly. She could bear no more. Not only had Sebastian been a smuggler, and *that* was bad enough—but he was a confessed pirate as well, one of those bloodthirsty, merciless scoundrels who preyed upon honest seamen.

She rose to her feet, throwing her napkin down on the table and pushing back her chair with a force that drew all eyes. 'No wonder you're rich, sir!' she cried, staring at Sebastian. 'Is my father aware of this? I can't believe that he would have agreed to the marriage had he known.'

Sebastian did not condescend to look at her, lazing in his chair, an indifferent expression on his handsome features. 'Sit down, Berenice. You've no idea what you're talking about—'

She cut him off, protesting, 'Stop treating me like a child. I thought you were a planter, a fur trader. No one told me that I was married to

220

a pirate king! You, sir, have been flying false colors!'

She was shaking with rage. The thought of him striding the decks of some lawless frigate filled her with disgust. And worst of all, she had just begun to believe in his sincerity. Now she was ashamed, feeling that somehow he had taken advantage of her. He had said nothing of his past, and she realized how little she really knew about him. She was overwhelmed with a sudden wave of homesickness. The room and everyone in it became dreadfully alien to her, the land, too, seemed unfriendly.

Through the open glass doors, she could see the black night, hear the whine of mosquitoes, and the strange cry of a nocturnal bird seeking its mate. How she longed to go home! There, men did not plunder and rape—they were hanged if they did. Pirates, rogues and vagabonds were frowned upon, not half encouraged, as here.

Pirate! The word filled her with terror. Often she had heard the officers aboard *La Foudre* talking of their savagery, their greed, their contempt for life and honor. The scum of the seas, they had called them. Sometimes, when they had thought she was not listening, they had regaled one another with even more horrible yarns concerning the torturing of prisoners and ravishing of women. Had Sebastian taken part in such barbarity? Now she could understand his hardness; no doubt he had learned it from those debased sea wolves with whom he had sailed.

He looked at her sternly. 'When I first came

over, I found the plantation neglected. It needed money spent on it—a large sum of money, and we'd been able to bring little out of France. I would have stopped at nothing to raise the cash needed to restore it.'

'That I can well believe,' she flashed back. 'I thought you were a gentleman who considered *some* things unworthy. Now I see that you're totally without principle or honor.'

A hush descended on the table, the ugly scene between man and wife disturbing. 'That's pretty strong, ma'am,' commented Greg. 'Many a likely lad hereabouts has taken part in activities on the wrong side of the law.'

She rounded on him, sparking with indignation. 'I think it's disgraceful! Piracy's no fit occupation for a well-bred man.'

'They're usually the ones most deeply into it,' Greg laughed, winking at Damian, who was squirming with embarrassment at his sister's outburst. 'The lifestyle of the Quality's devilish expensive.'

'Enough of this!' Sebastian shouted, mortified by such an unseemly spectacle. 'We'll discuss it in private, madame.' Ignoring her further, he turned to the colonel. 'What d'you say, sir? Will you help me to flush out Modiford?'

'Depends what I'm letting myself in for,' hedged the old soldier.

'I can't tell you exactly. The matter needs thrashing out, but I think we should make for Mobby Cove and see what's afoot,' Sebastian said crisply.

'Damme! I'll go with you!' The colonel

slapped his massive thigh, inspired by Sebastian's verve.

'And you, Damian? Do you fancy a skirmish with pirates?'

Damian's face was glowing. He had come to the New World in search of adventure, and was about to find it. 'You can rely on me.'

Peregrine sat silent under Sebastian's imperious stare. He was always ill at ease in his presence. Resentment smoldered in him. He hated the Frenchman with the bitter enmity which only a weak man can feel for a stronger. He blamed him for his treatment of Berenice, yet despised himself for lacking the courage to defend her. It was true that his motives for coming to America had not been selfless. London had become too hot for him, and he had hoped to make his mark in Georgetown. His feelings towards Berenice were confused—he desired her, yet was afraid to put it to the test. Even so, he wished to look well in her eyes.

'You, sir,' Sebastian demanded, staring at him keenly. 'Have you the stomach for such an operation?'

Just for a moment a bright vision floated somewhere in Peregrine's imagination. In it, he saw himself returning to Charleston in a cloud of glory, having performed some incredible feat of valor, perhaps bearing Modiford's head on a platter to lay at Berenice's feet, while beautiful daughters of the Quality wept tears of joy, and showered him with flowers.

'You'll not find me wanting in courage, Comte,' he answered, almost without knowing that he spoke. 'I'll be honored to accompany you.'

Berenice stood there feeling lost, forgotten in this important conference. She rested her hand on the chiffonier as she listened to them, numb with misery. Animals! she thought scathingly. Men are like animals—or silly children! She recalled hearing women friends in London declare in amused, indulgently superior voices that men were but boys after all. Now she understood the truth of that remark. They *were* nothing more than little boys playing at soldiers! Even Peregrine was joining in the game.

Sebastian had asked her to play for his guests. She would have refused, but now she wandered listlessly into the music room. Melody had always comforted her, and tonight she was in need of solace. She sat down at the walnut pianoforte, an oblong case supported on turned legs with a pastoral scene painted on the lid, showing nymphs and shepherds flirting against a backdrop of Arcadian columns. Flipping through the sheet music, she selected a saraband and set it on the stand.

A footman brought over a branching candlestick to give her more light, and she began to play. Her fingers fumbled at first, for she was accustomed to the crisper action and plucked strings of the harpsichord. This newly invented keyboard sounded strange to her ears, its hammers striking clearly, bell-like in tone. Momentarily she forgot her cares and homesickness, losing herself in the harmonies.

Sebastian stalked into the room and leaned

back in a padded wing chair, smoking and watching her. Berenice was unaware of the perfect picture she made—a beautiful woman, illumined by the soft, golden candlelight that formed a halo around her curling hair—shadows playing over the gracious sweep of her neck, the swell of her breasts, her rounded arms and slender hands. The jewels he had given her sparkled against her skin.

He closed his eyes and surrendered to the enchanting sounds, though rage still simmered beneath the surface. Whatever Berenice might say, he had been successful in carving out a new life for himself, God damn it! He had fought and worked and done many things of which he was not proud, but the result had been the restoration of Oakwood Hall, and he was not ashamed. No chit of a girl was going to make him regret a single deed.

SEVEN

It was most peculiar, her calm—somehow unnatural. Berenice wondered how long it would last, dreading a resurgence of feeling. She was standing alone in the bedchamber, listening to Sebastian outside talking to Damian. The hour was late, and Dulcie had retired, but Berenice's gown was so easy to unfasten that she could manage herself.

As Sebastian entered, he was jerking im-

225

patiently at his collar, coat slung over one shoulder, looking distinctly piratical with his blue-black hair mussed, one lock falling forward over his scowling brow. He shot her a look charged with annoyance, and instantly Berenice's composure wilted.

'You made a damned disgraceful exhibition of yourself tonight!' he began, striding to a side table and picking up the decanter. 'What the deuce ails you?'

Ready temper rising, Berenice flashed back at him, 'It was something of a blow to find that my husband is a pirate!'

'*Was,*' he corrected her coolly, pouring brandy into a glass, holding it to the light and admiring the color. 'It was a long time ago, *ma belle*—when you were a schoolgirl.'

'I don't care. The fact remains that you tricked me.' She was watching him guardedly, ready to run if he so much as moved towards her, but he was lounging with an elbow on the mantelpiece, regarding her in that mocking fashion which she disliked so much.

'Well, madame, you'll be pleased to know that I'll be removing my obnoxious presence shortly. When I've finished making preparations, I'll be off to Mobby Cove,' he informed her with a crooked smile.

Berenice felt an odd pang of disappointment. A vista of empty days and lonely nights stretched ahead. He was leaving—no more Sebastian, to bully, tease, and rouse her emotions. She knew that she should be glad. Maybe he would even be killed and she would be free of him at last.

She wondered why her heart did not lift at the prospect.

'How nice,' she said sweetly, going to the toilet table and taking the riband from her hair. Her eyes were full of questions as she stared at him in the central mirror, the ones each side giving her a different view of him, three Sebastians, each of them alarming. 'I'll be able to go visiting, and make myself known to Charleston society.'

'True. The ladies will be leaving their calling cards in the morning, everyone panting to meet someone from the old country. You'll be lionized, *chérie*, and, knowing you, it'll probably go to your head. Mine is an old and respected family, so I warn you not to disgrace our name. My mother was English, her forebears settled here early in the last century, my father's a little later, migrating from Louisiana, so I have both French and English connections in the area.' He was considering her carefully, never quite sure what she was going to do or say next. It was unnerving.

'La, such fine ancestry for a pirate!' she remarked flippantly, wondering why he was bothering to tell her the Lajeaunesse history at this particular moment.

Sebastian gripped his glass tightly. She had no notion of what life was about. He had experienced it in all its aspects, terrible as well as good. No one of his class could have survived the French Revolution and not been scarred. The air seemed to crackle with emotion. Berenice felt its power, her pulse racing as she

227

met his brooding eyes.

'Be quiet, madame,' he said coolly. 'You begin to bore me.' With that he turned away, so lordly and arrogant that she longed to hurl herself on him, and thump him till he saw reason.

She controlled the impulse, a taunting smile on her lips. 'You lie, Sebastian. You may resent me, even hate me—but you're not bored by me.'

This was true, and Sebastian recognized it. She was an exasperating enchantress who haunted him night and day, no matter how hard he tried to forget her, tormenting and vexing him. She could be aloof and remote, withholding from him all that he knew her very capable of giving, yet at the same time she could squander her thoughts, the golden, joyous sound of her laughter on an empty-headed buffoon like Peregrine.

He could just imagine the commotion she would cause in Charleston—they'd be calling at the house in droves, every young rakehell vying to be allowed to escort her to some entertainment or other, taking advantage of her married state to make free with her. Why, not so long ago, he, too, preferred the company of wedded ladies, knowing them to be more generous with their favors than their single counterparts.

His eyes traveled down over her insultingly, and there was an edge to his voice as he replied, 'You flatter yourself, *chérie*. Just because I've taken my rightful place in the marriage bed, it doesn't mean that I require more than a responding body in my arms. What makes you think I'm interested in the contents of your vain little head? You're my wife—the bridge between myself and my children. That's all I ask of you. Your thoughts are not necessary.'

Berenice was speechless with anger. How dare he! Children? She would rather be barren than bear children for such a villain. It was not right that a woman should conceive when she resented the man in her arms. Surely, children were the symbol of devotion and respect—the product of two caring human beings who wanted them as living proof of their love? But she could feel only hatred for him.

When she did find her tongue, he almost recoiled from her flashing, tearless fury. 'You bastard!' she hissed through her teeth.

Sebastian's laughter rang out. Hands on his hips, he goaded her. 'Bravo! Encore! Where's the refined town belle now? That viperish tongue suits you far better than the simpering lisp you use when addressing Peregrine.'

Berenice looked about wildly for something to throw at him. Her eyes alighted on the sapphires, which she had taken off and placed on the table. Her hand closed on them and she spun round, hurling them at Sebastian's mocking face. A flashing cascade of valuable gems struck him smartly across the cheek.

'By God, I'll die before I give you a child!' she stormed. 'Take your damned present! I want none of it! You can't buy me with pirate's loot!'

Pain crossed his face. It was instantly controlled, but nonetheless gave her savage satisfaction. Sebastian did not even glance at the necklace sparkling at his feet.

'You're wrong, madame,' he said evenly. 'They were once worn by a most gracious lady, and I had hoped that you would prove worthy of them. I see now that I was mistaken. They're not plundered goods, as you suppose. They belonged to my mother.' With quiet dignity he stooped to retrieve them, turned his back on her and strode from the room.

Berenice stood perfectly still, her knuckles pressed to her mouth. Suddenly she was aware of the enormity of her action. This time she had gone too far. But how was I to know? she argued with herself. He never said who they belonged to.

She flung herself on the bed, and tears coursed down her face. What was she to do? That blackguard had forced her to come to this remote country and it was the very last thing on earth she had wanted to do. He had wrenched her from her world, destroyed her for mercenary reasons, leaving her nothing to believe in or trust. Damian had changed almost beyond recognition, taking Sebastian as his role model, and Peregrine seemed to have deserted her for dreams, proving himself unworthy of her love.

Where were the Lancelots and Tristans whose images had filled her girlish imaginings, culled from books? They had honored and worshiped their ladies—the blessed Guinevere—the adored

Isolde. That was true love, she decided firmly, not the lust she had experienced with Sebastian. She writhed with shame, heaping maledictions on his head, but even as she cursed him, her blood clamored, wanting to feel him, to smell him, to have his hands work their magic on her body.

With a muffled cry, she twisted on the pillows, thumping them with her fists, steering her willful thoughts back to the safe, though annoying, harbor of Peregrine. He was a poet. Surely poets never hurt their ladies? In their verses, they crawled, implored, wept for the reward of the smallest chaste kiss. But Sebastian? Ah, that wretch! He had been a pirate. How could he know the meaning of noble love when he had spent his time terrorizing prisoners and falling into the arms of coarse strumpets in the seedy ports where he must have returned to spend his ill-gotten gains?

She cried until it seemed that she had no more tears left to shed. Her face felt puffy, the skin stretched and stiff, and her eyes were sore and red. She knew that such weeping would not profit her cause, for if she were to escape, she would have to lure Peregrine into helping her, and to do this she must armor herself with beauty, her strongest weapon.

Finally the night closed about her. She was no longer angry with Sebastian, not even furious with fate. She accepted her misery, too tired and sick at heart for further tears, brooding on life which had promised so much and in which, after all, she had found so little joy.

'Madame, wake up!' It was Dulcie, standing by the bed holding a salver containing a cup of steaming coffee and several miniature white envelopes. 'These have been arriving since early on. They look like invitations to me.'

Berenice sat up sleepily and examined her mail. She opened the envelopes one by one. They contained cards from ladies with impressive names—each requesting that they might drop by at her convenience, to make her acquaintance and welcome her to their town. She hated to admit it, but Sebastian was right—all of Charleston was eager to meet the Comtesse Lajeaunesse.

—Thus began a hectic week of entertainment, during which Berenice discovered that far from being a colonial backwater, the capital of South Carolina was culturally vibrant, nurturing music, the theater, a fine choice of smart shops, a lively interest in current fashions, and offering an enchanting way of life, gracious, easy and enormously wealthy. She quickly made friends with the married ladies and their daughters, softly spoken, elegant women who comported themselves like aristocrats, proud to be called the Quality.

Accompanied by her brother and Peregrine, who was an instant hit—so much so that Berenice became quite jealous as she saw how envied she was of her cavalier—she entertained in the house in Meeting Street, and went visiting. There was never a moment when she was not involved in some amusement or other, impressed by the magnificent mansions surrounded by lovely gardens, some of which faced the harbor. The climate was warm and humid and the colonists had built houses with high ceilings and rooms opening on to broad piazzas to catch the refreshing sea breezes.

Though the plants and shrubs were tropical, Berenice felt at home in the town itself, for the architecture was mostly of the eighteenth century, and comfortingly reminiscent of the most select parts of Bath, Brighton and London, with numerous church spires punctuating the skyline. When being taken on a sightseeing trip in the splendid carriage belonging to Mrs. Rowena Wilkins, Charleston's most popular hostess, she had even discovered a church modeled on London's St. Martin-in-the-Fields. Berenice started to rethink her feelings about Carolina. Maybe she could settle there after all. She found time to note this in her journal, and also in letters to her father, Lady Olivia and Lucinda.

Sebastian was hardly ever present, not even for dinner or at night; she could only assume that he was fully occupied with the organization of his expedition to Mobby Cove. Her heart grew even lighter at the prospect of being a grass widow during his lengthy absence.

'I shall be free,' she caroled joyously one morning, rummaging in a drawer for a pair of gloves as she prepared to go out.

At that moment Dulcie came sailing in carrying them. 'Here you are, milady. Clean as a new pin and fresh from the glove stretcher.'

'Free! Free! Free!' Berenice beamed, taking them from her and working her fingers into the tight kid. 'Just think, Dulcie—weeks, maybe months, without him.'

'You'll be queen of Charleston by the time he returns,' Dulcie agreed, yet she was already alarmed by the number of young men her mistress had managed to gather in so short a time. They positively flocked to meet her every day, putting Peregrine's nose out of joint.

'Come along, Dulcie. Don't hang about, my dear,' Berenice ordered jovially and rushed out of the room.

Dulcie followed thoughtfully, unconvinced that her mistress's loudly expressed gaiety was genuine. She was just too frantically festive, too excited and overenthusiastic. In Dulcie's opinion, it was false, covering a maelstrom of bewildered emotions that centered on Sebastian.

Although the maid was the same age as Berenice, she had been reared in the brutal environment of the London slums and this had rendered her years older in experience. She accepted that human beings were greedy, weak, selfish and lascivious. It was no one's fault that they were like that, it was simply how things were. They could also be kind, loving, generous and self-sacrificing, and somehow one had to find a balance between the two. In her plain, uneducated manner, Dulcie was something of a philosopher, thankful that she had clawed her way out of the mire and been given the chance to better her lot.

Ever optimistic, she had a sisterly attitude towards Berenice and, considering the short time they had been together, understood her as perhaps no one else did. Dulcie was enjoying Charleston as much as her mistress, and now they were about to depart on a picnic.

Berenice ran lightly down the curving staircase with its wrought-iron handrails, her white gown floating out behind her, big picture-hat dangling by its ribbons over her arm. Damian looked up as she descended, pleased at the change in her; she was much more like the gay girl he had once known. Yet it saddened him to realize that the major contributing factor to her happiness was Sebastian's preoccupation elsewhere. With Dulcie and Chloë in attendance, both wearing identical sprigged muslin and mobcaps to mark them as their maids, Berenice stepped into the chaise with Damian and Peregrine at her side, the coachman flicked the reins and they were off, bowling through Charleston towards the headland.

The rest of the party were already there when they arrived, reclining on cushions and rugs spread on the grass under the shade of palmettos. It was a young crowd, for that day Berenice had escaped the older ladies. There were some half-dozen pretty girls, with their duennas fanning themselves and gossiping beneath the trees a little further off, and an equal number of good-looking men, as *tonnish* and fashion-conscious as any in England.

The chaise parked alongside several others and Berenice walked the short distance to the rendezvous. Footmen moved about, serving food from the hampers. And what food! Berenice feared she would start to put on weight soon, for the local dishes were quite irresistible. The bucks saw her and leapt up, vying with one another to be the first to reach her and offer her an arm, but it was Greg who succeeded.

'Good morning, Berenice,' he said, his deep blue eyes smiling at her. He had appointed himself as her guide during that week, but had also decided to keep a close watch on Sebastian's flirtatious bride, doing it so subtly that she was not aware of his intention.

They were not the only people to enjoy the lovely day. Several others strolled about or sat admiring the view. There was even an artist, busy at work with his sketch pad and pencil. Families were eating in groups under the trees; lovers wandered hand in hand; a little covey of gentlemen were playing cards. Were it not for the sea, the magnolia bushes and exotic flowers, they might have been in St. James's Park, Mayfair.

Berenice settled herself gracefully on a heap of cushions and Greg fetched a selection of dishes, spreading them out before her. She was still unfamiliar with the Low Country specialties, and he suggested that she try the sautéed shrimps, pecan pie, quail stuffed with cornbread and shellfish served in peach sauce, crab cakes dipped in basil tartar sauce and scollops garnished with roasted pine nuts. For dessert, he fetched her strawberry mocha mousse.

'Ummm,' she gave a drawn out, contented sigh as she wiped her fingers on a pristine white napkin. 'Oh, that was delicious! I love the food here.'

'Not only the food, I hope, Comtesse,' said one of the young bloods, a handsome boy named Bradley Banis, brown-haired and grey-eyed, with a lean, rangy body most elegantly clad. Son of one of the town's leading citizens, he had been the most persistent of her admirers since she arrived on the Charleston scene.

Berenice glanced at him from under her long lashes. She had not intended to encourage him, far too wary of Sebastian, but it was pleasant to flirt again, to see a man's eyes light up when he looked at her, to accept his compliments, to promise—half promise—

'Why, no, sir,' she said softly. 'I love many things here.'

'Dare I hope that this includes me?' he whispered in her ear, close to her now, his shoulder pressed against hers.

'I'm married. You seem to forget.' For the first time, Berenice appreciated the advantages of a wedding ring; such a useful thing for deterring a too-ardent swain.

'Oh, no, ma'am, I don't forget that. How could I, when your husband is one of the most feared marksmen in these parts? No one in his right mind would want to be called out by him. But I think he neglects you shamefully. I'd not leave you on your own, were I your husband.' Then, seeing Greg eyeing him as he returned carrying two glasses of wine, Bradley moved away from her a shade.

Berenice accepted a glass from Greg and then, prompted by a spirit of pure mischief, she said, 'Bradley thinks Sebastian neglects me.'

Greg's brow furrowed a little as he stretched out his legs on the grass beside her. 'He's busy right now.'

She sat back on her heels, teasing him by trailing her feather fan across his face. 'Do you know where he is at this very moment?'

'Sure thing. He's at Monsieur Etienne's fencing academy.'

She had not expected that. 'Why?' she asked.

'He likes to keep in trim, and, where we're heading, he'll need to be fighting fit.' Greg looked at Bradley meaningfully.

'Can we go and watch?' Now why am I saying this? she wondered.

'If you want.'

'You're leaving us so soon, Comtesse?' Bradley stood as she did, a boy with impeccable manners. It seemed the Americans remembered that no gentleman worth his salt ever remained seated while a woman was standing, unless, of course, she was a servant.

'I fancy a trip to the fencing school,' she said lightly, beckoning Dulcie and Chloë. They came reluctantly, having their own coterie of admirers among the footmen.

'Will you be attending the play this evening?' Bradley asked, though restraining his eagerness because Greg was listening.

'I wouldn't miss it for anything,' and Berenice gave him the benefit of a dazzling smile,

238

unfurled her parasol and walked off on Greg's arm.

Monsieur Etienne's house, situated in the Old Market area, had once been a dwelling place, but now the large drawing room on the lower floor had been stripped of furniture and carpets. There were racks on the walls holding foils, and shelves filled with protective clothing and face masks. The school was popular among the Charleston beaux, who liked to keep up with the finer points of fighting with rapier or épée. Though dueling had been outlawed, a Carolina gentleman might still have occasion to defend his honor. Pistols were popular, but the sword was sometimes used.

Peregrine had elected to remain with the picnic party, but Damian had come with Berenice and Greg and, as she entered, she saw two combatants hard at it. The room echoed with the clash of steel and the stamping of feet. Both men wore masks, white quilted cotton jackets, nankeen breeches, stockings and pumps. It was difficult to see who they were, for the full masks had close-woven metal mesh to shield their faces. Monsieur Etienne, a compactly built Frenchman of fiery disposition, was standing to one side, watching them keenly, highly critical of their performances and calling out instructions now and again.

For a while, he did not notice the new arrivals, and Berenice took one of the chairs ranged around the walls. Greg leaned his shoulder against the door, watching points, making the occasional continent of encouragement

239

or reproof. The taller of the men, whom it was impossible not to recognize as Sebastian, even though he was masked, was the more experienced of the two. He seemed almost indolently relaxed, yet parried every thrust with lightning speed, giving his adversary no chance to pierce his guard. The other man was not lacking in skill or courage. A fierce fighter, sometimes rather rash, but unable to beat down that flashing blade.

At length, Monsieur Etienne saw that he had visitors and called for a rest. He greeted Greg, bowing and smiling, 'Ah, Dr. Lattimer. Have you come to perfect the art?'

'Not today, sir,' Greg replied. 'The Comtesse wanted to see her husband fight.'

'Comtesse—I'm honored.' The Frenchman hovered over her hand, lifting it to his lips.

Sebastian came across, removing his mask, his face running with sweat. He pulled off his gauntlets and took the towel which Quico handed him. 'To what do I owe this visit?' he asked, his breathing rapid, chest heaving from exertion.

She had no ready answer, impressed by his fencing skills, and watching as he stripped off his padded jacket, and then his shirt, standing naked to the waist as Quico toweled over his chest and back. He had such a perfect physique, iron-muscled arms, wide shoulders tapering to a narrow waist and hips, his torso scarred here and there from old wounds. Greg was amused by the unguarded expression of admiration he was surprised to see on her face.

'Madame was curious to know how you passed the time,' he said laconically, grinning at his friend.

'In a more productive way than herself,' Sebastian replied, his black hair tousled as he held out his arms and slipped them into the shirt his valet held up. Then, after tucking it into the top of his breeches, he shrugged on his coat, picked up his hat and prepared to leave.

Berenice, offended by his brusque manner, could not help comparing it with the attentiveness of Bradley, but even so, she stepped towards him hesitantly, impressing the susceptible Monsieur Etienne with her beauty. The sunlight, streaming through the window behind her, rendered her gown semitransparent, silhouetted her figure and formed a halo round her abundant hair.

'Can I expect you for dinner tonight, Comte?' she asked, her voice trembling slightly.

He spared her a single glance, but it was one that shocked through him, making him long to yield to his desire to be with her. But he could not, *dared* not risk another upset which might distract him from the dangerous mission on which he was preparing to embark. He needed his wits about him; those who accompanied him to Mobby Cove would be dependent on his cool nerve. No one and nothing must stand in the way of this, least of all a flighty woman who, so the scandalmongers had been only too eager to inform him, was playing fast and loose with every beau in town.

'No, madame.' His voice had never been

more controlled. 'I am too busy. We leave tomorrow morning.' He snapped his fingers at Quico and left the room, the Indian padding silently after him.

'Damn him,' Berenice whispered to herself, but not so low that Greg was unable to hear. Such vehemence made him smile, for he suspected that it indicated disappointment rather than anger.

The fencing room was filling up with others eager for the exercise, so he took her arm and, after they had said farewell to Monsieur Etienne, they walked out into the street where the white walls were dazzling to the eye, sliced across by inky shadows.

'Where do you wish to go now, Berenice?' he enquired, though knowing that he should be consulting with Colonel Perkins.

'Take me back to the house,' she said, a dispirited droop to her shoulders. Then she looked up at him. 'Did you know he was going in the morning?'

'I thought it likely.'

'And you will go, too, and Damian and Peregrine?'

'Yes.'

She sighed heavily. 'Then I shall be alone.'

Greg laughed, pushing his palm-woven hat to the back of his blond head as he opened the door of the chaise and stood aside so that she might climb in. 'Hardly, I think. There will be plenty for you to do while we're off hunting Darby Modiford.'

'Dock Street Theater was built early in the last century,' said Mrs. Wilkins, her voice holding a ring of civic pride.

She had taken Berenice under her wing, a stately dame whose soirées were so exclusive that people positively fought for invitations. Berenice, Bradley and Peregrine were visiting her box during the interval, not surprised to find that she, too, had decided to attend the performance that evening. Mrs. Wilkins had told Berenice that she adored going to the theater, and questioned her closely about plays she had seen in England, conversant with the most famous of the actors and actresses that trod the boards over there.

'Take careful note of the ceiling, Comtesse,' the mature, poised and perfectly attired lady continued. 'It's decorated with most exquisite paintings.'

'I noticed them. They're tearing fine.'

'I do deplore the behavior of some of the audience.' Mrs. Wilkins raised her lorgnette and, with a pained expression, gazed down into the pit where a collection of gentlemen were arguing, laughing loudly, leaping over the seats and ogling the women. She turned that basilisk stare to Bradley, saying censoriously. 'I hope you never act like that, young man.'

'Oh, no, ma'am, never,' Bradley lied. Mrs. Wilkins knew his mother and he needed to foster that lady's illusion that he was a perfect son. Mama doted on him, and this kept his pockets full and the prospect of stirring himself from his idleness, no matter how slender, firmly at bay.

243

'It's the same at the Theatre Royal, Drury Lane or at Sadler's Wells. The audiences are always rowdy,' Berenice asserted, sipping at the glass of iced lemonade that Peregrine had fetched from the refreshment room.

'I'm sure I don't know what's gotten into the young these days. They show so little respect,' Mrs. Wilkins complained, waving her fan in an agitated manner.

'Please don't feel bad about it.' She had been kind and Berenice did not want her to be unhappy. 'The play is awfully well acted and I'm enjoying it tremendously.'

'The actors are convincing, aren't they? A touring company from New York.' Mrs. Wilkins sounded as proud as if they were blood relatives, though, according to the rules of conduct, she would never have invited them into her house.

'I've not seen better,' Berenice agreed. 'Even in London.'

'Oh, look!' Mrs. Wilkins suddenly exclaimed, forgetting the disagreeable antics in the pit. 'Well, I declare—isn't that your husband in the next box, madame?' She leaned over the red plush rail, making her presence known.

Berenice shrank into the dimness, but could not avoid the piercing stare of a pair of tigerish green eyes. Sebastian raised one eyebrow and then his glance slid to Bradley and Peregrine. Was it a trick of the light, or did his mouth really draw down in a sneer? Berenice was so consumed with guilt that she might have imagined it. Then she saw that he was seated by a beautiful woman wearing the latest in gowns,

244

and a silver turban fastened with a brooch containing an emerald the size of a pigeon's egg. Her other jewels sent out brilliant flashes of light, and she was looking at Sebastian from under lowered lids, one of her hands resting on his arm in an intimate gesture. On her other side was a grey-haired gentleman of courtly bearing, dressed in black with diamond buttons.

Civilities exchanged, Mrs. Wilkins sank back in the crimson and gilt chair, her eyes gimlet sharp as she asked, 'How is it that you're not with him, my dear?'

'Oh, it's a business matter.' Berenice was amazed at the quick excuse that sprang to her lips, and even more astonished because she cared. He had said he could not spare the time to dine with her, and yet he was out with someone else—a very lovely someone, at that.

The bell rang then, warning the audience that the second act was about to begin, so she and her escorts returned to their own box. The house lights dimmed, the curtains parted with a swish, and once more the actors played out the comedy on the stage.

Later, Berenice recalled that she had not the smallest idea what had happened in the last act, or, indeed, how she got back to Meeting Street. Everything had been blanked out by her obsession with Sebastian and the pain that gnawed inside her. Another woman? Somehow, it had never crossed her mind that he would be unfaithful, not now that they were married. She remembered him being seen with Mrs. Jermaine, or so Lucinda had reported, but since that time she had come to believe that he did not agree with adultery.

Pacing her room after Dulcie had helped her undress and then retired, anger began to surface. How could he do such a thing when he was forever accusing her of dalliance with Peregrine? Then she realized that he probably could. He was, after all, a man, and men possessed double standards. They demanded purity from their wives, but behaved like whoremasters themselves. And he would be gone tomorrow, giving her no chance to confront him, and what she most wanted to do was give him a piece of her mind.

She was about to climb wearily into bed, her Charleston triumph reduced to ashes in her mouth, when Sebastian suddenly came in. She was so surprised to see him that the angry words she had been rehearsing in her head deserted her.

He gave her no chance to recover, going into the attack at once. He had come to a lightning decision when he saw her at the theater, and now had no intention of leaving her where every philanderer in South Carolina could try his luck. What she needed was a severe lesson—something that would make her more human, and strip away that brittle veneer brought about by easy living. There would be no more servants, no soft beds, and the sun would be her only cosmetic. No fancy foods either, only the animals he could kill and cook over a campfire, and she would sleep in the open, under the stars. He smiled grimly at the thought of her annoyance when her fine clothes were torn and muddied, and she found that she had to perform menial tasks. Perhaps it would bring the real woman to the surface, make or break her. She would soon change her tune and forget her fads and fancies.

'Put away your calling cards, madame, and give your followers their marching orders,' he said crisply, drawing himself up to his full height. 'You're coming to Mobby Cove.'

'What!' Berenice shouted, one hand going to her throat. 'You can't make me! I'll not be dragged off to the wilds!'

'I can, and I will. As for being dragged, I think you've been watching too many melodramas performed on the stage.'

Now it had to be voiced, before Berenice exploded with rage. 'Why did you lie? You said you couldn't dine with me, then I see you at the theater with another woman. Explain yourself, sir.'

'I don't need to explain anything to you.' Her outburst surprised him. 'You were there with your foplings, if I recall.'

'I only went because I don't like being alone. You're never with me these days. Indeed, I might as well not be married.'

'I thought that was what you wanted—for me to leave you alone.' *Dieu!* he was thinking, is there anything more complex and illogical than a woman. Chase them, and they hate you. Ignore them, and they hate you even more.

'Don't change the subject.' Berenice was too cross to be prudent. 'Who was that woman?'

'Madame de Courcey,' he replied, keeping his face impassive. 'And the gentleman is her husband, the Chevalier. She is my cousin—not my mistress, as you seem to think. They were in town for one night only. I hadn't seen them for many months. It was a duty that I couldn't avoid.'

'Why didn't you tell me the truth? Why say that you were busy?' The relief was making her weak, and other feelings, too—that deep stirring within her when he was near.

He shrugged. 'I didn't know they were here until I got back to the house. Then it seemed a pointless waste of time to try and make you understand. It's no lie. I intend to spend most of what's left of the night concluding plans.'

He didn't want to stay with her? I'm glad, she told herself firmly. 'Very well, sir. I accept that you're speaking the truth,' she said, moving to the open window and looking out at the deep blue night where the moon sailed serenely across the sky, accompanied by her retinue of stars. Then she said, over her shoulder, 'You jest, surely, when you say that I'm to go with you into the wilderness?'

'No. You'll come. Get to bed, Berenice, for we start early. I'll tell Quico to find your maid and instruct her to prepare a few necessities.'

'You can't be serious—'

'I've never been more serious about anything in my life.' He gave her a long, steady look, then let himself out of the door very quietly.

A loaded wagon and armed escort were waiting

outside the house at daybreak. Having spent a miserable, restless night, Berenice rose and summoned Dulcie.

'We're going on the trek with the Comte,' she said angrily.

'I know, milady.' Dulcie was already dressed for traveling. 'Quico told me, late last night.'

'You saw him?' Berenice found the energy to be surprised, for Dulcie maintained that she could not abide the manservant.

'Yes, milady. He's difficult to avoid, for he always sleeps across his master's door, wrapped up in a blanket. On guard, I suppose.'

'I'm not surprised he needs a guard,' Berenice muttered darkly. 'There must be many people who'd like to murder him. Myself included.'

'There's nothing else for it, madam. We'll just have to make the best of a bad job, won't we?' Dulcie was trying to be cheerful, but could not help adding, 'I can't pretend that I'm not put out.'

'*You're* put out. How do you think I feel?'

'Sick as a pig, I imagine.' Dulcie was folding garments into a valise as she talked. 'I was looking forward to mixing with the servants of the important Charleston folk. It's a real nuisance, that's what it is! How am I ever going to find myself a husband at this rate? Not someone suitable, that is. Trappers! Backwoodsmen! Forget it!'

'What do you want a husband for?' Berenice almost yelled, as she rummaged in the wardrobe. 'Heavens above! You're better off single.' Her hands came to rest on a new and beautiful

249

carriage costume. She had not worn it yet. A mischief-inspired smile lit up her face. 'Ah, this will do admirably! Take me into the wilds, would he? I'll show him!'

So when she eventually descended the stairs to the hall where an impatient Sebastian was striding up and down like a caged lion, fuming at the delay, she was wearing a long fitted coat of military cut in claret velvet. It was lined with white satin and trimmed with rich gold frogging, with a skirt to match. Crimson half boots encased her feet, while her hat was like a soldier's calpac, set at a dashing angle and sporting a yellow plume.

'*Sacrébleu!*' he exclaimed. 'What's all this? We're hardly going for a canter in Rotten Row, madame.'

'Standards must be maintained,' she retorted loftily, and stalked past him with her head held high.

Outside she found Peregrine, Damian and Greg, already mounted and ready, accompanied by Colonel Perkins riding a stout cob and leading a motley collection of men, mostly members of the regiment he had once commanded. A groom was holding the head of a steady gelding, while another bent with cupped hands at the stirrup. Berenice slipped her foot into this improvised rest, gripped the pommel and swung up, spending time afterwards arranging her skirt so that it draped itself gracefully over the animal's flank. The procession of men, provisions and horses started off through the town. When they reached the wide river mouth, the whole party embarked on flat-bottomed, schooner-rigged barges, paddled by slaves.

'The barges form the bulk of river traffic,' Damian explained as he helped her aboard. 'Great craft, aren't they?'

'They're used for almost everything,' Greg added, assisting her to the wooden bench in the stern. 'To float rice crops downriver for export; to fetch supplies back from the stores or, well scrubbed out, to take planters and their families to and fro. There's a deal of traveling about as the fashionable season shifts from the plantation mansions to the town houses.'

Sebastian seemed to have planned the trek with the precision of a military operation, and the hard-faced men in his pay were used to obeying his orders, as Berenice quickly gathered from scraps of conversation heard as the barge was steered along.

The Santee River was bounded on either side by swamplands. Mangroves trailed their roots in the mushy soil, and the smell of decaying leaves dissolving in mud, the choking stench of brackish water, mingled pungently with the overpowering scent of wildflowers. Hidden in the trees, birds screamed and chattered, and mosquitoes gave out their infuriating, high-pitched whine, swarming under the peak of Berenice's hat so that her face became spotted with her own blood where she had slapped at them. Dulcie did nothing but complain, seated glumly in the stern.

'We're doomed to be eaten alive by insects or scalped by roving bands of Indians,' she moaned, whisking the flies away with her hand.

'The people won't hurt you, if you're with me,' Quico offered, staring ahead of him up the river.

'Thanks for nothing!' the maid retorted crossly. 'I don't know which would be worse— capture by them or rescue by you!'

'Be quiet, both of you,' Berenice rapped out, thoroughly uncomfortable and realizing that her carriage costume had not been a wise choice.

She assumed that this was to be their mode of travel throughout the journey, but by noon they landed at one of the stages along the wide Santee, and set out on horseback. Conditions improved for a while, as they left the fever-infested swamp behind, heading south, following a trail that wound deep into the forest. A close column of horsemen led the way, cropping watchfully through the maze of oak and cypress and regiments of tall, loblolly pines. Most of Sebastian's troop were bearded, battle-scarred veterans, and there were several freemen among them, on equal terms with the rest. Each man was armed, including Sebastian, who wore a sword hanging from his belt, and each had a pair of serviceable pistols in holsters each side of his saddle.

On and on they rode, coming out on grasslands where the sun blazed overhead, a merciless white disc set in a flat blue sky. Berenice felt dwarfed by the vastness of it all—rather like the English countryside, but huge—stretching as far as the eye could see, dark masses of woods and hills in the far distance. Big—so big—stunning the mind and eye.

Would they never reach their destination? Her body quivered with weariness, unyielding leather prodding her with every lurching step of her horse. Rest was all she craved—to be allowed to fall to the ground and sleep, to forget her pain, her thirst, her despair, but still, mile after weary mile was covered without respite. She was too proud to ask if she might ride in the wagon for a change, having rashly boasted to Sebastian that she was a good horsewoman, a member of the Church Stretton Hunt, where no man could best her.

She brushed the perspiration from her eyes and frowned at Sebastian. With the shackles of civilization behind him, he seemed at home in this barbaric wilderness. He looked like a savage in his cape of Indian weave, dirty linen trousers and dusty boots. His palm-fiber hat was pulled down low over his forehead, those arched black brows scowling as he stared into the distance through half-closed lids. He rode his horse as if he were a part of the animal.

They moved in silence mostly, only the sounds of nature, shrill birdcalls and the humming of insects, marked their passage through the forest that surrounded them again. Occasionally, Greg cracked a joke that promoted laughter, mingling with the squeak of saddle leather, the jangle of harness, the slither and clop of hooves, the rumble of the wagon's wheels. Once again, Berenice fell to thinking of how little she knew her husband, glancing sideways at his profile as he rode beside her, only too aware of those muscular thighs which gripped his mount so confidently. Once they had folded around her in passion. The memory made her shiver.

There was no way of telling the time, but the sun was lower now, the sky a tawny red on the horizon. The colors started to fade slowly as evening softened into cool shadows, and the cavalcade came out through an avenue of trees into a clearing. Sebastian barked an order and they halted. Berenice slithered to the ground, vaguely conscious of the others swinging from their horses with groans of relief, talking and laughing, stripping off harness while their tired beasts lowered their heads and nuzzled the short, springy turf.

She was so exhausted that her head swam. Every inch of her body had its own particular ache. If the opportunity of escape from Sebastian had presented itself, she would not have had the strength to attempt it. She sank to her knees, head bowed, hat off, hair falling forward like a tangled curtain in the twilight. Some of the men were crashing about in the bushes, collecting wood. Others were getting fires going, or taking blankets, utensils and guns from the wagon. The trees shivered and whispered and, somewhere, an animal gave a spine-chilling cry. A bird called fearfully, sadly, caught by a predator, and between Berenice's head and the teeming stars, nightjars cut the air with a whickering of wings.

She saw someone approaching, and coiled her limbs, ready to leap up and defend herself,

254

then Sebastian spoke, bending over her with a canteen of water in his hand. 'Do you want a drink?' he asked.

Rigid with pride, even now, 'Go away,' she said.

He squatted on his heels beside her, commenting, 'You'd be really annoyed if you died of thirst.'

'I don't care,' she muttered.

'Very well.' He stood up and made to leave her, but she put out her hands and he placed the canteen in them. 'Don't drink too fast. It's not good for you.' He was a black shape against the backdrop of firelight, the cape slung across his shoulders. She could not see his expression, but he sounded amused.

'You're enjoying this, aren't you, you devil?' she croaked.

'No. And it's not as bad as you think. You'll get used to it,' he said, then pointed to where some of the men had slung a billy can over the flames and were preparing their supper. 'Keep away from them. Quico has built a fire for you and Dulcie yonder. He's making food. Go and eat.'

He disappeared into the darkness and Berenice, after watering her horse and making sure he was comfortable and securely tethered, went in the direction he had indicated. There she found Dulcie and Greg, with Quico leaning over the flames and stirring something in a cooking pot. It smelt rich and gamy, stomach cramps reminding her that she had not eaten for hours. Quico looked different, taller and more dignified in his native costume of doeskin trousers, with a beaded belt and necklace. His straight ebony hair fell across his shoulders, and around his brow was a painted leather strip.

Berenice sank down on the blanket that Dulcie had spread out, the whole scene seemed so unreal that it came as no surprise to find that Greg was also wearing Indian gear; moccasin boots decorated with colored beads, thigh-high buckskin leggings with fringed outer seams, a long, loose deerskin hunting shirt with further fringes at sleeves and hem, and a cap made of a whole coonskin with the tail dangling down behind.

'You've gone native, too,' she said, stretching out gratefully on the rug, certain that she would never be able to move again.

'Oh, this—' he answered casually, trying to coax a smile from her lips. 'It's pure affectation, ma'am. Sweaty in warm weather, chilly in cold, but what every well-dressed trapper wears. It sets off a tall, good-looking kind of person mighty well, don't you think? And draws the eye of every woman. Why else do you suppose I've adopted it?'

He was teasing her gently, and she smiled at this endearing man who seemed to be Sebastian's closest friend. She was sure that his indolence was a cloak behind which he hid his real nature, realizing that he was probably just the sort of person to have on hand in a crisis. He would be quick-witted and cool-headed in action, and she noticed that he had added a cutlass to the hunting knife which he wore

256

in a fancy sheath at his belt, while a long, wicked-looking musket lay at his side.

'You look magnificent,' she answered. 'But don't pretend with me. I'll wager that you're no stranger to the wilds.'

'You've got my measure.' His sharp blue eyes considered her anxiously as he wondered if Sebastian was pushing her too hard. 'Even these fancy fringes have their uses—they tend to drain off the rain, and they're also a ready source of binding thongs. So, if your garters break, come to me and I'll lend you a couple.'

'D'you think there are Indians about?' Berenice asked, nervously listening to the unfamiliar night sounds echoing through the forest.

Greg took a bowl to the pot suspended over the crackling logs, ladling out hot soup. 'I expect they know we're here. This land once belonged to the Cherokees, and in the early days there was bitter fighting between them and the settlers. Ain't that so, Quico?'

The Indian nodded, standing just within the light of the flames, arms folded, head at a haughty angle. 'Yes, Dr. Lattimer,' he replied, in his deep voice. 'Now they're mostly employed in the peltry trade. The Comte knows them well—he buys their skins. They won't attack us. Sometimes there's violence, when the young braves have too much liquor.'

'Don't worry, Berenice,' Greg said. 'Sebastian's mighty sharp when it comes to posting guards, and he brings me along as his medicine man.'

'If you're so skilled, can't you give me something to put on these insect bites?' she begged, her skin sore and itchy, though she was feeling better, now that she had food inside her. She was young and resilient. Sebastian had been right when he predicted that the journey would not do her any lasting harm.

'I could,' he said, 'but Quico's the one who knows about herbs. He'll give you some salve.'

'Try this, madame.' The Indian produced a small stone jar from his pouch. When she lifted the lid, the contents had a strong smell that made her nose wrinkle but, after applying it to her face and neck, she was aware of instant relief.

'You know an awful lot, don't you?' Dulcie said, beginning to revise her opinion of Quico.

During their stay in Charleston, Dulcie had been conscious of Quico's presence, wondering whether he was spying on her mistress or guarding her. There was no denying that he had always been somewhere in the vicinity. He looked totally different in Indian clothing—dignified—almost lordly. Dulcie had always dreamed of marrying a nobleman, and scoffed at herself for her foolishness. How could she, a baseborn thief, ever hope to achieve such an ambition? Now she looked at Quico in a new light, seeing his almond-shaped eyes, those high, flat cheekbones, his magnificent build. Why, he could even be labeled handsome!

'I learn much at my grandmother's knee,' Quico told her, the shadow of a smile lifting his chiseled lips. 'I teach you, if you want.'

'Would you? I'd be interested.' Dulcie inched nearer to him. 'I worked for an apothecary once, not for long, mind you—he was a mean old skinflint and wouldn't pay me, but I was fascinated by the things he had there, and the bunches of herbs hanging from the beams. He distilled them into lotions to cure everything from a raging toothache to a boil on the backside.'

Quico gave a rumbling laugh. 'I do all that, and more.'

'I'd like to hear about it,' and Dulcie smiled up at him, feeling much better, warm somehow, and protected.

Berenice sat beside Greg on the springy turf, arms clasped about her raised knees. She had peeled off her velvet coat, and her blouse felt clammy. There was too much of it, the full sleeves gathered in at the wrist. She unbuttoned the cuffs and rolled them back. The neck plunged deeply, showing the curve of her breasts, and her bare head shone in the fire's glow, hair spreading across her shoulders like a dusky cloud. Greg studied her face with his slow, warm smile.

'You should wear something simpler to-morrow,' he advised. 'Trousers would be more convenient.'

'Really! I've never worn such things. It's not the done thing where I come from,' she shot back, then began to mull it over. Maybe he was right. It would be easier to ride astride; sidesaddle was not comfortable on a long journey. 'And where am I to find a pair to fit me?'

'I'll make some enquiries. There are several lads among us about your size. Leave it to me,' he promised, lighting up a cigar and drawing the aromatic smoke back into his lungs. 'I think Sebastian would agree.'

She stiffened, that nice, relaxed feeling vanishing. 'I shan't ask him. If I want to wear trousers, I shall.'

'Berenice, why d'you turn everything into a battle?' Greg asked, cigar between his teeth as he started to hone his knife on a whetstone. 'Sebastian takes some knowing, but it's worth it.'

'You've a high opinion of my husband, haven't you?'

'He's one of the best. There's no one I'd rather have as a friend, or fear more as an enemy. Why do you ask? Is something bothering you?'

He slipped his knife into its sheath and rested back on his elbows, regarding her seriously, sensitive to the hostility between Sebastian and his bride. She had been something of a surprise, for he had been expecting a demure English rose, not this stormy creature with her independent attitude, and almost pagan beauty. In many ways he was glad, knowing that Sebastian would never have been happy with a compliant wife. He needed all the stimulus she could give him, yet Greg was worried by her unhappy eyes and the rebellious slant to her mouth. And he agreed one hundred per cent with Sebastian's decision not

260

to leave her to her own devices in Charleston.

Berenice shrugged, tossing her loosened hair. 'What do you expect, sir? I was compelled to give up my life in London, for this!' She cast a shuddering glance at the shrouding trees that looked so black and menacing. 'I didn't want to marry him in the first place, and his behavior towards me has done nothing to make me alter my opinion. I've never met such an overbearing person!'

Greg shook his head dubiously. To his way of thinking, they were perfectly matched, two proud, headstrong individuals who would end up either murdering one another or falling deeply in love. He had watched them, knowing from his experience in amatory matters that there was only a thin line between the two emotions. So often quarrels could end in kissing, the lust of hate merging into the lust for love. If they settled their differences, he could see them becoming a formidable team, faithful unto death. But if not, then their disagreements could end in a violent explosion, the shock waves of which would be felt by everyone around them.

'I'd sure like to see you two happy one day.' Devoted to Sebastian, he wanted to convince her of his sterling qualities. 'He's full of plans for Oakwood Hall.'

'The plantation house?' Berenice was interested, despite herself.

'Sure, he's already made many improvements. He's ambitious, Berenice, but is renowned for his just treatment of his slaves, black or white. I think he'd free them if he could. The trappers and traders respect him for his fair dealings, those who are any good, that is. And he's popular with the Indians.'

'You make him sound like a saint,' she remarked acidly, refusing to betray the eagerness with which she snatched at each crumb of information, denying even to herself that she longed to know her husband's heart and mind.

Greg's face became serious. 'Look here, Berenice,' he began. 'He had a difficult time in France. I don't know everything that happened—he won't talk about it much—but things were bad. When I met him, he'd been on the high seas—'

'A pirate!' she spat out the word in disgust.

'Yes, a pirate, but only taking ships that belonged to the Revolutionary Government. Can't you understand? He'd been robbed by them—had lost everything—he wanted to stop them.'

'That's no excuse.' She could bear no more, and tried to struggle to her feet.

Greg pulled her down again, making her listen. 'Don't be so goshdarn stubborn! The man has suffered more than you or me will ever know, but he has tried to build up a new life. Not only for himself, but for those around him, too. He's talked to me at length, telling me that he believes in order, in progress, in justice, and for a long while now has felt that his life was incomplete, lacking in a vital element. He needed a wife and children to impose a kind of symmetry on his existence. He was so excited when he left to fetch you from England.'

'He was?'

'Like a kid.'

'Then what went wrong?'

'*You* tell *me.*'

For a few minutes she sat there turning over all he had just said, but then the insect bites started to smart again, and her muscles ached every time she moved. Why should she give Sebastian any quarter? He showed her no mercy. She got up, trying not to groan, and stood above Greg, her face sullen.

'Don't waste your time trying to whitewash him. It won't work with me,' she said, and left him to find Peregrine.

EIGHT

The alteration in Sebastian was subtle but marked. All that day Berenice had witnessed his ease in the saddle, his habit of squinting up at the sun, his smile when one of his men made a joke, the confidence with which he handled his musket and sword. She did not know him at all—he was even more of a stranger.

Now he was with his men. She could see his tall figure outlined by the leaping scarlet flames. Some of the men were kneeling by the fire, consuming their supper; others, replete, had wrapped themselves in their blankets and were already asleep; some sat smoking and talking quietly. Damian was perched on a tree stump, tipping a bottle to his lips, head tilted back, Adam's apple bobbing up and down as he swallowed. It had been passed to him by Colonel Perkins. She felt neglected because her brother had not come to find out how she fared, but could see that he was too busy with his companions.

Pressing needs of nature had to be met before she did anything else, no matter what lurked in the bushes. So Berenice crept into a hollow behind a gnarled tree, its roots twisting into the soil like deformed limbs. All the while, she cursed Sebastian for bringing her to such a pass, feeding her anger, making it flourish within her. Rearranging her clothing, she went across to Peregrine who was hunched against the bole of a pine, looking every bit as miserable as she felt.

He glanced up, saying fretfully, 'My dear lady, are you quite exhausted? What a grueling day? So long in the saddle. I swear I'll never be able to close my knees again.'

'Such an adventure doesn't appeal?' Poor Peregrine, she was thinking, it's because of me that he's enduring this discomfort.

'I don't believe that I'm designed for adventure,' he observed wryly.

'But you enjoyed yourself in Charleston?'

'Of course. I was among people of the first consequence, and I don't think I boast when I say that I cut rather a dash,' he smirked, and she smiled at the fashionable cant he habitually employed.

'Then it stands to reason that you'd do as

well in Georgetown, doesn't it?' she hinted, wondering if she could rely on his courage. She decided to try, resting her hand on his arm. 'Peregrine, listen to me. Shall we run off, as we once planned? I think I can remember the route to the river. There we could be ferried to Charleston, and find a ship to take us north.'

The idea appealed to him. He was already tired of being ordered around by Sebastian and shouted at in that rude, sergeant-major manner by the colonel. A single day of it had been quite sufficient. Unlike Damian, he was finding it impossible to fall in with the rough, bawdy humor of the others, and was outraged that Berenice had been forced to ride among them. Admittedly, they were far too well aware of their leader's watchful eye to attempt any familiarity with his wife, but this did not protect her from their stares, and murmured comments concerning her face and figure. The distance which Sebastian placed between her and the men he employed was almost feudal, even Dulcie was kept away from them, but nevertheless, Peregrine was anxious. Supposing Sebastian met with an accident? What then? The colonel was an elderly man who would be quickly overpowered. And Greg Lattimer? Peregrine didn't much like the way the Southerner looked at him.

All things considered, he was inclined to fall in with Berenice's proposal, though alert to the hazards. Not only was there Sebastian's wrath if they were discovered, but the dangers of the journey were manifold, since neither knew the terrain. How could they hope to reach Charleston safely?

'Shall we do it?' Berenice was pressing close to him. 'Shall we ride away tomorrow, while the others rest in the noonday heat?'

'What of the guards on watch?' he demurred. Berenice found his caution discouraging, but told herself bravely that it was due to his concern for her.

'I'll go into the woods on the pretext of relieving myself, while you make it known that you're taking our horses to the stream to drink.' Her face was eager, and Peregrine began to take fire from her daring. 'I've some money—enough to pay for the ferry, and then I can go to my bank. I'm sure we can find a captain in the port who'll take us as passengers to Georgetown. You do still want me, don't you, Peregrine?'

'Of course I do, my angel,' he whispered, his fingers closing on hers, happier now that she was his companion again. He had rather missed her amid competition from such forceful rivals as Bradley Banis and the like.

She darted a glance across the clearing, but it was too dark for them to be seen. He attempted to kiss her but, made clumsy by nervousness, he missed her mouth, his lips finding her cheek instead.

Her brain was working feverishly, planning every detail of their escape. As yet she had only the vaguest notion of what she would do if they succeeded in reaching Georgetown. No doubt there would be a hue and cry. Perhaps she could throw herself on the mercy of Peregrine's aunt; all she wanted was to return to England, explain everything to her father and ask that the marriage be annulled. It would not be easy and might take years, but she was convinced that anything would be better than the servitude which Sebastian expected.

She left Peregrine and went back to where Dulcie was still deep in conversation with Quico. 'You can't read?' she heard her maid saying, and smiled when she added, 'I'll teach you! And how to write, too.'

Sebastian came across, carrying some blankets. He tossed them to her, saying, 'Lay them out under that tree over there. There are enough for the two of us.'

'You expect me to sleep beside you? In the open?' she gasped.

He gave her a sideways glance. 'Would you prefer to lie near the men?' he asked with a lopsided grin.

'I thought—naturally assumed—the wagon—I could make up a bed there.'

'No room. It's full of goods.'

'Then I'd rather have a corner of the forest to myself,' she began, but stopped, remembering the wild beasts, maybe poisonous snakes and stinging insects.

They might come crawling towards her once the camp was quiet. With an exasperated snort, she tramped over to the spot he had pointed out and started to arrange the blankets. He was the most infuriating of men. Since their latest quarrel his manner had been cool to the point of indifference. Beyond seeing that she was as comfortable as conditions would allow, he ignored her, staring right through her when their paths crossed. This rudeness was exasperating. He was behaving as if she hardly existed, and Berenice was insulted. If he intended to keep up this behavior, then she certainly had no intention of remaining with him—the boor!

But as she tossed and turned on the uneven ground, she became frightened by the dense blackness of the woods, and alarmed by the grunts of animals prowling the camp's perimeter. She heard stealthy rustlings in the undergrowth, and was sure they concealed stalking Indians. She pulled the rough blanket over her head, longing for the comfort of a strong body next to hers, and Sebastian's arms offering protection. As she fell into an uneasy doze, she thought of how it would be to snuggle against his broad chest, knowing that he would shield her from the dangers of the night.

She dozed at last, and then woke in a panic as she thought she felt someone touching the coverings. In an instant she was in Sebastian's arms, clinging to him, and, somehow, they were beneath the blankets and he was still holding her, his hands moving soothingly over her back as if she were a terrified child. Reason told her to tear herself away from him, but she could not do it, burying her face in his cloak. She was shivering, worn out, unable to register any emotion but the need to have him there. He shifted so that her head rested on his shoulder, and a feeling of calm stole over her.

Sebastian did not speak or move, lying flat on his back, staring upwards. Everything was very clear and dramatic in the moonlight, and he was in an unusually introspective frame of mind, touched by Berenice's need of him, aware of that soft body curled trustingly next to his. He came to the disturbing conclusion that he was a cad. He had no right to bring her to this place, no right to force her into marriage. The agreement could have been broken without too much trouble on either side. Had he not vowed, once upon a time, that if spared death on the guillotine, he would spend his life making amends for any wrongs his family might have inflicted on the peasants, and ensure that he never hurt anyone in the future?

Revolution! How ugly a word, and how terrible it had been to see his country torn apart by bloody conflict. The revenge of the downtrodden masses had been swift and brutal—anyone vaguely connected with the hated *aristos* condemned without a trial. That devil-inspired machine of death which the rioters had called Madame la Guillotine, set up in the center of Paris, its blade flashing up and down ceaselessly, spouting blood—the tumbrils rumbling over the cobbles bearing hundreds of men, women and children to their doom, their only crime that of coming from a privileged class.

He could see the rabble now, hear those vicious voices screaming, '*À bas les seigneurs! À bas les tyrans!*'

They had executed King Louis XVI and his

Austrian-born queen, Marie Antoinette. And I survived that Reign of Terror—Sebastian thought—and believed that I had been spared to fulfill some god-given purpose. He remembered the girl he had loved, who had not loved him back, Giselle, who had become the leader of that fearsome band of women known as the *Megaera,* merciless harpies who had laughed to see suffering and torture, glutting themselves on blood and vengeance.

He had thought of taking his own life then. Now he smiled bitterly, stroking Berenice's back, and recalled the many other women he'd had since that time. He thought of all the dreams and passions, the longings and agony. How important it had all seemed once and how trivial now. But when he had met Berenice in her father's house, he had thought, for one flashing moment, 'She is the one!'

I was wrong, he concluded sadly, holding her in his arms through the night. Nothing matters really, life but a space between birth and death. He had dwelt on this often during other starlit treks when he had hunted with only Quico for company. It was a time for serious contemplation—the vastness of nature, the endless space of the universe. He had stretched out to the remotest regions of his mind, seeking answers which would make sense, but had always returned as perplexed as ever.

Berenice was still awake, reflecting as well. She could not fathom her mood of troubled happiness. Here she was, in a fraught situation, yet hardly aware of any reality except that of the muscular shoulder under her head. Sebastian was a shield against terror, and it was humiliating to have to confess her weakness. He was her enemy and she hated him, but somehow that hatred was burning low. He was a bully, a dreadful man, and yet sometimes, just sometimes, he could be warm-hearted, even charming, as he had been in Madeira with that dear old Spaniard, Don Santos, and she wished that he had never displayed this side of his character. It was far easier to think of him as a ruthless pirate.

She turned on her side in the crook of his arm, feeling it tighten momentarily. She was glad he was there; the world seemed very empty and primitive. Then, incongruously, strains of melody crept over the clearing. One of the lads was playing the flute, a sweet, trilling sound. It was the last thing Berenice heard as she drifted into sleep.

She awakened as the first faint flush of dawn spread like a gauzy veil over the sky and banished the clouds. The sun came up in a flourish of rainbow hues, and the birds started to chatter. The air was cold and dew lay heavily over the blankets. Berenice was aware of a loss of heat at her back. She sadly realized Sebastian was no longer there.

The men were stirring sluggishly. There were laughs and curses and prodigious yawns. Two were already squatting near the embers, warming their hands round steaming mugs of coffee. A third stood over them, stretching and rubbing his knuckles into his eyes. But where was their leader?

Berenice's overstrained muscles protested when she moved, and she did not know how she was to endure another day in the saddle. There were two things she craved above all—water to wash in and a cup of strong coffee. Normally, such comforts were served automatically, but here, it seemed, she must fend for herself. Her eyes roamed the clearing, unconsciously seeking Sebastian. Though she would have died rather than admit it, she was wondering why he had left her. Angrily she scrambled to her feet, trying to smooth out the creases in her crumpled skirt. Pushing the tangled hair back from her face, she caught sight of him near the fire and watched him covertly. He seemed to be happy in these primitive conditions, and friendly to his men, that evil-looking bunch who persisted in calling him Captain. It shamed her to think that the hard-visaged man, who commanded them like some brigand chieftain, was her husband.

'Oh, milady, is that you?' Dulcie said, coming awake to find her setting the metal coffeepot on the remains of the fire. 'Let me do that,' she insisted, throwing aside her blanket. 'It's not right and proper that you should soil your hands.'

'Don't be a goose,' Berenice smiled, fastening her heavy hair back with a ribbon. 'We're in this together, aren't we? But we could do with a bucket of water.' She saw her brother coming out from the trees. 'Damian!' she shouted. 'Will you fetch me some water, please?'

Sebastian was standing by the main campfire and his head went up as her voice rang across the glade. He was unshaven and his hair was uncombed and, in that clear morning light, he seemed so alien. Part of her said that she preferred it that way—wanted him to keep his distance. And yet, there were those nights of passion she had spent in his arms—and the bitter-sweetness of his gentle embrace during the dark hours just passed.

'Did I hear you shouting for water?' He rasped, halting before her, his tanned face unsmiling.

Berenice's chin lifted; eyes flashing at him. 'You did. I want to wash away yesterday's dirt. You may not do so, but I make a habit of cleanliness.'

'Then you'll have to take a bucket to the stream yourself,' he answered, hands on his hips, legs spread. 'Madame la Comtesse must learn to provide for her own wants.'

'Surely my brother can help me?' she began, aware that his men were grinning at her.

An unpleasant smile formed around his lips. 'Oh, no, madame—you'll fetch and carry for yourself.'

'I'll go, Sebastian,' Damian broke in, looking anxiously from one angry face to the other. 'She's not used to work of any description.'

Sebastian hesitated, then shrugged and said, 'You're not doing her any favors by encouraging her. She's got to learn to survive out here.'

'She'll learn, I promise. Give her time,' and Damian picked up the bucket and, putting his arm round her waist, said, 'Come along, Sister. Let's do it together, eh?'

Dulcie was embarrassed, feeling it her duty to wait on her mistress, but she could see that Sebastian was talking sense. To be helpless was a definite disadvantage here. So she started to collect kindling and helped Quico to cook breakfast. A street urchin, who had never lived in the country and whose only experience with cattle was when the drovers herded them through London for slaughter at Smithfield Market, Dulcie was enchanted by the woods, the birds, the sense of limitless freedom.

'I think I'd like to be a farmer's wife,' she confided in Quico, who did not answer, but merely looked at her with sparkling black eyes.

On her return, Berenice was experiencing hunger pangs, and readily accepted the food which Dulcie offered, adding it to maize cakes that the maid produced from her basket, brought all the way from a Charleston bakery. She was allowed little time to do more than splash her face and brush her hair, when Sebastian gave orders to break camp. But before they left, Greg brought over a bundle and gave it to her.

'What's this?' she asked, viewing it with distaste.

'Boy's clothing.'

She retired behind a tree and presently emerged wearing a shirt and waistcoat over a pair of cotton trousers held up by a belt, as they were too large for her. She had retained her red leather boots. Sebastian grinned when he saw her.

274

'That's much more suitable,' he said. 'But you'll need a straw hat.' And he found one in his knapsack, along with something else.

'What do you call that?' she wanted to know. It was of coarse wool, patterned in broad stripes.

'A *chiripa*.'

With an agile swing, he tossed the shawl-like cloak over her head, settling its round opening about her throat and arranging it so that she could move her hands. It reached halfway between her knees and ankles, and he girded it in with a leather thong. For an eternity that lasted no more than a second, she felt his hands at her waist, tying the makeshift belt, and could not meet his eyes, remembering another time, another place, when those well-shaped fingers had had intimate knowledge of her body.

'I hope the thing is clean,' she said pithily. 'I don't fancy playing the host to fleas.'

'It's clean,' he said, smiling grimly.

In the saddle once more, Berenice guided her gelding over the rough ground, while the sun climbed steadily, relentlessly sucking every vestige of moisture from the scorching earth. It was appallingly hot by noon, and Berenice rode in a daze, her clothing sticking to her, the sweat trickling down her face from beneath her hat. All around her, thick forest dipped and swayed, filled with creatures who fled away as the riders approached.

It was as if they were traveling through a vivid curtain of green, the foliage closing in on them, shielding them from the sun yet adding to the humidity. Gnats and flies plagued them as they went, and the birds jabbered and shrieked like fiends amidst the brilliant, sickly-sweet blossoms. Jogging along, her eyes fixed on Sebastian's straight back just ahead, Berenice found it most disheartening. Oh, there were towns, of course—much of America had been settled for years, but here it was still untouched, almost a jungle, as old as time itself. God! How could she ever live in such a place?

She glanced at Peregrine who was riding at her side, and could see by his expression that much the same thoughts were running through his head. Damian, however, was completely captivated, engaged with Greg in lively conversation, of which she caught odd snatches.

'I very much regret not being among the first men to conquer this land,' he kept saying. 'I'd like to claim a stretch of it as my own.'

'That could be arranged,' Greg answered reassuringly. 'I'll have to teach you how to hunt with a bow and arrows, and how to fell those towering trees so much in demand for timber. A man can make a good living out here, if he knows how.'

She had never seen Damian so happy, his fair skin kissed by the sun, impatient to don trapper's clothing, like Greg's. Berenice sighed. She had lost her ally. Close though she had once been to her brother, he was now infatuated with America, busy striking up friendships with those tough fellows who followed Sebastian.

'I don't think I'll ever be able to settle

here,' she butted in, gentling her horse who had spooked himself by the sudden twitching of a branch. 'I want to go home.'

'To England? Don't be silly, Berenice. This is your home now,' Damian answered, with unusual briskness.

Berenice shriveled. Her brother had never before spoken to her thus. Peregrine was her only hope, and she knew that they must act soon, before putting further miles between themselves and civilization. When they paused to rest and water the horses, she whispered to him as they dismounted.

'Are you ready?'

'All right,' he muttered, but seemed less than enthusiastic.

'Dulcie.' Berenice had decided to take her into her confidence. 'I'm leaving.'

'Leaving, my lady? What d'you mean? You can't!' Dulcie, hot and flustered and certainly not enjoying the ride, gripped her mistress by the arm as if she would forcibly prevent her.

'I can. Even if I perish in the attempt, it will be preferable to living in my husband's satanic shadow. Don't worry, I'll send for you later, hopefully.'

The men were tired and hungry, tethering their animals in the shade where they could crop the turf, and throwing themselves down under the great trees, enjoying a siesta. Some took turns on guard duty, muskets primed and ready, weatherbeaten faces alert, hardbitten fighters, many of whom had seen active service in the Indian wars.

Nervousness was making Berenice's stomach muscles tighten. It was not going to be easy, even though Sebastian lay on his back on the grass, hands locked beneath his head, eyes closed. Colonel Perkins had been put in charge and she noticed that in the sleepy atmosphere of the quiet clearing, his head was starting to nod.

'I need privacy for a moment, Dulcie,' Berenice announced loudly, and started to stroll off down a small, overgrown path that connected to where Peregrine was standing by the stream, the reins of two horses held lightly in his hands.

Once the bushes screened her from the camp, she hurried to join him, her heart beating like a drum. His anxious face did nothing to reassure her, and she felt angry with him, wishing that he could have showed more élan. It seemed that she had to make every decision, and she found herself doubting his ability to carry off such a venture. There was nothing for it but to try—it was now or never.

'Shall we go?' she whispered.

'Yes,' he answered, impressed by her bravery and fascinated by the way the sunlight caught her eyes, turning them to sapphires, slanting across them to spill down to her lips.

She was a woman in a million and he wanted her. He had been deprived of women for too long. In Charleston there had been no opportunity to find a brothel, and Peregrine was not used to curbing his desires. He was unable to think further than the fact that they would soon be alone and he might be able to make love to her.

Berenice strove to be practical. 'Did you bring some food, a water-bottle—pistols?' she asked, trying to keep the nagging edge from her voice as he inveigled an arm round her waist. Now was certainly not the time. Lord! There'd been chance enough for him to show affection. Why must he choose *this* moment?

'Yes, yes. I've brought everything you said.'

'Good. Come along, Peregrine. We must hurry!' she urged.

'Don't worry, darling,' he murmured, thrilled by the idea of abducting another man's wife. It was not the first time—he preferred women of experience—whores or bold-eyed matrons. He found Berenice even more attractive for knowing that she had been possessed by Sebastian.

'We mustn't delay.' Berenice was suddenly uneasy at the look in his eyes. He was her savior, her gentle knight; with her bruised emotions she was not ready to accept him as a lover—not yet.

She mounted quickly, the horse quiet under her sure hand, and Peregrine jogged beside her as they went deeper into the forest. They would have to retrace their steps of that morning, but did not dare to do so for a while. First, they must put several miles between them and the uproar which was bound to arise when their escape was discovered—and this could be at any moment.

As soon as it was prudent to do so, Berenice urged her beast into a trot, controlling her longing to go faster, her ears straining for any noise from the rear which would tell her that they had been missed. But all was quiet, the forest a thick wall of dense green, the stream winding along on their right. The afternoon heat was remorseless, but still they dared not stop, until at last they broke out on clearer ground and burst into a gallop. With every thudding beat of her mount's hooves, Berenice's spirits rose in wild elation.

She had done it! She was free! Sheer joy made her reckless, and she gave the beast its head, bending low over the withers, holding on to her hat with one hand as she clung atop her surging mount, jumping fallen trunks, feeling the lower branches whip her face.

Caution prevailed eventually. She knew that she must not tax her horse, for they had a long ride ahead. As she slowed to a walk, Peregrine drew up alongside, and they rode for a while in silence, then she said, 'It's essential that we find a safe spot to camp before nightfall. Do you know how to light a fire, Peregrine?'

'I've a tinderbox in my pocket,' he replied, then added doubtfully, 'But I've never been called upon to use it, other than to ignite a candle.'

Berenice began to worry. Their flight had been well enough in theory, but now the reality scared her, and she sent up a fervent prayer that they should not fall into the hands of marauding braves. An apprehensive glance at the sky showed her that the sun was much lower now, casting mysterious shadows which would bring the blessed relief of coolness, but also meant darkness.

They followed the stream which twisted and bubbled, finally widening between low banks and flowing into a weed-edged pool. After dismounting and taking their horses to the water, Peregrine flung himself, face down, scooping up handfuls and pouring it over his head. He had long since discarded his jacket, and his shirt was sweat-stained, his breeches muddied to the knee, his boots caked in dust. Berenice pulled off the *chiripa* and her hat with a grateful sigh, shaking her head to loosen her hair. She dabbled her hands in the stream. Her skin prickled all over with heat and she longed to bathe.

After a moment, she announced, 'I'm going to swim. We're well away by now, and I can't go any further without resting. Turn your back, Peregrine, while I undress.'

He began to protest, thinking it far too dangerous to linger, but one look at her determined face told him that argument was useless, so he presented an obliging shoulder. Berenice stripped, leaving her clothes in a heap on the grass and stepping into the shallows, forgetting Peregrine's presence, in her desire for coolness. Even the thought of alligators, which had terrified her when she had first seen them in the creeks, could not deter her.

She lowered herself, then struck out boldly, calling, 'It's lovely!'

Peregrine looked round, gasping at the vision she presented. She was like a naiad. His eyes were transfixed by the grace of her slim form glimpsed through the water, hair floating behind her, her breasts rising up for a moment as she waved at him. The frustrated lust which he had controlled for so long nearly overpowered him and he knew that he had to assuage it.

Berenice, blissfully unaware of his turmoil, was lost in the new sensation of swimming naked. When joining Brighton bathing parties, she had always worn a decorous long flannel gown. This was an entirely novel experience, and she found herself wishing that Sebastian were there to share it. She permitted herself to dream of how it would be if he *was*—his strong, sun-browned body close to hers in the water—diving beneath, touching, playing, kissing.

Telling Peregrine to look away, Berenice climbed on to the bank and dressed herself again, finding the boyish attire unrestricting and pleasant, much more convenient than trailing a skirt. 'I think I'll have a suit made when we reach Georgetown,' she said. 'It might start a new fashion.'

'Indeed it might.' He was prepared to agree to anything, if only he could kiss her.

'Wouldn't it be wonderful if we could live here forever?' she romanticized, rolling up her trouser legs and sitting at the pool's edge, dabbling her bare feet in the water. 'You could build me a loghut, and we'd be as happy as the babes in the wood.'

Peregrine came to sit beside her. 'Darling, Berenice—stop talking nonsense,' he said gently. 'I don't think I could—but when are you going to let me make love to you?'

'Soon,' she promised vaguely, aware of his tension, his arm around her waist, his hand sliding towards her breasts. 'Not now, but soon.'

'When we get to Charlestown?' She had been teasing him too long and Peregrine was losing patience. He deserved some reward for laying his life on the line, for he entertained no illusions. That was exactly what he was doing.

He alerted suddenly, hearing a twig snap, but by the time he had swung round, it was too late. The glade seemed to erupt as a crowd of men came charging out of the bushes. Peregrine was too late to get to his pistols, for he was set upon by two ruffians. Berenice found her feet, scrambling up and facing their assailants, imagining for one frantic moment that it was Sebastian's men who had found them. In an instant she knew her mistake. A gang had taken possession of the clearing, shouting, pointing at her, a dozen unfamiliar scoundrels, grinning lewdly, making her burn with fear. One of them, dressed in soiled finery, swaggered to the front, and she had the quick impression of a viciously handsome face, a big frame, and a definite air of authority.

'Stow that bloody racket!' he bellowed, silencing the others.

He stared down at her and she held his gaze. His was a darkly jowled countenance, with a prominent nose, and black eyes set in smudged hollows. A smile began to deepen the curves of his thick, sensual lips, and he murmured,

'Well, here's a slice of luck! Come closer, darling, so that I can have a proper look at you. Wearing men's duds, eh? But you can't hide those womanly curves from me.'

'Stand aside,' she commanded, managing to keep her voice steady. 'I don't know who you are or what you're doing here, but you have no right to detain us.'

Her imperious tone sent the men into fresh gales of raucous laughter. 'Listen ter that!' chortled one broken-nosed hellion, giving his leader a poke in the ribs. 'A lady, by Gawd—an' she wants ter pass, the pretty little thing. You goin' ter let 'er?'

Obscene comments followed this sally, and Berenice darted a frantic glance at Peregrine, but he was shaking with fear, his captors grinning evilly as they pushed him about. Then one of them fetched him a backhanded blow across the face that brought him to his knees.

Their leader held out a grimy, beringed hand to her, saying in a crooning voice, 'Don't be shy. I won't hurt you.'

She had never seen such cold calculation as that which gleamed in his close-set eyes as he assessed her value, as though she were an animal brought to market. From the bottom of her heart, she wished that Dulcie was there—she would have known how to deal with this terrible man. One of the others ducked under his chief's arm and tried to touch her. She shrank back, longing for a weapon—a knife, a cudgel, anything.

The leader thrust him away, roaring. 'She's

mine! Maybe I'll turn her over to you later—when I've had my fill.' Then he lunged towards her, seizing her wrist and, at the touch of his fingers, she started to scream. So great was her terror that she did not realize the name that sprang to her lips.

'Sebastian! Sebastian!' Her anguished cries rang through the evening air, echoing among the treetops, reaching out across stream, forest and hill.

Sebastian heard that cry as he rode in search of her. He reined in for an instant, then urged his beast into a gallop, following the direction of the screams, his men pounding along behind him.

Rage beat like thunder in his head, and at the same time he sweated with fear for her. Running off with Peregrine! How could she have done such a foolhardy thing? The terrain was not easy, the country hard and deserving of respect. Now it sounded as if she were in trouble, and worry gained the upper hand. She might be hurt! Dying! And as he heard her shouting his name, he was overwhelmed with the desire to save her. Pray God, he'd get there in time.

When he charged into the clearing and saw her struggling in a man's arms, something snapped in his brain. He leapt from his horse and was on him like an avenging angel, seizing him by the collar and dragging him backwards. Instantly he recognized him, shouting,

'Darby Modiford! You dog!'

Modiford, recovering quickly, tore himself

free, bunching his muscles, and snarling, 'Lajeaunesse!'

'*Canaille!* Still up to your games!' Sebastian stormed. 'Can't you get a woman without forcing her? You've picked the wrong one this time—the lady is my wife!'

His men were covering Modiford's gang, the fading light winking on pistols and muskets. Damian ran to Berenice who sat huddled on the grass, arms wrapped round her body. Shamed though he was by his sister's conduct, his first instinct was to comfort her but, above all, he was furious with Peregrine. He hurled himself on the dandy, pulling him to his feet by the shirt front.

'Is this the reason you came to America, to rob my sister of her honor?' he cried, glaring into his face. 'I knew you had a dubious reputation—a gamester—a seducer, but I believed that our friendship meant something to you. God, man, how long have we been companions? How many times have you enjoyed the hospitality of my father's house? And this is how you repay him! I should call you out! Make you face me with a sword in your hand!'

Peregrine spluttered, and shook Damian off. He was still reeling from the fright of Modiford's attack and the even worse threat of Sebastian's vengeance. 'I didn't mean harm to her,' he muttered. 'Quite the reverse. Surely, you can see that she's miserable?'

'She's young and willful,' Damian answered, his eyes holding a new hardness. 'Given time, she'll settle down, but not if fools like you intervene.'

Half fainting, the scene swimming before her eyes, Berenice was aware of a great upsurge of relief. Sebastian had come! He was there, conquering that vile beast who had threatened to have his will of her.

Modiford was sneering at Sebastian, lips curled like a wolf's. 'So she's yours, is she? I might have guessed. Come back from your trip to England, bringing a bride to warm your bed. And I almost made a cuckold of you, by thunder!'

'You always were a treacherous cur, Modiford.' Sebastian's eyes were like spears. 'What are you doing on my land?'

The clearing fell silent, every eye on this confrontation. The men of either side were easily swayed—this Sebastian knew. Only a handful among his followers could be relied upon implicitly—the colonel, Greg, Quico, and a few who had sailed with him and bore personal vendettas against Modiford and his crew.

Seeing that Sebastian was not about to attack him, the unrepentant pirate preened himself in front of Berenice, as he said, 'Your land, Lajeaunesse? I question that. It was bought with the proceeds of one of our raids. You cheated me of my dues. Therefore, I've a right to come here.'

'You lie, *crapule!*' Sebastian rasped. 'You had your share. It was fairly divided. If you chose to spend it on gambling and whoring, that's not my concern. I want you off my property *now.*'

Modiford spat out an oath and sprang, agile as a cat. A knife blade glinted for an instant as he smashed the pistol out of Sebastian's grasp and brought his weapon slicing down. But, Sebastian sidestepped, whipping out his dagger. The strip of steel seemed like a living creature in his hand, spitting viciously, eager for blood. The two men circled warily, bathed in scarlet as the sun sank on the horizon, setting the pine tops aflame, darkness reaching up swiftly like spilled ink engulfing the heavens.

Berenice stumbled to her feet, her eyes enormous with terror. Damian's arms came out to hold her, sensing that she was about to rush forward and fling herself between Modiford and Sebastian. She struggled in his grip, crying, 'But he may be killed!'

Damian gave her an angry shake. 'Isn't that what you want? You've made it quite clear that you hate him and wish him dead.'

Hate him? Suddenly she wanted to hit Damian for saying that—for standing there so calmly, as if this were a game, not a grim fight in which Sebastian might lose his life. As if she were tottering on the edge of an abyss, she visualized a world in which there was no longer Sebastian to mock her, goad her, drive her crazy with desire. In a blinding flash of revelation she realized that she had fallen in love with her husband.

She could no longer deny it—it had been there from the start. That was why she had fought him so desperately, terrified of her own passionate feelings. It was insane! He disliked her, even hated her, and her action of running

288

away with Peregrine would have intensified this hatred. But she was trapped by this handsome aristocrat who had forced her to love him, even while her soul mourned the loss of its freedom. Now that he might be going to die, she could face the truth at last, trembling with fear for him, following his every move with anxiety and dread.

The contenders were well matched. Both were quick, wily and alert, and when their bodies did come together it was with a speed which drew a gasp from the men who had formed a circle round them. Berenice shut her eyes, hearing the grate of steel as the knives met. When she next looked, it was to see them struggling in close combat, glaring into each other's faces. The wicked blades were held high while each had his free hand clamped round the other's wrist to prevent that murderous steel plunging downwards. They broke suddenly. Modiford was beginning to feel the strain, his years of debauchery taking their toll. He tried to keep out of Sebastian's reach, gasping, grimacing, on the defensive, stepping backwards and sideways. Then Sebastian sprang, his weight knocking Modiford from his feet.

They rolled over and over on the grass. Then Modiford was underneath while slowly, inexorably, Sebastian brought his dagger closer to the pirate's face, inch by inch, gradually forcing back the hand that gripped his wrist. Berenice shuddered as she watched, seeing the veins standing out on Sebastian's brow under the strain, his mouth twisted into a grim smile, the sinews showing starkly on his bare throat. With every passing second, Modiford's arm weakened and the knife slid nearer to his bulging eyes, ready to plunge into his brain. The spectators leaned forward, waiting for the death blow, some grinning excitedly, others looking on calmly. For them, violent death was an everyday occurrence.

Closer the knife edged, and still closer. 'Have you had enough?' Sebastian gasped, voice tense with effort.

Modiford was not prepared to die for a principle—that was not his way. 'Very well. Let be. I'll trouble you no further,' he snarled up into the relentless face above him.

Greg had his flintlock trained on Modiford as Sebastian relinquished his hold. 'Finish him off,' he advised his captain. 'You should know better than to take his word.'

Sebastian was standing, thumbs hooked in his belt, sweat forming great dark patches on his shirt. 'I don't want his blood on my hands,' he replied, then addressed the scowling pirate. 'The next time you cross me, you'll be pulling my sword out of your bowels!'

Modiford got to his feet, staring about him truculently, while his men slowly collected their discarded arms, ready to saddle up and get away. As the pirate passed Berenice, he paused, and said,

'So, you're Madame la Comtesse? Your husband thinks he's got the better of me, but we'll see about that. I'm your servant, madame—your humble, devoted servant. Remember that.' And he swept her a deep bow before going to where his horse waited.

Berenice swayed towards Sebastian, glorying in the fact that he was still alive, longing to feel his arms round her. But she was halted by the fury in his eyes as he towered above her—savage—indomitable, still possessed by the lust to kill which it had taken every ounce of willpower to control. He vented his rage on her.

'You fool!' he thundered, gripping her by the shoulders as if he would shake the life out of her. *'Mon Dieu!* How dare you run off?'

Part of his anger was because she had caused him so much anxiety. When he realized that she had given him the slip, his first thought had been of the dangers lurking in the forests. He knew that both she and Peregrine were ignorant of trappers' lore, and would probably die unless he could find them. In a ferment, he had organized a search party and scoured the countryside like a madman, giving his men no respite.

Now that she was safe, he exploded into rage as a parent will who snatches a disobedient child from the edge of a precipice. But his anger went deeper than that. Berenice had insulted him by running away with Peregrine, making him appear the wronged husband and thus lose face. *That* he would not tolerate!

At his harsh words every sensitive feeling that had been blossoming in her heart withered and died, to be replaced by misery. He was right, of course. But even now it was hard to say what was in her heart. All she could whisper was, 'I'm sorry.'

The look in his eyes told her that he did not believe her, his lips contemptuous as he jerked his head at Peregrine. The dandy stood there uncertainly, fearful that he was about to challenge him to combat.

'And to choose *him* as your lover!' Sebastian grated. 'That mincing fop! I suppose I should be glad that it wasn't a more lusty fellow! Did he manage to roger you? Or is he incapable?'

Sick with disgust, he remembered Peregrine's face when he had burst into the glade. He had seen him, straining in the arms of his captors, watching Berenice being molested, watching with *excitement*—yes, definite excitement shining in his eyes, his body betraying all too plainly his inner emotions. The wretch was a voyeur. Sebastian had heard as much in London. Gossip had hinted that Peregrine was willing to use any crooked pathway of perversion for arousal. The thought that he might have laid a hand on Berenice drove Sebastian to the point of frenzy.

'Why did you encourage him to come with us if you hate him so much?' Berenice was so ashamed that she wished the earth would open and swallow her up.

Sebastian's face was drawn into those somber lines which betrayed the bitterness lurking in his soul. He let his hands drop to his sides, his eyes smoldering. 'I wanted you to see him for what he is—a man of straw. Had you remained apart, he'd have become sanctified in your heart.

292

You'd have genuflected each time you thought of him—pined for your lost love—blamed me for the parting.' Then, nostrils flaring, he added savagely, 'I'll share you with no one—not even a dream lover. You are mine!'

At this, Berenice flew into the worst rage he had yet seen. She stamped her bare foot on the grass, screaming, 'Damn you! I'm not yours! You don't own me just because a priest mumbled a few phrases over us!'

'Those phrases were enough, *ma doucette*,' he drawled, faking a maddening superiority. 'No matter how many tantrums you throw or how badly you behave, in this land I've the power to treat you as I think fit.'

His eyes had frozen into chips of green ice, and this statement drove her further into a blind, passionate fury. Unable to restrain herself, she flew at him recklessly, hands curved to claw at that swarthy, mocking face, but he caught her wrists as she fell against him.

'Oh, no you don't, you hellcat!' he muttered. 'It's high time you learned, once and for all, the future pattern of our life!'

She found herself lifted bodily from the ground, and even though she tore at his arms, he held her prisoner. Waves of shame laved her as she heard his men laughing, evidently delighted by the way their captain was handling his viperish woman. His fingers twined in her hair, dragging her head back, and abruptly his mouth came down on hers in a hard kiss. She stopped struggling as his lips demanded her surrender to his will. Suddenly he raised his head, and with a deep rumbling laugh, tossed her over his broad shoulder and strode to his horse. The breath was knocked out of her as he threw her across the saddle and vaulted up in front.

Once on the path that led back to the camp, he shifted her struggling body until she sat sideways, her heaving breasts pressed to his chest, held by arms that refused to let her go. Unwilling to submit, she strained away, but he gave another laugh and pulled her easily to him.

'Are you happy now, you savage?' she asked in icy tones. 'You've succeeded in humiliating me.'

'Shut up!' he growled, his tight expression giving way to a smile. 'I've not finished with you yet.'

They rode through the gloom in tense silence, his men surrounding them, the night filled with the sound of hooves. The trees thinned and the campfires glowed a dull red. When they reached the clearing which Berenice had left with such high hopes that morning, Dulcie ran to the stirrup, her face awash with anxiety.

'Oh, my lady,' she gasped, reaching out her arms to Berenice as Sebastian dumped her on the grass.

Feeling Dulcie's tender hands upon her, Berenice's knees buckled and she would have fallen had not her maid held her tightly. Gratefully, she laid her head on that soft, womanly breast, ready to give way to tears, but Sebastian would have none of it. He loomed over the two women, his face grim as his eyes raked them.

'Leave her be, wench!' he ordered.

Dulcie faced him stoutly. 'My mistress needs attention, sir.'

He frowned darkly, still beside himself with rage, recalling the ghastly sight which had met his eyes at the pool. Darby Modiford, that scoundrel whose name stank in every port! He had dared to look at her, to lay his dirty hands on her—lusting to join his poisonous body with hers. And that little fool had put herself at his mercy.

'I don't give a damn what she needs!' he lied, managing to convince even himself.

'But she's exhausted, the poor dove,' Dulcie expostulated. Much as she might consider Berenice's actions unwise, she would defend her to the death.

'Exhausted! Bah! Worn out by bad temper, more like,' he shouted, his face devilish in the dancing firelight. 'I'll have no one running errands for her. Mark this well, Dulcie, for if you disobey me, back you go to Charleston.'

'It's no use arguing with him,' whispered Berenice, reluctantly leaving the haven of Dulcie's arms. With as much dignity as she could command, she walked towards the wagon.

He delivered a final barb. 'Don't bother to try and avoid me, madame, for you'll be sharing my sleeping place tonight!'

She shuddered at his words, and with trembling fingers found a chemise, petticoat and dress in her valise, going behind the trees and changing out of her trousers and shirt and wrapping her cloak closely around her. She wanted to hide from all eyes, still visualizing Modiford's, and cringing from the thought of what might have happened had Sebastian not arrived when he did. Never had she felt so guilty and ashamed.

Greg came over to the fireside, dropped on his hunkers, and said, 'Jeez, girl, you had a narrow escape. Modiford's about as nasty a piece of carrion as you'd find this side of the border.'

'Don't remind me,' she begged, shivering. 'I know I've been a fool, and I fear that Sebastian will never forgive me.'

'Dammit, sweetheart,' he said with a light laugh, 'can't see why you're in such a fret. Sebastian cares, all right. An indifferent man would never react so strongly.'

Sebastian, however, was being coldly, calmly efficient, posting guards in case Modiford should decide to retaliate during the night, giving orders that everyone be ready to move on at dawn. The camp grew quiet, those not on watch rolling themselves up in their blankets close to the fire. Even Dulcie slept, worn out after so much stress. Berenice huddled near the steps of the wagon, staring into the darkness. Here and there, by the glow of the embers, she could discern the shapes of sleeping men and, on the far side, she saw Quico, his brown skin gleaming, immobile as he merged into the shadows.

What were Sebastian's intentions? The

thought nagged at her unmercifully. He had said she was to share his couch, and a half-frightened, half-anticipatory thrill coursed along her nerves at the idea. She was in a wavering mood of deep confusion, not knowing what to expect. This evening he was ignoring her again, and yet she could not forget Greg's words. It *must* be true. His attack on Modiford surely showed that he possessed some feeling for her. She was so lost in thought that she jumped when a figure materialized out of the gloom.

'Spying on me again?' she snapped in fright, as Sebastian's face appeared above her.

'That's a hell of a greeting from a newly wedded bride,' his deep voice answered.

An arm shot out and reached for her, crushing her against his body. The smell of him mingled with that of the night air, a stirring combination of tobacco, rum and leather that tingled through her senses. With a muttered oath, he swung her up, his mouth seeking hers. Vainly she sought to fend him off, but at the touch of his firm lips she was fighting herself, not him, hopelessly battling to control the desire sweeping her away.

Her response deepened Sebastian's cynicism. How was a man to probe the complexity of women? Who was Berenice, this witch whose body enflamed him? Was she the cold actress who paraded before the world? Or the hot-blooded wanton whom he could so easily arouse? This girl whom he had taken to wife had the power to destroy him, if he let her.

It was not only her body he wanted—there was something else which he dared not even

297

contemplate, much less put into words, as if a roaring furnace consumed him, a fire that could only be quenched by possessing her entirely. He needed her love, her laughter, her tears—even her damnable temper! It was inexplicable and it terrified him. He recognized these feelings only too well. They were akin to those which he had once experienced with Giselle—Giselle, who had betrayed him, and through whom he had almost lost his life.

He fed his bitterness, a screen against softer emotions, distrusted of this bewilderment which was clouding his usually clear judgment. Ignoring her protests, he carried her off with fast, long-legged strides, away from the slumbering camp, and deeper into the bushes. At last he found a bower where moonlight shone through the trees between whose tracery of branches the star-stabbed vault of heaven could be seen. There he spread his blanket on a carpet of pine needles and laid her gently on it.

Though her blood was rushing at his nearness, Berenice made a last, weak effort to resist. She tried to be detached, to pretend that it was some other woman lying there under the stars. Unable to stop herself, her lips responded to his, and her hands reached up to caress his dark head. His own hands were skimming delicately over her, wooing her. She was drowning in a sea of sensations, her mind bright with flame. The smell of him, the sweet drug of his mouth where she could almost breathe the perfume of his blood as the night thickened around them like a wall. How splendid it was, the whip of desire making life run through her veins, the interplay of hands and limbs moving her to ecstasy.

'Don't deny me,' he muttered thickly. 'How I will make you feel...'

'I know—I know—'

Then he was kissing her again, his hand on her breast, opening her bodice, and her nipples rose at his touch. She pressed down on the hard thigh between her legs as he pushed up her skirt. She gasped at his experienced touch, now firm, now gentle, his fingertips expressing his joy in the warm, moist feel of her, making her shiver with delight. Their mouths came together again, and she met the searching of his tongue with flickering movements of her own. His fingers continued their delicate rhythm and she could feel herself soaring to the highest peak, mindless, abandoned, and when she climaxed with a sharp cry, she felt him raise her hips and enter her.

Then he was the sliding stave of pleasure and her body expanded to take him, aware of intense satisfaction at such melding, as if they were fused into one being. Her tears flowed like crystals, like roses spilling out of a crimson fountain, her nails curving, growing, a cat's claws marking his back.

His mouth was hers again, and she was rocking, rocking on the strong waves of a primordial ocean. Drunk, in love, she plunged and drowned, controlled by feelings above and beyond comprehension, forgetting everything, only wanting this force to sweep her forever, knowing Sebastian was trapped in the magic of it, too. The sap of life flowed hot, carrying them to the peak of pleasure.

Dying, but for an instant free, Berenice drifted down, and languor poured invisibly into the deep night of her heart. She cradled him in her arms, making him her captive, waiting with indrawn breath for the declaration that would seal his fate, but he did not speak, releasing himself from her sorceries, relaxed and spent, his eyes closed.

The exaltation diminished, and she was lying on a blanket in the middle of a forest. Already she was gathering the shreds of logic around her, sheltering behind them, feeling shame where but a few moments ago she had been ringing with triumph.

Then he spoke, 'I'll carry the marks of your nails on my back for weeks.' But his voice was gentle, pleased, and Berenice was too tired to think further. Tomorrow he would drive her to distraction again, but now there was only the ensorcelled night, bright with moonlight and filled with the drowsy churring of insects.

She coiled closer to him, her lashes like silky fans against her cheekbones. 'Sleep, *mon amour,*' whispered Sebastian and, very softly, he began to sing an old French nursery tune, rocking her gently, all passion spent, his lips caressing her hair.

'A lullaby? For me?' she murmured, lost in wonder.

'But yes,' he replied softly, and there was a sadness in his voice which touched her. 'I used to sing it to a very dear little child.'

Berenice would have liked to question him,

but found herself unable to form the words, slipping away on rosy clouds of slumber. Soon, by the evenness of her breathing, Sebastian knew that she slept, and was glad. Somehow, the fact of her sleeping meant that she trusted him. It was almost as if she had given herself, body and soul, into his keeping. He lay awake for a long time, watching the moon glide across the sky, finding an odd satisfaction in holding her, as if her body were a barrier against the ghosts of his past and the vagaries of fate, giving him the courage to face whatever life had in store.

Berenice woke before Sebastian, in that hush which precedes dawn. She lay savoring the warmth of his body, his long legs twined with hers beneath the covering, the feel of his strong shoulder under her head. She smiled, half dreaming of the night just passed, yet basking in the sweet moments of the present, a tiny oasis of peace and harmony. She sighed contentedly, nestling against him.

During that tumultuous union when she had been conquered by her own longings, it had seemed that something had flown from her body to join his, taking all fear, all bitterness with it. But as she became more fully awake, the memory of her boldness made her blush, and the thoughts which she had successfully pushed aside, returned once more to snap at her mind. Not once, even at the height of their passion, had he spoken of love. Oh, he had beguiled her with heated words such as a man would say when his blood was roused, but at no time had he given her any indication that he required more than a desirous female in his arms.

Berenice turned on her back away from him, hurt welling inside her, squeezing her heart with yearning for what might have been if only he loved her. The thought of further nights of being possessed by him in lust was repugnant to her. Yet now that she had admitted her true feelings to herself, how would she ever have the strength to refuse him?

She got up in an unsettled state of mind, looking back regretfully at his sleeping face. She ached with a love so deep that she knew it could destroy her, if she allowed it. This warmth, this pain, this sudden rush of tenderness weakened her defenses. She did not want it, had not asked for it, and longed for her freedom again—longed to know that she belonged to no one but herself. Sebastian had the power to trample on her, wound her as she had never been wounded before—by his absences, his indifference, his scorn. Maybe he would even parade his mistresses in front of her, and she would be helpless, a victim of her own absurd infatuation.

He looked different somehow, as he slept. The harsh lines had been smoothed away, and there was a boyish expression on his face under the three-day growth of beard. Despite her inner confusion she longed to hold him and brood over him with an almost maternal care, but her heart was heavy. She knew perfectly well that as soon as he woke, he would revert to the sarcastic, harsh rogue who terrified and angered her.

Moments later, he awoke and roused everyone swiftly, and within half an hour they were in the saddle. This time there was no respite. He rode like the wind, covering the miles with unusual speed, so that before noon they had left the forest behind, and were coming out on a rough track which wound along the edge of cliffs, the sea pounding and breaking against the razor-edged rocks far below. Finally, they halted, looking over the great curving bay, where a spread of dazzling white sand met an expanse of blue ocean. Mobby Cove—their destination.

The path led downwards, and Berenice was surprised to find herself before a pair of rusty spike-topped gates which stood open, half buried in weeds and undergrowth. Beyond lay an overgrown driveway leading to a ramshackle house which must once have been splendid, but was now in a sad state of dilapidation. This was a totally unexpected turn of events. Somehow, Berenice had never thought their journey would lead them to a dwelling place—and such a place as this!

It was large, rambling, and constructed like an English Tudor manor, built of stone and timber with a gabled roof. Part of this had caved in and, from under the broken eaves, latticed windows with tiny panes stared down like empty eye sockets. The ornamental stonework had crumbled in many places and the heavy oak front door hung from blackened hinges. Berenice dismounted, while from an equally

303

derelict building at the back a large man came out to greet them. His eyes and teeth gleamed in the blackest face she had ever seen, and his wide smile did much to dispel the sense of doom which had overwhelmed her at the sight of her new home.

'Master! I bid you welcome,' he addressed Sebastian in a rich, rolling voice which seemed to rise from the depths of his massive belly. 'It's too long since you were here. Just you wait till Jessy sees you!'

Greg whispered to Berenice the man's name was Adam. Adam was dressed in a shabby scarlet coat that did not meet over his ebony chest, while breeches of a peculiar mottled green fell to his knees, and his bulging calves and large flat feet were bare. He bowed, grinning with delight to see Sebastian again. Now others came running, an assorted collection of men, women, and children, some white, some brown and some of various shades between. Dogs barked somewhere at the rear, and Sebastian's men climbed from their mounts with shouts of glee.

There was a good deal of back-slapping and embracing, and Greg buffeted Adam affectionately, crying, 'Hi there, Adam! How goes it at Buckhorn?'

Berenice and Dulcie stood forgotten in the excitement, then Sebastian took her by the hand and presented her. 'This is my wife—Lady Berenice, Comtesse Lajeaunesse.'

His staff smiled in a friendly way, but there was a hint of suspicion in their eyes as if they were not sure what to make of this astoundingly beautiful woman who held her head so high, and had a hard, wary look in her blue eyes. Who was this creature the master had brought home? They had expected a gentle English rose, but she had the brilliant coloring of a jungle orchid.

Adam was the first to speak, a large-hearted man, devoted to Sebastian. He would be proud to serve the Comtesse, just as he was proud of Sebastian's trust in him, for he had been left in charge of Buckhorn House during Sebastian's lengthy absence. Adam was always eager to prove his loyalty to this man who had given him his freedom.

'You are most welcome, Lady Berenice,' he said, bowing. 'You just call for Adam if you want anything.'

'Aren't you going to introduce me, Sebastian?' A voice rang across the courtyard, lilting and melodious.

Berenice's eyes lifted and she stared in the direction of the stone steps that led to the entrance of the house. A woman stood there, tall, arresting, wearing a low-cut white lace blouse and a pleated scarlet skirt. Gold rings flashed in her ears against the fall of straight, ink black hair, and necklaces glittered round the olive skin of her throat. She was a beauty, long of limb, full of bosom, moving with the grace of a sleek animal as she paced towards them. Her dark eyes came to rest on Berenice, and her face was cold, but when she switched her gaze to Sebastian, warmth transformed those thin features. Berenice saw him smile back, his hands meeting the woman's, holding them in a tight grasp, as he answered,

'Juliette! *Chérie,* how are you? Come, meet my wife.'

Unable to speak for the agitated pounding of her heart, Berenice noted how Juliette hung possessively on his arm, while he continued to smile down into that dark, lovely face. Juliette gave her a hostile stare, and any hopes Berenice had been harboring with regard to her husband, died in the presence of this powerful rival.

NINE

It was the most devastating moment of Berenice's life, calling for a fortitude which she did not dream she possessed. All that she could do was shelter behind an icy, indifferent calm, so that no one would guess the fury boiling within her.

'So, you are the English lady who has dared to enter the lion's den, are you?' Juliette mocked.

'Not by choice,' Berenice retorted.

'No?' The finely marked brows lifted. 'That's hard to believe. Aren't you pleased with your bridegroom?'

Without deigning to give her an answer, Berenice looked down her nose at Juliette, then turned to Sebastian and said,

'Are we going to stand here all day? I've had enough of the heat. I want a bath.'

'A bath, Madame la Comtesse?' Juliette interrupted rudely, eyebrows shooting up. 'This isn't one of your fancy hotels, you know.'

'Even you, must wash sometimes.' Berenice pushed back her snarled curls, furious because she looked a mess at the very moment when she needed to put this woman firmly in her place. 'I suppose you've heard of hot water and soap?'

The stunned silence that followed was almost deafening, then the men burst into laughter, while Juliette almost danced with fury. 'Tell her!' she shrieked at Sebastian. 'Tell her who I am!'

His smile faded. 'And just who *are* you, Juliette? I don't recall giving you any authority around here.'

Juliette flounced off, but not before flinging Berenice a glance of undiluted venom. Sebastian and Greg exchanged a glance. 'Sebastian, you should've shown her the door long ago,' said the young doctor. 'I've always said she wasn't no good.'

Berenice was thankful that Juliette had left before she yielded to the desire to throw herself on her and claw the eyes from her head. It was horrible! Had Sebastian brought her here with the intention of making her meet his mistress? She was convinced that this is what the woman was. Could he be so heartless, so vile? Shame engulfed her as she remembered how close she had come to admitting her love for him last night, letting him use her as he would, reveling in the sweet conquest. Never again! she vowed silently. Damn him to hell, and her with him!

A pair of brazen savages, well suited to one another. Juliette could share his bed in future.

This dreary recital went on in her head as she was conducted up the steps and into the decaying grandeur of the hall. Plaster flaked from the once-magnificent ceiling, paint peeled from the woodwork, and the paneling was eaten out with deathwatch beetle.

The big kitchen appeared to be used as the central living room, and this had been patched up. A fire was crackling brightly on the wide stone hearth, cooking-pots and sooted kettles swinging on cranes over the logs. A spit spanned the flames on which a joint of beef revolved, fat dripping down to hiss and splutter. The furniture consisted of a long refectory table littered with wine jars, plates and mugs, with benches on either side of it. And there were people everywhere, women cooking, children crying, men laughing and talking, dogs and hens running about the stone floor. Everything was dirty and untidy, but even the hostile Berenice could not deny that it had a warm atmosphere, as if this was the center of a happy little community.

It also appeared to be a temporary resting place for some trappers who had driven their pack horses into the yard and were haggling over pelts with Sebastian, who had dropped everything to attend to them. Berenice told herself that she disliked the place intensely and failed to comprehend why he didn't have it razed to the ground and rebuild, if he *must* have a property in this remote region.

At the same time she began to understand why he surrounded himself with ruffians. This rambling ruin was surely the ideal headquarters for a gang of desperadoes. The bay provided a convenient hideaway for lawless ships, and few constables would venture into the Indian-infested territory in search of smugglers. No wonder Modiford coveted it. It seemed that he had taken over during Sebastian's trip abroad, and moved out in a hurry just before they arrived.

'Where is he now, Adam?' Sebastian wanted to know as, business with the trappers concluded to the satisfaction of all parties, he prowled over to a trestle that stood in an airy corner and drew himself off a mug full of strong beer.

Adam looked at his splayed feet, his eyes gleaming. 'He's the other side of the creek, Master. That's a fact. He were scared when he heard you was on your way back, and got out of here double quick. I couldn't stop him taking over—none of us could. He came like a thunderstorm—we couldn't do nothing about it—that's the truth, before God, it is.'

His wife, a woman who kept house in a haphazard way, stood at his side, nodding in agreement, her ample body seeming to burst from her vivid blue cotton dress. Sebastian nodded slowly, believing them. He had not expected such a move from Modiford, and had left it sparsely guarded, having never really had much use for Buckhorn House, simply buying it from a member of the Quality down on his luck. He could have got there quicker by sea, but had taken the long way round by land to surprise Modiford.

There were many tales told about this old place that had been built in the seventeenth century by a nobleman exiled from England during Oliver Cromwell's dictatorship after the king's men had been defeated in the Great Civil War. He had purchased the plot and lived very much the recluse, apart from one son. Sebastian had done little to restore it; he had always been too busy in Charleston or at Oakwood Hall, or engaged in profitable ventures. Yet he loved this part of the country and was glad to be back, looking round the shabby, homely kitchen with all the relief of the prodigal returned.

Even the annoying sight of Berenice's angry face could not spoil his contentment. His soul seemed to stretch itself as he anticipated living off this bountiful land, hunting when he needed food, consorting with Whirling Hawk, the wise chief of the forest Indians with whom he had spent so much time. As he stood gazing into the flames leaping on the hearth, he remembered recent campfires and the smell of fresh meat roasting. He straightened his shoulders, determined to organize a hunt and restock the larder with venison and buffalo. Glancing at Berenice again, his mouth set grimly as he saw the disdainful way in which her eyes were studying the room and those in it. She was still so self-opinionated and proud. It was only in his arms in the dark hours that she became a warm, vibrant human being. Even her shocking experience with Modiford appeared to have taught her little humility.

She was seated at the knife-scarred table with Greg and Damian. 'Have something to eat,' Sebastian suggested, pushing over a bowl of food.

'And drink,' added Greg, lifting a tankard to his lips.

She was hungry and the food was good, and the comings and goings in the kitchen gave little opportunity for brooding. Juliette sulked in the background, and with a laugh, Greg spoke to her as he went over to the fire, took out his knife and hacked off a thick, dripping slice of meat.

'What's the matter with you?' he asked, ignoring her glare. 'Such an expression! It's enough to turn the milk sour.'

She gave vent to an oath, and tried to hit him, but he merely went on laughing and jeering, moving out of her reach, while she screamed abuse. Sebastian ignored the uproar, digging his strong white teeth into a hunk of steak, and making short work of hard-boiled eggs and wheaten bread. He can't think much of her, Berenice decided, calming down slightly, and taking satisfaction in the fact that Greg was insulting the girl and Sebastian appeared not to care.

Once she had eaten and taken a few sips of wine, she became conscious of her weariness. It was hot there, filled with the odors of braised meat and unwashed bodies. She wanted to discard the itchy *chiripa* and her soiled shirt and trousers, and suddenly leaned forward.

'What about that bath?' she asked Sebastian,

who was lounging back in his seat, booted feet propped on a strut beneath the table; lord of this thieves' den, she thought.

'Ah, a thousand pardons,' he drawled sarcastically, and slowly crushed out his cheroot, then pointed to a wooden tub hanging on a hook against the stone wall. 'I'll order my minions to carry it to my room, right away.'

'Don't bother!' she said crisply. 'You surely don't expect me to wash in that, do you?'

He shrugged as if the matter were too trivial to warrant serious consideration, swinging his legs to the floor, spurs ringing as he got up. 'The only alternative is the stream outside. And you won't find much privacy there.'

'You're nothing but a barbarian!' Berenice sprang to her feet in disgust. She always disliked sitting while he was standing, feeling dwarfed by his height.

'No, I'm not,' he said, grinning down at her. 'Merely a rough sort of fellow with a sense of humor.'

'A warped one!' she retaliated, and walked towards the door.

'Jessy,' he commanded Adam's wife. 'Take the Comtesse to my bedchamber.'

Berenice hoisted up her bag, and Dulcie went with her, the light of battle in her bright brown eyes, in high dudgeon because her lady must do her own chores. Berenice left the kitchen with her head in the air, though imprinted on her mind for all time was the picture of Juliette and Sebastian standing together, with her tugging at his arm and launching into shrill

312

complaints about Greg.

She could not forget her face, those baleful black eyes so full of hate whenever they looked at her, that curved nose and full red mouth, and that long hair—falling to below her waist in one straight, unbroken sweep of burnished ebony.

Jessy led the way as they recrossed the hall, pushing open a battered carved door and standing aside for Berenice to enter. She smiled widely, spreading her plump arms in a gesture of apology, saying, ' 'Course, it's a mite dusty.'

Viewing the chamber, Berenice dourly considered this to be the understatement of a lifetime. It was a huge room which must once have been an imposing salon, the lofty ceiling crusted with crumbling plaster and faded gilding. Perhaps, longing for England, the gentleman who had built it had added the large fireplace made of oak, carved in a pattern of acanthus leaves, with two nearly life-sized Titans supporting the massive, ceiling high chimney breast.

Tall double windows with tattered brocade curtains led out on to a terrace, where weeds sprouted between the paving stones. Insects scurried for cover across the scuffed cedarwood floorboards as they entered, and a huge, furry spider remained stationary for a moment, before scrambling through a hole in one wall. Dulcie gave a horrified snort. Filthy though the room was, she did not doubt her ability to render it habitable, but she was upset that Berenice should be forced to use it in its present disgusting state.

'It's the master bedchamber,' offered Jessy, exuding a friendly warmth, watching Berenice closely, curious about her.

Berenice wanted to sit down and cry, but fought against her sinking sense of failure. Tears were for weaklings. She would show Sebastian that she was made of sterner stuff, and so she became brisk and businesslike.

'I want lots of hot water, and dusters and brooms,' she began, ticking off the items on her fingers, but Jessy lifted her shoulders in a shrug.

'I've had my orders, my lady. I can't help you. The master, he say you got to work yourself. I'll show you where everything is, though. Follow me.'

For hours Berenice toiled with grim determination, stripped to petticoat and shift in the heat, one of Dulcie's aprons fastened round her waist, her hair caught back with a thong. Cursing Sebastian with all the vehemence of her strong-willed nature, she swept and polished, scrubbed and cleaned, sweat dripping off her flushed face, and wet patches staining her chemise.

Dulcie helped her, in direct defiance of Sebastian's edict, and together they took down the drapes from the windows and the huge tester bed, dragging them outside and beating them. When she went through the kitchen, Berenice met Sebastian's eyes and gave him glare for glare.

From his comfortable position in his great armchair, feet resting on the table, he asked,

314

'*Ma foi,* madame, and how d'you like working for a crust?'

She dumped the heavy wooden bucket on the floor, careless of its slopping, and stood with her hands on her hips, such fury on her face that Sebastian pretended to cower. 'You'll not find me wanting in application,' she said. 'I'm not accustomed to living in a pigsty, even if you are!'

By early evening, both she and Dulcie flopped down in two padded chairs in the bedroom, utterly exhausted, but satisfied with their handiwork. Although the chamber was still in desperate need of redecoration, they had cleaned it thoroughly, and Berenice experienced a sense of personal triumph at its transformation.

It glowed in the late sunlight, the old carved pieces of furniture shiny with beeswax, the brass glittering like gold. The bed was a truly remarkable object, an oak four-poster with a solid paneled tester and bulbous supports. The headboard was inlaid with lighter wood and bore a coat of arms, and there were broad, low steps at each side. Berenice presumed that it had been transported from England, for Jessy had recounted the story of the exiled cavalier, and she had found it sad and romantic. Was that his family crest carved at the head? Now, with its hangings brushed, the bed looked magnificent, a couch fit for an emperor and his consort, or maybe—the unpleasant thought rushed in—a pirate king and his doxy!

'Oh, Dulcie,' she sighed, brushing her hand over her damp face. 'Do you think Juliette

315

has ever lain there with Sebastian? Is she his mistress?'

'I wondered too, when I first saw her, but I've asked Quico and he says no,' Dulcie answered. 'Don't worry about her, my lady.'

'I wasn't at all worried,' Berenice said, unconvincingly. 'She doesn't bother me in the least, but I don't like being made to look a fool. If she's his paramour, then I should know about it.'

'Yes, my lady,' said Dulcie, without believing a word.

When they had stripped the bed earlier on, they had been appalled by the dirty sheets and blankets, and had wondered what to do for the best. There was no time to wash and dry them before nightfall. Then, on one of Berenice's frequent trips to the kitchen, Sebastian had suddenly tossed her a key, muttering something about a linen press. On investigation she and Dulcie had found this to be a large closet which contained, not only linen of the finest quality, but many other treasures which they had used to turn the room into a place of beauty and welcome.

Berenice had unearthed a pair of silver candlesticks and wax candles, as well as woven rugs of Indian craftsmanship and a shawl of unique, glowing purple that she had pinned on the wall to cover an unsightly damp stain. In the bottom of a worm-eaten coffer, she had found a tarnished silver toilet set which, when buffed up, took pride of place on the heavily ornamented bogwood dressing table. They had then spent time polishing the mirrors which, though blotched, had been much improved by their efforts. All in all, the bedchamber could now almost pass as the guest room in a stately English manor.

Berenice wanted nothing more than to crawl between the fresh sheets and sleep, but she was still in a mood of defiance, her pride insisting that she put off her soiled garments and don the one fine gown which she had been able to pack. That strumpet would be green with envy when she saw her!

'I want a bath now, Dulcie,' she announced in that imperious voice which her maid knew spelled trouble, and they went to fetch the tub.

More work, more humping of buckets, but at last Berenice tore off her sweaty garments and stepped into the round wooden bath, sinking down slowly into the warm water. As she did so, she gave a long-drawn, tired sigh of relief, soaping herself languorously. Every part of her ached; she felt as if her bones and muscles were crumbling with fatigue, and there was a nagging pain in the small of her back. She held up her hands, scowling because they were red and roughened.

That fiend of a husband of hers! How dare he put her through this? She had been reared as a lady, groomed to become the dignified mistress of a great establishment, only to be brought low by a scoundrel! She slithered down in the tub, knees under her chin, brooding on her misfortunes, daydreaming of having Sebastian

317

grovel at her feet whilst she, triumphant, reviled him. It might not be too late. Surely there must be someone who would pity her and take her away from that exasperating individual?

As she pondered, her thoughts flew to Sebastian and Juliette, and the idea of them together angered her so much that her enjoyment of the bath was ruined. She finished washing hurriedly, rising and folding herself in the towel which Dulcie proffered. In no time she was dried, dusted all over with sweet-smelling powder, and ready to dress.

The gown was made of sarcenet in a popular shade known as Amaranthus, a purple with a pinkish tint. With narrow straps and a little bodice, the skirt falling from a ribbon girdle fastened just under the bosom, it was as diaphanous and fragile as a nightdress, drifting to Berenice's white kid pumps.

'Why, Dulcie,' she said, twirling before the cheval mirror, and viewing herself from all angles. 'I could almost believe I'm off for an evening at Covent Garden Theatre, to occupy a stage box, smile at the gentlemen, maybe flirt a little, and employ the language of the fan.'

'Dear old smelly London. I'd like to see it again,' Dulcie agreed, putting the finishing touches to Berenice's toilette.

'Riding in Hyde Park, escorted by gallant hussars in beautiful uniforms,' Berenice sighed.

'Ladies strolling on the grass, looking like flowers under the gentle sunlight,' Dulcie chimed in.

'The balls, the dancing-rooms where I used

318

to enjoy the company of civilized people. In London I never saw threats or bloodshed.'

'I did, madam. It was different for someone like me.'

Berenice swiveled round on the stool, gazing up at her. 'Tell me about it.'

'Oh, no, milady. You don't want to hear about things like that.' Dulcie wanted to forget the past.

'I do. I must. I fear that I've been blind and selfish. Help me to understand.' Berenice looked at her with wide, earnest eyes.

'Well, madam, it's like this. There's parts of London where you never had no call to go—Whitefriars, St. Giles, full of dark, narrow, stinking alleys where the folk are so violent that the watch won't go in there, unless they've got soldiers with them. These places offer sanctuary for thieves, and people get sort of drawn into them.' Dulcie sighed, then, continued. 'It's lack of money that does it. If you're starving, then you'll do anything for a crust of bread. Like I stole that length of silk, remember?'

'And it's impossible to escape from the trap?' Berenice was sitting upright, very quiet and serious.

'Pretty nigh impossible, I should say. If your parents were poor, then you stay poor, too. There's no money for food, and the children cry all the time—no fuel, so it's freezing cold—underpaid slave labor, greedy factory owners. I can remember fights every night, the men shouting, the women shrieking—too much gin and opium. It's cheap, you see, milady—a pennyworth can make you forget that you're tired and cold and hungry and hopeless.'

'You survived all that? Dulcie, you make me feel ashamed.' Berenice reached out and took her hands in hers, and her eyes shone with tears.

'Don't be. It's the way of things. They tried to change it in France, killing thousands of aristocrats, but I don't think it's made much difference. I'll wager that the poor citizens are as hard up as ever they were, and they're at war with us in the bargain.'

'I'd like to do something to help, if ever I get back to England,' Berenice said. 'I did try, taking baskets of food to needy villagers on our estate, but Miss Osborne used to hustle me away if ever I wanted to stop and give money to little beggar children in the London streets.'

'I know, my lady. Don't feel bad about it. You helped me, after all.'

'I'm so homesick,' Berenice confessed.

'So am I, madam,' Dulcie agreed. Then she pulled herself together, tweaked one of her mistress's curls into place, and handed her the perfume flask. Berenice dabbed the crystal stopper against her wrists, temples and throat.

'Will I do?' she asked.

'Oh, madam,' Dulcie breathed admiringly, standing back to view her. 'You look a treat, really you do. That Juliette creature can't hold a candle to you. He won't even notice she's there.'

'D'you think I'm doing this to impress him?' Berenice demanded, wondering if she

320

had betrayed herself in any way.

She could feel her face growing hot. Had Dulcie noticed something different about her? Had she seen her following Sebastian's every movement whenever they were together? Had she observed her fight to control her stumbling tongue when every coherent word fled under his disconcerting gaze?

'Certainly not, my lady.' Dulcie kept a perfectly straight face.

'It's quite immaterial to me whether he notices me.' Berenice's tone was acerbic. 'I've not changed my opinion of him one jot.'

She paced to the door, reminding Dulcie of an untamed creature resentful of the bars of its cage. Yet, experienced as she was in matters of the heart, she remained unconvinced. Though loyal to a fault, she recognized that her mistress needed some curbing and that Sebastian was the only man capable of doing so. Despite his aggressive manner, Dulcie liked him, responding to his undeniable masculinity. Peregrine was no match for the Comtesse, and Dulcie had never trusted him, recognizing his type—a self-seeking weakling, out for his own gain.

Quico, now—there was a man! He had begun to appeal strongly to Dulcie. She had never met anyone like him, a 'noble savage' indeed! As soon as Berenice had departed for the kitchen, the maid took off her clothes and used the bath water, paying attention to her own appearance. With any luck, she might see Quico later.

Earlier, Berenice had been aware of a commotion outside, voices raised in greeting and the clatter of hooves, and when she entered the large, warmly lit room, she was astonished to find it crowded with a further group of tanned, leather-clad pelt traders bringing their furs for Sebastian's inspection. Swarthy-skinned, tough and boisterous, they stared when she appeared, falling silent for a moment.

She was looking exceptionally lovely, her gown drifting about her slender limbs, its very fragility accentuated by her graceful walk, languid yet vital, her body swaying rhythmically from the hips; a woman aware of her own power, and proud of it. For modesty's sake, she had added a purple velvet spencer to her outfit, a short jacket that hugged her figure in front but swung out into a full, capelike back, the sleeves long and tight, the edges encrusted with silver embroidery. Pearls gleamed against her throat and ears, her hands bare save for the single band of gold on her ring finger. These were the only gems she had brought; for once, she had heeded Sebastian's advice and left the rest in his strongroom in Charleston. Looking about her at the bearded, roughly clad men now swarming in the kitchen, she was glad of it, for they seemed villainous enough to murder for a single diamond.

But if their appearance was alarming, their response to her was not. She discovered them to be polite, congratulating Sebastian on his good fortune in having obtained so charming a bride. To her intense and very feminine satisfaction, she totally eclipsed Juliette. A picture of annoyance, the woman was seated in the inglenook, giving ear to an ancient crone whose black and wrinkled skin resembled a walnut, and whose clawlike fingers were busy with rows of strange-looking beads that dangled round her scrawny neck, as if she were reading a rosary. Berenice was chilled by the malevolence in their eyes and, because she was nervous, she talked too much, enchanting every man present—with the exception of her husband.

He was staring at her with creased forehead and compressed lips, his hair steel blue in the shadows, looking harder, bigger and more menacing than ever, at one in this setting where savagery lurked just under the surface. He wore fawn nankeen breeches tucked into high-topped boots, a silk shirt open over his brown chest, and a pistol stuck in his wide leather belt.

Inwardly, however, Sebastian was tormented by shame when he thought of how selfishly he had dragged Berenice here, perhaps to her and his own destruction. Looking upon her, he was bewildered by such a confusion of feeling that he dared not speak. Her beauty hurt him almost physically; she was so rare, so lovely a creature. And yet she hated him so! Every word he uttered, every action he performed seemed to drive her further from him. But, *ah Dieu,* if anything should happen to her because of his pride which had insisted that he punish her! He remembered Modiford, and it was like a hot iron twisting in his gut, making him clench his big hands into hard-knotted fists.

Eventually, the trappers stopped circling round the Comtesse and returned to their drinking and bargaining, but still they smiled at her, teeth flashing in their hairy faces under the racoonskin caps, jabbering in a mixture of French and English. Sebastian slipped back into his native tongue when he talked with them, which made Berenice feel excluded, since this gave Juliette the chance to come to the fore. Berenice went across to join Greg who stood with an elbow on the corner of the mantel, a glass of beer in one hand.

'Who is she?' she hissed, giving a jerk of her head in Juliette's direction, while being careful to hold her fan as a screen between her complexion and the flames. To her horror, she had discovered that her face was turning golden brown, kissed by the sun through the days of riding.

His blue eyes laughed down at her, hinting that he knew a good deal about the state of her emotions. 'Juliette Pascal is from New Orleans. She's European—French Creole—though born here. She's got no mixed blood in her veins, witnessed by that straight hair. Her father was a rich Louisiana planter, but he gambled his money away and shot himself. Because he had been a friend of the old Comte, Sebastian promised to look after her and she came here to stay. A strange woman, very much under the thumb of old Leah, who was her nurse. It's said she's versed in voodoo, learned at Leah's knee—the crone being a native of Haiti, hotbed of that religion.'

'Voodoo?' Berenice was mystified and oddly chilled as she saw the wizened hag staring at her, lips moving as if she were holding a conversation

324

with invisible entities. 'What is voodoo?'

He hesitated a moment as if wondering how to frame his reply, then continued. 'It's a curious religion—pagan yet mingled with Catholicism. Some call it witchcraft,' he answered slowly, watching her reaction. 'A form of sorcery brought over by Africans. Some say that its rites include human sacrifice and cannibalism, but this is probably an exaggeration.'

Berenice shuddered. 'Superstitious nonsense, surely—to frighten children?' she protested, but to her alarm the smile left Greg's lips and his eyes grew unusually serious.

'Don't underrate it. I'm a doctor, a man of science, but I've seen a few strange happenings out here that are difficult to explain.' He was playing thoughtfully with the fringe on his jacket—then, seeing that he had scared her, he smiled again reassuringly. ' "There are more things in heaven and earth, Horatio, than are dreamt of in your philosophy." Speaking of which, I saw a performance of *Hamlet* recently in Charleston. You've visited our theater, haven't you?'

Berenice sensed that he was steering the conversation into calmer channels and was grateful for the change of subject. Soon she found herself telling him about London and showing off a little, whilst he good-naturedly played the ignorant colonial.

Dulcie, meanwhile, was enjoying the company of so many fascinating men. Though they had brought along several sluttish camp followers, they were delighted to find this bright-eyed girl

325

in their midst, laughing loudly at every pert sally she made. She looked spruce and fresh in a pastel cotton dress, her full bosom rising above the round neckline, but her eyes kept returning to the lanky figure of Sebastian's manservant. Presently he stepped out of the shadows and moved towards her.

'Can I fetch you a glass of beer?'

'No, thank you,' she answered, confidence fled and suddenly she became shy.

Quico tried again. 'Well, then, do you want to talk?'

'No.' She shook her head, hand raised as if to ward him off, though he had stopped feet away from her.

A faint smile touched his lips. 'Would it be in order if I asked you to walk with me under the moon?'

She nodded, then slipped away, making for the rear door. Quico looked round to make sure that his master did not need him, and followed her with studied carelessness. Berenice noticed her maid's departure, and was puzzled. She felt as if she had been abandoned by this last link with home, and even kind Colonel Perkins's conversation did little to alleviate her sense of isolation. Sebastian was taking more notice of the pair of shaggy hounds lying by his chair than of her. He dominated the gathering effortlessly. There was something so dazzling in his personality that he arrested attention wherever he went, and he seemed perfectly at ease with these hunters, whilst they obviously admired him hugely.

Berenice fidgeted as the soft pelts were spread out, examined and handled, while foreign voices talked on interminably, and Sebastian, inspecting each fur carefully, nodded and gestured with shoulders and hands, a cheroot between his lips, the blue smoke coiling up towards the blackened rafters. Berenice was about to retire to her room, when there was a noise at the door.

A guard holding a musket, stuck his face through the opening and shouted, 'Captain, there's Modiford and some of his men just come into the yard, and he's asking to speak with you!'

'Let him enter,' Sebastian said with a frown, laying down the beaver pelt he was admiring, and getting to his feet.

Modiford swaggered in, backed by some of his crew, all armed to the teeth and glaring round fiercely. Berenice pressed her back against the wall, memories of the previous day returning with horrible clarity. Modiford's black eyes found her, and he bared his teeth in a vulpine grin. He had been searching through his possessions to find a tidy suit and was certainly more presentable, no longer so filthy or alarmingly ferocious.

He wore a cutaway jacket, a striped waistcoat, a frilled shirt worn open to reveal a tanned, hairy chest, and white pantaloons which met the tops of his leather boots. His oily curls had been brushed back into a semblance of order, and he had taken a razor to his chin. But even though he had the trappings of a gentleman, he could never pass as one; on him such things as rings

327

and fobs simply looked tawdry and vulgar.

'What do you want?' Sebastian viewed him with suspicion, not a wit deceived by his friendly manner.

Uninvited, Modiford took a chair, and eyed his former associate closely. His men slunk to the table, forming a half circle about him. The trappers instinctively knotted into a group on the far side, keeping their eyes on their valuable furs, hands creeping to the hilts of the long knives glittering at their belts.

Sebastian was aware of the tension, knowing that there could be bloodshed. These men were volatile. They did not wear weapons as mere ornaments. Fights among them were frequent and vicious. Here the law was to hit first and ask questions afterwards, and with a man of Modiford's ilk, human life was held as cheap as honor.

The pirate's coarse face twisted into a grotesque travesty of a smile. 'Oh, come on, Lajeaunesse. Why be so damned uncivil? Me and the lads have come to trade—all legal-like. We've got money and we need food. What about a bit of barter, eh?'

'I don't like the way you've been using this place, but I admire your deuced nerve in visiting it now,' Sebastian remarked icily. 'Particularly in the light of what happened yesterday.'

'Well now, since you've mentioned it, that's part of my reason for coming—to offer my apologies to the lady. I'd no idea she was your wife, damn me if I had!' Modiford protested.

His eyes shifted to where Berenice stood.

He had never seen such a woman, and he had inspected many at close quarters. There was something about her which he had been unable to put out of his mind. He had been thinking about her for hours. Why, his men had even mocked him slyly, hinting that he was lovesick! He had snarled in angry denial, but there was a grain of truth in it—he was haunted by memories of her beauty, and the refinement of her speech and bearing.

Seeing her again, dressed in that purple gown which showed the curves of her body, he was even more excited and perplexed. He found himself longing to win a smile from her carmined lips, his unsatisfied lust working inwards like a slow poison, burning in his belly, gnawing at his vitals. He had so very nearly taken her! If only he hadn't been prevented by that accursed Frenchman! The hot remembrance of her struggles was enough to drive him mad. It was that—though he dared not admit it—which had projected him into this hazardous visit with his enemy.

'Would it have made any difference if you had known that she was mine?' Sebastian asked heavily.

Modiford tried to shrug this off, rising to take up a canvas bag that had been carried in by one of his henchmen. Out of its depths he pulled a mantilla of gossamer black lace which spilled over his brown, ring-laden hands as he offered it to Berenice.

'I've brought you this,' he said, his voice dropping to a husky growl. 'Will you accept it? I regret treating you so roughly yesterday.'

Berenice felt sickened and afraid as she stared into his eyes. He seemed to exhale evil. She felt dazed by his glance, but kept her self-control, realizing suddenly that his desire put him in her power. A hatred of all men rose chokingly in her throat. They were animals—arrogant and cruel! It was a man's world that she inhabited, unloving and insensitive. Very well, she would play them at their own game. Let this fool gloat on her beauty while she remained cold. She would trick him, use him as a pawn in her scheme to win her freedom from Sebastian.

Giving him a gracious smile, she reached for the mantilla, but Sebastian's lean hand shot out, snatching it before she could even touch it, and tossing it back to the pirate. 'She takes nothing from you. I can provide for her needs.'

Modiford shrugged and stuffed the gift back in the bag, his eyes speaking volumes. 'Not so hot there, cully. I meant well. You've got yourself a lovely wife, my friend. Never seen such a bonny bird, not in all my travels.'

With a quietness which held the hidden menace of a tiger's purr, Sebastian replied, 'Take yourself off, Modiford. My temper is notoriously short fused.'

Modiford's hand rested on the hilt of a cutlass that was suspended from an embossed baldrick slung across his deep chest. His men closed in, a solid wall of muscle at his back. 'That's a mite unfriendly, ain't it? But if I'm not welcome by an old shipmate, then I'll go. No call to take that tone with me.' He half turned to the door, then looked back over his shoulder, a smile playing around his lips. 'Oh, by the way, did you know that Whirling Hawk is having trouble with his sons again? Copper Hair and Eagle Fox—they're always at each other's throats.'

'Why do you tell me this?' Sebastian scowled, his distrust deepening with every passing moment. The scoundrel had dared offer Berenice a gift, and she had been prepared to accept it.

Modiford paused, glancing at Berenice impudently, and his men eyed her too, stripping her in their minds. Their captain was a spry fellow, they thought, he'd get her, by fair means or foul, and more than likely he'd give her to them when he tired of her. They knew his way with women—he was the sort who got more pleasure from rape than from having a female go willingly to his arms. They grinned as they imagined her sufferings in his hands. She'd get little mercy from the likes of Darby Modiford.

'I thought you'd like to know that Copper Hair's left the tribe,' Modiford stared arrogantly at Sebastian. 'He came over to offer his services to me, along with a band of warriors.'

'So you think you've scored a point by recruiting a band of Indians on the warpath?' Sebastian's tone was one of contempt.

'Certainly I do. All I needed to give them in exchange was whiskey and a few muskets.'

Sebastian almost yielded to the overpowering longing to smash his fist into the unsavory countenance smiling so triumphantly at him. Both men were aware of the trouble that was

331

brewing among the braves. There had always been antipathy between Copper Hair and Eagle Fox, hotheaded sons of the proud, honorable old chieftain. Copper Hair was treacherous and easily led, while his brother followed their father's example, embodying the finest qualities of their people. Their rivalry might well turn the whole area into a bloody battleground.

'It's in both our interests to keep the peace, if we can. We don't want braves butchering each other on our territory,' he said quietly, his hand coming to rest on his pistol butt. The fact that he did not bother to draw it, seemed to give him added authority. The room became quiet as he outfaced Modiford, forcing him to look away at last, unable to meet that scornful stare.

Modiford shrugged contemptuously, then bowed to Berenice with nauseating affability. 'Your humble and devoted servant, ma'am. Ever at your call, should you need me.' Continuing towards the door, he fired a parting salvo at Sebastian. 'Watch her well, my fine bucko! Wouldn't surprise me if somebody didn't try to abduct her.'

'Like you?' Sebastian asked, while his men held their breath.

'Like me,' Modiford answered, from the threshold.

'If I catch you on my land again, I'll kill you!' Sebastian warned. The door slammed shut behind the pirate and his men.

Berenice listened and watched with a chill smile on her lips. She had enjoyed their quarrel, excitement coursing through her veins. She'd make them suffer! They'd be cutting each other's throats before long! A curious feeling of ecstasy lifted her spirit, like that of a saint who dedicates herself to martyrdom.

Something of her emotion communicated itself to Sebastian, and he clenched his fists tightly. How he wished he could make her see sense. She had no idea what sort of men she was dealing with. Modiford was a devil, cruel, unprincipled and totally without conscience. She wouldn't be able to twist *him* round her fingers as she had done weak fops in the past. She was a bloody nuisance and a thorn in his flesh! He bitterly regretted his rash impulse to bring her there, for now it would mean watching her constantly to prevent her doing something idiotic and self-destructive.

The trappers and Sebastian's own followers had settled down to the serious business of the night—gambling and getting drunk. The light from the candles glowed like blood on the bottles of rum, the tankards, the piles of gold, the cards and dice. Knowing that soon the gathering would degenerate into drunken brawling, Sebastian suggested that Berenice go to their room, his tone indicating that she had better not argue.

She resented being sent to bed like a child, while he remained there with Juliette. Not quite convinced by Dulcie's assurance to the contrary, she had wanted to ask Greg if the woman was Sebastian's mistress, but had been reluctant to show so much interest; interest suggested caring, and she would never have admitted that she cared for her husband. If she confessed it to Greg, then what was to stop him telling his friend? She blushed at the thought of giving Sebastian such an advantage, picturing his mockery, imagining how he would use such knowledge to degrade her.

Struggling to remain controlled, she gave him a frigid nod and passed through the throng, but just as she reached the door, she overheard Juliette saying to Sebastian, 'Come to my cabin, Comte. I've something to show you.'

— Berenice willed herself not to glance round. Pain shot through her, the terrible, consuming fire of jealousy. The hurt in her heart so wounding that she pressed her hands to her breast as she ran across the hall. Alone at last, she leaned against the bedroom door, taking comfort in the improvement that she and Dulcie had made. The room now had that snug intimacy which only a woman can create, and she had an inexplicable longing for Sebastian to see it, for his eyes to light up and for him to give her his rare, charming smile—perhaps even praise her a little.

Dolt! she told herself sternly as she undressed, flinging her gown on a chair, pulling the chemise off over her head, sitting on a stool to unwind the lacing of her pumps, and peel down her white stockings. Why do you yearn for his approval? He cares nothing for you. He may never even enter this room. He'll spend his nights with Juliette. Didn't you hear her openly inviting him to her cabin?

Wearily she slipped on her nightdress, worn

down by physical toil and heaviness of spirit. Even Dulcie had deserted her—she was out there somewhere in the moonlit garden with Quico. She envied her maid's attitude to men—she seemed to fall in love without hesitation. Berenice could not love so casually. She was one of those deeply passionate women who could only give her mind, body and soul to one man for the whole of her life. It was hard to possess so intense a nature—hard and extremely painful, as she was beginning to discover.

She wandered restlessly to the window, pushing open the broken glass door and stepping out on to the terrace beyond. Night shrouded all—cool, blue night that seemed to drip out of the clouds. A pale moon rode high, bathing the clearing and the trees with a mellow loveliness. Berenice stood lost in wonder, such peace acting like balm to her troubled soul. Resting her hands on the stone balustrade, she gazed across the grassy stretch that had once been a lawn.

Suddenly her eyes sharpened as two figures strolled over it, making for the huddle of palm-roofed huts on the other side, where some of the servants lived. Sebastian's height was unmistakable, and there was a woman hanging on his arm, pressing close, their shadows intermingling. It was Juliette.

Berenice drew in a shivering breath, gripped by a paralysis which rendered her helpless for a second. It was true. She could no longer even hope. Juliette *was* his mistress. She felt naked, as if she had been brutally stripped of her desirability, all her womanly power, her magic torn rudely from her. Abruptly she forgot how she hated him, and how she had contemplated locking the bedroom door against him. Now all she wanted was to weep. The fact stood out, stark and inescapable. He did not want her.

It was humiliating! Maddening! Oh, the hours she had wasted cleaning that room, just to prove herself to him, and all the time he and Juliette must have been laughing up their sleeves at her. She wanted to dig her nails into his cheeks, to hit him! The thought of hurting him restored her a little, giving her a surge of energy.

She paced the floor, her negligee floating behind her like the wings of some giant moth as she clenched her fists and worked herself into a passionate fury to numb the pain which made her feel that she was bleeding to death internally. To see him flinch—how wonderful that would be! Yet last night she had wanted to protect him, to love him, to die for him if need be, gladly accepting the words of the marriage service—to love, honor and obey—in sickness and in health.

Presently, the frenzy burned itself out, leaving her drained, but even so, she resolved not to occupy that flamboyant bed. He would not find her waiting there when he crept back in the small hours, reeking of another woman's flesh. There was a daybed in the room, a dainty thing of walnut and cane, with loose feather-filled cushions of crimson plush, so faded that they had the soft, dusky hue of a musk rose. Berenice dragged a blanket from the bed and settled down there, too tired for tears, falling at last into a deep sleep.

An hour later, Sebastian entered the room. As he tossed his coat over one of the high-backed chairs and divested himself of his boots, his eyes searched for her, noting the feminine garments lying about, and the gleaming air of cleanliness. He prowled across the polished boards on bare feet, then stopped when he saw Berenice asleep on the couch. His frown vanished as he stood looking down on her, replaced by a curiously gentle smile, noting the soft movement of her breasts beneath the lacy robe as she breathed, the hair spread out like a cloud over the rose-colored cushions, and her dark lashes sweeping the peachlike bloom of her cheeks.

Such innocence, such helplessness, reminded him of evenings when he had crept into the nursery to watch over Lisette. It seemed a lifetime ago, those months he had spent in the Chateau Hilaire where he had kept his mistress and their child, thinking that he had found peace and eternal love. The chateau! What had become of it? Had the revolutionaries burned it down? Would it ever be safe for him to return to his home and stand in its magnificent grounds again? Did he really want to? Or would the memory of dead parents and friends be too much to bear?

Sebastian heaved a deep sigh, his face sombering, taking a modicum of comfort in reaching out and carefully lifting a lock of his wife's hair, twining a curl about his fingers. She stirred, as if aware of his touch, then burrowed

337

deeper in to the cushions. He longed to scoop her up in his arms and carry her to the bed, but could not stomach the thought of rousing her into screaming, hellcat fury. So, disturbed and distrustful of this sudden wave of tenderness, he turned away, taking off the rest of his clothes and throwing himself on to the four-poster.

Sleep, he discovered, was impossible, not now, not there in that chamber which he had always loved and considered truly his—not with his wife lying so close on the couch. The candle burned near her, transforming her into a thing of darkness and silver highlights. Sebastian heaved up, leaning back against the pillows. He took a cigar from the side table, lighting it and blowing smoke rings. She woke, stared across at him, and asked sleepily,

'Why are you here?'

'It's my room and my bed.' He regarded her levelly. 'You've made it look nice.'

'Yes, I have.' This prosaic conversation in the middle of the night was odd. She wanted to ask him about Juliette, but how to do so without giving the game away? 'You're late,' she began. 'Did you have business with the woman?'

'I did, but it's nothing that concerns you.' He was watching her with a faint smile on his mouth.

Ah, God, she thought, that mouth which had made forgetfulness its country. A shiver rippled over her skin. The silence stretched between them till she wanted to scream.

'Not my concern, when my husband chooses to visit another woman by invitation at dead of night?' She sprang into the attack, fighting to control herself and repair the havoc that he had wrecked on the order of her existence.

'No more than mine when your would-be lover is still on the loose. I'd like to put him under restraint.'

'He hasn't committed any crime.'

'Neither has Juliette.' He stubbed out his cigar in the brass ashtray, shrugged on his robe and came over to where she lay, stretching out a hand and playing with a lock of her hair that lay across her shoulder. Berenice trembled.

'Perhaps not,' she whispered, wishing he would tell her about the Creole.

'Aren't you in love with Peregrine, and longing to be his?'

'I've never said I was in love with him,' she corrected, nerves tingling.

'I didn't think you were,' he shot back, face hardening, his hand still holding her hair but now resting it against her breast. 'I've not seen you shed a single tear on his account.'

'You don't know what I feel.' She arched her spine to get away from his hand.

'Oh, yes I do. I can read you like a book, cool Comtesse.' He smiled, not his usual mocking smile, but one that was rueful, almost tender. 'If you hate, you show it. If you love, you show it, but if you desire, *Dieu!* It vibrates through your whole being—like this.' His fingers traced across her face, drawing a moan from her lips. 'Or this?' His hand was traveling down the center of her body, and she stiffened in a desperate attempt to ignore the sudden leap of longing.

She struggled with this paradox of loathing him and at the same time having her entire being dissolve at his touch. In a tight, defiant voice, she hissed, 'Then recognize how I feel about you. I hate you.'

'That's what I expected you to say, *chérie*,' he teased, and drew her up into his arms. 'I don't pretend. I want you. Come to bed.' And he chuckled with the assurance of a strong man who knows that the woman he desires is responding to him. 'There's so much I can teach you—so many wonderful ways to make love.'

Strange bed beneath her, soft mattress—a different odor—how alien new beds always seem. She was naked now, the herb-scented sheets smooth against her skin. His hands were moving confidently over her, finding that sensitive point where her shoulders met her neck, then down over her back, her hips, caressing her pleasure-hungry skin. This time he controlled his own needs, wanting to linger over each delight. With slow deliberation, he explored her ribs, drifting down across her stomach, and her heart thumped. She wanted to touch him, to fondle him as he was doing her. Her fingers, shy at first, grew bolder, having a will of their own, enjoying the rapture of the senses. He was on the edge—the tension was building too high, and he knew that he must either stop her or accept his release and disappoint her. He extricated himself, rolling her on to her side, her spine molded to his chest. His breath was like spice on her nape, shivering over that sensitive zone. She pressed back into

340

him as if they were one person, her buttocks curving against his belly, her legs following the long, strong lines of him. He found the core of her, his touch like slippery silk and she gave herself up to him. He did not interrupt her pleasure, judging the moment when she overflowed into completion, hearing her cry, feeling her spasms, then entering her welcoming warmth. She joined him in fulfillment, making his possession smooth, encouraging him so that he, too, knew the glory.

Bemused, Berenice came back to earth, finding herself lying in the curve of his arm. Very slowly, the room righted itself, no longer a dizzy cloud of intensity. The candles had burned out, and she was glad of the darkness, filled with self-knowledge. Now she understood the insanity that drove women into the arms of the most unsuitable men. Passion, hunger—that madness which so often resembles love. She knew, firsthand, that blinding force. She loved Sebastian, and would have given almost anything not to.

TEN

In the drowsy moments of dawn, Berenice woke and imagined that she was back at Stretton Court. It was the thick pillars at the foot of the bed, outlined against the light from the windows that had created this illusion,

341

reminding her of her four-poster at home. If she kept her eyes tightly shut, this escape into nonreality was nearly complete. It was possible to believe that the aroma wafting on the breeze was that of English roses, not hibiscus, and the sound of cattle lowing in the distance those of sturdy Wiltshire herds, instead of foreign stock. But she could not deceive herself for long, other sensations impinging on her dreams. She was conscious of a draft down one side of her back where, not long before, there had been a furnace. She stretched out an arm, but encountered empty space. Sebastian had gone.

She sat up sharply, glancing round the room, uncertain whether to be relieved or upset. The place where he had lain still retained traces of warmth; the pillow bore the imprint of his head. She ran her fingers over it, prey to memories of him—his finely drawn lips, the firm line of his jaw, the sometimes aggressive thrust of his cleft chin, and the shock of those green eyes in that tanned face—features she would never be able to forget, ever.

It was then that Juliette appeared, unannounced, a fearsome light in her dark eyes. 'I had to see for myself!' she said, her tone bitter. 'Madame la Comtesse installed in her husband's bed. I curse the day he went to England for you. You'll bring nothing but ill fortune.'

Berenice was dumbstruck. She instinctively pulled the quilt higher over her breasts. All trace of sleep had gone, her senses honed. The woman was dangerous, maybe insane.

'What are you doing here?' she said coldly,

looking at Juliette as if she were a cockroach.

For reply, 'I was in this house long before you,' Juliette snarled, glowering at her.

'So you may have been, but I'm mistress now, and you'd do well to remember it.' Berenice was about to order her to leave, when an idea struck her.

With a flash of insight, she knew that she was about to behave foolishly and felt a twinge of shame, but her original course of action had become too deeply ingrained to change overnight. She leaned forward and, making her voice more friendly, said, 'If you want me out of the way, why don't you help me? Once I leave here, you'll never see me again, I swear it.'

Juliette did not answer at once. Then, 'You're asking me to betray the Comte?' she asked thoughtfully, her expression guarded.

'If that's how you see it, yes. I must get away from here. I've little money with me, but once I reach Charleston, I'll arrange for you to have some.' In her eagerness, Berenice rose to her knees, the sheet slipping, displaying her shoulders and arms.

Her hair shone, and her blue eyes were wide with hope. She had all the fair-skinned beauty that Juliette envied—an English aristocrat, pampered, spoilt, enjoying the privileges that the Creole had lost, and bewitching Sebastian, into the bargain. Juliette wanted to take up a knife and cut out the Comtesse's heart, offering it as a sacrifice to one of her gods.

Then Berenice asked the question that had been trembling on her tongue ever since she arrived at Buckhorn. 'Are you, or have you ever been, Sebastian's mistress?'

Juliette's smile was poisonous. 'That's for me to know and you to find out, madame,' she answered, enjoying Berenice's torment.

'You won't tell me? But will you help me?'

'I may. I must think it over carefully.'

The moment was so finely balanced that the scales could have tipped either way, but in the next instant Sebastian strode in, his brows winging down in a scowl as he saw the Creole.

'Juliette!' he barked. 'What's the meaning of this?'

Eyeing him insolently, 'I came to see if madame wanted anything,' she lied.

'Did you indeed?' he replied sharply. 'I decide what happens here and, at the present time, madame is learning how to be a competent housewife.'

Berenice was disappointed that he had interrupted their discussion, more than half convinced that Juliette had been about to agree to her proposition. She sank back against the pillows. Juliette was most anxious to get rid of her, though Berenice still could not quite understand the nature of her relationship with Sebastian. It was baffling.

Pale with rage, Juliette gave him a searching glance and took herself off. Unaffected, Sebastian strolled to the bed, and seated himself on the side. 'Trying to bribe her, were you, *mon enfant?*' he asked nonchalantly. 'Working on the theory that everyone has their price?'

'And what if I was?' she answered crossly.

His mouth turned down in cynical amusement. 'Such a change in you. I see that your petal softness of last night has gone, replaced by thorns.'

Berenice had the grace to blush. 'Those aren't the words of a gentleman, sir.'

Sebastian threw back his head and laughed. 'You want to forget when daylight comes? Is that it? Very well. I'll play the game your way—for the moment. As for bribing Juliette? You'll not succeed. She's loyal, besides which, she fears me.'

'What a tyrant you are!' But even as she spat out the angry words, Berenice wanted to go into his arms. It was degrading and she despised herself, certain that he read her mind. 'Is she your mistress?' she shouted.

He looked pained, but his eyes were twinkling. 'Madame la Comtesse! What a question for a wife to ask her husband! I'm shocked that you should even think such a thing!'

This answer was no answer, and she saw that it was useless to probe further. Yet did she really want to know? Her heart felt as if it was being squeezed by a giant fist when she visualized them together.

It looked as if he had been up some time, his jaw freshly shaved, his hair combed back, an outdoor air about him that hinted of an early morning canter. Then, with one of his mercurial changes of mood, he said, 'If you want any breakfast, you'd better get down to the kitchen.'

An angry retort was on her lips, but one glance at his face stopped her from uttering it. She contented herself with tossing her head and pacing to the window, the sheet wrapped around her like a toga. Sebastian said no more, and she heard him cross the room, then the sound of the door shutting behind him.

Later she stood in the vast, untidy kitchen across the hall, a pan of eggs boiling on the fire. She was beginning to discover that she quite enjoyed cooking, remembering lessons learned under the tutelage of Lady Olivia. There was no sign of Dulcie, and Berenice guessed that, with her head in the clouds and a new lover, she had temporarily forgotten her mistress. The kitchen was the heart of the house, and Berenice was growing used to having Jessy and Adam and a half a dozen of their children wandering in and out. Hens clucked, and scratched about in the refuse on the floor, and a couple of mongrel dogs nibbled at their fleas on the hearth rug. A lame gull stood on the threshold, getting in everybody's way, perpetually wailing for tidbits.

Berenice, becoming less fastidious by the second, was sitting at the cluttered table when Dulcie rushed through the door, out of breath as she cried, 'Oh, madam, I'm sorry that I'm late.'

Berenice paused in slicing the top off her egg, looking up and saying with a smile, 'Don't worry about it, Dulcie. I'm not supposed to have servants anyway, according to the rules of my Lord High and Mighty Lajeaunesse.'

'Well, we know that's foolishness, don't we, my lady?'

'We do, but we'll pretend, shall we? Just to keep him sweet.' Berenice did not need to ask where Dulcie had been. She was wearing a string of Quico's beads around her neck. 'Have some toast?' she suggested. 'And this quince jelly that Jessy made is truly ambrosial.'

After they had eaten, Berenice heaved the big laundry basket to her hip and went down to the stream. There, with Dulcie's help, she beat her washing on the round white stones over which the brook gushed and gurgled, then laid the garments across the bushes to dry in the hot sun. She 'was relieved that Sebastian had not asked her to include his dirty shirts, collars, drawers and hose. Jessy saw to all that, and the household linen, too.

It seemed to Berenice that she had been at Buckhorn House for an eternity, surprised to realize that had been a matter of hours. She was starting to find her way around and put names to the faces of the various members of that disorganized household. The trappers had departed at daybreak, leaving the kitchen in a greater state of chaos than usual, with a mountain of used dishes, cooking-pots and tankards, Berenice had no intention of clearing up behind them and trusted that Adam would attend to it. They had ridden off noisily with money bags swinging from their saddles, and the pelts had been stored until such time as Sebastian took them to Charleston. And when would that be? she wondered as she worked, pausing to wipe the sweat from her brow, raking the surrounding area with anxious, puzzled eyes.

All morning she had been uneasily aware of Juliette or Leah watching her, coming upon one or other of them at the turn of a stair—in some unexpected corner of the garden, their eyes boring into her as if to unravel her innermost secrets.

She was missing Peregrine, seeing him from the distance only. Obeying Sebastian's orders, he was keeping very much to himself, hanging around on the periphery, eating alone, spending most of his time in the room alloted to him. Damian, too, seemed to be avoiding her, or maybe it was simply that he was finding so much of interest in and around the house and grounds. Sebastian and Greg absented themselves for the whole of that day, returning late, when she had gone to bed. She slept alone, and was thankful for it, needing time and seclusion in which to come to terms with her emotions. It was impossible when Sebastian was in the bed.

She even got out her diary, much neglected of late, and wrote in it, 'I'm shocked by a side of my nature that has been startlingly revealed. I never dreamed I could be so abandoned. I enjoy my husband's embraces. In his arms I play the trollop. Surely no cultured lady could behave like that unless she were in love? Sometimes I think I am. Sometimes I *know* I am! How can this be when he annoys me so much. He's the most mystifying man I've ever met. As for Juliette Pascal? I'm half inclined to fancy that she's his slut. And I care. Oh, yes, I care. I'm so confused and feel that I must get away if I can. Maybe if I go to Charleston, I can think quietly, and decide whether I want to leave him for good and all.'

She was awakened next morning by the sound of horsemen riding in, and peeping from her window, saw a band of Indians. Their coming brought confusion until Sebastian appeared and invited them to dismount. The sudden arrival of these deerskin-clad men with their dark complexions, their prominent noses and haughty expressions unnerved Berenice. Some of them had vivid patterns painted on their faces and porcupine quills stuck in their long, braided hair, and their leader was a greying, elderly man resplendent in a feathered headdress, who stood with Sebastian, resting a hand on his shoulder as if he were his son.

Indeed, Sebastian was like a savage himself, a transformation which became more marked with every passing day. He was tanned almost as brown as the Indians, his hair had grown longer and more tousled, and his clothing always consisted of fringed breeches and jacket nowadays. He welcomed his guests with grave courtesy and, before long, he and Greg had joined them in the large circle which they had formed, seated cross-legged on the ground, entering into the solemn, serious conversation, which included much sign language, the drawing of diagrams in the dust, and the passing of a long-stemmed pipe from lip to lip.

This debate continued while the sun climbed

high, beating down on their heads, the tall pines whispering at their backs. The scene was timeless—men of different race and color meeting to talk over their affairs with mutual trust, the elders quiet and dignified, tempering the fire of the young braves with comments born of wisdom and experience.

'Why aren't you out there with them, Quico?' Berenice asked as the two of them paused in their labors.

'I'm not a Cherokee,' he answered, his eyes expressionless, his face as impassive as a statue's. 'Indeed, madame, I belong to no tribe at all. My mother was an Indian squaw, but my father was a white man.'

She had never heard him talk of his past before. Since Dulcie was now having an affair with him, Berenice viewed him with new respect. Before that she had treated him with indifference; at best, as a strongly built bodyguard; at worst, as her husband's spy.

'Do you mind belonging nowhere?' she asked.

He did not look at her, his eyes remaining fixed on those engaged in the powwow. 'This no longer troubles me. The Comte is my leader now, almost my father. I follow him as I would have followed my chief. I've pledged my life to him.'

Berenice was touched by the simplicity of this statement, and by his composure. 'Tell me of your mother's people,' she asked.

Her interest was genuine, for she had been moved by the mien of Whirling Hawk and his braves. Until that moment she had thought of

Indians as monsters of violence and barbarity, but seeing them in the garden of Buckhorn House, her ideas were changing dramatically.

Quico did not speak for a moment, then he said, 'My mother used to tell me how, in the beginning, the Indians welcomed the white man but could never understand his greed for land, his destruction of nature's gifts, or his blindness to all that makes life beautiful and peaceful. I've found this to be true. So many white men destroy like wanton children, ruining that which offers so much. It is a violation of everything we hold sacred—an affront to the Great Spirit.'

There was no anger in his voice, only a deep sadness, and she felt tears springing to her eyes. As she turned back to her work she pondered on this information, forced to face issues of which she had been ignorant. She was sharply aware that she had left girlhood behind, a woman now, facing a woman's problems in a world only too eager to strip her of her innocence and faith, and to shatter her belief in the innate goodness of human nature.

She thought of home with a poignant longing for the security that had once been hers, wondering briefly how Lucinda would have coped. A smile lifted her lips as she stood before the stone sink, scouring dishes with a handful of sand. That strong-willed young lady would probably have managed very well indeed. There was a steely strength about her, and Berenice wished wholeheartedly that she were there. She needed guidance desperately, needed a woman in whom she could confide, someone who would advise her on how to deal with the difficult Sebastian. Her thoughts were heavy, filling her mind with gloom. What did he intend for her?

The Cherokees did not leave till late in the afternoon. Greg and Sebastian strolled into the kitchen, and even Colonel Perkins, who had also sat in on the conference, seemed satisfied. Berenice was ironing, having filled the heavy flatiron with smoldering charcoal. She was laboring diligently over her task, and looked up sharply as they tramped over to fill glasses at the beer keg.

'Whirling Hawk'll give us his support if it comes to a battle with Modiford,' Greg was saying, winking as he saw her.

Damian come to put an arm lightly about her waist, giving it an affectionate squeeze. Her brother had changed, becoming more like the men he strove so earnestly to copy, his new growth of beard making him appear much older. Greg and he spent hours at the rifle range, improving their aim.

'He's a grand old man,' commented Sebastian warmly, long body stretched out in the carver, tankard to hand. 'I've a lot of respect for him and his tribe.'

'Aye, the Indians are a fine people and it's a pity they're being corrupted by the white man's diseases and his whiskey,' put in Greg. 'Are you expecting trouble?'

'Modiford still hasn't left the area. I think he's planning something. When I went for a swim in the sea this morning, I noticed that

352

he's moved his ship to the next bay, ready for a quick escape, perhaps. The scouts tell me he's taken over that abandoned stockade on the other side of the forest. I wouldn't trust him further than I could throw him.'

A month passed, and still they remained at Mobby Cove, Modiford making no move, therefore preventing Sebastian from doing so either. They had reached a deadlock. He could not leave the area while the pirate insisted on staying, and there was no way he could get rid of him unless they engaged in a full-scale battle, a risk to his men's lives that Sebastian was reluctant to take.

Berenice had mastered the art of housekeeping, surprising Dulcie with her aptitude. 'My word, madam,' the maid was fond of saying, 'You'll be a real tartar when you get into a proper home. No butler will be able to cheat you, or servants get away with shoddy work. You won't settle for anything slapdash.'

'That's as it should be, Dulcie,' Berenice would answer, busy with her baking, or ironing or polishing. 'But I don't intend to slave like this forever. Oh, no, when I get me back to civilization, I'll take up the gay life again. It'll be balls and parties and shopping sprees, just you wait and see.'

But inside she wondered—would it ever be the same? Wouldn't that empty round of pleasure pall? She might grumble about the basic conditions at Buckhorn House, but she had grown to love it, the rambling, weedy garden, the rocks leading down the sea—the miles of golden sand.

The days took on a settled routine of sameness, and she made friends among the people who lived in the house and those who owned homes further away, with half-acres of land where they produced vegetables and kept pigs, goats and the occasional cow. Some of them were tenants, paying Sebastian rent, but he was a liberal landlord and no one had ever been evicted. The kitchen became her haven by day, where she hobnobbed with Adam and Jessy, but at night she retired to the master bedchamber with her husband where, in the darkness, she accepted her frailty, a slave of her own desires.

It was as if something had passed from Sebastian to her, filling her as lightning fills a cloud at sunset. And not only when he touched her. Now it came every time she looked at him, even at a distance, or heard his voice. If he was out of sight she felt only half alive, restless until they met again—yet when they did, she sometimes wanted to run away and hide.

She tried to discuss it with Greg when she came upon him one afternoon, sitting by himself, mending some portion of his horse gear. He looked up, pleased to see her. One of Jessy's lads had taken the scythe to a patch of grass near the back door, and Berenice settled down there on a white-painted garden bench, the hard seat softened by the addition of threadbare cushions.

'I'm bored,' she announced, watching his

354

strong fingers drawing thongs together tightly. The sunlight filtered through, the leaves of an enormous, spreading oak tree, dappling his face. 'The chores are done, the food heating up, and now—what? Is this what domesticity brings forth? A cessation of everything, once work is over?'

'Sebastian is a busy man,' he said, smiling, aware of her agitation, and its cause. 'He can't spend all day with you—as well as all night. You've sure put paid to our card parties. At one time he never left till the small hours.'

'Maybe we could find a harpsichord somewhere. I used to love playing,' she sighed, unaccountably restless.

'I know. I've heard you on the pianoforte, and you're good. You'll have to wait till we go to town, honey,' he soothed, and laid aside his work. Resting on the grass, he lit up a cheroot.

'Must you smoke?' she asked, moving further down the bench. 'I can't bear the smell. It makes me feel quite sick.'

He gave her a lazy look from behind his blue smokescreen. 'You sure it's the tobacco?'

'What else could it be?' she stared at him blankly.

'Oh, nothing, I guess,' and he went on talking about Sebastian, and the fun they used to have, racketing around, turning night into day with their furious life, or off bashing pirates.

Greg was a great talker, but she was too embarrassed to tell him the real reason why she had come, so she resigned herself, lying full length on the bench, and soon fell into a deep sleep. When she woke, she found him still holding forth, fresh as ever and quite unaware that she had hardly heard a word. She got up groggily and returned to the kitchen, no nearer finding a solution to her dilemma.

One morning she woke early, roused by the numerous barnyard cocks. Sebastian had already gone, and the house was stirring, an air of anticipation ripping through it from attic to cellar. A gala had been planned, a break from the daily round when the men rode off about their activities, nefarious and otherwise, and the women worked the fields. A number of wild horses had been captured and horsemen from far and wide were coming to test their skills at breaking them.

Berenice dressed with care, putting on a freshly laundered gown, and ornate hat, for this was an important local event and people who had not already met her would be curious about the new Comtesse. It was a glorious morning, not yet too hot, and a colorful crowd was gathering on the stretch of grass that lay beyond the gates. Some arrived on foot, others in wagons, gigs and donkey carts; couples with their children; single men on the lookout for strong, healthy girls who would make good wives; young lads seeking adventure; gamblers eager to make a quick guinea.

Bets were being placed on the riders most likely to break the fiery mustangs. The Comte was voted favorite, and Quico had a reputation as a horseman of courage and élan. Greg had added his name to the list of contenders, and Colonel Perkins, who had set himself up as the doctor's trainer, was passing the whiskey bottle to him frequently, by way of Dutch courage. Berenice strolled there with Dulcie, delayed along the way by folk who wished to offer their best wishes and welcome her to America. Eventually she took her place on a stand that had been erected under a shady tree. She could see Juliette in the distance, very grandly arrayed, her hair drawn back into a knot, her lips painted crimson. The Creole seemed so much a part of the scene—at ease and familiar with the people, whereas Berenice still felt herself to be an outsider, not yet fully accepted.

Greg saluted Berenice as he rode by on his steed, making for the corral where the feral horses stamped and snorted. He had a woven hat tipped forward over his eyes, a cigar jammed between his lips, and was wearing a white shirt and trousers, and coltskin top-boots. Quico passed next, every inch the warrior, nodding to Dulcie who blew him a kiss. A murmur of approval rose from the onlookers, and this swelled to a roar as Sebastian made his entrance on his high-stepping beast, a gleaming black thoroughbred, reminding her of her own team at home.

Berenice sat motionless, staring at him from under her parasol. He looked spectacular, wearing a broad-brimmed grey hat, his suit made of costly material, the breeches snug fitting, the coat well tailored, emphasizing the breadth of his shoulders. His whip handle; the sheath of his long knife and his rings were of glittering silver. More of this precious metal ornamented his spurs, the pommel of his saddle, his stirrups and the headstall of his bridle. He knew the importance of putting on a show to keep the people happy, and he was a sight to stir the blood.

A rider of some repute herself, Berenice increased her admiration as the morning wore on, and she watched her husband perform stunning feats of horsemanship. No one else stood a chance—not Greg, skilled though he was—not Quico, who was next in the popularity stakes—not those others who resorted to hard handling and cruel spurs, heckled by the crowd for their pains. Sebastian's ability was unquestionable, and the final animal he selected was as unbroken and vicious as they come.

Between man and horse, on that ring of sunbaked earth, the struggle for mastery raged. The stallion reared, plunged and bucked, putting into practice every conceivable trick to rid itself of its burden, while Sebastian applied tremendous energy and strength, pouring out torrents of strange, violent expletives. He triumphed and, as the crowd surged forward, cheering, so Berenice saw Juliette running up as he dismounted, flinging her arms around his neck and kissing him, just as if *she* were his Comtesse—his bride, his love!

Instantly a fierce surge of jealousy sent Berenice jumping to her feet. 'Damn her!' she muttered to an astonished Dulcie, and set off down the steps of the stand, heading towards the cliffs, almost running.

She had thought no further than distancing herself from her husband and that woman. Juliette was always somewhere in the background following him around, there when he engaged in deep discussions with his men, watching her, watching *him*, waiting her chance.

Well, here it is, lady! Berenice raged. I know when I'm beaten. You can have him. I give him to you on a plate!

She stormed off, more frightened than ever before of her weakness where he was concerned. If she did not leave him soon, then she never would. She reached the screening bushes, hearing the cheers fading, finding the cliff path and starting to scramble down its steep face. The ground was crumbly, so she clutched at the prickly bushes. They, too, became dislodged, and she stopped to steady herself. There was no shade and the heat grilled her, sweat soaking through the thin material of her dress. The sea pounded the shore far below, and she was afraid of falling on the sharp rocks, to land in some crevice where the carrion crows would find her dead body and peck at it.

I'm mad, she thought. Why am I doing this? It was to worry him, to make him wonder where she was, and distract his attention from Juliette. At last she came to easier ground, though it still sloped rapidly, but it was shady there, a moist, overgrown gully filled with the sound of fresh, rushing water spilling down to pour across the beach. Her throat was parched, and her palms tingled with heat. She hurried towards the stream, promising herself a long, cool drink. On all sides there was a confusion of jagged rocks, mixed with a tangle of vegetation. A great blue-winged butterfly passed across, and above the dashing of the water, the clear warble of a bird startled her.

Berenice moved cautiously along till she came to where the stream poured into a rock pool. She dropped to her knees, plunging her hands into the icy water, scooping it up in her palms and drinking. She washed her face, and dipped her feet in it, sandals and all. It was quiet there, a quiet that was unnerving. Berenice listened intently, scarcely breathing. Whether real or imaginary, the silence became profound, and the gloom in the gully deepened. Berenice shivered. Quico had told Dulcie many Indian legends of the demons who haunted the woods, and Dulcie had repeated them to her mistress. There was one in particular, a misshapen, man-eating monster who beguiled his victims by mimicking the human voice, sometimes using the cries of a woman in distress or singing beautiful melodies.

'Don't be such a ninny!' Berenice lectured herself out loud, yet was afraid to turn round lest she catch him stealing towards her on his big feet with the toes pointing backwards, mouth open in a horrible snarl.

But it wasn't a monster who came out of the bushes, it was one of Sebastian's men, someone she recognized, a Mexican called Lopez, not the most trustworthy of individuals. 'Señora, may I help you?' he grunted.

'I don't need your help,' she shouted, angry with him for frightening her.

Lopez had been drinking and watching his leader's wife. He had seen her go towards the cliffs, and done something that he would never have attempted if sober. He had followed her. There had been no plan in his slow brain, though, like many others, he considered her to be a desirable woman. Now, finding her there alone, the demons of alcohol were whispering in his head.

'You'll be nice to me, won't you, señora?' he panted, blowing his sour breath into her face.

Then everything seemed to happen at once. Greg came crashing through the undergrowth, followed by Sebastian. He had a gun, but Lopez's knife flashed in the sunlight, aimed directly at Sebastian's throat. Then there was the sound of a shot. Lopez's fat body jerked. He gave a choking cry and slumped to the ground. Damian stood at the head of the gully, a musket in this hand.

'Are you hurt?' Greg asked Sebastian.

'No.' His face was stony as he stared down at the dead man. Then his eyes went to Berenice. 'Why did you run away? Now I've lost a good fighting man!'

She had been so terrified as that knife hurtled towards him, her one thought for his safety. Now he was acting as if he did not care about her, more vexed by the death of his man. She began scrambling down the slope, panicky, angry, hurt. It was impossible to stop, the loosened stones slipping beneath her feet.

The strain was too much for her sandal and it broke. Her right foot twisted under her with such force that she heard the tendon snap like a dry twig. Agony shot through her and she cried out, clinging to a clump of thorns, heedless of the barbs entering her palms. The pain in her foot was making her feel faint, black flecks swimming before her eyes.

The blood was running from her pierced hands, the blue sky, that hot landscape revolving madly. She let go, dropping through the foliage, grabbing at a branch as she fell. For a second, she was halted, then it gave way, and she went spinning down into oblivion.

Berenice floated back from the void, finding that she was lying somewhere warm and soft. She felt bruised all over, content to remain there without moving. Pain throbbed up from her ankle. Though too sleepy to lift an eyelid, she could hear Sebastian's voice and, after a while, peeped through her eyelashes.

She was in the four-poster, and the master bedchamber was flooded with the red, elongated shadows of evening. A quilt covered her, but under it she still wore her dress. Dulcie was there, hovering anxiously, and Damian, too.

Greg saw that she was awake, and said lightly, 'Feeling better, ma'am?' And his fingers rested on her wrist, checking the pulse.

A figure moved out of the shadowy bed curtains and, 'Fetch warm water, soap and towels,' Sebastian ordered Dulcie. 'And will you take yourselves off, my friends? I want to be alone with Berenice.'

'Sure. She's not much hurt,' said Greg.

'Is that true? It was an awful tumble.' Damian was looking at her with a worried expression on his bearded face.

'You shot a man,' she whispered.

'I know. My first, but I guess it won't be my last.'

'Don't you care?' Where had her gentle brother gone? she wondered. That dear lad who had covered for her, taken the blame for her pranks, supported and loved her.

'Of course I care. But it's a case of kill or be killed out here,' he said gruffly, and she realized that he was still her champion, killing in order to protect her.

'Off you go. The festivities are still in full swing.' Sebastian was almost hustling them out of the door.

Dulcie came back with the things he had requested. 'Shall I help wash my lady?' she inquired.

'No. Put them down and go away. Meet Quico and put him out of his misery. I'm tired of seeing him mooning about. You can marry him, if you want. I'll give my permission.'

'Thank you, sir,' Dulcie said, astonished. Not that she hadn't already thought about it.

When she had gone, Sebastian poured himself a glass of brandy, and stood for some time looking down at Berenice's motionless body. She could not be bothered to talk to him, emotionally and physically spent. She wished she was dead. No, she thought suddenly, I

363

wish Juliette was dead. And she spent a few fruitless seconds envisioning horrible and painful methods for her disposal.

Quietly and efficiently, he gathered up the bowl and hot-water jug and walked towards the bed. He hesitated, and then said, 'You've a nasty sprain. Greg has left me to dress it. I'll try not to hurt you.'

He stripped back the covers and lifted the torn hem of her skirt. She was too weak to protest, sickness bringing her out in a cold sweat, the heavily carved tester undulating. She flinched as his hand touched her injury, and he smiled in commiseration.

'This wouldn't have happened if you hadn't tried to hightail it. Why did you?' he scolded, more in sorrow than anger.

'I wasn't running away. I just wanted to be on my own.'

Greg had said that her ankle was not broken, but it was very swollen. Berenice was surprised by Sebastian's skill as he bound it, using strips of linen. When he had finished, he added a few drops of sleeping potion to a brandy tot and told her to drink it.

'What's that? Are you drugging me?' she asked suspiciously.

'Yes, I am, and stop glaring at me. It's for your own good. Now sleep.'

With a resigned sigh, she swallowed the contents of the glass, and, lying back, wondered what he would do next. She was feeling more eased, the pain in her strapped ankle subsiding to a dull throb. The drink was taking effect, blunting the edges of reality. He took the empty glass and set it on the table, then, propping her up against his shoulder, removed her dress, laid her down again, and began to bathe her entire body, shaking his head over the cuts and bruises. Absorbed in his task, he bent over her, toweling her dry. He found some dusting powder and sprinkled her, the pungent perfume rising.

When he had finished, he tidied everything away and, going to the armoire, selected a white silk nightgown. Carrying it carefully, spread over his arm, he coaxed her to sit up and then helped her into the garment. Finally, he took up her silver-backed brush and worked the tangles from her hair.

Berenice was filled with a sense of well-being, happy to be cared for, the medicine making her sleepy. She fretted vaguely as to how she could possibly trust him, but even this did not seem to be significant. He went round the room, touching a spill to light the candles, then drew the coverlet over her, picked up a book and sat by the bed, reading.

Once, he looked across and caught her watching him. His lips formed into a smile, and he said something that sounded like—'Later, *chérie*, I'll eat you,' but she was not sure if those were really the words or part of a dream.

Much later, it might have been a hundred years for the opiate had made a nonsense of time, she was aware of him in the bed with her. Her reflexes were clumsy and she floated off again, hearing him chuckle. It was so peaceful in the chamber, with only the gentle soughing of the trees outside the windows. Berenice thought she felt a light kiss on her brow, a kiss such as Damian might have bestowed on her.

As was his habit, Sebastian was awake at daybreak and lay staring into the dimness for a while. Berenice's body in its silk covering was warm and soft as she lay sleeping. By the regularity of her breathing, he could tell that it was a healing sleep, and he was glad. It meant that she felt safe with him and had delivered herself into his care. He savored this idea, sitting up and staring down into her dreaming face. Her features still carried the unlined innocence of youth, the lashes lying like thick fans against her skin, mouth curving tenderly, a burnished curl waving across one cheek. She was so lovely, intelligent, too, and had a strong body beneath that fragile appearance. He knew that she could hold a man well, and could imagine her nursing a child equally warmly. He shook his head to clear it of such fantasies, allowing desire to rise in him. That was safe, reasonable, something he could understand.

Dreaming, her arms crept up to cling round his neck, her fingers caressing the thick hair that grew at his nape, and he reached down to lift her nightdress, pushing it back to expose her thighs. Berenice, still half asleep, arched her body to meet his hand. His mouth was on hers and, cradled in languor, she became pure sensation as that mouth left hers, traveling slowly over her throat, her body—down—following the tingling path of his fingers—while she lay there in a pleasure trance.

This kind of loving excited him, and he muttered thickly, 'Ah, darling—you are like a flower opening to the sun.'

In the quiet spell of that dawn-brightened room, the endless caressing, that mingled scent, raised her on a huge bubble of ecstasy. Sebastian slipped his body into hers, and she felt the eruption of his held-back passion, holding him close. The past was behind her, the future not yet revealed—now there was only the present, and she could think of nothing else.

Berenice was confined to the bedroom for several days, and he was with her for much of the time, her close companion. When he was away she was stricken, hobbling about on the stick he had given her, her ankle too sore to bear her weight. As time passed, her injury healed, but they remained enchanted with each other's society. When they wandered hand in hand on the edge of the cliffs, watching the sunset kindling earth, heaven and water with a mystic fire, it was as if no one else existed.

The change in their relationship was obvious to Dulcie who, in love herself and wanting everyone to share this bliss, began to dare hope that the situation would last. Her mistress was so much easier to deal with now, more patient—no longer flying off the handle. Even when things returned to near normal and Berenice once more took her turn with the chores, that tranquillity still shone through.

But idylls rarely last, and Sebastian became caught up in the troubles with Modiford, who had been raiding remote homesteads, foraging for food, arms and money. He was away for several days, along with Greg, Damian and the colonel. Peregrine took the opportunity to visit Berenice. She enjoyed being with him, chatting about the old days, commenting on the new friends they had made in Charleston, speculating on how they might have fared, had they been successful in reaching Georgetown. Berenice no longer blamed him for his sorry part in the affair, glad of his company. It helped to mitigate the loneliness that swamped her, and she sat up late with him, avoiding the bed which seemed far too wide for one person.

Sebastian returned, stirring everything into life again with his fire and force, filling the kitchen with his dominating presence, and Berenice was engaged in cooking when he entered, both of them aware of a certain estrangement. He had been living rough, camping out, visiting tenants who had suffered at Modiford's hand, his anger mounting. It was a man's world out there in the wilds, where soft emotions were best kept in check.

Yet it was a domesticated scene that greeted his return and, for an instant, Sebastian dreamed of coming back to her thus every day. How would it be, he wondered, to find her with a meal prepared for him and maybe children gathered round the table—tiny, sturdy replicas of themselves? Such yearning was painful and he cut short this reverie, brooding on remarks dropped by Juliette as soon as he set foot in the stable, before he even had had time to speak to his wife.

Of course, the Creole was a troublemaker, jealous of Berenice's position at Buckhorn House. As he had entered the kitchen, he was sure that he had seen Peregrine sneaking away through the hall door. Sebastian wished he could justifiably put him under guard. Was Berenice still encouraging the fop? It drove him mad with frustration, and he could not shake off the desire to look at her, gloat on her; he wanted to keep her a prisoner, hidden from all other eyes.

It was foolhardy. Ridiculous! But ah, if only she could learn to love him. If only he could take her in his arms and say to himself, she is mine. If only he could believe that she was his on every level—this creature of flesh and blood, sparked by an immortal soul—his to protect, to cherish, to revere.

His face betrayed none of these confusing thoughts as, deliberately testing her, he said, 'Berenice, I'm going hunting tomorrow. Do you want to come?'

She swung round, startled, and he noticed how lovely she was in her sudden excitement, her eyes as bright as jewels, her lips glistening where her tongue had steadied them.

'I'd love it, Sebastian!' she replied breathlessly, unable to credit that he was actually including her in such an outing.

'Are you quite sure?' he questioned gruffly. 'Can you bear to spend a few hours in my company?'

She controlled the sharp retort that hovered on her tongue, afraid that he might snatch the treat from her. Studiously, she kept her eyes on her work, knowing that if he started one more of those hurtful arguments which seemed to lead nowhere, she would dissolve into tears.

Berenice knew that she would suffer, riding astride again. But Sebastian insisted that she wear breeches, throwing over a pair that he thought might fit her. She held them out at arm's length. Trousers had been bad enough, but tight breeches, known by the *ton* as 'inexpressibles,' were most immodest garments for a woman to wear without the addition of a flowing skirt, which is how the fashionable rode back home. There had been a frightful scandal when one of the court ladies had appeared at a ball clad in flesh-pink ones, worn beneath a transparent Greek-style gown. The lady had been forced to retire to the country for a spell, till the talk died down.

So, embarrassed, face burning hotly, she joined him outside the house dressed in buckskins which fitted her slim hips closely. In addition she had on a full-sleeved white linen shirt, a beige leather jerkin and a wide-brimmed hat. Sebastian had even found her a pair of high, Indian-style moccasin boots, which she was certain made her look even more absurd than ever.

She was slightly mollified when Greg gave a slow, admiring whistle as he helped her into the saddle, for she needed aid, as her ankle was still troublesome. It was only then that she realized she and Sebastian were to be the sole members of the hunting party. With her jogging quietly behind him, they left the grounds of Buckhorn House. As she rode, she watched the play of early morning light over his broad, leather-covered shoulders, feeling the dew wetting her face as they brushed through the bushes, taking a narrow track which meandered between the dense mass of oak, beech and pine.

Alone last night, she had not slept well, wondering why Sebastian had elected to spend the hours of darkness drinking with Greg. Even so, she had awakened with a shivering sense of anticipation, like a child on Christmas morning, knowing that something wonderful was about to happen.

Sebastian was in a genial mood, talking to her as they went, telling her the names of the trees, pointing out birds and animals, his voice ringing with passionate enthusiasm for the glorious scenery all around them. Berenice was entranced, never having seen this side of him. He had become a different person, patiently explaining when she questioned him about the terrain, displaying a knowledge of and love for the country which astonished her.

Eventually they came to a wide stretch of open grassland. A west wind had sprung up, huge clouds throwing their swiftly moving shadows over that vast expanse of brown, gold and purple. Patches of sunlight broke through to cast a radiance, made even more dazzling by contrast.

Sebastian turned in his saddle, jammed his hat down on his head and shouted, 'I'll race you, Berenice. Show me what a fine rider you are, Lady Charioteer! I'll wager a pony on the outcome!'

'Only twenty-five pounds, sir? That's not very generous. Why, back in Bath, you said you'd have offered a monkey had you known I was competing in the phaeton race!' she responded, eyes shining.

'I must have had more money then!' Sebastian leaned over to slap his impatient horse's neck gently. The animal sensed a gallop and was restive. 'Besides, I expect to win, and don't imagine you'd be able to meet your debt if I pushed the stakes too high!'

Damned sauce! she thought happily, saying, 'Is the great horse breaker really intending to pit himself against a woman? Where's the finish line?' Her mare was nervous, too, pawing the ground, eager to be off.

He pointed to a clump of trees. 'Over there!'

'Right!'

They exploded into flight, two streaks of color, one chestnut, one black. His mount was larger, but the mare was spirited and lively. Berenice had been schooled by a wonderful old trainer at Church Stretton, and she loved horses, respecting their moods, their great hearts, their bravery. Not for her the spur, the cruelly tight bit sawing at a tender mouth, the continual use of the whip. It seemed as though the animal knew the stakes involved—not only a sizable sum of money, but Berenice's pride, and ran with speed and grace.

She loosened the rein, drummed her heels

against the mare's sides. The animal's neck was tense, her nostrils flared and her ears lay back with the speed of the wind whistling past them. Sebastian's horse's pace was less that of a racing gallop than flight itself. But the mare kept up with him, stretched in the air, touching the ground only to leave it again with a single strike of her hooves.

Berenice, her face against the flowing mane, her hair streaming out behind her, felt as if her body was light. She had become as one with her horse, wanting nothing but to float over the grass forever—the earth, the sky, the mare, all mingling with her own being.

Sebastian was gaining and he gave a wild, barbarous cry. It was flung by the wind, tossed and echoed. His horse neighed, the foam of this mad race pouring from his coat and mouth. Berenice shouted encouragement, and the mare responded, giving of her all. The trees were coming nearer, huge and black and, with one last gigantic effort, woman and mare reached there first. Berenice slowed the animal to a walk, lovingly patting her steaming neck and praising her.

'Well done, girl! Lovely girl! Pretty, clever girl!'

Sebastian drew up alongside. 'Congratulations,' he said, and he was breathing fast, sweat coursing down his face. 'I thought Damian exaggerated when he said you were an Amazon on horseback, but I admit that I was wrong.' He paused and gazed at her a beat longer than necessary 'Your hat blew away, but no matter.

You look even lovelier without it.'

Pink with heat and his praise, she dismounted, still petting the mare, who was recovering her wind. The warmth of her deep breathing wafted over Berenice's skin; her head, hot and moist, nuzzled gently against her shoulder.

'She's a fine animal,' Berenice said, glancing up at him and then looking away. 'We must find water for them. They've both done well.'

'Yes. Well, this fine animal's name is Saffron.' He cocked a foot out of the stirrup and swung down. Then he pulled a purse out of his jacket pocket and tossed it over. 'She is your gift. This is yours, too. Twenty-five pounds, I believe.'

Sebastian had planned that they should race on this particular spot, knowing that there was water close by. So they rested there, and Berenice brought out the food which she had packed in a knapsack—maize-bread and fruit, cold chicken and yams, together with a canteen of rum and lime juice for him and a bottle of wine for herself. Sebastian lay on his back after they had eaten, his arms pillowed under his head, staring up at the swaying tops of the trees.

'And later, *m'amie*, you shall sup off venison if I've not lost my skill with the musket,' he said, glancing over at her with indolent amusement. 'Maybe you'd like to learn to handle a firearm?'

'What makes you think I can't?' she perked up at him.

'Can you?' His eyebrows rose, and his lips quirked.

374

'My dear sir, my father, the Marquis, shoots game on his estate—pheasants, partridges. Ever since I could toddle, I've had ample opportunity to handle guns. The gamekeeper was closer to me than my nursery maid.'

'Point taken,' he grunted, picked up his musket and disappeared into the woods.

He shot two bucks before noon, somewhat put out when he found that she already knew how to paunch and skin them, standing upwind while he slit open the stomach and then buried the contents. Berenice watched and listened and learned, just as she had done on her father's lands, a good, warm feeling growing within her. Out there in that plentiful wilderness it seemed that they were the only couple alive, and it filled her with contentment. Work over, they sat by the deep pool shaded by trees, and Sebastian announced his intention of taking a swim, stripping off his clothing with complete lack of self-consciousness.

Berenice hurriedly averted her eyes, but the desire to look grew too strong. Turning towards him, she took pleasure in the sight of his movements, for he was as fluidly graceful as a puma, for all his size. The sun glittered on the heavy lids of his eyes, the proud curve of his nose, the sensitive, sensual lips. He stood there enjoying the heat on his skin, magnificent body superbly nude. She could not help admiring the splendid width of his chest and shoulders, the narrow waist, the tight muscles of his arms covered with soft black hair, the hard thighs and long, well-formed legs.

He looked even more powerful naked. It frightened her, excited her, the restrained, almost brutal virility of that body, and she drew in a shuddering breath. He caught her studying him and grinned, his straight white teeth flashing. She blushed furiously, hanging her head so that her hair curtained her features.

'Coming in?' he asked, and when she next looked up, the smile had been wiped from his face and she was startled to see passion shining in his emerald eyes.

She nodded, her heart pumping madly, turning her back to him and divesting herself of her garments, curiously shy, wanting to cross her arm over her bosom and place a hand at the apex of her thighs. To her relief, she heard a splash as he dived in, and she crept to the water's edge, lowering herself into the pool, giving a little shriek as its icy contents stippled her skin. With long, lazy strokes, he swam across to join her, tossing back his streaming hair, and for a while they forgot their differences, happy as children, racing, splashing and laughing. Then Berenice lost sight of him as he dived beneath the surface, giving a startled shriek as his arms came up about her and his head reappeared close to her own.

Her laughter died on her lips as she stared into his eyes. His grip tightened and she was very aware of that hard, wet body, his chest and shoulders glistening with water. Unable to restrain himself, Sebastian clasped her to him with both arms, dragging her against him with savage intensity while his mouth came down on hers, his lips tasting of the pool, cool as ice, yet burning, too.

Her limbs losing all rigidity, Berenice surrendered, letting her head fall back while his mouth explored her face, her chin, sliding over her fragrant, damp flesh, down to her throat and breasts. She experienced an exquisite delight, a sense of emptiness as his lips found hers again. It was as if he sucked out her soul so that she became a part of him, mingling with his spirit in those kisses. Her lips opened, smiling; her eyes were shut, and one arm stole up about his neck, the other round his bare waist. She felt deliciously small and crushable, of no account before the urgency which he expressed in his quick breathing and the trembling of his hands.

Still clasping her close, as if afraid that the glassy dazzle of sunlight in water might come between them, he carried her to the bank. There he released her momentarily, spreading out his buffalo cloak at the foot of a giant tree, and pulling her down on it. He was cool to the touch, and the water dripped from his hair. In her nostrils was the fresh, clean smell of him and the faint odor of wine on his breath.

The sun warmed and dried her, and she stretched luxuriantly, catlike, purring, as his hands and lips moved over her face and body, delighting in the feel of her satiny skin. It was like no other time that they had lain together; perhaps it was the freedom of being naked in the forest like two primitives, the sun burning down on them, the warm breeze rustling the leaves overhead, the soothing murmur of water in their ears; perhaps it was because they were alone at last, with nothing to remind them of their past.

Whatever the cause, this time their love-making took them to a different stage of intimacy. They knew each other now, no longer strangers, their coming together a peaceful one, as both began to dare believe that their mating had its roots in something finer and more lasting than mere needs of the flesh. Berenice had never before felt such hunger to be united with him. Sebastian could think of nothing save the joy of her quiet acceptance, and the bliss of her mouth.

I do love him, she thought. Why fight it? His every caress sent swirls of desire coursing through her, and she met his need with her own, no longer playing a passive role, but boldly, wantonly, moving her lips across his with sweet provocation, her fingertips sliding across his back, wandering down to his hips, learning to know the shape of him, excited by the way that sinewy body quivered at her touch.

With a low growl, Sebastian slipped a knee between her thighs, spreading her legs, and she gave a sigh of satisfaction as he slid into her body. Soon she was aware of nothing but his movements within her, his hands gripping her buttocks, raising them to meet his every thrust, taking her into a world of blazing excitement, body, soul and mind shivering.

Time was of no account then. It could have

been moments or hours—she did not know or care. At last, as she lay quietly in the sleepy afterglow, he stirred, laughter threading through his voice as he said tenderly,

'*Mon amour*, you bewitch me from my duties. But we must saddle up if we're to make Buckhorn House by nightfall.'

He got up, pulling on his breeches with swift, controlled movements and thrusting his arms into the fringed jacket. Following his example, Berenice dressed, too, though reluctantly, wishing she could have kept him longer, still needful, knowing that she could never have enough of him.

They were almost ready to leave, the deer carcasses hanging one each side of his saddle, when a slight sound made him whirl round, fists bunched, automatically adopting a fighter's stance. Berenice stared in alarm as a painted and feathered brave leaped from behind the trees. His dark face contorted with anger, this ferocious aspect accentuated by the livid scar running down one cheek. His head was ornamented with scarlet feathers, and from his belt dangled the fiery locks of a white woman he had scalped, thus earning his name.

Everything happened with horrifying speed. The warrior's arm went back, a tomahawk arced through the air, and Sebastian cursed as the weapon sliced his coat, pinning his left arm to the pine at his back. The brave sprang. Sebastian jerked himself free, blood spreading over the leather as he met him. He wound a leg between his and twisted him to the ground.

They rolled together viciously, quick as striking snakes. Sebastian found himself pinned under his attacker, but his steely fingers found the Indian's throat, his grip closing with murderous force. With desperate strength the man tried to break that deadly hold, twisting and thrashing. Berenice woke into life, seizing Sebastian's musket from the saddle bow, standing over the battling men, and aiming it at the Indian's face. He surrendered immediately, and Sebastian sat up, kneeling over him.

'Copper Hair!' he panted, fingers still pressed to his windpipe. 'Who sent you to kill me?'

'Modiford!' Copper Hair gasped, his eyes on the musket.

Sebastian relaxed, getting up and looming over the brave, taking the weapon from Berenice's hands. 'I thought as much. I should kill you, but I won't. You'll be spared for the sake of your father, my old friend, Whirling Hawk. But run quickly, before I change my mind!'

Copper Hair scrambled to his feet. With a glare of pure hatred, he merged back into the forest as swiftly and silently as he had come. Berenice did not give him a second glance, turning to Sebastian, her hand on his injured arm, taking out her handkerchief and trying to stem the flow of blood seeping through the rent in his jacket.

'Oh, my love!' she cried. 'Thank God you were wearing it. It saved you from a deeper wound.'

'That's why we favor leather,' he replied, grimacing with pain. 'It's not just for show, as Greg might lead you to believe.' His eyes twinkled with amused pride. 'You acted promptly, *chérie*—I'd never have thought it of you. Becoming quite the pioneer, aren't you?'

He looked at her face, filled with concern, as she tried to examine his wound. Her calling him 'my love' had amazed him. There were streaks of blood from his injury smearing her cheek where she had pressed to it in her anguish. Though she was ashen and he could feel her trembling, he saw that she was smiling. She looked up at him, overcome with relief at finding him still alive. She begged him to let her wash and bind the wound, but he would not delay, insisting that they mount at once and return to the house, lest Copper Hair bring more braves and repeat his attack.

It was a breakneck ride home, with Sebastian growing steadily weaker through loss of blood. In the end, she had to lead his horse while he slumped low in the saddle. She was riven with fear, expecting a band of warriors to descend on them at any moment. Berenice was never more thankful than when she saw the house rising out of the trees, and she practically fell from her mount in the courtyard, yelling for help.

Adam and Quico came running, an anxious gaggle of spectators gathering at the commotion. Greg appeared instantly, and Sebastian paced the kitchen, eyes like granite as he told him what had happened.

Then the doctor said, 'Stop prowling around like a goddamn cougar and let me take a look at that arm.'

'Later! There's a crisis looming,' snapped Sebastian, but he came to rest near the hearth, leaning on the stone overmantel, kicking at a log with his booted foot till it collapsed in a shower of sparks.

'Don't act crazy!' Greg stood squarely in front of him. 'Sit down before you fall down. You're bleeding like a stuck pig!'

Sebastian did as he suggested, taking a stool by the fire. Then Greg set to work, pulling off the fringed jacket. Berenice stared in horror at the blood seeping through the sleeve of his shirt. She met his eyes, and tried to say something, but her tongue would not obey her and she was shaking so much that she had to cling to the back of a chair. She felt hot and sick. Then the room blurred, everything spinning as she sank to the floor in a dead faint.

She came to herself slowly, attended by Dulcie, just as Greg washed Sebastian's wound with rum while the injured man shouted, *'Dieu!* That hurts!'

His roaring brought Berenice to full consciousness. Dulcie was smiling at her, and saying, 'He'll be all right. You must rest, my lady.'

Berenice groaned, the room heaving. 'Oh, God—I feel so ill! What's the matter with me?'

Regarding her with amusement in her eyes, and something else, too—a kind of excited glow, Dulcie whispered, 'It's your baby making you sick.'

ELEVEN

Dulcie's whispered words hit Berenice with the force of a thunderclap. She held herself still, hardly breathing. It couldn't be true, could it? But then she realized that it very well could be true, in fact, it would have been unusual if it hadn't been!

She looked up and stared into Dulcie's smiling face. The maid nodded, put an arm round her and helped her to her feet. Berenice was still reeling from shock. She felt strange, wobbly, hardly able to believe that Dulcie was right. It was hard to think clearly, for she was still possessed by the horror of that fight in the forest—the vicious Copper Hair and Sebastian fighting to the death if need be. And now this shattering news!

'How can you be sure?' She kept her voice down, though the others were so busy with Sebastian that no one was paying much heed to the women.

'I've been wondering for some time. You've not had a flux of blood since we reached Carolina, have you?'

It was part of a personal maid's duty to supply her mistress with small cotton napkins every month which, after use, were boiled, dried, ironed and returned to a drawer till they were required again. Thus, if she kept a check on dates, she often suspected that a baby was on the way even before the lady whom she served was aware of it.

'I haven't thought about it,' Berenice stammered, pressing a hand to her hot forehead.

'I dismissed it as due to the change of climate, but lately—I've noticed something different about you. Your bodices are tighter, you've complained of dizziness sometimes.' Dulcie was half afraid of how Berenice would take this revelation, yet could not repress her own joy. Babies sometimes built bridges, and she longed to see Berenice and Sebastian lay down their arms, declare a truce, and live in peace together.

Greg and Quico had managed to get Sebastian to his feet, though, shamed by his weakness, he pushed them away, staggered across the kitchen and hall and into the bedroom without their aid. Berenice gripped Dulcie by the hand saying, 'We'll talk about this later. Now I must go to him.'

'I'm coming with you,' Dulcie declared, though her major concern was for her mistress, not the master. She was convinced that he was made of iron and would survive almost anything, whereas Berenice, conditioned by upbringing and breeding, was more vulnerable, and needed love and understanding, never more so than now.

Quico laid back the sheet and Sebastian sprawled heavily across the bed. The Indian hauled off his boots, advising, 'Rest. You've lost a lot of blood. We'll take care of everything.'

Greg stood at the bedside, cool and efficient, opening his bag of medical paraphernalia. Berenice, panicking, grabbed him by the arm.

'He's going to bleed to death! Do something!'

Her eyes were wide, her clothing disarrayed, but he merely smiled, laying his instruments on the table. 'Calm down, Comtesse! It's flattering to be so much in demand. Maybe I should turn your room into a hospital ward, it's been used so much of late—first you—and now him. Be good and fetch the brandy. I'll lace it with opium. When I stitch him up, it's going to hurt like hell, and he's already been cursing me most horribly, threatening to tear my heart out and eat it stewed in cumin seeds!'

'You're a butcher, Greg,' Sebastian growled, impatient with any form of disability that prevented him from operating at full stretch.

'Shut up, you bad-tempered old devil!' Greg retorted cheerfully. 'You sound like a grizzly with a sore arse. Here, drink this, and give us all a break,' and he thrust the glass under Sebastian's nose.

'Get on with it,' he muttered ungraciously, tossing back the draught. 'Put in your stitches and be damned!'

'And you, girl,' the doctor swung round on Dulcie. 'Make yourself useful. Go ask Jessy for a sheet and start tearing it into dressings.'

Dulcie looked at Quico, and he nodded in agreement. Though never discussing it in any detail, they worked together for the mutual benefit of those two people who had given them back their lives, their hope and their dignity,

385

blessings never to be forgotten by either.

'Where's my brother?' Berenice needed him, dying to tell him he was to be an uncle, yet not daring even to mention it.

'He's on guard duty, madame,' said Quico, a considering look in his eyes which made her wonder if Dulcie had already informed him of her delicate condition.

With the drug stealing through his system, and already hazy, Sebastian had the impression that Berenice was floating above him, solicitous as an angel. She had probably saved his life, and he struggled to understand why. Was it just her natural instinct for self-preservation? Fear of being captured by Copper Hair? Was it, impossible idea, that she cared what happened to him? His eyes met hers, and she was transfixed by what she read in them. A quick surge of hope flared in her breast, but was dashed when, as swiftly as it had come, his tender expression changed, replaced by hardness.

Sebastian refused to allow his physical weakness to trick him into believing her capable of becoming his helpmate, his partner for life. Soon, he suspected, this lovely dream-woman tending him so gently would revert to someone changeable and unpredictable. He dared not soften or put his emotions in jeopardy.

He shifted impatiently, 'This isn't women's work, Berenice. Get you gone.'

'My place is here, with you,' she said firmly.

Sebastian was prevented from saying more, for Greg began to suture the wound. It was an agonizing process, the long needle and gut thread gradually drawing the jagged edges of skin together. Quico and Adam held Sebastian steady, ignoring him as he cursed.

Giddiness threatening, Berenice could not watch, convincing her that Dulcie was right in her diagnosis. She *was* pregnant. A slow ripple of excitement started to pervade her whole being as she finally accepted the truth. She could feel within herself a new life beginning to flower.

She had the almost uncontrollable urge to tell Sebastian and see his reaction, then her spirits plummeted as she guessed what it would be. Distrust, and disbelief that it was of his begetting. But surely he didn't believe her wanton, still? His anger over her running off with Peregrine loomed in her mind. Before any public announcement could be made, she must decide the future of herself and her unborn child. She felt heavy with responsibility, and stood for a moment, hands pressed to a belly that was not even rounded as yet. She tried to imagine what it would be like. A handsome little boy with Sebastian's features, or a dainty girl who resembled her? Though having some experience with Lady Olivia's children, enjoying romping with them, newborn infants alarmed her. They were so small and helpless and cried such a lot. As for giving birth! Lucinda, who'd never done it, and several other ladies who had, had recounted bloodcurdling tales of week-long labors, of agony and forceps and stitches.

Where would she be, she wondered, when she was near her time? With Sebastian? It was doubtful. Her heart ached as she finally admitted that she was in love with him—no passing infatuation, but a love that would endure for the rest of her life. With a sad little smile, she realized that half her anger and hatred of him had been a defense against this mighty force that could tear her apart.

A knock at the door disrupted her thoughts, and all the worry, fear and pain exploded into rage when she found Juliette there, demanding admittance. Leah was with her, carrying a basket of herbs on top of which lay a strange object comprised of chicken feathers and twigs.

'What on earth is that?' Berenice cried.

'A spell for making the master heal quickly,' the old woman mumbled.

'Bad medicine,' observed Quico, long features dour.

'Be silent, savage.' Juliette tried to step into the room.

'What do you want?' Berenice barred the way, eyes blazing like those of a lioness defending its cubs.

'He needs me.' Juliette returned that glare, a powerful woman, her face framed by her straight black hair.

'He needs no one but me. I'm his wife,' Berenice replied grittily, refusing to be intimidated.

Juliette was as still and watchful as a snake. 'What d'you know of him? You, with your prissy airs and silly gentility! What can you offer such a man?'

Had Berenice been holding a weapon, she would have struck her dead. Rage boiled in her, an overpowering murderous rage that set her trembling.

'Get out!' she spat venomously, hands clenched into fists, legs tensed to spring, a virago itching for a fight. 'And take that damned old witch with you! We don't want your evil charms and incantations. I'm warning you—keep away from him in future, or you'll have me to reckon with.'

Juliette stared at her through slitted lids, an icy smile lifting her lips. 'I'll go, but don't think this is the end of it. I never give up. My gods will punish you.' She turned away, still with that secretive, menacing smile.

Sebastian heard the disturbance, his body limp against the pillows. 'Those damned women,' he complained weakly, as Greg completed his task, binding the arm with a strip of bandage. 'Can't they quarrel elsewhere? Send 'em packing, there's a good fellow.'

Quico, starting to help him out of the rest of his clothes, pursed his lips and said, with a faint air of reproof, 'A wife should stay with her sick husband.'

A sour expression crossed Sebastian's haggard features. 'They're all the same, every one of 'em!'

'That's one hell of a sweeping statement,' Greg said in a slow, considering way. 'What makes you think she's any different?'

'Sometimes for an intelligent man, you can be mighty stupid. She's a fine woman. I tell you, if you weren't my friend—and you can be an infuriating bastard at times—I might have

389

tried to lure her away. I could've got rid of you in a hundred and one ways—an accident out hunting, a chance arrow, the silent knife in the back. But she loves you, you fool, and you can't see it.'

Oh, God! He mustn't say that! Berenice thought. I don't want Sebastian to know. But Greg *had* said it, and it couldn't be recalled. She looked at her husband anxiously, wondering if Greg's statement had penetrated the fog of pain and exhaustion.

The anger had died from his eyes, leaving them unreadable. Greg assumed wryly that his words had fallen on stony ground, but next time he looked at his patient, he saw that he was asleep. 'That's the best cure for him,' he said, smiling at Berenice. 'Make sure he doesn't try to get up—and don't encourage any activity that'll make the wound burst open. You know what I mean?'

'I think I do,' she mumbled, blushing as she tidied away the bowls, stained linen and general mess which any operation, minor or serious, leaves in its wake.

'Fine. Then I'll see you in the morning. Come along everybody,' and Greg hustled the others out of the room.

The night had rushed in unnoticed, the stars twinkling like diamond dust in the sky, and Berenice was strangely content, even amid the furor of her turbulent emotions, wanting nothing more than to anticipate Sebastian's every need. For once, he was very nearly helpless—and dependent on her.

He slept and she sat beside him, feasting her eyes on every contour of his face, and she daydreamed of remaining at Mobby Cove, never returning to the town, wandering the forests and plains with him. Of camping beneath a starry canopy, of feeling the baby moving inside her and telling him, laughing, that he was to be a father. Most of all, she dreamed of him being pleased at her news, wonder and joy widening his eyes. Perhaps he would swing her up in his arms and hug her, calling her his treasure, as he had done in those rare moments of accord.

She lit the candles and undressed, washed away the dirt of the journey then, naked, slid between the sheets, feeling the heat of his sleeping form, her shoulder pressed against his, thigh following the line of his leg as he lay on his back. She did not want to sleep, hating to lose contact with him for even a moment. There might be too many lonely nights ahead when she would be unable to look at him, or touch him.

She had to fill herself with him, saturate every fiber of her being with memories, and his scent was in her nostrils, that musky, sense-stirring tang that was essentially Sebastian. She pressed closer, lipping over his skin, tasting the salt of his sweat, returning to his sleeping mouth, yearning to absorb and be in turn absorbed. She was careful not to put pressure on his damaged arm, but longed for him to wake. As if she were a succubus sent to haunt his dreams, he became aware of her and stirred as she ran her fingers down to his groin, knowing how to pleasure him. Then he woke more fully, said nothing but touched her face. Smoothly, tenderly, silently, they became one. When he withdrew, Berenice ran her hands over him, not with passion, but just for the sheer delight of it. He leaned over to kiss her parted lips, then fell asleep again.

Berenice stayed awake, her mind working feverishly. She had lost him to slumber and felt this remoteness as a shivering chill. To comfort herself, she thought of the new presence within her, and this was so sweet that it made her heart ache. She turned on her side towards Sebastian, wanting desperately to share her news, yet was afraid to speak. He might not want it, but it was there, growing larger by the minute. A few weeks more and she might feel the baby move inside of her. How long could she conceal it? And what would he do when he found out? The inability to guess filled her with despair. But she knew that no matter how harshly he treated her, there was nothing she could do to save herself, caught in the snare of love.

Yet confessing this did not bring the hopelessness she had expected, quite the reverse. She curled at his side, watching the play of shadows in the warm intimacy of the room, content to lie and listen to his steady breathing, to rest her hands on him and know that he was really there, a living man of bone and muscle, not some apparition created from her own romantic longings.

Sebastian woke first, as grey fingers of light were creeping between the brocade curtains.

He was instantly alert, jerking into complete consciousness as a trained fighter will, aware of the stiffness of his arm and, at the same time, realizing that he was not the sole occupant of the bed. He did not move, slowly savoring the presence of Berenice, sleeping peacefully beside him. He felt the softness of her silken skin brushing his thigh, and the warmth of her body beneath the sheet.

It seemed so right somehow, that he was scared by it, knowing that she was weaving a subtle spell about him, trapping him in a web from which he would never want to break free. And this was the same woman who had once fought him and damned him with every breath! As she slept on, he studied her face, grimacing at his folly. This girl he had married, this mystery of loveliness, touched by a strange, magical alchemy—why should she mean so much? Why should she bedevil him so that his hands trembled as if he were afraid?

She stirred, dreams penetrated by his watchfulness, and her lids fluttered open. Instantly remembering that she was with child, her eyes widened, all her fears rushing up.

'Go back to sleep,' he said. 'Yesterday was hard. You need the healing power of rest.'

She shook her head, every nerve in her body responding to his nearness. 'I can't sleep any more. How are you, Sebastian? Does your arm hurt?'

'You're mighty concerned about my health all of a sudden. Why? Do you hope to become a widow?'

Cast down by his reply which indicated that he had wakened in exactly the mood she most feared, Berenice bit her lip to still its trembling, sitting up, her hair falling about her bare shoulders, eyes pools of sorrow.

'Oh, Sebastian, you're always so distrustful of my motives,' she cried. 'What have I ever done to harm you?' She knew his body, his passions, but he had kept the secrets of his soul from her.

His eyes were hard when he looked at her, but the morning light fell on her face, showing up that fine bone structure that would make her beautiful still, even when she was old. Sincerity shone in her eyes, and he was moved by her concern for him. He made up his mind that she should hear the truth.

'Not you,' he said gravely, avoiding her gaze now, staring up at the paneled tester of the huge bed. 'You've done me no real harm, but there was another woman—long ago—in France.'

'Tell me,' she whispered, eager to know his secrets, trembling on the brink of discovery.

'You don't really want to know my past, do you? You'll find it monstrously boring.' His reply was sarcastic, but when she tentatively groped for his hand under the covers, his fingers closed round hers, and he began to talk in a flat monotone, speaking of things which he had never revealed to a living soul.

Berenice was caught up in wonder, and also a pride that made her throat ache with unshed tears, quite overcome by the strangeness of that moment. It was so unusual for them to be lying together without passion. She hardly dared let the breath slide through her nostrils lest it snap that tenuous thread of communication. He spoke of many happenings; his life in France before the Revolution, his family, the Chateau Hilaire, and her heart sank like a stone when he mentioned a woman, whom he had loved in his youth.

Then she wanted to stop him from going further, wanted to place her fingers over his lips and prevent him uttering those words which pricked her like needles, yet she did not move, eager to hear, but fearing to do so. Instead, she clung to his hand and let him talk on without interruption.

'She was so beautiful, and I was very young and impressionable,' his deep voice ran on, and it was as if he had forgotten her presence and was speaking to himself. 'She was older than me, and experienced. She loved power and wealth above all else. She wanted more than I could offer, playing political games, becoming involved with those who were plotting to overthrow the monarchy. I, too, listened to her, and to the stirring words of my greatest friend, Jacques, who longed to free the oppressed, to feed the poor, starving in the squalor of Paris, whilst the *aristos* squandered vast fortunes in gambling and high-living. Oh, yes, I admit there was much that needed reform, but in the bloodbath that followed, the innocent suffered with the guilty. Thousands were dragged to the guillotine, a public spectacle for the mob crowding the *Place de la Révolution.*'

He paused, as if the memories of that turbulent time were too painful to put into speech, but Berenice pressed against him, at last able to ask him questions to which she had been longing to know the answers ever since they met.

A rush of questions escaped her lips. 'Did she love you, this woman? What happened? Why did you leave France if you were sympathetic to her cause?'

Berenice felt the tension in him, and his voice hardened. 'No, she didn't love me, and I couldn't agree with everything the Jacobins were doing. It was Jacques whom she adored—Jacques with his high words, his fanatical fire! She had been my mistress for some time, but her lowly birth prevented her from taking her place in society. This angered her. She considered it her right to do so and hated those who scorned her, doing her utmost to help bring about their downfall. I was a fool, and she used me ruthlessly for her own ends. When the mob finally came to Chateau Hilaire, she was at their head, flaunting the tricolor. She'd hoped to take over the place as a reward for her services. Perhaps she succeeded, I don't know. All that I found out later was that our child was dead.'

Berenice froze. 'A child?' she exclaimed.

'A little girl called Lisette. She was two years old.' He said it softly, and there was something in his tone which sent a shiver down her spine.

It was difficult to stop herself from flinging her arms about him, kissing away that terrible look of grief and telling him that there would soon be another child—their child, a precious gift for them to love and care for. Now she understood everything. The fine steel of which he was shaped had been tempered by fire. It was awful to feel so young, so ignorant, and she wished she were more worldly, unaware that it was her very youthfulness and optimism that could be his salvation.

He leaned back against the pillows, cheeks pale under the tan. Her love gave her the courage to push the covers aside and roll against him, clinging to his shoulders before he could stop her. 'Oh, darling, why didn't you tell me this before? I didn't know—didn't understand.' The relief was tremendous. He had been a youngster struggling to rebuild his life—not some outlaw driven by greed.

Shaken by her show of emotion, he picked his next words carefully, still hardly daring to trust her. 'We've never really talked until now. You seemed to hate me so.'

'We must talk much more in the future. Perhaps I need to be listened to as well,' she said tentatively, feeling her way.

Even now she was holding something in reserve, vast areas of her life and his still to be explored—as large as the plains, almost. She would take it step by step, one day at a time and, just for a while, she would keep the baby a secret, a wise move under any circumstances as miscarriage was not uncommon and, should she be unlucky enough for this to happen, then her own disappointment would be enough to endure, without the additional burden of his.

He kissed her, a warm, affectionate kiss, almost that which a man gives a beloved wife of many years. Then he shifted her down so that she lay with her head against his chest, while his fingers stroked her hair. Presently his hand grew still, and stealing a glance up at him, she saw that he slept. The lines had been smoothed out of his face and he looked very peaceful, as if the action of confiding in her had lanced a septic wound and released the poison within his mind.

Berenice slid out of bed, tiptoeing about so as not to disturb Sebastian as she dressed and hurried through her toilet. Though queasy with morning sickness, she was determined to hide it and go to the kitchen to prepare nourishing food that would make him well again. She thought no further than this, leaving the future to take care of itself. Later, I'll decide what I'm going to do about the baby, she promised herself, and Sebastian and Peregrine—and everything.

It was still early, and the sun was creeping from behind the retreating clouds, coming up in a blaze of glory—sweeping fans of orange, vermilion and green spanning the sky in the east. Berenice stepped out into the dewy freshness, filling her lungs with the crystal-clear air. The world seemed to have extra sparkle that day, as if the scales had fallen from her eyes and she was seeing it for the first time.

She wanted to be alone there, communing with nature, appreciating every birdcall, each branch shimmering with diamondlike droplets, every blade of grass holding a wonderful message of hope, illumined by love. Then she come upon Peregrine lying in a cane armchair on the verandah, his face pallid after a night of heavy drinking.

'You're an early bird,' she said, thinking how rough he looked and wondering what she had ever seen in him. The memory was misty now, as if it had happened to someone else.

'They catch the worms, so it's said,' he answered wearily, so different now, compared to the dashing young blade who had enchanted her in the days when he pursued the pleasures of town with unrivaled glee.

'What's the matter, Peregrine?' she asked gently, for, no matter what had happened, they were friends and she was concerned for him.

He sighed heavily, his clothing crumpled, his linen far from clean. He was unaccustomed to looking after himself and Sebastian had forbidden the servants to wait on him. 'This adventure is not what I thought it would be—or rather, it's precisely what I expected, but I permitted myself to be swayed by others. Your brother, for one.'

'Ah, come, be fair. You can't blame Damian.' She sat on the top step of the verandah where vines with purple blossoms snaked upwards. A green, jewel-bright lizard skittered up the white stuccoed wall, stopping for a split second, motionless, its sides palpitating, before darting off again.

'I was a fool allowing Lady Chard to persuade

me into coming. All that fine talk about her relatives in Georgetown. It was a trick. The old bawd wanted me off her hands.' Peregrine never had been able to take responsibility for his own actions.

'Oh, dear, you are in a mumpish humor! I'm sure she acted with the best of intentions. You need a change of life. You're drinking too much, and should find yourself a young lady.' She tried to stir him out of his gloom by speaking in a light vein.

'And how, pray, am I to do that, marooned out here?' he asked pettishly. 'But when I get back to somewhere that remotely resembles civilization it will be a different story.'

'I'm sure it will. You must be patient.'

'Patient! Rat me, madam, I've had a troubled night, brooding about it,' he replied slowly. 'It's no use. I just can't fit in here. These men—so rough, so crude—not what I'm used to at all. Dammee, they're more savage than the Indians. And your husband! Zounds, every time he looks in my direction I fear he's about to strike me.'

Berenice's lips quirked into a smile at his woebegone expression. 'You've given him enough provocation. I think he's shown admirable restraint. He could have had you clapped in irons for mutiny.'

Peregrine frowned, sitting up, his hands dangling between his knees, a frill of soiled lace cuff part covering them. 'I thought Damian was my friend, but now he's siding with the Comte. Oh, it's all very well

400

for him. He's taken to the life like a duck to water. You too, Berenice.' His eyes were filled with reproach. 'You avoid me now.'

Once, his sorrowful, little-boy-lost look would have made her heart flip over, but not anymore. She rested her hand on his as a reassuring gesture. 'Sebastian doesn't like our friendship.'

He snatched his hand away as if stung. 'So you must do what your husband orders, must you? That's devilish beastly! I never expected to hear such a confession from the self-willed Lady Berenice. You're becoming as meek and obedient as a parson's wife.'

This riled her, for no lady of spirit liked people to think that her husband had the upper hand. 'If this appears to be the case, then it's because I want it,' she said sharply. 'I've learned a lot since we came here. So much, that I can't begin to tell you. I couldn't go back to the old ways now.'

'I don't suppose he'd let you. Probably lay his cane across your backside. Maybe you'd like that? Is that the secret of his success with women? Is he something of a brute in the boudoir? I've been told that some ladies find a cruel fellow exciting.' Peregrine was hurting inside, and this made him spiteful. He was lonely and bored, and felt like a fish out of water at Buckhorn House.

'Please, don't.' Berenice was genuinely sorry for him, wishing she could do something to make him feel better. 'You used not to be so unkind. I've found love, Peregrine. That

401

emotion you've written of so beautifully in your poetry.'

'Love? You're in love with *him!*' Peregrine stared at her blankly noting that she had never looked more beautiful, even though her dress was plain, her hair untended, and not a trace of paint or powder colored her complexion.

'Don't scoff at me. It's true, and I thank God for it.'

Peregrine sobered. 'And he? Does he return your love?' He would have given anything to have her speak thus of him. He wanted her, but more than this—he realized, too late, that she meant more to him than anything on earth, in heaven or in hell.

'I don't know how he feels.' She was speaking low, as if to herself. 'Indeed I've done much to make him hate me. All I can say is that if ever harm should come to him, I'd want to die. Life would hold no meaning for me. I can only pray that I may earn his regard, given time. It's a great thing to be able to love, and one is never the loser if one gives more than one receives.'

'Quite the sage, my sweet.' He gave a crooked grin, a flash of his old charm shining through. 'So, I see that I must concede defeat to your husband. How very unfashionable of you to fall in love with the man you married.'

'Then we can still be friends?' Her face seemed to be translucent, lit from within.

Peregrine could not help responding to this appeal. 'I'll always serve you, Berenice, in any way possible,' he said sincerely. 'I'm a rascal and unworthy, but you can rely on me. However, I'll be going away as soon as I'm able. I must reach Georgetown and visit my ratted aunt. My purse is woefully thin, and a gentleman needs to find a way to keep up appearances. But I'll never forget you and, if you need my help at any time, you've only to ask.' He took her hand and bore it to his lips, for an instant becoming the noble knight of his poems, wearing his lady's colors on his lance and swearing to champion her forever.

Berenice left him soon after, saddened by the picture of his figure slumped in the chair. Yes, she thought, he is out of place here. He needs the setting of coffeehouses, elegant streets, shops, clubs, pleasure gardens, and the stimulus of irresponsible companions. Once upon a time, she, too, had been convinced that this was the only way to live, but that was in the past and she now saw it for what it was—an empty, frivolous existence.

She made her way towards the kitchen with a light step, looking forward to those small yet essential chores which hold a home together, and through which she could express her devotion to Sebastian. Trivial services such as she might once have left to the servants; preparing his breakfast tray, making sure that he had clean linen and a supply of cigars to hand. She embraced such wifely duties willingly, wanting to weave herself into his life so that she became as indispensable to him as breathing.

For the whole of that morning, Berenice felt as if she were walking on a rainbow, expression dreamy, a smile curving her lips.

Dulcie eyed her with amusement, and asked

as they worked together, 'Are you well, milady?'

Berenice did not answer at once, afraid that by putting her emotions into words, the reality might fade—so delicate, so sensitive a thing was love. What awakens it? she wondered. What keeps it? What is this magic which suddenly transforms two people, making them hungry to possess every part of one another?

Then she said, 'A little sick, but better than I was, Dulcie. When do you think my baby will be born? Can we work out the date?'

'We can try, but perhaps you should ask Dr. Lattimer.' This was to be an important child and Dulcie was anxious that Berenice have the best of attention.

'Not yet. I want to keep it a secret for a while longer.'

'But you're not still thinking of leaving the Comte, are you?' Dulcie had hoped that her mistress would put such thoughts behind her now.

'We'll see.' Berenice was still unprepared to commit herself completely.

Yet she felt so different. It was as if she had become an adult overnight. In her most secret heart, she had thought this would happen when she lost her virginity to her husband on their wedding night, but instead she had fought him every inch of the way, refusing to accept that she loved him, when the truth was plain to all around her.

Tears filled her eyes when she remembered how he had behaved, forgiving him now that she understood the cause; it was not her, per se, but visions of the woman in France. Looking back on her own actions, she blushed with shame. How proud she had been, believing every male should be her doting slave. How quickly she had flown into a temper when she did not get her own way. How both of them have changed, she mused.

'Oh, Dulcie, isn't it a beautiful day!' she cried rapturously, up to her elbows in soapsuds as she scrubbed at the washing by the stream, no longer caring that the sun was scorching her back, only aware of the brook frothing over the mossy boulders and the gaudy birds caroling in the branches above her head.

'Yes, madam. Everything takes on an added lustre when one is in love,' Dulcie agreed, wringing the clothes, her skirt wet to the knees as she worked. She was in a hurry to get through it and meet Quico.

Never, in Dulcie's wildest dreams, had she, a child of the slums, imagined she could find contentment with a man so vastly different in every way, but the miracle had happened. Quico revered and respected her; a gentle, caring, passionate lover. She was learning to know his world, to appreciate his values, willing to throw in her lot with him. He wanted to marry her, and she had agreed.

'I've not said I'm in love,' Berenice reminded, sitting down on the bank and drying her hands on the bottom of her petticoat.

'There's no need, my lady. I can see it by the stars in your eyes.' Dulcie was rolling down her sleeves and buttoning the wristbands. 'Can I go now, please?'

'Yes, of course. And what will you be learning this afternoon, I wonder? More Indian lore?' Berenice asked with a chuckle.

'I expect so, madam. He's teaching me the language—'

'The language of love, more like.'

Dulcie laughed, then her pretty face became serious. 'I want to spend my life with him. Men have always used and abused me, even when I was a child. I trusted none of them, till I met him. He's not like that. He treats me as his equal, asks my opinion and listens to what I have to say. This means more than gold and riches. I've agreed to marry him. He'll build a cabin for us, a real home that I can furnish as I want. For the first time, I shall have something of my own—a house, a bit of land to farm and, God willing, children who I can bring up in clear, sweet air, and educate so that they have a chance in the future.'

'Does this mean that you'll be leaving me?' Berenice found it hard to imagine life without her.

'Bless you, no! Not for a while, at least. Quico is loyal to your husband, and he'll not abandon him! We shall stay, for as long as possible—certainly till you're settled here. But one day we'll branch out on our own.'

'My dear friend, I wish you the greatest happiness.' Berenice rose to her feet and embraced her maid, kissing her warmly.

Dulcie returned the embrace, sniffing and

wiping away the tears, then she laughed again. 'You don't think I'd leave you to have that baby all on your own, do you?'

'I trust not, for I shall be frightened to death!' Berenice answered, her own eyes wet. 'Now, off you go and find your man.'

In an exultant frame of mind, she watched Dulcie tripping lightly off in the direction of Quico's quarters, then laid the wet clothes in the wicker basket, and sauntered towards the house. On the way, she smiled gaily at a few of Sebastian's rapscallions who were lounging in the sun near the stables, and their pleased response made her realize that she had never gone out of her way to be friendly to them before.

She intended to peg the garments on the line to dry and then go indoors, her thoughts already leaping ahead to the moment when she would enter the bedchamber. Greg would have been in to change the dressing on Sebastian's wound, and she planned to take up the tray of food that she had prepared herself. They would spend the afternoon together, with him talking to her as if he had suddenly discovered that she was an intelligent human being instead of a vapid doll—and then, oh, then—her breath shortened and her heart beat rapidly, then he would make love to her.

Desire tightened like a coil in her loins, her nipples rising almost painfully against the thin material of her dress as she imagined them lying in that great bed through the torrid heat of siesta. The things she would do to him! Bold things which she had wanted to try, but had never quite dared—till now. She'd show him how consummate a lover she could be, his mistress as well as his wife. And then—just maybe, she might drop a hint about her pregnancy.

Lost in this wonderful vision; she stopped abruptly when she found someone in her path. Coming back to earth with a bump, she saw that it was Juliette. Berenice tried to push past, but the Creole stood her ground, her black eyes shining like glassy pebbles under the sun's harsh glare.

'Move aside,' Berenice said haughtily. 'I've work to do.'

'Still busy caring for Sebastian?' There was an ugly, sneering quality in Juliette's voice.

Berenice was suddenly aware that the garden around them had become a jungle, filled with the raw passions of hatred, jealousy and anger. The sensation was so intense that she could feel her scalp rising. Two strong-willed women in love with the same man; a potent and fatal brew.

'He needs me.' Berenice strove to maintain her dignity, refusing to sink to vulgar name-calling and invective.

'So you like to think,' Juliette said, on a menacing purr. 'But I sat up all night working strong magic to make him whole again. I've a salve here. His wound will heal at once if this is placed on it.'

'It's more likely to poison him,' Berenice said scornfully. 'I don't need your magic. I'm using proper medicines—things you wouldn't begin to understand.'

'I understand plenty. What can you do for him, eh?'

'More than a draggle-tailed slut who can't keep her nose out of other peoples' affairs!' Berenice shot back, refusing to be frightened by Juliette's baneful glare, but if ever she felt the force of undiluted evil it was then.

Juliette stared at her, still as a snake before it strikes. 'I was part of his life before he met you. Why don't you leave as you said? You don't belong here, and mean less than nothing to him.'

Berenice's hand itched to strike her, the instinct for murder making a red mist float before her eyes. It was degrading to feel this so intensely, but strangely satisfying, too. She felt tinglingly alive. Nothing Juliette could say or do would hurt her now. She was with child and, then and there, she made up her mind to tell Sebastian right away. No more delay. No more hesitation. She would triumph over Juliette, and persuade him that the woman must leave at once, for the sake of their heir. Sebastian was hers, and no one was going to take him from her.

Juliette did not move, the two women caught up in a situation as old as time, then, 'There's something you should know. Come with me,' she said.

'No,' Berenice replied and turned to walk away. She was mistress of this house and Juliette could not order her about.

Juliette's hand touched Berenice's shoulder. 'I think it's best that you come with me. I have something to show you. Something you would want to see.' Her eyes were inky pools in which Berenice felt she might drown in if she looked into them for too long. Unwilling to let the Creole take the upper hand, she grudgingly agreed to accompany the woman. Soon they reached her log cabin on the other side of the garden, a large wooden structure with a palm-leaf roof. Juliette held aside the striped Indian blanket that covered the door, and Berenice stepped inside.

It took a second or two for her to become accustomed to the gloom. Light slanted through the small, unpaned windows, dazzling rays in which dust motes and flying insects whirled in ceaseless dance. She glanced about nervously at the surprisingly sumptuous furnishings, the crimson hangings on the walls, the patterned rugs on the floor. Evidently this was the domain of someone well used to luxury. There was a large bed along one wall, canopied in vermilion silk, with a velvet counterpane, and gold-fringed cushions taking the place of pillows, a large carved armoire, an old, heavy, Spanish-style table and four matching chairs. It was a magnificent lair, bizarre and frightening.

As Berenice gazed around with growing dread, she saw other things, too. Tarot cards, strings of beads, crude pots containing bunches of dried herbs. There were piles of books; bones, counters and reptile skins. A skull grinned from the table, which was spread with a purple and gold cloth, and a long-dead alligator, teeth agape, hung from hooks in the rafters, as if suspended in water. A strong odor filled the air, spicy, sweet, yet with rotting overtones, as of meat kept too long in the heat. Berenice felt icy shivers creeping down her spine, recalling Greg's talk of voodoo.

Her fear mounted when she caught sight of Leah hunched on a stool by the hearth where embers glowed like red eyes. The stones of her many rings shone dully from the dirt-encrusted crevices of their settings, a half moon of grime under each nail. Her eyes rolled up towards Berenice's face, covert under slack lids that drooped at the outer corners, lips moving silently. She was rocking to and fro, a bundle clasped in her skeletal arms.

Juliette walked swiftly over to her, pulled back the covering and revealed a sleeping baby with a thatch of black hair. 'This is my son,' she announced, voice vibrant with pride. 'I bore him here, six months ago. Isn't he lovely? And can you guess who fathered him?'

'No,' Berenice whispered, the cold spreading from her spine to encase her whole body, like corpse wrappings.

'You can't? Then you're a bigger fool than I imagined,' Juliette responded contemptuously, picking up the child. 'It was your husband, Sebastian Lajeaunesse!'

Her voice was a roll of doom, reverberating under the rafters. Silence followed. Juliette and the crone watched Berenice with the avidity of vultures about to swoop on a carcass.

411

Not Sebastian! Dear God, *not that!* The thought was a knife-blade driven into her heart. For a moment, she stood absolutely still, staring down at the infant. No! It was not possible. Life could not be so cruel. Why not? whispered an insidious demon in her brain. He has confessed to one babe in France. Why shouldn't there be a score of others scattered about the globe?

Berenice felt her reason tottering. Her rage was directed not toward him, but to this woman who had callously destroyed her dreams. 'Liar!' she cried, almost springing at Juliette. 'How dare you say such a thing?'

Juliette drew herself up, gathering her brilliantly embroidered shawl about her baby. She was awe-inspiring, her beauty a part of this untamed country—as was Sebastian. In that dreadful moment, Berenice saw her as an altogether fitting mate for him, painfully reminded of her own inadequacies.

'I say it, because it is true,' Juliette replied. 'How can you, a callow girl, begin to plumb the depths of a man such as he? We jested before he departed for England—laughed at the thought of the simpering miss whom he was pledged to marry. Has he ever said he loves you?' Juliette continued before Berenice could answer. 'No, I thought not. Sebastian loves no one. He has a heart of granite!'

'Be silent!' Berenice shouted.

But the cold voice went on remorselessly, stripping away her hopes, leaving her bereft. 'I *will* have Buckhorn House! It shall be mine, and my son's.'

'Why wasn't I told before? You've hidden the baby here. Why?' Ask rational questions, her brain insisted. Don't let them scare you. There must be some other explanation.

'He wished it to be kept a secret. It suited his plans.'

'Plans? What plans? I don't understand.'

'Hasn't your father given you a large sum of money, separate to that which came as your dowry?'

'He has. Some of it is in the Bank of Charleston, and the rest invested.' Too upset at the time of her marriage to listen properly as her father explained this, Berenice now realized that it had been important. 'But how do you know all this?' she gasped.

'How do you think? Sebastian tells me everything,' Juliette said, with a confidence that was shattering. 'He can't touch that money while you're alive, but if you die it will be his.'

She handed the child back to Leah. He had awakened and was whimpering. The crone cackled with mirth, jiggling him against her shoulder. Berenice watched them with sickened fascination, the heat of the fire, the strong odors, all those eerie objects conspiring to drain her senses.

'But I shan't die,' she cried, gripping her hands together. 'I'm young and strong.'

'Accidents happen, and there is always sickness. There are poisons that are impossible to detect,' she said ominously.

'But,' Berenice found her faith wavering. 'He wouldn't do something so diabolical! Why

413

should he? Sebastian's rich in his own right.' Berenice's face was white as a winding-sheet.

'Wouldn't he? That shows how little you know him. Sebastian is a greedy man, besides which, he wants me—and his son.' Juliette gave the baby a rattle to play with, made out of tree branches and cocks' feathers. He gurgled, waving the toy while Leah crooned at him,

'Ah, my good little boy, in your dimpled hands lies your mother's prosperity, and mine, too.'

'Unfortunately, Sebastian didn't anticipate the disruption caused by that piece of scum, Darby Modiford,' Juliette continued. 'Had he not come to Mobby Cove while the Comte was away, then you'd have never been brought here. He'd have disposed of you somewhere else—in Charleston, or maybe at Oakwood Hall. But he's told me that he intends to attack the pirate without delay, then he'll carry out his plans for your demise.'

The room seemed to quiver with dark force, pressing in on Berenice's head until she felt that her eardrums would burst. 'I don't believe you!' she cried.

Juliette smiled and lifted the boy from the old woman's arms, holding him closer to Berenice. He was a handsome baby, the innocent cause of her misery. Although he was illegitimate, would he be Sebastian's heir? Sebastian was a law unto himself and, with her out of the way, he could marry Juliette and legally adopt the child. The Marquis would be stricken with grief when he heard of her death. Would Damian remember Sebastian's desire for her and attest to Sebastian's innocence? Then her husband would inherit everything she possessed, and her father, out of pity for the sorrowing widower, would never think to contest the will.

Juliette's next words were so extraordinary and unexpected that they seemed a part of the madness that had invaded the hut. 'I'm giving you a chance to escape with your life.'

'You are? Why should you do anything to help me?' It's a trick, Berenice thought, while thought was at all possible.

'No trick.' Juliette spoke slowly, deliberately prolonging the agony. 'I don't want your ghost haunting me. I simply want you gone. Sebastian won't know that I've had anything to do with it, and he'll get over the loss of the money. In fact, if he can prove your adultery, he'll sue the Marquis and gain anyway. Why don't you leave now? Run away into the forest. Find Darby Modiford. He'll be only too willing to take you wherever you wish to go. Follow my advice. You'll never be happy here, madam, I'll make certain of that. Every day I'll make sure you'll know when Sebastian is visiting me, as he has since you arrived, making love to me, playing with our child who'll be the future master of Buckhorn. And you'll never be certain when death will come. You'll be afraid to eat, terrified to sleep. Run away, Madame la Comtesse, before you go out of your mind!'

TWELVE

Berenice clapped her hands over her ears and ran from Juliette's house—sobbing—shaking—blinded by tears, keeping to the path because there was nowhere else to tread, not knowing why she was there or where she was going. Out of the sunlight and into the woods she ran, crashing through bushes, heedless of the brambles that tore at her skirt. As if the devil himself were after her, she ran, almost insane with grief and bewilderment.

At last she came to where the stream flowed into a shallow pool, her heart drumming, pain slicing between her ribs with every struggling breath. She slumped down on the bank and wept, leaning her arms on her knees and pressing her face into her hands. Over and over she heard Juliette's mocking voice saying, 'Has he ever said he loves you?' And back came the answer, like the doleful tolling of a funeral bell—No! No! No!

And then the ominous echo 'He's going to kill you!'

Her whole body was shaking. Every word the Creole had uttered was branded into her mind, the memory of the baby boy made her want to scream. She moaned, rocking in anguish. Listening to his tragic story last night, she had so much wanted to tell Sebastian about

416

the child, to give him joy after the death of Lisette—but now it was too late. Someone else had already done it—

Since waking that morning, she had been dreaming of a bright future, of warm houses filled with possessions beloved by both of them, of comradeship and affection as they grew ever closer together. She had even pictured the moment when Sebastian crept in to see their first-born; she, pale and weak after labor, he, cradling the baby in his strong arms, a smile lighting up his eyes as he looked at her with love and admiration. Their child—heavy, yet so soft to hold, warm and living.

Feeling sick and weary, she rubbed the salt tears from her cheeks with the back of her hand. Juliette was right. She had to get away. Knowing what she did, she was afraid for her life, and could not bear to have him touch her again. Feverishly, her eyes searched the forest, shimmering hotly under the blaze of noon, alien and alarming. She must think, plan, curb the impulse to take to her heels, and steadily fuel her wrath in order to give her the impetus needed to escape. That black-hearted villain. He had planned to kill her from the beginning, even when he charmed her father and her brother—lying, scheming—monstrous!

If only she had not known that he intended to harm her, then she might have been able to live with the fact that he had a mistress and a bastard living right under her nose. It was commonplace among others of her station; wives were often little more than glorified housekeepers, expected to entertain, and dutifully breed legitimate heirs, while their husbands took their pleasure elsewhere. Perhaps, in time, she might have become as hard and brittle as the married ladies she had known in London who, once they had filled the family nursery, carried on their own adulterous liaisons behind the backs of their bored, indifferent husbands who turned a blind eye to any late arrivals who did not resemble them in the least. But now that she knew that Sebastian wanted her dead, it was impossible to spend another night under his roof.

'Never!' she cried aloud. Better far to leave him, find Modiford and bribe him to help her, rather than risk her life and that of her child.

Bitterly she imagined Sebastian's rage when he discovered that she had flown, and it would anger him even more when he found out that she had asked his enemy for aid. I'll do it, she resolved. Modiford was a scoundrel, but money talked, and she had plenty of that in Charleston. He was her only hope, for she knew she could never find her way back to the town without an experienced guide. Once, she had thought it possible, but she realized how foolish this idea had been. Now, more familiar with the difficulties involved she knew that scouts would be needed, tough men who would protect her and lead her to safety.

It was wise to plan her escape this time so, after tidying herself as best she could, she retraced her steps, with feelings numb, brain clear. No helter-skelter flight for her. She

418

needed a horse, a gun, ammunition, a map and money. It was only midday, and she had heard Greg and Damian say that Modiford's stockade was situated less than a hour's ride away. Thus she would be able to reach him before it grew dark. She resolutely pushed from her mind any thought which might suggest that she could run across hostile Indians, or that the pirate would behave in anything other than a gentlemanly manner when she arrived. She dared not consider either of these alternatives.

The yard was deserted, so was the kitchen, apart from the odd menagerie of stray animals that resided there. Berenice filled a covered basket with bread, cheese, some fruit and a water bottle. She remembered to include a tinderbox; should she be delayed or unable to find the stockade before nightfall, then she would need to light a fire in order to keep prowling animals at bay. Carrying the basket over one arm, she stood at the door leading into the hall, listening intently. The next part of the operation was a tricky one, entailing stealing Sebastian's keys. Her mind was cool and clear, with that desperation that drives a person to take the most appalling risks.

She could hear the rumble of male conversation coming from the direction of the front verandah. It was shady there at that time of day and they sometimes lunched outside, lingering over coffee and cigars. She caught the sound of Sebastian's voice. So, he was well enough to get up, was he? Like a phantom, she slipped across to the bedchamber, an excuse on her lips should she find that she was mistaken and he was in there after all. The room was empty. The next question was whether he had left his coat behind him. He had; she found it hanging on the back of a chair. It took but a moment to feel inside the pocket. Her fingers closed on a cold bunch of iron keys.

Berenice breathed a sigh, too tense to feel anything but relief. There was no turning back now, and she returned to the door, glancing up and down the passage that led to his study. She had never been invited into this place which he used as an office and once inside, she found it to be tidily kept, having a businesslike atmosphere. There were shelves containing ledgers, bookcases filled with leather-bound volumes, windows that looked out over the stables and a large desk with carved legs and ball feet, its top covered in green leather. Papers were strewn on the surface, and Berenice riffled through them. She was certain that someone, maybe Greg, had mentioned a map of the area, with the stockade indicated. Notes, receipts, addresses, bills of sale—some in Sebastian's large, sprawling hand. A rough sketch of the coastline—a printed street guide of Charleston, then a scrappy, dog-eared paper which proved to be the one she was seeking. She slipped it into the basket. There were rows of small drawers down each side of the desk front and, holding the keys carefully so that they did not clink, she tried each one. He must have some money hidden somewhere. To bribe Modiford, she needed more than she already had.

The first drawer yielded nothing, but there was a small metal cashbox pushed to the back of the second. Nervously, she retrieved a purse containing gold pieces. When she accidentally brushed the bag against the desk, the coins resounded like bells. But there was one thing that she had to do before she left.

She drew out a sheet of paper, her trembling fingers taking up a goose quill from the brass pen tray and, pausing for a moment only, she plunged it into the inkwell and started to write,

Monsieur le Comte,
Today Juliette Pascal told me that she was your mistress and that you were the father of her infant son. She also told me of your wicked intention to kill me. Therefore, I am leaving. Do not follow me or hinder me in any way. If you do, then as God is my witness, I swear to bring you to justice, so that you may be hanged as a pirate and a murderer.
Berenice, Comtesse Lajeaunesse.

She left this open on the desk along with the keys, and angrily stabbed it through with a paper knife. It would be the first thing he would see on entering the study. Then, her control weakening, she snatched up the money, lifted a pistol from the gun rack, along with a powder horn and some balls, and fled the room.

There was a good chance that Dulcie would be with Quico, and Berenice had cause to be thankful that the two servants had fallen in love or else they would have been more alert. Dulcie slept in the dressing room attached to the master chamber, among her own and her mistress's clothing. Berenice was right in her assumption that she would not be there. The maid did not own many clothes, but the things that she had were plainer than anything Berenice possessed, so she took Dulcie's one best dress from a hanger and changed into it.

Because they were of similar build, it fitted reasonably well, of plain tobacco-brown cotton, with a bodice buttoning high at the collar and long sleeves. The effect was puritanlike and ideal for Berenice's present mission. She scraped her hair back into a severe bun, covered it with a cream linen sun bonnet, and put on her crimson riding boots. A woolen shawl would be useful if the evening grew chilly, so one was added. At the last moment, she remembered her journal, that old friend who had been the recipient of so many of her secrets. This, too, must go with her.

So far so good, she thought, and let herself out through the kitchen. The guards in the yard were sleeping, feet propped high, hats over their eyes. Only a tabby cat, basking on the wall, followed her progress with gleaming yellow eyes. But Damian was in the stable, expressing mild surprise to see her there.

'I'm riding over to the Martin place,' she said, astonished by the quick, face-saving lies that tripped so readily from her tongue. 'Annie Martin gave birth last night, and I have some things for her.' She held up the basket, hoping he would not look inside and see the pistol.

'Shall I come with you?' he asked, helping her to saddle Saffron.

'No,' she answered, ever so casually. 'Stay here and keep Sebastian quiet. He's not taking kindly to being ill.'

'I know. We've just had lunch and he's in a devilish impatient mood,' Damian said ruefully. 'You're lucky to have an excuse to escape, but don't be late back or I shall worry.'

'Oh, Damian, my dear brother—' Berenice threw herself into his arms, her overstrung emotions nearly betraying her.

He was surprised and touched by this display. 'There, there,' he soothed, patting her gently. 'Yesterday was an ordeal, I know, and you were so courageous. Sebastian told me.'

At the mention of this, she tore herself away, head bent as she fastened the basket into position at the back of Saffron's saddle, then stuck her foot in the stirrup, and swung herself up.

'Goodbye, Damian,' she cried, nudging the mare into a trot and leaving the stable. She did not look back, but knew he was standing there, watching her go with a puzzled expression on his face.

Once the stretch of grass near the house had been covered, the forest enfolded her, and it was like parting a dark green curtain stretched between earth and sky. Berenice halted some way in, listening for the sound of pursuit, but a hush held everything in thrall. She rode on, using the map and the sun as her guide.

'Come on, girl,' she said to the mare, whose ears twitched in response. It was good to speak to something alive, and she wound her fingers in the chestnut mane for comfort.

She was frightened, a cold fear engendered by the woods that seemed to breathe animosity, the rustling of branches, the movement of hidden creatures. She clutched the reins till her wrists ached, whispered to Saffron, endeavored to be as quiet as possible though the brushing of leaves against her sounded like thunder. In vain she told herself that she was lucky to escape, and more fortunate still to have money to buy her way to Charleston. It was no use. She was alone, scared and heartbroken.

She paused when she came to a stream, dismounting and bathing her tear-stained face. This weak crying would do nothing to further her cause. It was essential that she appear calm and strong, beautiful, but not too attractive. Modiford should not touch her. No man would ever touch her again. She would become as a goddess, shutting herself away in purity, remaining aloof, devoting her life to her child.

Modiford shall take me to a spot near the town, she said to herself to bolster up her courage. From there I'll find my own way, and visit the British consul and explain my position, and then I'll go to the bank. I shall book into a respectable hotel and wait for a ship homeward bound. Why, in no time at all, I'll be sailing for England.

The stream was marked on the map and she followed along its banks until, after what seemed like an eternity, it widened into a river and she saw a thin blue spiral of smoke rising above the wall of trees on its far side. The water was deep, but there was no alternative save to urge Saffron in, so after removing her boots, lacing them together and slinging them round her neck, Berenice ventured into the swift flowing current, the mare finally hauling herself out on the other bank.

At once there came a rustling in the bushes and a man appeared, poking a musket at her, shouting, 'Who goes there?'

'A friend,' she answered crisply.

He grinned, showing stumps of blackened teeth between a gingerish beard. 'What d'you want?'

Despite the fact that she was wet to the thighs, she assumed an air of authority. 'Take me to Captain Modiford,' she said and, drying her feet on her skirt, slid them into her boots.

After ordering one of his mates to keep watch, he led the way along a dirt path leading to a clearing surrounded by a rough palisade. In the center stood a large wooden cabin. The men were leaning lazily on their muskets or kneeling on the earth rolling dice, and looked up as she passed, their attention sharpening. With a start of fright, she saw Copper Hair and a group of rowdy, drunken braves waving spears and circling in a war dance.

The word spread that the Lajeaunesse woman had arrived. Berenice heard the talk and bawdy jests, but it was as meaningless as the rushing of the wind through the pines. She was eager to see Modiford and get the matter settled once and for all. She dismounted, tethered Saffron to a rail outside the cabin and, with her head held high, walked up the steps and went inside.

Modiford sprawled in a hammock slung between two of the tree trunks that supported the roof, a thin cheroot clamped between his lips. His eyes widened when she appeared in the doorway, thinking that he had dreamed up this vision. Her skirt was soggy, clinging to her legs; she was hot and tired, but she carried herself like an empress. He rolled out of the hammock and was on his feet in one lithe movement, snapping his fingers in dismissal at the Indian girl who had been waving a palmetto leaf fan over his head.

'Madame la Comtesse!' he cried, with an exaggerated bow, a broad smile on his coarse features. 'To what do I owe this honor?'

Now that she was trapped within this dangerous place, Berenice suddenly realized what she had done. Her nerve failed a little, yet she replied coolly, 'I've come to ask your help, Captain Modiford, recalling that you once offered it to me.'

'A seat for the lady!' Modiford roared, and one of his men dragged a cane chair forward. Berenice groped for it, her knees buckling, thankful that she had not fainted. She needed every vestige of strength if she was to bargain with this ruffian.

'Will you assist me, Captain?' she asked.

Modiford gnawed at a hangnail as he stared at her. She was even more lovely than he remembered, and he experienced an unprecedented feeling of awe. To be sure, there was no lack of wenches to satisfy his low-grade lust, but she was different, a dainty city lady. How would she act if he took her? he wondered, twitching at the thought. Would she scream and struggle? Or would she disappoint him and prove more than willing? He hoped not; he would prefer to shame her. He knew that his reputation was base even among the pirates, but he was proud of it.

A thief from the time he was a lad, abandoned at birth and brought up by a wily fence who taught him to pick pockets, he had learned through brutal treatment that the only way to survive was to be more ruthless than anyone else. He possessed a native cunning that had brought him, by way of cheating, murdering, becoming in turn a footpad and then a highwayman, to where he now stood—the leader of a gang of cutthroats.

He had never known love from anyone, and he despised it, using then kicking aside any woman who was prepared to share his bed. Yet he had always hankered after the impossible—a genteel, educated girl. And it was not only Berenice's body that he ached to ill treat—he wanted to torment her mind, to lay waste her spirit as well. He smirked across at her, smoothing down his greasy curls. His raffish attire consisted of velvet breeches, a gold chain shining against the black hair of his chest, revealed by a silk shirt unbuttoned to the waist, his feet encased in scarlet boots of supple cordovan leather.

'My dear lady,' he purred, 'didn't I promise to serve you? You can trust me. I'm a Londoner, too, first saw the light of day in a workhouse in Whitechapel—left my homeland ten years ago through a miscarriage of justice. They wanted to hang me for murder, you see—all because I'd accidentally shot a fellow when I was on the hightoby—but the judge was merciful and sentenced me to the colonies instead, as a slave, madame—but I escaped.'

His ingratiating smile did nothing to reassure Berenice, nor could he conceal the admiration in his eyes. The full awareness of her position rushed upon her with stifling terror. She saw how the Indian wench flinched at his every movement, all the spirit beaten out of her. What madness had possessed her to put herself in the hands of such a man? Juliette must have known full well what she was doing when she urged this action. Why, at this very moment, she was probably savoring the sweetness of revenge, whispering her lies into Sebastian's ear, telling him that Berenice had left him for one of the worst rogues in the whole of America.

'Captain Modiford, I need someone to take me to Charleston. You have a ship, and could do this easily or, if it's too dangerous for you, then provide me with an escort to go overland.' Berenice kept her mind firmly fixed on the image of her father, a sometime magistrate who had sent many to prison for lesser crimes than those Modiford had perpetrated. Her father would have crushed this villain with a few well-chosen words.

The pirate said, 'Ah, a pretty proposal, my dear,' rubbing his stubbly jaw with his hand thoughtfully. 'And what payment are you offering?'

'I have money, and will settle part of it now, and the rest when I reach my destination.' So steady the eyes that met his, so haughty and intimidating.

It was a novel sensation to be awed by anyone, least of all a female, and he enjoyed it. This was a rare woman indeed, one that he would like to keep longer than usual, and she belonged to Lajeaunesse, an added bonus. 'Why did you leave Buckhorn House, madam?' he asked, keeping his distance, but with difficulty.

'I have my reasons, Captain, and they don't concern you,' she answered, still subjecting him to a bright blue stare. 'I'm involving you in a monetary transaction, nothing more. Can you do what I want?'

'Well, now, let me see.' He pretended to consider it, then suggested, 'Why don't we discuss it over supper? Grant me this favor. It's a long time since I sat at table with a beautiful lady.'

Raking back through the mists of memory, he realized that he had never eaten with a lady during the whole of his checkered career—tarts perhaps, painted whores who aped fine ladies, but never a genuine one. The need grew in him, his brain, already damaged by too great a fondness for alcohol, becoming obsessed with the ambition to sit with her, converse with her, impress her—perhaps she might even take a

429

fancy to him. It was not beyond the realms of possibility. He was still a fine-looking fellow, and rich, too—he had a chest full of gems that he could offer her. He had never yet met a woman who could resist the lure of diamonds, gold, rubies or pearls. Yet, somewhere in the depths of his being, buried deep by years of debauchery and sin, there lurked the hope that she would refuse. If she did not, it would reduce her to a strumpet, like all the rest.

Berenice had more than herself to fight for now, she had her baby, and knew that she must be as devious and manipulative as Modiford to fulfill her aim. 'Thank you for inviting me, Captain,' she said graciously. 'It's so civilized to carry out business matters over a meal and a glass of wine. How thoughtful of you.'

Modiford, smiling widely, shouted for the girl to clear the muddle of bottles and dirty platters from the table and find a cloth with which to cover it. He implemented his orders with scowls and a series of vicious kicks, until Berenice could stand it no more, crying,

'Stop it, I pray you, sir! There's no need to treat the poor girl so harshly.'

She went over to the cringing girl and put an arm round her, thinking she was the oddest little creature she had ever seen. Even the way she held her head was peculiar, while the rest of her was swathed in tattered skirts and petticoats. She had small black eyes and ragged dark hair, and seemed half paralyzed with terror.

'She's not right in the head,' Modiford said, as if this explained his cruelty. 'We call her

Peggy. Her real name's unpronounceable. She lives with us and cooks the meals. If it wasn't for me, she'd have died long ago. She was a slave, but I freed her.'

'What a noble gesture!' Berenice's irony was lost on him. He took her remark as a compliment, and stopped bullying the girl.

His men were crowding the doorway, amused to see their captain entertaining like a gentleman. He frowned darkly and ordered them out, while Peggy set the table, her eyes darting towards Berenice, who smiled encouragingly. Silver plates were unearthed from a box, a pair of ecclesiastical candlesticks, too, stolen from a church. The girl filled a tureen with soup, ladling it from a smoke-blackened cauldron suspended over the logs in the stone fireplace.

'It's made from game I shot myself,' said Modiford, as he pulled out a chair for Berenice. 'And Peggy baked the bread.'

'How clever. It's delicious, Peggy,' Berenice replied, trying to control her uncertain stomach. And all the time she was trying to force down the food, she was thinking—what am I going to do?

She was between the devil and the deep blue sea. Modiford was unpredictable and Sebastian wanted to kill her. What a choice! At that moment, the pirate seemed the best of the two, and this was a dreadful admission. There was no doubt about it, whichever way she looked at it, she was in dire peril.

Modiford's manners left a great deal to be desired. He stuffed in the food; he talked with his mouth full; he belched loudly. After eating, he lay back in his chair and picked his teeth, then filled his glass to overflowing.

'I toast you, Comtesse. To the most beautiful woman in Carolina!'

She inclined her head in acknowledgement, then said, 'And now, Captain, it's time we got down to the crux of my visit.'

'You want me to give you an answer? Will I or will I not take you to Charleston?' He leaned closer and the reek of wine on his breath was almost visible.

'Yes.'

He gazed at her owlishly in the candlelight. 'Well now, that depends.'

'On what? I've already said I'll pay well.'

'Ah, but you see it ain't a matter of money. No indeed. I'm not interested in your cash.'

Her heart sank. 'Is that so? Piracy is profitable?'

He lowered an eyelid in a wink. 'I'm not short of a penny. Look at this.' He dragged a casket from the floor and placed it on the table, then flung back the lid.

It was as if the contents were on fire, a blaze of necklaces, tiaras, bracelets, rings, strings of pearls. He dug in a hand and pulled out a fistful, thrusting them towards her. Berenice did not take them and they cascaded down to lie in a glittering heap on the cloth.

'They are lovely,' she said slowly.

'Aren't they just? Worth a king's ransom. So you see, madame, though men call me venal, I can't be bribed with money, not by a beautiful

432

woman. I need some other inducement.'

Berenice sat motionless, while hope deserted her. She saw Peggy looking at her from her corner by the fireplace, black eyes brimming with pity. Dragging the fading remnants of dignity together, she said, 'In that case, I shall leave and travel on alone. Good-bye, Captain Modiford.'

She half rose, but he placed a detaining hand on her arm. 'Oh, no you don't, my dear,' he murmured. 'You're not going anywhere. You and me are about to concoct a plot to capture your husband. We'll write him a note, saying that I hold you hostage and demanding that he come here alone to treat with me—and you'll sign it.'

His manner had changed. Gone was that air of slippery friendliness. His hand moved up to her shoulder, while Berenice could only stare at him. 'You'll take him a prisoner? But why?'

'It's simple. He cheated me. I seek revenge.' His eyes narrowed, a thin smile playing about his lips.

'And how does this involve me?' Keep him talking, play for time, her mind insisted. 'What makes you so sure he'll come?'

'Oh, he'll come all right. You're his wife and he's a proud man.' Modiford looked deep into her eyes with a crafty smile. 'You've run away from him, haven't you? I could tell when I came to the house that you don't like him much. In a way, I sort of expected you'd turn up here some time.'

'He won't come,' she insisted. 'You're right.

I have left him, but it was by mutual agreement. Ours was an arranged marriage and it hasn't been successful. We have an aversion for each other.'

He shook with laughter. 'You're a bad liar, madame. If this were so, then he'd have escorted you back to Charleston himself. Even *he* wouldn't have let a woman roam in these woods alone.'

Suddenly, she felt hot and the room started to spin and Berenice lowered her head into her hands. 'Water,' she begged. 'Can I have some water?'

Peggy was there in an instant, without waiting for Modiford's assent. She held a pannikin to Berenice's lips, and she rested gratefully against that little body which felt painfully thin through the dirty clothing.

'Don't distress yourself, Comtesse.' Modiford slouched in his chair, never taking his eyes from her. 'Do as I say and we'll both get what we want.'

'How d'you mean? I don't understand.'

'I'll spare his life, providing he gives me Buckhorn House—and you. Then, later, we'll talk about letting you go—if you still want to, that is.'

Berenice leapt to her feet. She stood at bay before him, erect, her head thrown back, her eyes sparkling with defiance as she glanced at the men who had sidled in to watch. On no face could she find the remotest trace of pity. They bore the same expression that she had seen men wear at a cockfight, thirsting for blood and excitement. And despite her fear of her husband, she could not find it in her heart to let him walk into a trap.

'How long must I stay with you, if he agrees?' The prospect was unthinkable, but she would do it to save Sebastian's life.

Modiford's confident laugh rang out through the room. 'Till I'm tired of you, Comtesse.'

'And if I don't sign the letter?' she whispered.

'Oh, you will, my dear, and in it we'll say that if he doesn't come, I'll hand you over to Copper Hair who'll skin you alive, inch by inch. I've seen him do this and, believe me, he's most skillful with his knife. I'm sure he's itching to add your lovely scalp to the one he already wears.'

At hearing his name, Copper Hair came forward, smiling grimly and fingering the razor-sharp edge of his blade, while his braves, drunk on Modiford's whiskey, gave high-pitched cries.

'All right. Say he comes, and refuses to agree to your terms?' Berenice felt she was living in a nightmare.

The whole scene was like something out of Dante's *Inferno;* the men who would torture and kill her without a qualm; the native girl, so cowed that she dared not offer help; the dirty hut, its floor littered with empty bottles and garbage. Please God, let her wake from this hideous dream!

'If he's obstinate, he'll die a slow, lingering death, and I'll make you watch.' Modiford mouthed the words with relish, his eyes blazing.

'Have you ever seen a man pegged out under the scorching sun?'

'Stop it!' Berenice cried.

A vivid picture of Sebastian's features, so arrogant, so handsome, floated before her, and she saw him as she had seen him yesterday, with tenderness in his eyes. Then she remembered everything Juliette had told her, but even someone as wicked as he, should be given the chance to make amends.

'Make up your mind, madame,' Modiford urged. 'I'm eager to face him on my terms, not his. Will you sign the letter?'

'No,' her lips barely formed the word, and she shrank back.

'Don't be foolish, Comtesse. This is the only way,' he said and called to Peggy, 'Bring me paper and quill.'

'I'd rather die than have anything to do with it,' Berenice said, and meant it. Death seemed an easy option in that terrible moment.

'Would you? By Copper Hair's knife?'

The writing materials were hurriedly gathered and placed among the supper things on the table. Modiford stood over it, scribbling rapidly. After sanding the note, he slid it towards Berenice. 'I've put my signature. Now add yours!' he commanded.

Berenice tottered, hearing the blood singing in her ears, the badly spelled and ill-formed writing dancing before her eyes. Modiford pushed the pen impatiently into her hand and she wrote her name slowly. Sebastian was clever. He would think of some way in which to defeat Modiford.

With a satisfied grunt, the pirate took up the letter, folding it and giving it to one of Copper Hair's scouts with instructions to deliver it to Buckhorn House at once. Then he swung round to Berenice, aware that his men were watching and expecting him to act.

'What about a kiss to seal the bargain?' he said.

She drew back, felt someone beside her. It was Peggy. Then her palm responded to the feel of cold steel, and her hand closed round the handle of the knife that the girl had placed there. A weapon! It gave her strength. The pistol was still in the basket near her feet, but was a clumsy thing compared to a sharp dagger.

'I don't give my kisses lightly,' she answered playfully, while inwardly vowing to stab him if he took a step nearer. 'A man has to earn the right first.'

'Ha! That's it! Deny me. I like fire in a doxy.'

'Doxy, sir? You insult me and then expect me to feel like kissing you?' Berenice teased, wondering if the hollowness of her words rang in Modiford's ears.

This pulled him up sharply. He was confused, torn between the unusual desire to impress a woman and the knowledge that his men were waiting for him to force her. His hesitation was costing him their respect, and, if he was mot careful, someone else would step into his shoes as leader.

'I apologize, madam,' he growled, though with a mockery that pleased the spectators.

'We're coarse fellows and unused to dainty manners.'

'That is obvious, sir,' she answered scathingly, determined to keep him talking for as long as she could. 'You disappoint me.'

'I do?' Modiford was becoming more bewildered and agitated.

'Yes, indeed. I had thought, while we supped, that you were an unfortunate victim of circumstances and, had your life taken a different course, we might well have become friends,' and here she managed to cast her eyes down demurely, adding more softly, 'Perhaps even something more.'

'Is this the truth?'

'I never lie, Captain Modiford,' she lied with ease.

Modiford's face was working with emotion. 'You might have learned to like me?'

'I might, but you've lost the chance, haven't you? My husband will come now. And, if you force me to live with you, I'll never do other than despise you. What sort of man compels a woman to do something totally against her nature?' It's not so hard to trick him, Berenice was thinking. Remembering her flirtations of old, she noted he's a gullible fool—like most men. Appeal to his conceit and he's putty in one's hand.

But suddenly he stopped and she came to her senses. Aware of a change in him, she stared into his sweating face. He was alert, head lifted, listening to the sharp rattle of musket fire that suddenly echoed round the stockade. With an

438

oath, he reached for his sword, while his men ran to the windows.

Then a guard rushed in at the door, panting, wild-eyed, shouting, 'It's Lajeaunesse. He's attacking!'

'Impossible!' snapped Modiford. 'The scout couldn't have reached him yet.'

'He must have followed me,' Berenice said, while thinking, Juliette told him where I'd gone. But why did he come after me? Was he so concerned about keeping hold of his investment? She could feel uncontrolled laughter bubbling up in her throat, and added aloud, 'I don't understand!'

There was no more time for questions. The camp was under siege and pandemonium broke out as Modiford's men grabbed up their weapons and ran to defend the walls. Copper Hair and his braves had already leapt to the high platform that girded it, letting fly their arrows.

'Fire! Fire!' someone yelled above the din, and Berenice saw flames licking at the straw roof, the acrid stink of blazing palmetto in her nostrils as the crackle and roar increased.

'Jesus!' bellowed Modiford, sword in one hand, a dagger in the other. 'What the hell's happening?'

'They're fording the stream, Cap'n,' the guard declared, eyes rolling with alarm. 'And Whirling Hawk and Eagle Fox had stolen up through the woods on the other side.'

'Bastards!' Modiford shouted and leapt outside.

The surprise attack had given his enemy the advantage, but his men were recovering quickly, letting loose a volley that emptied saddles and set horses whinnying as they crashed to the ground in a flurry of hooves.

Sebastian's men rushed the gates with a battering rain, using one of the large logs that formed part of the barricade. With a splintering sound, the heavy gates groaned, screamed, and fell inwards. Modiford was furiously ordering every available bulky object to be dragged into place to form a further blockade; tables, chests, firewood and boxes were piled up in a ragged line, while the defenders knelt in the dust behind them and fired.

For a moment, it seemed that their fusillade would stop the attackers in full charge. Some fell sprawling, but others leaped over their bodies and hurled themselves at the barricade like a tidal wave, crashing over it and tumbling in amongst the pirates. But, at the same instant, Whirling Hawk waved on his warriors from the far side and Modiford's fighters were caught between the two.

Berenice crouched by one of the windows, her arm around Peggy, half concealed behind a shutter, knowing that she must run from the hut into the open. Men were choking in the fumes, struggling through whorls of smoke from the blazing building to join the hand-to-hand fighting that had broken out. It was nearly impossible to distinguish friend from foe in the mêlée, but she caught sight of the tall, unmistakable form of Sebastian, his

440

sword flashing as he dispatched one assailant and rounded on a second. The heat was so intense that Berenice was forced outside, sheltering behind Saffron who was neighing with fright at the uproar—battle-crazed men giving inarticulate cries, shouts of triumph or agony ringing across the clearing.

'We should escape in the confusion,' Peggy said with a voice Berenice never imagined she had. 'You have a horse, lady. Let us ride into the forest.'

'You know this area? Would you guide me to Charleston?' Was it possible that help could come from such an unexpected source?

'Yes, I could do that,' the girl answered, then added, almost shyly. 'Can I stay with you? You are the only one who has ever been kind to me.'

'Of course. If we get out of this alive, I promise you can stay.' Hope was striking a timid root into Berenice's heart. She placed the basket in Peggy's hands and gave her Saffron's reins. 'Wait here for me, and be ready to ride when I come back. My husband is as bad, if not worse, than Modiford. Whichever of those devils triumphs, I shall be their prisoner.'

'I'll do anything you say, lady,' and Peggy held the basket close to her chest and quieted Saffron, as Berenice left her to find out what was happening.

Modiford and Sebastian had come face to face. The pirate leapt at him with a great shout, his cutlass coming down in a whistling sweep which Sebastian caught on the quillon

441

of his sword, arm rock-steady under the blow. Blind to everything but their hatred, they fought with purpose and energy, the blades grinding against each other. Sebastian stood erect in the French dueling style, moving his feet constantly like a dancer, charging, side-stepping, feinting and lunging, while Modiford employed crude, slashing force, the steel singing as he whirled it furiously around in mighty sweeps.

All about them, little groups of men were still fighting, though several of Modiford's crew had thrown down their arms. But Berenice could see nothing, hear nothing, aware only of Sebastian's danger. She stood near one of the stockade posts in agonized concentration, unable even to pray. Her heart seemed to stop as she saw Modiford raise his cutlass, bringing it down in a swishing cut which could have severed Sebastian's head from his body had he not stepped neatly aside. Before Modiford could recover his balance, Sebastian leaned forward, his blade sliding into the pirate's chest till the hilt was pressed against his shirt and the tip appeared between his shoulder blades, lengthening into inches of steel. As Sebastian withdrew his sword, Modiford gave a shuddering howl, then crumpled and fell slowly to the dust, where he lay staring upwards, choking on the blood that gushed from his mouth.

With their leader slain, Modiford's men ceased combat and stood dazed. Then Copper Hair leapt the barricade, knife raised to hurl it at Sebastian. Suddenly a shot rang out, and the Indian bent backwards, blood fountaining from his side. Peregrine, breathing heavily, was holding a smoking pistol in his hand, and gazing down at the Indian's inert form, as if unable to comprehend the deed he had just committed.

There was a split-second pause, then one of Copper Hair's braves threw his lance. It transfixed Peregrine and he fell, his hands spread wide as if trying to pluck support from the air. He was dead before he hit the ground, the spear quivering in his back. Berenice screamed and ran to him.

'Peregrine! Oh, God! Help him someone!'

'It's too late,' Sebastian said calmly.

He was leaning on his sword, the point buried in the sand, his bandaged arm crooked awkwardly. He was smoke-grimed and bloodied, sweat running down his face in rivulets, and soaking into his shirt. He stooped to wipe the blood from his blade on Modiford's corpse, before slipping it back into the scabbard. His expression was stern as he watched Greg bend over Peregrine and shake his head gravely. At this, Sebastian turned and began to stride away.

Berenice, the paralysis leaving her limbs, flew after him. 'Sebastian!' she cried, pushing through the victors who were rounding up prisoners and attending to wounded comrades.

He stopped, his teeth clenched and the muscles each side of his jaw quivering with nervous rage. 'What the hell—?' he began. 'Two of your lovers have just died because

443

of you! Doesn't that satisfy you? What do you want with me?'

She stared at him, stunned by the contempt she read in his eyes. Tears were coursing down her cheeks. 'Why are you looking at me like that?' she gasped.

'What else do you expect?'

Sebastian was still caught up in the fury and concern that had beset him when he first realized she was missing. Damian had said he had seen her leave for the Martin farm, but Juliette had sidled up with the tale of her riding off to join Modiford's gang. Though never entirely trusting the Creole, his jealousy had overruled him. Refusing to listen to Greg, who warned that his wound might open, he had rounded up his men, distributed arms, sent a runner to Whirling Hawk, then ridden like a fury for Modiford's hideout. He was filled with pain, rage and disappointment. Berenice had seized upon the chance to escape while he was still weak, after lulling him with her apparent devotion.

What a fool he had been, and how easily she had duped him. More than that, she had plunged him into a fight which he had wished to avoid. His anger against her mounted steadily as he gazed upon the dead bodies of some of his finest men, lost because of her. And here she was, looking up at him with tear-filled eyes, expecting him to take her back once more.

She was shaking, terrified of him. 'What's this, sir! Have you come to haul me back to my doom!'

'What do you mean? What lies are you concocting now? Don't waste my time, madame!' he shouted. 'I've far more important things to do than bandy words with you.'

At that, her temper flared up and all the reasons why she had fled from Buckhorn House came back in full measure. He dared to look at her as if she were dirt, yet all the time his mistress and his bastard dwelt on his land, and he had planned to kill her. Almost insane with rage and despair, she drew back her hand and struck him squarely across the mouth with all the force she could muster.

'I did this once before!' she shouted. 'And, by God, my first impression of you was a true one!'

He stood there silent, eyes glittering in a face gone suddenly pale, but before he could move, she had whirled round, running back to fall on her knees beside Peregrine's body.

She could not believe that he was dead, that once light-hearted companion, her only link with the past. Her thoughts were wild and disjointed. She had to escape, yet she must see that he was taken to Mobby Cove and buried with due honor. She would tell Damian, that was the least she could do for the man who had fought for her, redeeming himself at the last. He lay in the dust, and she lifted his head into her lap, gently wiping the blood from his face, her tears flowing unchecked.

'I'm sorry, Peregrine,' she sobbed, her arms about him. 'So sorry—'

Damian found her there some minutes later, raising her up. 'Why did you lie to me?' he said, eyes and mouth stern. 'Will you never learn, you foolish girl?'

She wanted to explain, to tell him about Sebastian's wicked plans, but knew that it would be hopeless. He would not believe her. 'I must go away,' she said, her shoulders bowed, her dress smeared with Peregrine's blood. 'You'll see to him, won't you? Mark his grave so that he isn't forgotten.'

'Go where? Haven't you caused enough trouble?' Damian gripped her arm and shook her.

'I must! I can't go back with him! He'll kill me!'

Damian gave a bark of grim laughter. 'He may be damned annoyed with you, and with good cause, but I hardly think he'd go that far.'

'You don't understand. Listen to me—'

He broke from her impatiently. 'I can't waste time now. There's a lot to do—pirates to bury, our own dead taken home, and prisoners to be chained. Why don't you do something useful, and help Greg with the wounded?'

'Damian! Keep a strict eye on your sister,' Sebastian shouted, and she saw that he had recognized Saffron and set a couple of men to guard the mare and Peggy.

Berenice sank down on a log, defeated. It was useless. She would never escape him, and her danger had been increased because he now knew that she was on to him. Dulcie might be able to help her, but not Quico. He was Sebastian's servant, faithful unto death, no matter what he did.

'What are you going to do? Tie me up?' she asked her brother. She was so pale and exhausted-looking that he pitied her, even though she infuriated him.

The Marquis's last words to him before he left to board *La Foudre*, had been instructions that he should look after her, but she now was too much of a troublemaker for him to manage. If someone as strong as Sebastian found it impossible, then what chance did anyone else have?

'Of course, I shan't tie you,' he answered angrily. 'But you'd better behave yourself. Wait here till we're through.'

Sebastian was fully occupied during the next hour placating Whirling Hawk. The venerable old Indian was sorrowful, but he regarded Copper Hair as a renegade who had atoned for his betrayal by dying. His body would be borne away to be lain on a wooden platform in the tribe's sacred burial ground, where rites would be performed to send his soul winging away to become one with the Great Spirit.

When at long last they were ready to leave, the sun was sinking and the long shadows of evening lay across the devastated stockade. Berenice was in a state of depression and hopelessness as Damian helped her into Saffron's saddle, with Peggy seated behind her. Greg swung up on his bay, preparing to ride beside her. My guard, she thought sadly, another of Sebastian's cronies who'll not hear a word said against him.

'Won't there be trouble with the authorities about this—the killing of Modiford and the others?' she asked him, a faint flicker of hope arising as she thought of what might happen, if and when the news of the fight reached Charleston.

He rode on one side of her with Damian on the other, and he did not look pleased with her, and neither did her brother who was so angry and ashamed that he could hardly speak. She could feel him slipping away mentally, becoming a stranger, no longer the loving comrade who had smiled indulgently at her adventures. Now he was deeply offended by her actions and made no secret of his disapproval.

Greg bobbed his heels against his mount's belly, urging him into a walk as he answered her question. 'We'll get nothing but praise for ridding the territory of such vermin,' he told her, a grim smile touching his lips.

Berenice looked back at the deserted stockade where the fire was still blazing like a red dust storm, rearing into the sky. Spangled with starry sparks, a huge column of smoke slowly unwound and drifted up to meet the clouds of night. Dully she wondered what lay in store for her when they reached Buckhorn House, and she was chilled by thoughts of the future. She was still Sebastian's wife, his legal property. He could do with her as he wished and no one would stop him.

THIRTEEN

Berenice was practically ignored during the excitement of their return to Buckhorn House. Those left behind had been waiting anxiously for news, and now a crowd gathered from every quarter, not only those immediately concerned, but others from outlying homesteads. Everyone would sleep more easily in their beds now that they knew that Modiford and his bullies had been vanquished.

There was sorrow, too, for six men had lost their lives. Weeping women and relatives gathered up their dead, and the next day there would be funerals in the tranquil graveyard near the church. Sebastian had given orders for Peregrine's body to be taken to his room, where Jessy, together with the women who acted as midwives and nurses to the community, would lay him out decently. Already there was much activity and the sound of hammering from the carpenters' shop, as craftsmen prepared to spend the night making coffins.

Still keyed-up, their adrenaline pumping, those who had survived were reliving the fight, exaggerating their deeds, surrounded by an eager group of young lads and old men who had not been included. The horses were cared for, watered, given an extra feed of hay, and bedded down in the stable.

Berenice comforted Peggy, who was scared of so many strangers, settling her in the kitchen with Jessy's children. 'You'll be safe here,' she assured her, for the girl clung to her pathetically, so used to ill-treatment that she found it hard to accept kindness. 'I have things to do, but soon I'll return.'

Dulcie was relieved to see her mistress, but alarmed by the state of her. They cried in each other's arms in the dressing room, and Berenice told her everything that had happened, beginning with Juliette showing her the child she claimed to be Sebastian's and ending with the revelation concerning his murderous schemes, her flight to Modiford, his dastardly threats, the bloodshed in the stockade and Peregrine's death.

'The poor gentleman,' Dulcie said, shaking her head at the pity of it all. 'But oh, that evil witch!' She gave vent to anger after hours of worrying about Berenice, driving the patient Quico almost to distraction; he had been given the responsibility of guarding the house while the men were away. 'What a lot of trouble she's caused! D'you think she was telling the truth?'

'I'm sure of it.' Berenice was recovering her equilibrium, and her indignation along with it.

But surprisingly, she found that Dulcie did not agree when she raved on angrily about her devious, conscienceless husband. From Quico, the shrewd maid had garnered a lot of information concerning Sebastian, and had formed the opinion that he was nothing like the ogre Berenice imagined. She refused to believe that he was a potential wife-killer.

She clicked her tongue, shaking her head. 'Have you told him that you're pregnant, milady?'

Berenice had broken from her and taken to a restless pacing. 'Certainly not,' she cried in tones of mingled rage and pain. 'He doesn't deserve to know. I'm terrified that he'll try to take the baby away from me, if he hasn't succeeded in killing me before it's born. Oh, Dulcie, I must get away! Help me, please!'

'Be calm, my lady,' Dulcie urged, alarmed by her desperation. 'Let us think this through carefully. Now, about Juliette's story. He is aware that she's spoken to you?'

'How do I know?' Berenice snapped. 'We've been in the middle of a battle. No time to speak—no time to do anything but try to stay alive.' In her mind's eye she was seeing the flames, the blood, and Peregrine impaled on a spear. For a moment she wanted to scream in terror, but fought the impulse, saying, 'He must know. I left a note on his desk before I went.'

'He seemed frantic with worry when he found out you'd gone, storming around and giving everyone a hard time. It was Juliette who told him that you'd left him for Modiford. Quico says she's not to be trusted.' Dulcie wrinkled up her forehead in puzzlement.

'I don't care what he did! He's a liar and so is she. My life is forfeit if I stay here. I knew from the start that he was bad. I hate him. I've always hated him.'

451

Even as Berenice uttered the words, Dulcie knew that they were false. For a long while she had read the truth in her mistress's erratic behavior, had seen the way her eyes lit up when Sebastian approached, the agitation which had betrayed her chaotic emotions, those bouts of hectic gaiety that changed so abruptly to extreme melancholy.

'You can't leave, madam. Not now. I'm sure he means you no harm. I'd wager my immortal soul on his innocence.'

Dulcie wanted so much to convince her. She had recognized the signs. It had become perfectly clear to her that Berenice had fallen head over heels in love with her husband. Quico had nodded solemnly and agreed, saying that he was sure his master had lost his heart to his English bride, and they had decided that something must be done to make these headstrong lovers see sense. Now she could fully understand her mistress's devastation at being told that he had betrayed her.

'I'll fetch Quico,' she offered, needing him in this crisis situation. 'He's wise, and will give you his opinion of Juliette. I'm certain he'll say that it is impossible for the Comte to behave like that.'

'Do what you like, Dulcie. I don't know what I feel anymore,' Berenice sighed, collapsed in a chair, her face hidden in her hands. 'It's so hopeless. He says, and Damian believes it too, that I went to Modiford because I wanted him. He must be lying to everybody, for my letter explained my reasons for leaving.'

452

Dulcie narrowed her eyes in a considering way. 'You left it on his desk, you say? I wonder if he ever received it.'

'Does it make any difference whether he did or did not?' Berenice was too tired to cudgel her brains further.

Dear God, she thought despairingly, is there no cure for the pain of memory? Must I be tormented forever by the feel of his hands, the touch of his lips? Is there no escape from the thoughts cluttering my mind? Of course, I had begun to love him. I had recognized it by the trembling sensation whenever he turned and looked at me, by that bleak lost feeling when we were apart.

Dulcie took charge, briskly practical. 'All this ranting and raving won't help, my lady. Come—out of that dress at once.'

'Oh, Dulcie, I'm sorry. I've ruined it—it's covered with blood and the hem is muddy and torn. I shouldn't have borrowed it without your leave.' It was absurd to be worrying about such a trivial thing at such a time, but Berenice could not stop herself.

'Don't give it a thought,' Dulcie replied briskly. 'It'll wash, and by the time I've put a stitch in it, it'll be as good as new. Now come along. Bathe your face, and then we'll sort this matter out.' As she spoke, she was already searching through cupboards and ransacking drawers, assembling garments.

'I should wear black, in mourning for Peregrine,' Berenice said listlessly. 'But I've nothing suitable.'

453

'What about your mauve gown? If we add a black shawl, that will show respect well enough.'

Berenice nodded, and obeyed her. Soon her body was washed and scented, soft silk against her skin, and she was seated before the mirror, the candles flickering over her pale face. She closed her eyes with a tired sigh, as Dulcie brushed out her hair with long, soothing sweeps.

She knew that the confrontation with Sebastian had to come. She wanted it, she was ready for it. Dulcie was right, she must face him, and needed to look dignified and calm for the ordeal. It was hard to restore confidence to the crushed spirit which, not so long ago, had blazed in her, making her arrogant and defiant. Panic quickened her pulse as she recalled the look in his eyes when she had slapped his face, and she was racked with pain when she thought of Peregrine. Even at that moment, his body was being prepared for burial by Jessy and her helpers.

Why had he saved Sebastian? Had he been trying to compensate for his former cowardice? Had he really cared so much for her happiness, performing the one noble act of his life? Oh God, let him forgive me, she prayed. I didn't mean that he should die—that any one should die for me.

A peremptory knock on the door heralded Quico, who informed her that the Comte wished to see her in the study. 'Ah, you're just the fellow I want to talk to,' said Dulcie, adopting that bossy tone which she sometimes used with him. 'It's about Juliette Pascal.'

Berenice left them and made her way down the passage. Sebastian rose as she entered. So did Greg, Damian and Colonel Perkins. The atmosphere was so dense that it could have been cut with a knife.

The colonel broke the silence. 'What are you going to do with the prisoners, Comte? Hang 'em?' he said, as she sat down and the men resumed their seats.

'I'll give them the option of working for me,' he answered, and he winced as he nursed his wounded arm. 'Those who refuse can take their chance in the forest. They'll be issued food and horses and sent on their way. It will be in the lap of the gods whether they die at the hands of vengeful braves.'

I can't stand it if we're just going to sit here and pretend that Sebastian and I don't have vital issues to thrash out, Berenice thought impatiently. She stood up slowly, standing with her back pressed to the table, face guarded, wary eyes on her husband. He had changed into a pair of white linen breeches and black boots, his shirt frilled at the cuffs, his hair shining damply as if he had stuck his head under the pump to clear it. Images of him dueling with Modiford superimposed themselves on the present scene. He had run him through, wiped his sword on his corpse—a man hardened to killing. Her vision cleared and she saw him as he was now—plainly tired, his arm hurting him. The day's strife had not helped it to heal. Little lines of strain creased his eyes.

'We must talk, sir,' she said, as the men stood in deference to her. 'I'd prefer for us to be alone.'

'You can say what you have to say with my friends here,' he replied, and she noticed how he leaned on the back of his chair as if weak.

'If you insist.' Berenice shrugged, and drew the black shawl more closely around her shoulders. The evening was warm, but she still shivered with shock-induced cold.

'I do, madame. What have you to say for yourself?' He asked sternly. 'I'm becoming bored with rescuing you.'

His sarcasm infuriated her, and his nearness scattered her thoughts. She had prepared a speech in her head while she dressed, an impassioned tirade in which she lambasted Juliette, himself and his plots. But now that the moment had come, she had serious doubts as to her ability to deliver it.

When she finally answered him, her voice was tight. 'How can you speak to me iike that, after what you've done and planned to do? You know full well why I ran away. It was to save my life.'

He frowned at her. 'You're talking in riddles, madame, trying to throw me off the scent. I know why you went, right enough. It was to be with Modiford.'

Berenice walked slowly towards him, glad that the others were in the room, filled with an overpowering urge to expose him. She longed to see him brought to book.

'You lie, sir! I left you a letter, here on this

very desk. In it I wrote that I'd discovered the enormity of your crimes,' she replied in a low but very clear voice. 'Have you no conscience? Have you no heart? Did you really think I would stay after I found out that Juliette is your mistress and that you are the father of her little boy? And when she told me of your intention to get rid of me and inherit my money, I had no alternative but to go.'

'What!' he barked, drawing himself up and towering over her. 'What nonsense is this? There was no letter. As for the rest, I don't know what you're talking about!'

'Don't damn yourself further, pretending that it's not true.' Her hands were clenched into fists. 'She took me to her cabin and showed me the baby, and then she said that you were going to kill me.'

'But this is false,' he exclaimed, as clarity began to dawn, and with it a stirring of hope as he read the jealous torment in her face. '*Mon Dieu*, so that's why Juliette came to me with the story of you going to Modiford's camp. I remember thinking at the time that she seemed unduly pleased. I swear that it's a pack of lies. She must have stolen the letter, afraid of what I might do. You must believe me, Berenice. I've been many things, some of them not good, but I'm no liar. Ask any of these gentlemen.'

'He's known for his honesty, Comtesse,' averred the colonel, confused by her outburst. 'His plain-dealing manner has got him into trouble on more than one occasion, when it would have been more prudent to varnish the truth.'

Berenice was bewildered, groping in the dark, not knowing who or what to believe. 'You're his friend,' she said, suspiciously, 'and are bound to uphold him.' Her sapphire eyes were filled with accusation as she looked at the doctor. 'You, too, Greg. How can I expect you to believe that he's—'

'Capable of murdering you! Impossible!' Greg interrupted in angry denial.

'That traitorous Creole bitch!' His old companions had seen Sebastian angry on many occasions, but never like this. 'Greg, get rid of her!' he raged. 'Now! She must leave at once, and that damned old hag with her! I can't do it, for if I set eyes on her, I'll not be responsible for my actions.'

'It'll be my pleasure.' Greg was already halfway to the door. 'When I visited here to see how things were going while you were in England, I found her behaving as if she owned the place. I think she's capable of any trickery, even of having conspired with Modiford.'

'I agree,' Sebastian said, as he and Greg exchanged a stern, uncompromising glance. 'See that she has an escort out of here, for I owe it to her father to ensure that she doesn't come to harm. But my debt to him has been paid in full now.'

'I'll organize everything. Leave it to me,' Greg promised, eager to give the Creole her marching orders, and see the expression on Leah's face when she learned that their easy life at Buckhorn House was over.

'Thanks, my friend.' Sebastian clapped him on the shoulder, and Greg left the room with a purposeful ring to his step.

Damian had been listening in silence till then, but now he approached his sister hesitantly. 'Forgive me,' he blurted out. 'Oh, Berenice, why didn't you tell me about this in the stable? You couldn't confide in me? Have we grown so far apart that you don't trust me anymore?'

She raised her eyes to his, still unsure, clasping her hands against the shawl covering her breasts, saying, 'Would you have believed me? I doubt it. You were so much Sebastian's man. I was afraid to tell you—afraid to ask for your help. I thought you'd stop me from leaving him.'

He shook his head and groaned. 'What a pigheaded fool you must think me.' He took her hand and she gave a stifled sob and leaned into him. He hugged her awkwardly, adding, 'I want the best for you. That's all I've ever wanted. Your unhappiness has grieved me.'

Something incredible was happening to Sebastian as he watched the brother and sister together. He could feel every one of his carefully constructed defenses crumbling bit by bit, and in their place a fantastic notion was dawning; Berenice had been heartbroken at the idea of him loving another woman, and unable to bear the thought that he cared so little for her that he could take away her life for the sake of her inheritance. Could Greg be right? Did she love him after all?

Sebastian went to her then, and said humbly, 'Juliette has never been my mistress. She was already with child when I met her again in Charleston and brought her here. The father, a man from New Orleans, was already married and abandoned her when he found out she was pregnant. He's a powerful, influential politician, and she dared not harm him.'

'But why did you have to help her? Who is she?' It was hard to trust again, and Berenice wondered if she ever would—entirely. Or had this searing experience drowned her innocence forever?

'I knew her when she was a girl. Our fathers were friends. When her father died, my father promised to take care of her, but Juliette had always been strange, influenced by her old nurse Leah. I took on the burden when I, in turn, lost my parents, but she disappeared and I didn't see her for years, until that fateful day when I picked her up off the Charleston streets.'

'She loves you.' Berenice was convinced of it, still harboring that knot of resentment.

'Maybe she does. I don't know.' Sebastian smiled, but there was sadness in his eyes. 'I think she loves my money and property more. She must have seen you as a terrible threat.'

'Why didn't anyone tell me about her baby? Can you understand how such secrecy made me doubly convinced that he was yours?'

'Few people know. She told me, of course, when you and I first came here, but said she was so ashamed that she wanted to hide him. A very plausible liar, my dear. You wouldn't understand that, being so honest yourself.' He paused. 'Do you believe me now?'

'Yes, I think I do,' she whispered, so low that he had to bend closer to catch the words.

He reached out and placed his hands on her shoulders, holding her a little away from him and looking down into her eyes that glistened with tears. *'Ma doucette,'* he said softly. 'Can we make a new beginning?'

Damian touched the colonel on the arm. 'Come along, sir,' he said. 'I don't think we're needed here any longer.'

He gave a last glance back at Sebastian and Berenice, but they were so absorbed in one another that they did not notice as he and the old soldier quietly left the room.

A hush fell on the candle-shadowed chamber. Sebastian and Berenice stood without moving, gazing wonderingly into each other's eyes, unable to grasp fully what they saw mirrored there. The evening was cool, a breeze lifting the window drapes and, outside, the moon rode high across the starry heavens, but it was beginning to streak with clouds. The distant noises of carousing drifted in from the compound—laughter and shouts, the faint strumming of guitars, but sad sounds, too, as people mourned their dead. Yet these intrusions only served to emphasize the lovers' solitude, wrapping them in a private oasis of peace.

Without a word, Berenice went into his arms, and he stared down into her face, half dazed

461

with wonder at this miracle. He was afraid to kiss her lest this be some glorious illusion which might vanish if he tried to grasp it, leaving him floundering amidst the old pain and despair. But when he felt her sweet breath on his lips, he eased her head back, pressing his lips to her throat, and feeling her shiver as his hands moved lightly to her breasts and then supported her under the arms. Her eyes had been closed, but now she opened them and stared at him as if he were a god. He shook his head, unable to believe that she was eager to have him touch and kiss her. He moistened her lips with his tongue, and her mouth opened beneath his. Holding her with his right arm about her waist and his left cupping the back of her head, his grip tightened, and she reached up to him as high as she could, and he bent so that her arms could encircle his neck. He wanted to shout aloud with the joy of that moment, so unexpected, so splendid.

Berenice surrendered completely to his embrace, feeling as if her bones had dissolved, leaving her lax, a dead weight in his powerful arms. Sebastian kissed her eyelids, and the tip of her nose and her chin, kissing her again and again, running his mouth over hers, still fearing that something might break the spell and reawaken the Berenice who had fought him so bitterly.

He took his lips from hers, his eyes glowing as he gazed at her. Her face was pale and small in the frame of her hair, which swept over her shoulders and his arm. 'What's happening to us, Sebastian?' she gasped, her hands touching his face.

'Madness, I think,' he murmured into her ear, his breath sending shivers along her nerves.

'Love—I think,' she whispered shyly, hardly daring to voice it.

'Ah, that's a word I don't trust.' Something of the old mockery crept into his voice, bringing doubts surging up, but her newfound courage would not be denied.

'You mustn't be afraid,' she said. 'I know I'm young and foolish, but I love you. There—I've said it! I love you. You can use the knowledge to destroy me, or you can accept it and return it. The choice is yours.'

His arm tightened. *'Ma chérie,'* he said shakily, terrified and overjoyed to hear her confess her feelings. 'You've given me so much, things I thought I'd forgotten, feelings I'd buried deep in my heart. Your thoughts, your laughter, so much! Ah, Berenice, my beloved!'

'Do you love me, Sebastian?' she asked, her fingers in his hair, shivering because of the way he was looking at her.

'Hell!' he growled, face stormy, catching her to him and crushing her against his chest wanting to hold her there forever, armored by his devotion. 'I've been in love with you since I first saw you, only I was too blind and stupid to realize it.'

Such happiness was almost too sweet to be borne, and Berenice was crying and laughing all at the same time, clinging with her arms about his neck. Then suddenly she grew still and serious again.

'I've something to tell you, but first I must pay my respects to Peregrine.'

'Of course, darling.' He lifted her hand and kissed it gently, his expression grave. 'May I come with you?'

'Do you really want to? You disliked him so.'

'That's passed. In the end, he was a brave man. I owe my life to him.'

It was very quiet in the little room that led from the porch where she had last talked to Peregrine. Was it only that morning? she thought as they walked in, hand in hand. It seemed an eternity ago. So much had happened in the space of a few hours. Peregrine had been unhappy then. She prayed that he was happier now. Perhaps fate had been kind in letting him meet a glorious end—otherwise he might have dragged on a fruitless existence—gambling, drinking, in debt, squandering his talents. 'Whom the gods love die young,' she thought. The poet had acted out his epics in his passing.

His had been the first coffin the carpenters completed, and it had been placed across a bier. Four candles burned in floor-standing torchères, two at his head and two at his feet; four women were seated on either side, black shawls over their hair, rosaries in their fingers, sitting with him through the night; four censers swung from the rafters, containing smoldering incense.

Berenice stifled a sob. She staggered, but was upheld by her husband's firm hand under her elbow. Her eyes were fixed on the coffin, a dark skein of sorrow knotting inside her. Slowly she walked towards it and peered in. Peregrine looked serene, his face handsome and unlined, his hair neatly combed back, his body draped in a white cerement. He's gone, she thought. There's no one there. He resembles a waxen effigy. She stood for a while, the candle flames as straight as if suspended by cords, the thin wisps of smoke from their wicks mingling with the aroma of the incense, rising heavenwards like a benediction.

'Good-bye, my friend,' she murmured, and placed a posy of night-scented blossoms on his chest then, leaning over, rested her lips on his cold brow.

Sebastian led her away, and they walked in the garden, neither desiring to return to the house just yet. It was nearly dark, the sky burning with coppery flame, great black clouds piling up. He stopped and drew her to him.

'You have something to tell me?'

'Yes, but not quite yet. Can't we ride somewhere, away from here. There's too much noise—too much sorrow—Peregrine—'

'All right, but it looks as if a storm threatens.'

'I shan't mind, if I'm with you.'

Two horses were harnessed, not Saffron nor Sebastian's black favorite, but fresh ones. The grooms smiled to themselves, seeing how it was with them, their glances, the way in which they could not help touching. Sebastian borrowed their cloaks, laying one over her shoulders and covering himself with the other. Then his hands were at her waist, lifting her into the saddle.

'Where are we going?' It hardly seemed important, but she asked anyway.

'To a place I've wanted to show you for a long time.'

They rode towards the coast, and the wind rose, thrashing the branches, whipping their cloaks and, before long, it started to rain. The air turned cold and there was a deep, explosive crack of thunder. The flash lit the sky and etched Sebastian in silver as he sat his horse confidently.

They had reached the cliff path, crowned at its southern end with a high rocky mass that resembled a crouching lion. Sebastian turned his horse's head and took a track winding downwards, that ended in a deep fissure. It was like riding into a tunnel, filled with the noise of rain. The sides were covered in dense undergrowth and, from far below, came the roar of the sea.

Surefooted as a goat, Sebastian's animal picked his way cannily, and he led hers along by the reins. They came out on a stony platform and the rain and darkness blurred her sight. 'Can't we find some shelter?' She had to shout to make herself heard.

'Over there,' he called back above the clamor of the storm, pointing to a ledge, partially covered by bushes and ending in a wall of rock.

She had no alternative but to follow him, but did so gladly, placing herself in his care. He stopped and dismounted, then helped her to the ground. Then he had his knife out and was hacking at the tangled growth. Another vivid flash of lightning revealed an opening, about half as high and twice as wide as a door. They left the horses outside, tying them securely, and groped their way in. Sebastian found some dry brushwood and, taking out his flint and tinderbox, made a primitive torch. Its smoky glare showed that they were in a cave, very lofty and with a sandy floor. He stuck the flare into a crevice and set to work cutting more bushes from the entrance to make a fire. The prospect of a cheering blaze made her work with him, and by the time she had dragged in a final load, the fire was alight and he was heaping wood on it lavishly, the billowing smoke drawn upwards by the draught from some unseen opening high above their heads.

Her face was wet with rain, clothing too, but she was loving every moment of it. Living at Mobby Cove had taught her so many valuable lessons, stripping her of pretense, making her face life with all its pain and joy. There was so much to fear there, so much to love; why, even to exist took courage. Yet those very hardships sharpened the awareness, honed the senses, forced one to tread carefully, lest precious things be snatched away: most of all, that treasured possession which one could never truly own—love.

'What a wonderful place!' she cried, gazing round the cave.

'You like it? Good. It's my secret spot. I come here sometimes when I want solitude.' He was kneeling beside her by the fire, then he said, 'Get out of those wet things, before you take a chill.'

His clothes glittered with moisture, and he began to strip. Soon he was naked, hanging his things over a rack made out of branches. Berenice undressed more slowly, unusually bashful, and he took her garments and hung them near his. She huddled near the fire, knees drawn up, arms clasped about them, seeing pictures in the flames. She was very tired but excited, wanting him to take her in his arms, and make her feel secure.

He came to join her, and the sight of his muscular body, his lean face lit by the dancing glow, filled her with delight. He leaned forward to stir the logs, then glanced at her and said, 'What was it you wanted to say to me?'

She drew in a breath and met the question in his eyes. 'I'm expecting your baby, Sebastian,' she whispered.

Just for a moment, the brilliance of his smile almost blinded her. It was as if she had just given him the moon and stars. Then he caught her to him with both arms and kissed her, released her, shouted, 'A child! A child! Oh, my darling, you could not have made me happier!' Then he kissed her again.

All tension left her, replaced by unalloyed happiness. She felt an exquisite pleasure, as if his words had a healing power. She seemed to become a part of him, mingling with his soul, and the child in her womb was united with them, too, forming a mystic triad.

He suddenly frowned, saying anxiously, 'And I brought you here, on a night like this—in your condition!'

She gave a deep, warm, confident laugh, though keeping her fingers crossed lest she tempt providence, as she said, 'I'm strong and healthy, Sebastian. Nothing can harm me now.'

With a murmured endearment, he put her gently from him for a moment, gathering up a heap of leaves and spreading them before the fire. Then he took up his dried cloak and laid it over this simple couch. After this, he encouraged her to lie down and he stretched out beside her, his arms a safe haven. She welcomed the caressing of his lips, her tired body reviving and eager for him. There was no holding back of anything for either of them, no concealing of feelings, nothing but the intoxicating enchantment of their love.

Just before being swallowed up in the roaring of her blood, Berenice looked dreamily into his face. 'Say it again, Sebastian.'

'Women!' he chuckled. 'Must I spell it out? You know how I feel about you.'

'Yes, but I want you to repeat it,' she said with a laugh, then, strong in her confidence, pushed her fingers into his hair, lips close to his, demanding, 'Tell me!'

The feel of her body stormed the ramparts of his pride and he growled thickly, 'You're without mercy! All right—I'll say it again, as often as you want—I love you. Now will you let me show you how much?'

And he did, with Berenice responding as never

before. The leaping tongues of flame from the fire by which they lay was as nothing compared to the molten heat of their union. Later, problems might arise, no doubt quarrels, too, but now they thought of nothing but each other, hands seeking to bring joy, mouths murmuring love words between tasting and kissing. And when completion came, and faded, they still lay locked together.

Berenice woke as a smudge of greyish light came through the cave entrance. Despite her nudity, she was warm—heated by Sebastian's body on one side and the ruddy embers on the other. In that first drowsy moment, he was instantly awake, too, and she clung to him, arms twined round his neck, afraid that she had been dreaming and must now wake to lonely reality.

She became aware of hunger, but when she sat up, sickness rose in her, but now it was endurable because he was so considerate, making her rest with her head on his shoulder, his face contrite as he said, 'My poor girl—you're suffering because of me,' and ran his thumb over her lips and stroked her temples.

'It doesn't matter, darling. I'm so happy. You mustn't worry,' she said, wanting to banish the anxious expression from his face.

His eyes were so adoring that she drew in a quick breath, as he said with a smile, 'You must indulge me. I've not had a wife and child to worry about before. I find it quite amazing.' And his hands moved with infinite gentleness over her breasts and belly as if seeking confirmation of her condition.

With something akin to worship in her eyes, she watched him as he moved about the cave, putting on his clothes, fetching water from the stream. It was ice cold and quelled her sickness. She dressed, too, shivering now that the fire had been stamped out. Soon they were ready to go, and she stood at the entrance as he fetched the horses. The rain had stopped during the night, and only a few thin white clouds moved swiftly over the wide expanse of blue.

It was peace and harmony, its beauty filling Berenice's soul as she felt Sebastian's strong hands helping her to mount. She smiled down at him and the expression in his eyes was like fire and wine to her, as he murmured,

'There's something I want to say—something I should have said last night.'

'What is it, Sebastian?'

'Thank you for loving me.'

They rode back to Buckhorn House through the rain-washed freshness of early morning. No one was up yet, and after seeing to the horses, they went to the master bedchamber, still dark, with the curtains drawn from the night before. Berenice left him there for a while, going to the kitchen and loading a tray with food, a pot of hot coffee and substantial mugs. She was feeling extremely well, and just plain hungry. There was no sign of Peggy, but when she peeped into the adjoining room, she saw that she was asleep, tucked into bed with one of Jessy's daughters.

Berenice smiled to herself, and returned to the bedroom.

Sebastian had retired to the four-poster, lying there and smoking. He looked up as she walked in. 'Come to bed,' he said. 'We've hours yet before duty calls.'

She saw his arm, the bandage dirty and bloodied. 'That needs attention,' she reminded, as any proper wife would.

'Later,' he grunted, smiling as she set the tray between them.

It was so companionable and sweet, this first breakfast they had eaten together since this, their new consummation. She felt that it had been a true one, a union on every level expressed through the flesh, a symbol of a deep, abiding love that would last for all time.

When they had finished eating, she undressed and slid under the covers, winding her arms about him, thrusting her body against the muscled hardness of his, letting him know in every way that she was hungry for him. Her hands explored him, worshipped him. Her task in life would always be to support him, to make him aware of her adoration in every facet of their existence together. It was a task she was eager to accept, just as she was eager to carry his child inside her as a positive, living proof of their love. She was aflame with passion now, too long denied the freedom of expression, inhibited because she was so unsure of him. Her caressing hands roused him, her fingers playing with the black hair on his chest, wandering down over his flat, taut stomach, shivering with delight at the way his body responded to her touch.

'*Ah, m'amie,*' he groaned softly. 'I'm besotted by you—crazy for my own wife!'

His body strained against hers, his hands feverishly moving over her sweetly swelling contours, fondling the breasts which seemed to beg for his caresses. Over and over he whispered words of love in her ear, '*Je t'adore!* I love you, Berenice, I love you!'

He could think of no pretty speeches, too dazed by the keen desire which swept over him like a violent storm, too bewitched by the soft, passionate body in his arms, too eager to prove his love by giving her the deepest satisfaction, rousing her to that wonderful madness which demands fulfillment.

Berenice took the initiative this time, covering him with her body, stretching herself on top of him kissing his face, his throat, the edges of his lips, alive, brimming with love and wanting—his gentle strength, his wonderful body, his sex—moving down, her tongue making him larger. She was proud to be in control, touching him, her hair falling over him like some dark curtain. She straddled him, body straight, head thrown back, feeling him penetrate deeply into her, while his fingers fondled her breasts, circling each nipple, teasing it, till a moan broke from her lips at the overwhelming pleasure of this double sensation. She felt him tense, then he lifted her from him and lay her on the bed, her hair hanging over the edge, her throat curved, an arch for his kisses.

His hands caressed her taut breasts, flat belly,

going lower, and he moved carefully, shifting a little, slipping easily between her outstretched legs and she braced herself for his entrance. But he did not take her—not quite yet, Instead, he knelt before her and she felt his hair brushing her thighs, his hands lifting her hips firm and then his lips moving softly, deliciously, where she had hoped he would place them.

Riven with exquisite pain-pleasure, Berenice felt his tongue probe and explore, delicately flickering over that most tender, sensitive portion of her body, moistening and caressing the very core of her being. She urged him to increase the tempo, aware of nothing but the compulsion towards release, her groping fingers fondling his thick black hair. With the blood drumming madly in her ears, she twisted her head from side to side, sobbing, her hips straining up to meet the darting of his tongue, her incoherent cries driving him on until wave after wave of the most acute pleasure washed over her. Then she moved instinctively to join her body with his, drawing him down into her pulsating depths.

Then, and only then, did he surrender to his own pent-up passion, thrusting into her again and again. She clasped him close, feeling at last that convulsive shudder running through him and hearing the husky growl of satisfaction which told her that he, too, had reached the pinnacle of ecstasy.

Very slowly, Berenice came back to reality, to a beautiful world of touching and caressing, of warmth and love. Feeling limp and satiated, she lay quietly in his arms, his body still fused with hers. Her tender fingertips ran over his face in the dimness, tracing the contours of those handsome features, his eyebrows silky and thick, the high bridge of his nose, his sensual mouth. She could tell that he was smiling, and her own lips curved in response, body molded into his lean hardness, legs coiled round his. He kissed her wandering hand and nuzzled her neck, then raised himself so that he might look at her. She was not embarrassed, even though still tingling from the bliss which they had shared, each physical encounter, each diverse pathway of pleasure sanctified by love.

He was still bemused by the stunning revelation of the state of her heart. Had he tamed her, or had she tamed him? It didn't matter. The fact was that somehow they had found one another at last. Not that it would be a bed of roses from now on—Sebastian was too much the realist to expect that.

'I'll have to get used to being a husband, you know,' he teased her gently, kissing her hands. 'And learn to curb my love of independence. I'm unaccustomed to accounting to anyone for my actions.'

'And you must be patient with me.' Her hand sought his, slender fingers merging with those of toughened brown. 'I've so much to learn.'

'No doubt we'll still quarrel, my wild, willful love,' he whispered, his eyes so brilliant that she was dazzled by their promise.

The aftermath of loving brought no disillusion; indeed, it heightened their contentment. Passion spent, they could enjoy the satisfying delight of simply gazing upon each other, filled with happiness and dreams of the future. Berenice knew that she no longer hankered after the vanities of the world, for Sebastian embodied all the things she wanted. She asked for nothing but his love and trust. Gladly, she would have faced poverty with him at her side. She had no need of luxuries, for all the riches on earth could not compare with the touch of his hand and the light in his eyes when he looked at her.

It was as if she were suddenly suffused with energy. Tinglingly alive, she sat up beside him, her back propped against the white pillows. He poured two glasses of wine from a decanter on the side table, toasting her over the rim of his. For hours they talked and planned as lovers will. She told him of her desire to return to England one day, to show him off to her friends, and then drive to Wiltshire so that he might learn to share her love of that rolling countryside, with its pretty villages, parklands and forests. He confessed to the same longing to take her to visit France.

'One day, *m'amie,* we'll stroll the boulevards of Paris where once the mob roared for blood. Beloved, when the war is over, I'd like you to see the Loire Valley where I was born. It's so beautiful, with its wide, fast-flowing river, thick woodlands, and magnificent houses. The Chateau Hilaire stands there. You really must see it, for it is yours as well as mine.'

'Ah, yes.' She snuggled against him, her breast pressing into his shoulder. 'Our children should visit their ancestral home.'

His arm came about her, and her heart sang with happiness. 'That will come later, *mon trésor*. Firstly, I'll take you to Oakwood Hall, a fine place, built by the best of architects. I dare say it will remind you of mansions in England. The Quality imitate Europeans in their taste for having a town house as well as a country seat. Then, you must enter the society life of Charleston, properly this time, with your husband at your side, and not a fop in sight!'

He was about to continue when Berenice stopped him. 'But I want to stay here,' she protested, suddenly realizing how much Buckhorn House meant to her.

In this ancient, tumbledown dwelling, she had changed from a child to a woman. It had been a surprise, it was true, for she had been unprepared to find such a place in the midst of the wilderness, but now it spelled home for her and she loved every inch of it—its timbers, overgrown garden, sweet-smelling pine trees and towering oaks.

'That isn't possible.' He shook his head, smiling at her indulgently. 'I'll have to go to Charleston on business soon.'

'You aren't becoming involved in piracy again?' She frowned at him, eyes beginning to spark. Feeling her stiffen, he rolled over, trapping her beneath him, his hands buried in her outspread hair.

'Don't start telling me what to do, you shrew!' he said sternly, but there was laughter running through his voice. He held her tightly, though she squirmed, a hot retort springing to her lips.

'All right. Have it your way. We'll spend money on Buckhorn—make it our retreat, eh? I love you to distraction, and I will not do anything to dishonor you or our family.'

His mouth captured hers, silencing her declaration of love. He kissed her deeply, and soon her arms had closed about him, the fire of desire beginning to build up again. Life would be so good with him—unpredictable maybe, but exciting and challenging.

Her head was whirling with plans for Buckhorn House. Here, her children would be born, and here they would be reared, living free, learning forest lore. She had a vision of their descendants still keeping up the manor, preserving it as a warm, vibrant center of love, a real home. Oh, yes, she longed to see England again and to become acquainted with France, but it was here, in America, that she had been reborn—in this great, still partly untamed, magnificent country in which she had found true love.

With a contented sigh, she turned to Sebastian, feeling bliss running through her as his hands began their magic again. In the shadow of their marriage bed they lay together, as if protected by the wings of the angel of love, all doubts and uncertainties conquered.

The publishers hope that this book has given you enjoyable reading. Large Print Books are especially designed to be as easy to see and hold as possible. If you wish a complete list of our books, please ask at your local library or write directly to: Black Satin Romance, Magna House, Long Preston, North Yorkshire, BD23 4ND, England.

This Large Print Book for the Partially sighted, who cannot read normal print, is published under the auspices of

THE ULVERSCROFT FOUNDATION

THE ULVERSCROFT FOUNDATION

. . . we hope that you have enjoyed this Large Print Book. Please think for a moment about those people who have worse eyesight problems than you . . . and are unable to even read or enjoy Large Print, without great difficulty.

You can help them by sending a donation, large or small to:

**The Ulverscroft Foundation,
1, The Green, Bradgate Road,
Anstey, Leicestershire, LE7 7FU,
England.**
or request a copy of our brochure for more details.

The Foundation will use all your help to assist those people who are handicapped by various sight problems and need special attention.

Thank you very much for your help.